LATIN LOVERS

Edited by

MARCUS ANTHONY

Herndon, VA

Published in the United States by STARbooks Press

PO Box 711612, Herndon, VA 20171

Many thanks to graphic artist Emma Aldous:
www.arthousepublishing.co.uk

Printed in the United States

Herndon, VA

Contents

BRIDGING THE GAP
BY Logan Zachary

Logan Zachary (LoganZachary2002@yahoo.com) lives in Minneapolis, MN. His new book *Calendar Boys* is out, and his stories can be found in many STARbooks Press anthologies.

I ran full speed down the soccer field. The sun was behind me, and I had a great view of the net.

The goalie jumped from side to side, watching my hips to see which way I was going to run and when I would kick the ball.

Everyone from both teams was bunched up by our goalie, but I hung back. Sonny spun around and passed the ball to me.

I stopped the soccer ball and took off down the field. My white shorts clung to my butt as my blue and green striped jersey flapped in the wind.

The crowd cheered as I neared the goal.

I brought my leg back and kicked with all my might.

Whack!

Leather met leather, and the black and white ball spun over the goalie's shoulder.

He dove for the ball, but I never saw what happened.

All I saw was the world turned to the right, and the bright blue sky blurred over my head. White fluffy clouds floated as an ear splitting crack echoed through my body, and a burning sensation started in my leg. My body floated like the clouds for a second, and then the green grass knocked the wind out of me, and the world turned black.

# # # # #

I woke up in the hospital with my leg suspended from a traction device. An IV with a morphine drip was taped to my hand.

"You're awake," Rico said. "Can I get you anything?"

Rico was my best friend who got me to join his soccer team. I was the only non-Hispanic player on the team.

"What happened, Rico?" My mouth was dry, and my lips felt cracked as I spoke.

"We won the game. Your kick was the winning point."

"And my leg?" I looked at my orange stained hairy leg. "Is there any water?"

Rico handed me a Styrofoam glass. The ice sloshed inside as I brought it to my mouth. The cool, wetness quenched my thirst, and I licked my lips.

"They set your leg and as long as it stays in place, they don't think you'll need surgery, so that's why there isn't a cast on your leg yet. They want the swelling to go down, and then the doctor will decide what to do."

"When?"

"This afternoon. He wants to x-ray you again and then decide."

My finger pushed the red button, and the pain disappeared. I floated.

It was easy to see why these drugs were so addictive.

I clicked the plunger again on the IV drip and fell asleep.

# # # # #

"Rico, your friend's X-rays look great. All we have to do is cast his leg, and you can be on your way. Are you his ride home?" The doctor asked Rico.

"I can give him a ride home," he smiled at me as he spoke.

"Good, because he's going to be non-weight bearing on his leg for at least a month. He'll need a wheelchair and crutches."

"I have both at my house. I have him covered." Rico winked at me.

"Are you sure?" the doctor asked. "We usually like to check things out before we ..."

"My brother is a physical therapist."

"Okay," the doctor pulled the sheet down and pulled my hospital gown down to cover my lap. "Oops, sorry." He motioned for the orthotist to come in.

"What color cast would you like?" the man asked, as he donned a pair of rubber gloves.

"Blue with green strips," I said.

"Done." He rolled out a large stockinette and covered my whole leg. He pulled the top up, and his hand brushed over one of my testicles. I felt it pull up, and my arousal started to come up also. This wasn't the time to get excited.

Rico noticed my dismay and smiled. "Are you going to be able to get around your place in a wheelchair?"

2

"Everything is on one level, getting in and out will be tricky. I have that double deck on the back of the house."

"I've made lots of ramps for my brother's clients. I can make one in an afternoon for you."

"Thanks, but you don't ..."

"I am, and no arguments. If the other guys on the team want to pitch in they can. You won the game for us."

# # # # #

Rico was a man of his word. He brought me home and realized there was no way to bring the wheelchair into the house with me in it. He brought the chair up the stairs and returned for me. His hands slipped under my ass, and he moved me to the edge of the seat, left leg sticking straight out in a blue and green striped cast.

"You're not carrying me up the stairs."

"The Doctor said you couldn't walk on that leg for a month."

His hands cupped my ass, and my arousal grew. My shorts didn't fit well over the cast so the nurse slit the side all the way to the waistband. One of Rico's fingers slipped into my crease, and the thin shorts gave little to cover my tender opening.

I know I was the only white guy on the team, but the Latin guys never made me feel different. They welcomed me with open arms.

Rico carried me up the stairs and set me in the chair. "If I make a ramp from your driveway up the stairs and build a bridge over that open spot on the deck, I think you'd be independent to come and go as you please."

# # # # #

Rico returned within the hour with a huge bag and a six pack of beer. I have supper and *cerveza.*"

My stomach growled as he said food.

"I ordered lumber, which will be delivered here first thing in the morning, and my suitcase is in the truck. So you have a roommate for the night."

"You don't need ..."

"I want to. You didn't ask. I volunteered. Just accept it."

Supper was chicken enchiladas and pork tamales, the beer was Tecate, and I only drank one with the pain meds. Rico talked and talked, but my head swirled as my mind zoned out.

"Rodger, you should get to bed. Let me help you." He pushed the wheelchair to my bedroom and after locking the brakes, he pulled my T-shirt over my head. "Did you want a clean one to sleep in?" He tossed my shirt into the laundry basket in the closet and pulled his off, throwing it onto a chair in the corner.

His skin was a deep brown with muscles that rippled beneath. His nipples were the size of silver dollars and a dark brown. The nub in the middle rose up into a perfect bud. He had a spattering of black hair in the center of his chest, and it started again above the waistband.

"Let me help you into bed." His warm body pressed against mine, and I was instantly hard. I hung to the left and with the left side of my shorts ripped wide open to the waist, there was little to hold me inside.

Before I knew it, I was propped in bed and covered by the sheet.

"Did you want to take off those dirty shorts?"

The way he said that, the only answer was yes.

I pulled the waistband down and pushed them as far down as I could.

Rico reached under the sheet and fished the shorts down my leg and threw them into the laundry basket. "I'll be right back." He returned with a reacher, a glass of water, my pill bottle, and my cell phone. "Call if you need anything. I'm going to get my bag and put things away."

I settled back into the pillows and exhaled, allowing my body to relax for the first time.

What was the problem here? Aside from being naked with a half-naked handsome Latino male, a full leg cast which prevented me from moving, I had a raging hard-on under the sheets. What could I do?

Nothing.

# # # # #

I must have dozed off, because I heard a gentle rustling on the opposite side of the bed. I glanced over to the side in time to see Rico pull his shorts off. His beautiful brown ass had black hair that lined his crease. A pink pucker winked at me as a large pair of balls swung free as he dropped his clothes to the floor.

He sat down on the bed and slipped under the sheets.

4

My hard-on was back and with a vengeance. I pretended to still be asleep and inhaled his aroma, male, sweat, beer and spicy sex.

His hairy leg brushed against my good leg, and my whole body stiffened.

"Sorry, I didn't want to wake you." He moved over, closer, and his body barely an inch away. "I'm a cuddler, do you mind? Or is your leg too sore?"

"I'm fine," I lied.

His arm wrapped over my body, and he pulled himself closer. I felt his thick cock lay over my hairy leg. His arm slid a little lower and bumped the tip of my cock. He let it rest there and fell asleep.

I took a deep breath and passed out.

# # # # #

The next morning when I got up, a clean T-shirt and loose shorts with the left leg cut wide open were neatly piled on my wheelchair. The cell phone was on top. I quickly dressed with the reacher after figuring it out.

Coffee was brewed and waited in the kitchen as did a fluffy towel, washcloth and soap by the sink.

Rico came in from outside. "You're up. I hope you slept well. It's going to be a hot one. The lumber will be here in a few minutes, and now you're awake. I can start making noise."

"What's all this?" I pointed to the wash cloth and towel.

"I figured you'd want to wash up, and the kitchen sink was the best place to do it."

I nodded.

"If you could make iced tea and sandwiches as I work, that would help me a lot, and if you come outside and keep me company, the task will get done in half the time."

A truck honked outside, and Rico walked to the sliding patio doors and opened them.

I felt the wall of heat that entered.

"Yell if you need anything," and he was gone, to help unload the lumber.

I watched through the patio doors as he easily carried the 2x4s and set them into piles. He worked quickly and with a purpose.

I turned to the sink and washcloth. A sponge bath would make me feel human again. I ran the water and pulled off my shirt. I washed under my arms and across my hairy chest. I rinsed the cloth and thanked my guardian angel that I only broke a leg and not an arm.

I washed what I could of my leg, but my groin needed a going over. I looked out to see where Rico was.

The truck was gone, and so was he.

I pulled the shorts down in front and rinsed out the washcloth. I reached between my legs and washed my balls. My cock started to grow again as Rico's ass and chest came back into my mind.

His low hanging balls were full and heavy; a thick coarse black hair covered them.

I rinsed and washed along my ever-growing shaft, stroking up and down, feeling a little extra fluid ooze out of the tip ...

As the patio door opened, Rico walked in and said, "Oops."

I snatched the towel from the counter and covered my growing groin. "Just washing up."

"Did you need a hand?" and a look of horror came over his face. "I mean, did you need any help?"

My face burned. "I'm fine." My cock jumped under the towel, and I grabbed it, pushing it down.

"I just needed to use the bathroom, and I was ready to start building."

"You know where it is." I waved him in its direction. My erection waved at him, too.

Rico slipped by me. His face red also, and I wondered from the heat or the embarrassment.

A minute later, he returned and headed to the patio door.

"Once I'm washed and ready for the day, I'll make some iced tea and bring it out. Do you need anything else? Sunscreen? A towel?"

"Sunscreen if you have some."

"Okay, I'll be out soon."

He went outside and started measuring lumber, as I finished washing my dick and quickly dried off.

My cell phone rang, but I ignored it, as I made iced tea, filled glasses with ice, and made a plate of ham and Swiss sandwiches with horseradish mayo. I set the tray on my lap and realized there was no way I'd get all of this outside to the table. I grabbed a glass of ice and filled it with tea and carried that to the door, set it between my legs, chilling my nads and opened the door. I wheeled over to Rico and handed him the glass.

6

He noticed where it had been placed but didn't say anything. He drank greedily and wiped the back his hand over his sweaty brow.

"The rest of the stuff is on the counter ..."

"I'll be right back with it." He handed me the empty glass of ice and jumped onto the deck.

I noticed how short his cut-off jeans were and enjoyed his walk into the house.

Rico set the table with the food and drinks.

I looked at the ramp's frame and was amazed to see how much he had done.

He pulled his shirt off. His dark skin glistened with sweat. He wiped under his arms before he tossed his T-shirt to the ground. He turned his back to me and sweat poured down his spine, a wet spot grew at his waistband and the backside of his shorts.

"Wow," I said.

"Wow, what?" he turned and smiled.

"Wow," my eyes followed the sweat that rolled down his chest and over his belly and was absorbed into his shorts, "how much you have done already, but now it's break time." I offered him the empty tea glass back.

He filled it from the pitcher and wiped his brow with the glass, beaded with humidity. The hair under his arm was matted inside.

I could smell deodorant and male sweat. I inhaled deeply.

"I'll be ready to fill in the ramp next, and then we can bridge the gap of the deck, and you'll be set."

"Sit and eat, drink up, too. With this heat and humidity, you need to stay hydrated."

"Do you have a hose?"

"On the side of the house."

"After eating, I want you to hose me off, that will cool me off and ..."

Heat me up, I thought.

"... and then you can help apply sunscreen to my back."

FUCK! my mind screamed.

"Great sandwiches, I love horseradish."

"I really appreciate you building this ramp and bridging that gap on the deck."

"It's the least I could do." He drank another glass of iced tea before picking up another sandwich. "How's the pain today?"

"As long as I keep the leg up, the pain is down, and the meds help."

"Do you have sunscreen? I feel my pale skin burning."

"If you go into the cabinet in the bathroom, there are a few bottles in there."

Rico went in and returned with a bottle of oil.

I knew I had an easy-to-apply spray in there. "There was ..." but I stopped, "... a few choices."

"This will work." He handed me the bottle, knelt, and turned his back to me.

I poured oil into my palm and rubbed over his shoulders and up the back of his neck. His torso was muscular and triangled down into narrow hips. I applied more oil over his shoulders and worked it lower, down into the small of his back. I put more on along his side and up under his arms.

"Could you do my chest? That way the oil won't be on my hands. I hate to slip when I'm working with a tool."

I oiled both arms as he stood and faced me. I ran the oil over his washboard stomach and moved up his chest to the silver dollar sized nipples.

They rose under my palm as I worked the oil into his skin.

I pinched them as they rose into two sharp peaks.

He moaned. "I wish you could give me a full body massage."

I swallowed hard; I had been thinking the same thing. "When my leg is healed, it's a deal."

He pushed his pelvis toward me. "My waistband slips down as I work."

I applied more oil above his waist and then dipped my fingers into his waistband. I could feel the coarse hair that covered his lower body, and he wasn't wearing any underwear.

He closed his eyes, as my finger dove deeper.

I brushed something fleshy and pulled out immediately.

He turned his back to me. "Plumber's crack."

SHIT! my mind swore.

I rubbed more oil over his waistband and then down over the crests of his butt. A finger dipped into his crease and applied more oil, deeper. The hair in his crack tickled. He had buns of steel, and my hard-on was back. His brown skin glistened like caramel in the sun. The scent of Coppertone filled the air.

He turned and brought his face to mine.

At first, I thought he was going to kiss me, but he wanted sunscreen on his face. My fingers traced his face and protected every beautiful inch of his cheeks, nose, chin, and brow. I overlapped his neck and then thought about his legs, working up to his bulging groin.

But he never asked about it.

"Well, back to work. Keep the ice water and tea coming, and if I get really hot, I want you to spray me with the hose."

He could have asked me for a kidney, and I would have cut it out myself.

His shorts were oiled and sweat soaked, as he returned to the ramp. The nail gun made quick work of the ramp, and he started to build a framework for the gap.

As he bent over measuring and nailing, the top of his ass came out of his shorts. A deep tan line was easily seen, and I was glad I covered his sweet ass with sunscreen.

I resisted sniffing my hand. So I took my T-shirt off and wiped off the excess oil and savored the wonderful burning sensation of touching his hot skin.

Rico looked hot, so I went in to make more tea and bring out more water. When I returned, he was bending over, and I noticed something sticking out of one of his short's legs, brown, fleshy and covered in black hair, one of his testicles.

I hoped it wouldn't burn, but as he moved it slipped back inside.

The boards needed to bridge the opening were set in place, and Rico nailed them quickly into place with the nail gun. He raised his arm in triumph.

"Done?" I asked.

He nodded as he set the gun down. "Where is that hose?"

I pointed to the north side of the house and started to wheel in that direction.

Rico rounded the house and unrolled the hose. He turned the knob and pulled more slack in the green rubber as he brought it to me. "Rinse me off," he said as he handed me the silver handled grip nozzle.

I turned the chair to the side, aimed at his chest, and pulled the trigger. Cold water sprayed over him as he raised his arms up.

He spun around and around as I soaked him from head to foot.

I could feel the blow back, and the water felt great in the heat.

He opened his mouth and drank thirstily and then spat the water back out. "AHHHH, this feels great." He turned his back to me.

I enjoyed how the sun made rainbows around his glistening body, deep brown and perfect.

He bent over and pulled off his shorts and twisted them in his hands. Water poured out of them, and he tossed the shorts onto a dry part of the deck. He turned to me, and I almost lost the hose. He was hung, a huge uncut penis dangled from his torso.

I stopped pulling the trigger, hypnotized by the sight.

He smiled, and I sprayed him again. That bastard was playing me. He knew all along I wanted his naked body, and he had been teasing and flaunting it all over the place. He walked toward me.

I used the water to push him away, but it didn't work, the spray was set on shower and not on jet.

He stood near my chair as his dick began to grow, despite the cold water.

I stopped the spray and watched him grow.

The hooded cock swelled and grew, reaching toward me.

I reached for it. My hand opened up and caressed along the underside of the shaft. The foreskin pulled back and a pink mushroom head popped out of the collar. He was beautiful.

I leaned forward and brought his dick to my mouth. My tongue slipped into the end and tasted him, sweat, salt, and spicy sex. My lips drew him in, and I swallowed hard. My hand cradled his balls and squeezed and rolled them between my fingers. They were low, and full, and fleshy.

His hand came underneath my chin and guided me to look up into his brown eyes. They glowed an amber color I had never seen before.

"How's your pain?"

I had forgotten all about my broken leg, until he reminded me.

My backyard was secluded, and I enjoyed being outside in my underwear or naked, as I wanted. My next purchase was a hot tub for the corner, until I broke my stupid leg. Now, there was no hurry.

He bent down and kissed me, full and deep on my mouth.

My lips opened and sucked his tongue into me. I dueled with his tongue, and they rolled around each other, as we deep kissed.

The hose dropped from my hand. The trigger hit and sprayed a cold burst of water over us, but we didn't even notice.

His hand slid down my hairy chest, over my abs, and paused at my waistband. His finger entered my bellybutton. He opened his eyes and searched mine, asking for permission.

I blinked consent and opened my mouth wider, sucking him in.

His fingers slipped under the waistband and combed through my hair.

My cock shifted in its confines and slapped against his hand. I moaned into his mouth as his hand wrapped around my thick shaft.

He stroked me several times and pre-cum oozed out of the tip. He broke our kiss and licked the sweat down my neck. He continued to my nipple and sucked on it, bringing it to a sharp point. His teeth rolled the nub back and forth.

My hands grabbed his head, guiding it lower. He knelt and worked between my legs. His hand brought my cock to his lips, and he rolled the mushroom head around and around. He stuck his tongue and tasted the salty sweet before exploring the opening. He puckered up and kissed my cock. After the kiss, he opened his lips and swallowed my dick, inch by slow inch.

The stupid cast prevented me from thrusting my cock into his throat, but my hands pushed his head down.

His slow, deliberate motion was too slow for my nerves, and they needed more, now to end the torture of waiting. His mouth was hot and wet, skilled on how to pleasure a man. His hands reached behind me and worked my shorts down and under my butt. Carefully, they were removed and discarded on the deck with the rest of our clothes.

I let go of his head and grabbed onto the arms of the wheelchair, doing a modified push-up, I thrust my cock back into his waiting mouth. I could feel the pressure increase in my balls.

Slowly, he let my cock withdraw from his mouth, and he returned with a wooden ottoman on the deck. He sat down on it as close as he could and brought our dicks together. The wet tips touched and lightning shot through my body.

He pulled back his foreskin and guided my cock to his. He pulled the extra skin over both heads and made a seal between us. His wrapped over the junction and stroked back and forth, so slow.

Our pre-cum oozed out and filled the flesh chamber. Our tips slipped over each other easily, and the gooey fluid added a sensuous glide between us.

He increased his speed. The clear liquid escaped and ran down my shaft. His stroke increased, down the full length of both of our dicks. His other hand cupped my balls and rolled them like dice. One finger explored between my cheeks and touched my tender hole. He probed gently and almost made me come.

I rocked my hips for him as much as I could.

His hands worked magic along my cock and more pre-cum flowed out of our union. The pleasure rose and rose, as he stroked faster and faster. He bucked his hips into his hand as he jacked.

Coppertone filled the air as the heat made more sweat pour out of his body. Rivulets ran alongside my balls and into my crease as his finger drilled in deeper. He forgot to work my balls and focused his attention on my hole. The slippery finger entered and oscillated back and forth, sending a warmth through my pelvis.

My head fell back in the wheelchair, and I grabbed onto the armrests. It wouldn't be long now.

His finger entered all the way, filling and stretching, exploring and probing. His tip rolled over my prostate, and I felt a new wave of pre-cum gush out of my cock and into the chamber.

He stroked toward me and a trickle of pre-cum escaped. He fingered my gland one more time, and my whole body went rigid.

An explosion started in my balls and shot out of my shaft. The white, hot load filled the sac and added more pleasure to the overly sensitive nerves.

"Yes," I screamed as he plunged into me again.

His cock came at the same moment. His foreskin swelled to capacity and shot my dick out like a bullet. The tidal wave of come washed over me and splattered my abs and pubes. He milked his dick a few more times and cum poured out and over me.

I grabbed my cream covered dick and sent another wave of orgasm through my balls and out my shaft.

Rico collapsed on the deck and lay gasping for air.

Sweat and cum dripped from me and pooled around him.

He picked up the hose and rinsed himself off.

Drool rolled out of my mouth as I watched the water flow over his beautiful body.

Rico shook his head, and the spray of water went everywhere. "So?

"Should I rinse you off, too? You look like you really need it."

"If you can keep my cast dry, I'm sure it would help." I braced for the cold refreshing blast. A gentle sprinkle washed over my hot, sweaty body and rinsed all the fluids off me. I closed my eyes and savored the shower.

The rim of the cast was damp after washing, but in the heat, it would dry quickly.

Rico returned with two clean towels and dried himself off as I watched. "What would you like for supper?"

I rubbed my head and brought the towel down to my chest. "Haven't you done enough? Staying the night, the deck, this?" I motioned to his naked body.

He smiled. "You'd do this for me if I needed it. That's what friends are for."

"What we did was ..."

"Great, thanks for sharing."

"What I was going to say was that we are more than friends."

"I was hoping so ..." Rico walked toward me, naked, and his big uncut penis led the way.

I looked at it eye level and knew. This gap was so easy to bridge, over and over again.

ORCHARD AFTER DARK
By Jay Starre

Residing on English Bay in Vancouver, Canada, Jay Starre has pumped out steamy gay fiction for dozens of anthologies and has written two gay erotic novels. Contact Jay Starre on Facebook.

The first time Ryan saw the pair, he couldn't help noticing their obvious differences. One was slim and the other stocky, one was laughing and the other deadly serious. The older one placed a hand on the younger one's shoulder and left it there while they talked, a small gesture but one that revealed all. They were brothers. None of their differences would ever break that bond.

It was the end of the 60s, and California was wracked by social upheaval. There were the Black riots, the drug-enthusiastic hippies, and the war protestors. It seemed as if the world was careening into a future impossible to fathom.

Ryan was back from college in Los Angeles to northern California where his family lived. He escaped the restrictions of overbearing folks and three siblings to work among the rolling hills in the orchards north of town. It was quieter there, and he loved the trees. It also wasn't quite as hot as in the Sacramento Valley below.

It was tranquil and soothing working under the leafy roof. His own troubles seemed very distant. He didn't think of the draft, or the war, or his uptight parents. What he did think of was the hot tractor driver who picked up the apricot bins every couple of hours during the long summer days.

He was intrigued by the quiet power of the Mexican-American. Built stocky with massive forearms, he had the most beautiful dark brooding eyes and lustrous wavy black hair. Ryan attempted his usual friendliness with a toothy smile every time the driver arrived at his bins, but Pedro merely glowered back or ignored him entirely.

The blond student wasn't used to being dismissed like that. He was tall and very cute. His big white smile was stunning. Gorgeous pale blue eyes looked out of a round face with an upturned nose dotted with freckles and summer tan. He was athletic, and his body was symmetrical and alluring. Everyone looked twice and liked what they saw.

It was Rodrigo, Pedro's younger brother, who liked what he saw. He was definitely the friendly one of the pair. They looked a lot alike, the same broad faces with dark eyes under darker brows, but the younger one had a dimple in his chin and a rounder mouth with bright white teeth. He smiled every time Ryan looked at him, while the older brother hadn't cracked a smile once during the entire two weeks of the season.

With only that pair of sexy fellow workers to occupy his thoughts, the blond college student had little to do but work. He was ambitious, so hard work didn't bother him at all. Even though farm labor wasn't high paying, he managed to milk it for as much cash as possible. He worked relentlessly from dawn to dusk, snatching the golden apricots off the branches and dropping them into the bucket that hung around his neck. You weren't paid by the hour, but by the bin. The more he picked, the more money he made.

"You did well today, *chico.*"

The growl from close behind startled him so much he nearly fell into the bin he was emptying his bucket into. He turned to face Pedro.

Tall himself, he towered over the muscular tractor driver. But with a swimmer's body, he hardly outweighed him. They were close enough to touch. Even though Pedro looked him directly in the eye, and had just offered him a compliment, he still couldn't manage a smile.

Ryan's cock reared up to tent his cut-off jeans. He felt himself flush as the heat in his crotch flowed upward into his face. He was totally tongue-tied.

"Everyone else is gone. Time to call it a day, *chico.*"

It was true. The vast orchard was quiet, and it was starting to get dark. Pedro had arrived on foot instead of with his tractor, which is why Ryan hadn't heard him. He actually felt the Mexican's warm breath on his face, they were that close.

"Uh, OK. You're right. I won't be able to see the apricots any more. Nothing to do but quit, I guess."

He'd blurted it out in a rush, embarrassed by the hard-on sticking out from his fly and the pink flush on his face. He was afraid Pedro would interpret both as sexual statements, which they were of course.

Fingers suddenly surrounded his wrist. A hand thrust into his crotch and squeezed his boner. His mouth dropped open, and he emitted a startled cry.

"Don't complain, *chico*. You know you want it. *Venga*, under here."

Want it? What did Pedro have in mind? Ryan's entire body shook as the husky tractor driver yanked him forward and under the nearby branches of the sprawling apricot tree he'd just been picking from.

It wasn't yet dark, but the hovering branches offered a cozy gloom that would provide them some privacy, and Ryan suddenly felt a little encouraged. Whatever happened next, no one would see but himself – and Pedro.

The hand on his crotch released him as he was unceremoniously shoved to his knees. The hands on his shoulders pulled away and moved to the crotch looming in his face. The buttons of the fly were quickly opened and out popped a truly enormous dark dick.

He gasped as he got a good look at the rearing column. It was thick, and it was long. The head was a blunt knob. He barely managed to tear his gaze away to look up into Pedro's brooding eyes. They were unrelenting as he took hold of the base of the plump tool and waved it in the blond's face.

All Ryan's life he'd been around Mexican-Americans, Mexicans, or Spanish-Americans. Raised a Catholic, he went to Mass with them every Sunday and catechism every Tuesday. Along with the Spanish language, he was taught the history of California in school, which was dominated by the Spanish colonial period. Everywhere you went in California the place names were Spanish. The culture was familiar and comforting.

And there was no denying he'd always been attracted to the dusky, dark-haired looks of those Mexican and Spanish that surrounded him. Now, finally, he was being offered a chance to actually touch one of them.

He seized the opportunity – with his wide-open mouth. He leaned forward and wrapped his lips around the engorged head bobbing in his face.

"Suck it, *chico*. *Si*, use those pretty lips. *Si*, *si*, get it all in. I am sure you can do it, *chico!*"

Ryan slurped and smacked his lips, deliriously eager to please the stocky tractor driver. He shuddered all over as he realized what he was doing, then gurgled and nearly choked as the cock in his mouth shoved inward and banged against the back of his throat.

Instinctively, he opened up. Bulbous cock-head slithered into his gullet. Amazingly he felt no need to gag. He was hot all over and feeling light-headed as he held his breath, then with a snort, sucked in air as the gigantic crown pulled back out.

"Si, *chico*. Take some air, then take me to the balls again. *Si! Si!*"

Pedro hissed out his demands in the gathering gloom, his sturdy hips barely visible in Ryan's face. He unbuckled his belt and shoved his work jeans and underwear down to his knees as he began to fuck Ryan's face.

In and out, past his tonsils, filling his throat with pulsing heat, then coming back out and exiting past his smacking lips, teasing his open mouth, then pumping right back in. The kneeling blond took it like a champ, encouraged by a constant stream of whispered nastiness from the muscular Mexican.

Daring to reach out, he ran his hands over the smooth muscle of the bare thighs in front of him. Even in the dim light, he could see how dark the skin was. Some Mexicans were much darker than others, and Pedro was one of those. The chocolate hue of that firm flesh was darker still along the length of the purple-black tool he wielded to pump the college student's gurgling mouth.

Ryan fondled the solid thighs, then dared to slide upward. One hand slid around to roam over the heaving dark butt-cheeks while the other rose up to take hold of the dangling balls. They were enormous! He tugged on them lightly as he felt all over the solid butt and slurped loudly over the huge cock.

It ended all too soon for Ryan. In the midst of thrusting deep into Ryan's throat, Pedro emitted a deep grunt and pulled out. His cock erupted a steamy spew all over the blond's upturned face. The ripe smell of cock and balls was still in his nostrils, now the stink of cum was added to that. It was so exciting he almost came himself, although his stiff cock was still in his jeans untouched.

"Good job, *chico*. I think I'll need some more of that mouth soon."

He pulled up his jeans and slipped away, leaving Ryan there under the apricot tree on his knees with his face coated in cum. The blond didn't move, intent on savoring the experience for as long as possible. Now alone, he pulled out his cock and began to stroke it.

He licked the cum off his lips, then once he got the taste of it he wiped the rest off his chin and cheeks then licked that off his fingers. He couldn't help himself and moaned out loud as he pumped his pink cock and thought about Pedro and the juicy fat bone he'd just sucked on.

That's how Rodrigo found him.

"*Chico*, what are you doing? Do you want some company?"

The whisper startled him. What now? He recognized Rodrigo's soft voice right away and could make out his slender form in the semi-darkness. The moon had come out and offered a shimmering glow through the orchard's branches.

"I saw you with my brother. He is not very considerate. I think I can show you something better."

To Ryan's total shock, the slender farm laborer moved in between Ryan and the tree bole he knelt before. He was now standing exactly where his brother had a few minutes earlier. Only instead of facing the kneeling fruit picker, he turned around and shoved his round ass in Ryan's face.

His work jeans and his underwear were down to his ankles in a flash. His bare ass was right there in front of Ryan. Still trembling from the steamy interlude with his older brother, the college student didn't even hesitate.

He knew exactly what to do, exactly what Rodrigo wanted him to do and exactly what he wanted to do himself. He spread the smooth brown ass and began licking it. Now, he found himself sniffing Mexican ass instead of Mexican cock and balls. It was awesome.

The pert cheeks jiggled in his hands as Rodrigo squirmed backwards and moaned loudly. His little pucker was satin-smooth and twitching as Ryan's pink tongue found it and began to tickle it with big swipes.

"Ay, Ay. *Si, chico*. Lick my butt-hole. Then you can fuck it."

Ryan groaned as he dropped a hand to whip it up and down over his stiff cock while he continued to lick at the snug hole, imagining his cock going up it. How tight would it be? How hot? He groaned again and clamped his lips over the quivering hole to suck on it.

The slot responded by pouting outward. He stabbed at the entrance and managed to get his tongue past the ring of muscle defending it. Rodrigo cried out as he humped the mouth attached to his hole from behind.

"*Si!* Oh *Si!* Ay! Get my butt-hole ready for your cock! *Si*, like that, *chico!*"

Ryan let go of his cock and reached back up to seize the heaving butt, now with both hands again. The skin was warm and smooth like his brother's but not as rock-solid. The cheeks of the ass jiggled slightly as they squirmed against his face, and the hole itself had quickly become a gooey, mushy pit. He continued to suck on it and stab it with his tongue as one hand slid around in front of Rodrigo to find his cock.

It was fat and thick, just like his older brother's. It reared up from his slim thighs, stiff and slick with pre-cum. The head was slippery with it and Ryan rubbed it in while he tongued Rodrigo's hole, which had him bucking and crying out.

He knew what he needed now. Like most of the pickers, he kept a bottle of lotion in his pack to soothe his hands during breaks. Picking fruit in the California sun was hell on hands. He would have to use some of that lotion to lube up his stiff cock. He was going to fuck that brown butt!

All at once and so eager he couldn't contain himself, he pulled out of the warm ass and leaped to his feet. "Stay right there. I'm getting some lotion, so I can fuck you."

"Si, *chico*. Fuck my ass good. I know you want to!"

There was an eerie similarity between the brother's voices, which sent a shudder through Ryan's body as he trotted over to his backpack and snatched it up from where it lay beside the last bin of apricots he'd been filling, where Pedro had snuck up on him earlier.

The only real difference in their voices was in their intonation. Pedro snarled out his words, while Rodrigo gave them up with a gentle friendliness. But once back under the tree and staring at the younger brother's half-naked body, the brother's differences were more apparent. Rodrigo was almost willowy, while Pedro was a bull.

At the moment, the wriggling ass in front of him was all that mattered. It seemed to call out to him. He quickly shed his boots, jeans and underwear, now wearing only his tank top. Although he was a blond, he tanned well but was still much lighter than the chocolate-hued flesh he faced.

Rodrigo had also divested himself of his boots and jeans. He wore only his tank top, too. In the moonlight, the white shirt glowed against the darkness of the round ass and slender thighs. Barefoot in the grass, Ryan stepped in between the spread thighs and squirted lotion over the parted crack he'd just had his face buried in. He squirted more creamy lotion over his jutting boner.

He stepped in even closer. Their thighs touched as his cock pushed into the open crack. The copious goo created a slippery ride as he pumped up and down the smooth crevice. Rodrigo humped up and down at the same time, and both young men groaned with pleasure.

Running his hands over the heaving butt-cheeks, his fingers slipped into that gooey crack and found the hole. He couldn't stop himself from feeling it. The rim was swollen from his avid suck job, and the entrance pouted open. Rubbing it with his cock had only made it more swollen and eager.

His fingertips stroked the lips then as Rodrigo's butt-cheeks jiggled and jerked, he eased one finger inside. The sphincter yielded but still remained snug around his finger as he pushed it deeper and deeper. The steamy heat inside was unbelievable. He pushed all the way in then pulled all the way out. He did it again, this time twisting and probing. Rodrigo's entire body thrashed.

"*Si!* Finger me then fuck me, *chico! Por favor!*"

"Heck yeah! I'm going to do that, Rodrigo! Just let me know if it hurts too much," he whispered. He couldn't say he liked his older brother, but he sure did like Rodrigo, and the last thing he wanted to do was cause the slim Mexican any pain – as much as he wanted to fuck that warm hole!

For good measure, he eased a second finger between the quivering ass-lips. He might as well stretch it out now before he attempted to work the big knob of his cock inside. The slippery lotion helped as both fingertips began to slither inward, but it was Rodrigo himself who did what needed to be done.

He reared backwards, impaling himself on the pair of fingers and grunting at the same time. Ryan gasped as he felt those clamping ass-lips surrounding the base of his fingers. Inside, it was all gooey and pulsing. He had to stick his cock in there!

"Ready for it, Rodrigo?"

"*Si!* Fuck me, Ryan!"

He slid his fingers out and aimed his cock-head at the pouting hole left behind. The lips quivered and pushed outward as he settled between them. The head of his cock was broad like a helmet, but the shaft itself was lean and rigid. Once he got that big knob in, the rest would follow much easier.

Although he was dying to ram it right in, he merely probed gently, giving the lips time to accommodate the huge girth. Rodrigo stopped wriggling and held himself entirely still. He reached back and held his own brown ass-cheeks apart so that Ryan had a good view of his cock planted against that hole.

In the ghostly moonlight, his pale cock stood out against the darkness of that round ass. He watched as the lips slowly yielded, and the flared head began to disappear. Heated lips quivered and pulsed around him then suddenly parted and swallowed. He cried out as the entire head vanished beyond the dark ass-lips.

Pulsing flesh wrapped around his buried cock-head. Heat and tightness surrounded it. There was nothing to do now but fuck! He drove forward, just as Rodrigo heaved backwards. Half the length of his cock disappeared.

Neither of them were capable of any finesse by this time. The young Mexican-American bucked against the stiff rod drilling him from behind while the blond college student gripped his heaving ass-cheeks and pounded away.

The tight hole grew looser and looser as lotion squirted out around the pumping pink pole and dribbled down to coat both their balls. Rodrigo remained bent over with his own hands on his ass holding it open while Ryan gripped his hips and pummeled him.

There was a wild rhythm to the their thrashing bodies, which had them both on the brink of release before they knew it. Rodrigo precipitated their climaxes by achieving one of his own first. He didn't even need to touch his own cock. Ramming his hole back over that drilling pink cock was enough for him.

He shot a big load all over the tree bole in front of him. His asshole went into convulsions as his balls emptied, which did the trick for Ryan. Steamy innards pulsed around his pumping cock. He yanked it out and sprayed Rodrigo's sweet brown butt.

Rodrigo turned and pulled Ryan into his arms. Both still leaking cum, they embraced. They even kissed, which was a real treat for Ryan. Naked except for their tank tops, they huddled together in the moonlight under the tree branches, inhaling the stink of their own cum and sweat, and the smell of leaves and grass and ripe fruit.

The next day, the orchard seemed entirely different. There was a definite sensuality to the warm sunshine filtering through the gently waving branches. There was the promise of something exciting happening again that night, or the next.

Of course Pedro acted as if nothing at all had happened between them while Rodrigo continued to be as friendly and bright as ever, even winking conspiratorially when their eyes met.

He saw the brothers together again that next afternoon. The sun was shining down on them, a golden halo around their glossy black hair and dark-brown complexions. Rodrigo was laughing, while his stocky brother placed an arm across his shoulders and spoke straight-faced and seriously. It was strange how different the two brothers were, but how alike as well. Yet once he thought about it, there was perfect sense to it. It seemed an integral part of the California Spanish-American culture, that open friendliness and that brooding darkness side-by-side.

When the first day after their moonlight trysts ended, it was Rodrigo who came to him and offered up his chocolate-brown butt again with laughing eagerness. His older brother waited almost a week before he abruptly appeared at dusk to haul Ryan under a tree and unceremoniously fuck his face for the second time. Rodrigo watched, hidden behind a nearby tree, until they were done and then came to Ryan to help finish him off. Pedro was none the wiser, according to his younger brother.

So that's how Ryan spent the rest of his summer, picking fruit from dawn to dusk, and afterwards under those same trees either sucking Pedro's juicy cock or fucking Rodrigo's sexy brown ass, or both.

It was the best summer of his life.

THE GAUCHO AND THE TANGO DANCER
By Jay Starre

In a small tavern east of Buenos Aires in The Pampas a gaucho and his *compadres* were drinking the night away while watching the entertainment. The highlight of the evening was a group of tango dancers who had come out from the big city. One particular dancer stood out.

He was tall and slim, with an elegant grace to him that outshone all the others. His ink-black hair was swept back from a high forehead, while wide-set golden eyes hovered above a long Italian nose, pouting lips and strong chin. He was quite handsome, and he knew it.

Antonio watched him dance, as did most of the others through their wine and brandy. But unlike the others, the gaucho's gaze hardly wavered from the graceful prance he offered as he swept his partner around the dance floor in a dramatically rhythmic embrace. The pair moved in complete tandem, their bodies sharing a telepathic trust.

But, the gaucho saw more. Able to read the intentions of a horse, a dog, or a bull at a moment's notice, it was an easy matter to read these two. They shared the physical and the mental part of the intricate dance, but emotionally, they were two separate and two very distant beings. It was the tall dark-haired partner who created that distance.

Antonio knew. He knew if he waited, he could get what he wanted.

Dawn saw a golden sun rising over a green expanse of meadows and pastures at the edge of the small town. Here the gauchos made their living tending the cattle that fed the nation, and the world.

Antonio had waited for that dawn outside the tavern and was rewarded for his stoic patience. The dancer strolled out the back door, alone. The gaucho stood a half dozen yards away beside a hitching post where his horse was tethered. He stared directly at the exiting dancer and nodded.

The tall performer nodded in return and smiled. *"Papa, que tal?"*

Antonio offered his own smile, although it wasn't a particularly pleasant one. The young dancer had called him papa, obviously referring to their age difference. He was nearly thirty-five, after all. Hard living as a gaucho had definitely bestowed upon him a sun-bronzed, mature look. Yet able to lasso, ride and wrestle steers from dawn to dusk, he knew he could take the lithe dancer apart in two minutes.

"Niño, venga. Come on. I have something to show you. Something I know you will want to see."

His confident maturity easily matched the tango dancer's youthful self-assurance. The contest between them already had sparks flying.

"Now? Come with you on your horse? Why would I do that?"

"You will ride with me because I want you to. And because you want to. *Venga."*

The gaucho untied his horse and mounted without saying another word, although his dark eyes never wavered from their piercing lock on the tango dancer's golden orbs.

"I am Silvio, if you care to know. And you are?"

"Yo soy Antonio. Take my hand," the gaucho commanded with one arm outstretched.

Silvio laughed, truly delighted at the unexpected and spontaneous offer. Not that he hadn't noticed the brooding gaucho earlier in the night. How could he not? The man had watched him with a relentless glare, practically eating him up with his gloriously dark eyes. He was a big man, not tall but wide-shouldered and big-chested with mighty forearms and giant hands. His features were sultry and exciting, a broad nose, very plump lips and those intense black eyes. He had surprisingly light hair though, an auburn streaked with red from hours in the Argentinean sun. As well, a reddish goatee surrounded the full mouth. A green kerchief was knotted at his neck, and along with a clean white shirt set off his dark eyes and auburn hair.

Now, his wide flat-brimmed black hat covered the short mop of auburn, but his piercing eyes and full mouth were as alluring as they had been earlier in the night. Silvio willingly took that hand and allowed the gaucho to pull him up behind him.

Immediately, Antonio kicked them off to a canter. Silvio wasn't entirely inexperienced and was able to hold on without any problem. As a trained dancer, it was a simple feat to allow his body to ease into the loping stride of the horse beneath him.

Not wasting any time, his hands around the gaucho's waist dropped to grope his crotch. He discovered a large bulge beneath the heavy denim trousers. The bulge swelled the moment he groped it.

Silvio leaned in to croon a challenge in Antonio's ear. "Is this what you wanted to show me? *Esta bueno*, but I have seen many cocks before. What is so special about this one?"

The teasing tone was followed by laughter and more squeezing, which had that bulge stiffening up into truly prodigious proportions. Regardless of what he'd said, Silvio was impressed.

"Ay, this one is special because of what I can do with it. You will see."

"Promises, promises."

The contest that had begun the moment they greeted each other outside the tavern was now in full swing. Their canter through the morning sunlight lasted a mere quarter of an hour, but every moment of it was exciting and fraught with the promise of more. Silvio leaned in close, pressing his own stiff cock into Antonio from behind while he continued to squeeze and massage the fat pipe beneath the gaucho's jeans.

An expansive blue sky surrounded them while the rolling landscape embraced them in verdant green. They dropped down into a small valley where copses of acacia and mimosa offered some privacy from the open surroundings.

"My humble abode," Antonio announced as he reined in just before a small cabin. "Wait on the porch, *por favor*."

They dismounted and Silvio did as he was told. The morning sunlight streamed in from the eastern side of the roofed porch, and he sat in its warmth as he waited for Antonio to tend to his horse.

It wasn't long before the sturdy gaucho returned. His powerful stride carried him up onto the porch and in front of the seated dancer. "Have you ever danced? You have the grace for it, even if you are too muscular ..."

He was cut off in mid-sentence as Antonio reached down and yanked him to his feet, then covered his mouth with a kiss. His husky arms surrounded Silvio and pulled him into a fierce

27

embrace as his tongue stabbed between his plump lips and twirled in circles.

Silvio was hardly content to remain passive, even though he was trapped in those powerful arms. His own arms came around the bigger man's torso, and his hands fluttered up and down the broad back and jutting ass. He squeezed the large butt-mounds and pulled the gaucho even closer as their stiff cocks mashed together beneath the confines of their trousers.

He opened wide for Antonio's delving tongue then sucked on it with slurps and smacks. As that tongue swirled inside him, the clamping arms around his back suddenly released him enough to push him backwards a few steps against the porch railing.

It was so swift and unexpected; Silvio was not even sure how it happened. One moment they were kissing; the next he was lifted off his feet and twisted around, then bent over to straddle the porch railing. His arms and legs dangled down on either side of the smooth pole.

Startled but not daunted, he asked with a laugh, "Are you going to fuck me right here, gaucho? Bent over your porch railing and in the open?"

He choked that laugh back as he watched the quickly moving cowboy snatch his lasso from the wall where it hung on a peg, then whirl around and step back over to him. Before he could react, Antonio seized his dangling wrists and looped the long rope around them and between the posts of the railing.

He was tied in place!

Yet he was hardly frightened. Even though the powerful Argentinean cowboy displayed a dark and menacing façade, Silvio could sense there was no cruelty in the man's nature. As well, gauchos had a reputation to uphold and would do nothing to betray that. Yes, they were known to be hard-drinking and even hard-brawling, but their honesty and sense of justice were equally well-known.

The gauchos also were reputed to have an adventurous spirit. The moment Silvio took Antonio's outstretched hand and mounted his horse, he knew what followed wouldn't be ordinary.

"*Si*. I am going to fuck you right here over the railing of my porch. I am going to fuck you in that sweet mouth of yours, and up that beautiful ass of yours. You will love it."

"Promises, promises," Silvio challenged back.

Antonio smiled, but his eyes were hooded and intense. He was appreciative of the roped dancer's bravado, but knew his next action would have him less willing to bluster. The gaucho's tools included the lasso he'd just employed, but also a big and very sharp knife.

He slid that knife out of its sheath at his waist and went to work. As swiftly as he'd upended and roped the dancer, he ran the gleaming blade up the back of his ruby-red tango shirt to slice it in two. It fell in tatters around his dangling arms. Before Silvio had a chance to offer any kind of protest, that blade expertly sliced down the center of his trousers, from waist to crotch. The underwear exposed beneath immediately suffered the same fate.

Quickly, he gripped the torn sides of Silvio's pants and undershorts and ripped them wide open. He yanked downward then with another savage slice, cut them in two. With a deft toss, he returned the knife to its sheath then yanked down the split trousers even further to dangle at Silvio's feet.

Although the dancer was shaking all over and gasping at the suddenness of that savage strip, he managed to continue blustering. "I hope you've got something for me to put on afterwards!"

"No, *mi amigo*. I will make you walk back to town barefoot and naked, your ass and your mouth aching from taking my big fat cock."

He had hardly finished when he seized the dangling dancer by the hair and forced his face into his crotch. He tore his fly open and shoved his jeans down to reveal the cock he'd promised. And it was truly huge.

The head was a dark plum, round and blunt. He shoved it between Silvio's gasping lips while maintaining a grip on the hair on the back of his head. He began to pump it in and out of Silvio's gurgling mouth as his free hand reached back and groped the dancer's naked ass.

The sweet mouth yawned wide as Silvio did his best to swallow all he was offered. He managed a smirk around the thrusting knob, but that turned to a startled gurgle as the hand on his round ass rose and then fell to smack loudly against the amber flesh.

A series of smarting slaps rang out one after the other as more and more cock slithered into his mouth and toward his throat. His ass stung with a pleasant heat, which actually stimulated him enough to open wide and allow the burrowing cock-head to slide past his tonsils.

"*Si, niño.* Take that cock into your tight throat while I work over your ass! Now, how is that hole down there? Eager for the same treatment?"

The slapping halted, immediately followed by fingers digging between his pink-flushed cheeks and along his spread crack. The valley was wide-open across the railing, and the hole was clearly visible and undefended. Antonio grinned wickedly as he stared down at it and began to rub and stroke it.

Big gaucho fingers teased the snug ass-lips. The fingers strummed across it, spread it open, and then slapped it. There wasn't yet any attempt to penetrate it without lubrication to ease the way, but there was no question that was soon to come – though the manner of that penetration was not at all what Silvio might have expected!

Antonio slid his cock-head out of Silvio's tight throat and then out of his mouth. Drool followed the knob and coated his chin and full lips as he gasped for breath. His golden eyes followed the gaucho's naked hips as he turned to the cabin wall to fetch another of his work tools.

Three iron balls dangled from leather cords. It was the bola, the implement gauchos used to ensnare small game as they raised it, swung it, then let fly. Silvio had no idea what it would now be used for.

The sneering Argentinean kicked off his boots and jeans and tore off his shirt. He returned to his bound plaything naked, except for the green kerchief knotted around his thick neck.

"What are you doing?" Silvio bleated as those huge hands dove down between his splayed thighs and seized his cock and balls from behind.

"You will see. And I can tell you will like it."

Silvio bit back a smart reply as those hands gripped his defenseless ball sack and stiff cock. He waited breathlessly for what the gaucho had planned for them. He quickly found out. The strips of leather cord swiftly encircled the base of his cock and surrounded his sack. Tightly, but not too tightly, the leather was wrapped and tied, leaving those heavy iron balls to dangle down and stretch his tender parts.

His cock and balls now hung down on the porch side of the rail he straddled. His dangling nuts swelled up immediately, while his cock was already stiff and dripping. That pole was long and curved, with the foreskin peeled back to reveal the tapered head shiny with leaking pre-cum. He groaned aloud as he felt all that weight pulling down on his bound sack and rod.

But, he still had no notion of what the gaucho planned next. Writhing over the railing with that heavy weight pulling down on his cock and balls, his hands bound and unable to do much of anything to resist the stocky Argentinean's plans, he watched with a wary eye as Antonio returned once more to the wall and opened a small cabinet nailed to it.

Silvio couldn't help staring at the gaucho's chunky ass, two huge mounds of smooth brown muscle. He wondered if the man ever allowed a cock to burrow between the massive cheeks and his own cock throbbed and dribbled at the very idea. Perhaps if he played his cards right, he might get a chance to explore that powerful rear.

He almost laughed. He was in no position to do anything but go along for now. Even that notion had his cock jerking and leaking! Antonio turned and came back, his massive pole rearing up like a purple club at his crotch. Silvio gasped as he recalled how it tasted and felt in his mouth.

Now it would go up his ass! Or at least he thought that was the plan. Antonio held a small bottle of olive oil which would obviously serve to ease the way for what he intended to do with the pink hole he'd just rubbed and stroked.

Oil splashed over his rearing buttocks, the amber liquid almost exactly the same color as the smooth flesh. Both Antonio and Silvio were typical Argentineans. Antonio was descended from Spanish immigrants, with just a hint of native Indian in his blood, while Silvio sprang from an Italian background. These were the two dominant groups who had filled the Argentinean landscape over the years. Even their Spanish had a distinct Italian accent to it.

Silvio was a little bit lighter in complexion and skin tone, and a little bit smoother. Antonio was darker by a shade or two, while his chest was lightly furred with the same reddish hair as his goatee. His eyes were darker than the fairer dancer's, even though his hair was lighter.

The gaucho's massive hands, nothing like Silvio's slender ones, spread the oil over the round, hairless ass and into the crack. This time the blunt and oily fingertips not only rubbed the tender pink hole, but also, they found the center and stabbed deep into it.

"*Dios mio!* Ay, ay," Silvio cried out. The sudden probing wasn't painful; in fact it caused a throbbing ache that was so exciting, he found himself squirming upward toward it.

Antonio laughed as he twisted the pair of fingers up Silvio's tender ass. Without removing the big digits, he stepped back to the dancer's face where he immediately gagged him with that blunt cock-knob again. A few minutes of mouth-fucking and finger-fucking followed.

Silvio writhed over the railing, every squirm causing the dangling iron balls to tug at his nuts and cock. Regardless of the fact his mouth was stuffed with hot, pulsing cock and his asshole was stuffed with twisting, digging gaucho fingers, he was totally aware of those dangling iron balls.

He was about to become more aware of them.

"You will like this, *niño.*"

The growled promise was followed by something totally unexpected. The fingers slid from his throbbing asshole. A moment later something round and hard began to press against the swollen lips. It had to be one of the bola balls!

Antonio stared down at his handiwork and grinned. Such a sweet smooth body, so elegant and symmetrical in form, and now roped and tied and defenseless! The iron ball he placed at the entrance to Silvio's oiled and squishy slot was smooth and dark. He took great care of his tools, and had applied a black shellac varnish to each of the three bola balls so that they were shiny and very smooth. They weren't very big, yet were still large enough to strain the snug sphincter as he pressed inward.

Pumping his cock deep into Silvio's throat at the same time, he pushed against the resisting anal muscle and watched with satisfaction as the oily black ball finally popped within and disappeared. The leather cord attached to it lay along the smooth crack and down to the dancer's balls and cock where the other end wound around them.

There were still two more. As he slowly pumped in and out of Silvio's pulsing throat, listening to his snorts for air, he stared down at the wriggling round ass and the oozing amber hole. He slowly fed the next black ball into that oiled hole, then after that one disappeared, the next. Silvio reared and bucked now that he was full of three of the iron balls, but still he had no idea of what would come next.

Antonio laughed aloud as he gripped one of the leather cords and began to pull on it. Both ends tugged against Silvio's body parts. One end pulled upwards on his trapped cock and balls, while the other end pulled at the buried iron ball up the dancer's ass it was attached to. He knew exactly what he was doing, and with delicate precision held that iron ball just inside the straining sphincter, not yet allowing it to exit.

Even though Silvio was bound, he was not helpless. His asshole throbbed as the iron ball teased the inside of his sphincter, but wasn't quite yanked out. He sucked Antonio's huge shaft right to the balls and reared backwards. He willed his asshole to open.

The iron ball popped out with a splash of oil.

Antonio laughed with pleasure, and even though he had some respect for the writhing dancer's response to his teasing, he wasn't about to let him think he'd won the day. With a rapid tug, he yanked the second iron ball out unexpectedly.

Silvio gurgled and heaved. The third ball came quickly out with another slurp. The gaucho didn't wait for the writhing to abate before he crammed three fingers up the violated hole, twisted them to stab at the dancer's aching prostate, yanked them back out and began again to feed him the trio of iron balls.

While he fucked the dancer's drooling mouth, he stuffed his oiled hole with those shiny black bola balls, then yanked them back out. Silvio gurgled and heaved, attacked from either end and loving every moment of it.

"Time to fuck that plump, hungry ass. It is hungry for cock, isn't it *niño*?"

The husky growl was followed by a nasty laugh as cock slid from Silvio's mouth and allowed him to speak for the first time in several minutes. The dancer retorted with a nasty demand of his own.

"*Si, papa!* Fuck my fat ass! Take those bola balls out and shove in your cock!"

"Why should I take them out? You will like it better if I don't."

Now Silvio was shocked. How would that feel? The gaucho's cock was huge! He'd stretched his lips wide to take it in, and barely contained it in his tight throat. He shuddered as he contemplated that massive meat slithering into his gut, with those bola balls stuffed in there, too!

Antonio was true to his word. He moved behind Silvio and straddled the railing to plant his big bare feet right behind the dancer's shoes and torn pants. He pressed his powerful thighs against the dancer's lithe ones and aimed his gigantic purple cock at the oiled crack dividing the smooth round cheeks.

The three bola balls were buried in the leaking amber hole. The strips of leather they were attached to ran from the swollen ass-lips down to the trapped balls and cock. Oil smeared the wriggling cheeks and deep crack. Antonio grinned wickedly as he planted the slippery head of his cock on target and slowly began to press inward.

Silvio cried out as the plump knob stretched apart his quivering sphincter and slid into him. "*Dios mio!* Ay! Ay!"

"*Si.* I knew you would love it, *niño!*"

Antonio's nasty laughter rang out in the morning quiet along with Silvio's bleated cries. The sensation was incredible, for both Argentineans. The gaucho's burrowing cock was enveloped in trembling ass-lips and steamy gut. He could feel the iron balls sliding out of the way as his huge cock-head pushed deeper and deeper. Silvio felt all that stiff pole slithering into him, pulsing and hot, and the balls being shifted in his steamy bowels.

The gaucho took his time. He slid the purple meat in halfway, then slowly withdrew until it popped out into the open air, slick with oil and ass juices. He grinned as he pumped it back in, deeper this time. Silvio's lovely amber ass-cheeks shook and squirmed, but he was trapped over the railing and unable to do anything other than accept the deep probing.

Antonio pumped in and out, deeper with every slow insertion, until cock was finally buried right to the balls. Silvio gasped for air, never having been so stuffed before. Not only was the gaucho's cock enormous, but also the three iron balls in his gut added an aching pressure that had him shaking from head to toe.

The gaucho ran his massive paws all over the dancer's lithe back, ass and thighs. The calloused palms were rough, but the touch surprisingly gentle as the enormous cock slowly thrust in and out of his battered and quaking asshole.

Those hands eventually settled on the dancer's shoulder and pulled backwards as the fuck grew more vigorous. Now each thrust went balls-deep, and every withdrawal was complete. The thick shank disappeared entirely up the oozing amber hole, then came out to quiver and jerk in the sunlight before thrusting back in.

This deep gutting would bring the gaucho to his well-deserved release. His breathing grew ragged as he pumped his hot meat home, then yanked it back out. Grunting, he moved quickly. Suddenly he was no longer behind Silvio, instead hovering beside his face with that rearing cock aimed for his gasping mouth.

The head pushed between his lips just as it erupted. A spew of tasty nut cream filled his mouth. The dancer sucked it in just as a trio of big gaucho fingers drove up his ass to press against the buried bola balls.

He writhed all over the railing, his asshole on fire from those twisting fingers and the aching sensation of those iron balls being worked around in his gut. A river of spunk filled his mouth as he swallowed and swallowed.

Cock withdrew from his mouth and fingers from his asshole. He watched as Antonio stepped back to collapse into a wicker chair against the wall a few yards away. The bound dancer couldn't help grinning with a smug satisfaction as he noted how the hefty thighs trembled and the big chest heaved. Even though he'd been the one violated, he experienced an element of triumph in the way the fuck had seemingly exhausted the burly gaucho.

But, Antonio proved himself far from exhausted. He smiled at the roped dancer and winked. Then he lifted one powerful thigh and pulled it back to his chest. His deep crack was exposed!

A light reddish fur coated the hefty hamstrings, but the big ass was less hairy with only a light down of pale hair. Between the husky cheeks, a wrinkled slot pouted. Antonio slid a calloused hand down between his spread legs and began to rub and tease the hole. He laughed wickedly.

"You will get a chance at this hole soon, *niño*. You will lick it and then you will fuck it. But first, I will fuck you some more."

The promise of more fucking to come before the dancer had a chance to get into that gaucho hole was emphasized by the gaucho's other hand stroking his still-stiff cock. The big thing, slick with Silvio's spit, reared up from his crotch, obviously ready for more action. The combination of that one hand pumping the monster rod and the other hand stroking the pouting asshole was too much for Silvio.

He began to shoot. Straddling the railing, his hands tied with the gaucho's lasso, his balls and cock tied and his asshole stuffed with the gaucho's bola balls, he cried out as he stared at that lewd display and sprayed the pole between his legs.

As he bucked and quivered in the morning sunlight, Antonio laughed and laughed.

Then he got up and fucked Silvio again.

GAME BALL
By Landon Dixon

Dixon's stories have been published in the many magazines and anthologies, and he is a contributor to several STARbooks Press anthologies.

I was still upset with myself half-an-hour after the game. Everyone else had already changed and gone home, taking the 12-11 loss in stride. It was only a recreational indoor soccer league game, after all.

But I'd missed the tying goal with three seconds left. Faced with a goalie prone out of position, I'd sailed a shot right into the net – the net that hung from the ceiling of the arena to keep balls from flying into the stands.

I gripped the sink in the change room and hung my head, too disgusted to even look at myself in the mirror.

Smack!

I jumped up onto my toes, the swift whack on the ass waking me out of my misery. I stared into the mirror. Octavio was standing there, grinning at me.

"Still punishing yourself over blowing that goal, huh?" he said. "Mind if I lend a hand?"

Before I could object, the big, raven-haired guy smacked my butt again, jolting me a second time, this time on the other cheek. I was still wearing my game shorts, but that pitifully thin garment did little to take away the sting of the guy's huge right hand.

Octavio was completely naked. He'd obviously just come out of the showers located on the other side of the sinks and urinals. His smooth, rugged body glistened like copper, his cock sticking almost straight out from between his legs.

I got a weird feeling – in my mind and ass and groin. I stared at Octavio's long, hard prick in the mirror, my hands gone damp on the sides of the sink, my legs shaking.

And he swatted my bum again, and again. My butt flesh throbbed with heat, like my cock. I was actually getting turned-on by the guy's rough touch, the sight of his naked body and dick.

He got even more touchy, suddenly sinking his bare hands into the back of my shorts and splaying them out on my bare buttocks. "Want me to rub it better, baby?" he joked, massaging my burning bum. He was still grinning as if it was all in a day's work as team captain, his swollen cockhead sniffing up over my ass.

I gulped, my entire body shimmering with Octavio's hands plying my cheeks. First the pain, then the pleasure, then pain and pleasure together – from a guy! I'd never experienced anything like it before. But, so help me, I was truly getting off on it.

Octavio knew it, too. He pulled his hands out of my shorts and then pulled my shorts right down. My bubble-butt popped out nude and lewd right before the nude and lewd dude and his aroused cock, my own dick now fully poled out in front of me.

He clutched my cheeks and squeezed them, kneaded them, his dong bobbing.

"Jesus!" I breathed, on fire back and front. The guy's cheer job was sure as hell working; I couldn't even remember the score of the game we'd just played.

But, Octavio knew the score. He roamed his hands all over my butt, caressing and groping, getting himself a real good feel, and giving one. Then he released my right cheek and grasped his hard-on, slapped my buttock with the iron rod. I yelped, not from any actual pain, but from the blistering intimacy of skin-on-skin cock-to-ass.

Octavio whacked my left cheek with his dick, my right again, really laying down the lumber. I shivered with every sharp, sexual blow, my own cock jumping higher and harder.

Then I made my move, staring at Octavio's handsome face, his bright brown eyes reflected in the mirror. I grabbed onto my cock and started stroking, putting it all out there.

We were playing a better, hotter game than soccer now, one-on-one, and scoring was right at my fingertips. I fisted my cock from tightened balls to boiled-up cap, Octavio smacking my butt cheeks to rippling with his heavy dong.

It had all flared up so quickly and unexpectedly that I was ready to go off in seconds. Octavio sensed it, seeing my trembling legs and buttocks. He cracked my cheeks a couple more times with his prick and then cranked himself, stroking his cock fast and furious over my blazing ass.

I stared at the guy in the mirror, at his mounded, clenching pecs, his stiff, burnt-sugar nipples, his tight, muscled stomach, his hand shooting up and down the length of his tremendous erection. "Yeah!" I grunted, pumping to keep pace.

"Drop it!" he suddenly barked.

I wasn't sure what he was talking about. So he showed me, bending down slightly and reaching in between my legs and knocking my hand off my dick, replacing it with his hand.

"Jesus!" I gulped a second time. The guy's hot, smooth hand felt wicked good on my throbbing pole. He pumped back and forth, stretching me out with sensation, his forearm rubbing my balls just the right way.

I gripped the sink and held on for dear life, not wanting to come until we'd played every aspect of this new game. Because something told me we were still in the first half, the best, and Octavio and I, yet to come.

Sure enough, the big guy squatted right down in behind me, still jacking my cock. I felt a soft, warm pair of lips on my ass, kissing the sting out of my cheeks. Then a wet tongue, pressing against a lit-up buttock, swirling all over the burning skin.

I dropped my head almost right down into the sink, on fire with the strange erotic feelings of getting my cock stroked by another man, getting my ass kissed. My whole body shook, my dick a numb piece of meat in Octavio's caressing hand, as he lightly sunk his teeth into one of my seat cushions, the other one, then slid his tongue in between my cheeks.

"Fuck!" I cried, shooting up, jolted by the electric impact of his tongue on my crack.

He let go of my cock and planted both hands on my bum, spread my mounds, exposing my virgin pucker. He kept me in suspense like that for a moment. Then he blew on my asshole, and I just about went right through the mirror. He quickly followed up hot air with hot, wet tongue, pushing his neon-pink sticker against my starfish.

I bit my lip and dug my fingernails into the enamel, never feeling anything like it before in my life – someone licking my asshole. Fuck, it felt delicious! The guy bathed my ultra-sensitive manhole, stroked my pucker, lapped at my crack. He dragged his tongue up and down in between my cheeks, from balls to tailbone, over and over, leaving me breathless and blazing.

Then he really bit his fingernails into my cheeks and ripped the pair wide open, jammed his tongue right into my bung. I jerked, and groaned, the tip of his squirming mouth-organ and two more inches besides shooting inside me, invading my rectum with heat and dampness.

He pumped back and forth, fucking my ass with his tongue. I closed my eyes and tilted my head back, fully realizing what an erogenous zone I had back there. My straining cock twitched up and down, in rhythm to Octavio spearing my chute.

Then he plunged his tongue in as far as it would go, and kept it plugged there, writhing around. I full-body shuddered, arcs of joy sparking all through me, from the tongue-stuffed bung on up. He couldn't have jacked me up anymore if he'd stuck a live wire in my ass.

Finally, he withdrew his tongue, oozing it out slow and oh-so sensuous from my asshole. "Gimme some soap, playa," he growled, getting back to his feet.

I twisted my head around and stared at him. He nodded, his huge hard-on doing the same. We'd gotten this far into the game. There was no quitting now.

I pumped soap from the sink dispenser into my hand then handed it back to Octavio. He scooped it out of my trembling paw and slathered it onto his cock, grinning at me, greasing the full length of his prick. I watched him, my nerves screaming, my own cock pulsating. Then, I really did scream, when he slid his slippery fingers into my crack and lubed me up.

He scrubbed in between my cheeks, soaping my asshole, stroking my sensitive butt cleavage. "Let's see if you're game-ready," he said at last, then glided a long, thick finger inside of me.

"Yes!" I cried, his digit filling the aching emptiness his tongue had left in my asshole.

He gripped my waist with his other hand and dug his finger into my butt up to the third knuckle, pumped. He pushed me back and forth with the force of his stretching, probing finger, delving pleasurably deep inside of me. Then he doubled the pleasure, sliding another digit into my bung.

I groaned and glared at my sweating reflection in the mirror, getting finger-fucked by the stud. He slammed his digits in and out, his fist banging off my cheeks. My cock jumped wildly with each deep-body thrust, like my soul.

His fingers glided all the way out, leaving me with that savage emptiness again. But only for a moment. I felt something thick and meaty pressing against my bunghole – his cap. I stared at him. He was gritting his teeth and gazing down at my ass with a concentrated expression on his face, gripping my waist and his cock, pressing his hood into my pucker.

"Fuck, yeah!" I growled, the guy popping through, popping my anal cherry, his cap crowding the entrance to my chute.

Octavio didn't let up on the pressure, driving shaft through my ring, sinking his big cock slow and sure into my anus; all eight veiny, amazing inches. My ass was on fire like never before, swollen with pulsating dong, the blaze spreading to my balls and cock and all through the rest of my body. It felt weird, wonderful, wicked, having a man's beating cock jammed up my ass.

Octavio didn't waste any time mourning my loss of anal virginity. Instead, he celebrated it, gripping both of my hips and churning his, pumping his pole back and forth in my chute. I groaned my encouragement, my head spinning, eyes blurring, my ass getting stuffed full of feeling, fucked to the limit.

"Christ, you're tight, hot!" Octavio growled, pounding into my anus. His pecs clenched, and his stomach clutched, his heavy thighs banging against my battered cheeks, his axe just about splitting me in two.

I rocked back and forth to his brutally sensual rhythm. Then I grabbed up my own cock again, slid my soapy hand up and down its raging length. But I could hardly feel it, the awesome sensation of the big guy's plunging cock in my dirtbox overpowering all others.

Octavio slapped my ass, rippling my cheeks with the flat of his hand, as he rammed into them with his body. He stung me again and again, never breaking the plundering pace of his dick in my chute. The steamy air filled with the crack of flesh against flesh, the moaning and groaning of two men getting it on in the greatest sport known to man.

Octavio upped the tempo to frenzy level, grabbing onto my waist with both hands again and absolutely reaming my ass. My anus burned with the pistoning friction, his cock plunging down to the balls and back up again, sawing me in two. I fisted my own dick to keep up, glaring at the fucking stud in the mirror.

The tension swelled to a towering level, the air crackling, Octavio's thighs gunshotting off my buttocks. We breathed through our flared nostrils, concentrating full-bore on Octavio's cock thundering into my ass.

Then I danced up onto my tip-toes, my own cock going off in my flying hand. Just as Octavio threw back his head and howled, his dong exploding in my anus. He jerked around on the end of my ass like I was jerking around on the end of his cock, spurting fire against my bowels. He filled me to overflowing, as I jetted my own balls out against the sink, over and over and over again.

I would've collapsed into blissful unconsciousness and clunked my head on enamel, if Octavio hadn't scooped me up in his arms and held me tight to his heaving chest, his cock still buried in my simmering butt. We stood like that, breathing hard, melded together, trembling with the sweet aftershocks of our all-out ecstasy. Octavio cupped my pecs and kissed my neck, gently undulating his hips against my ass, rutting his cock around in my beautifully violated chute.

I leaned my head back on the guy's massive shoulder and sighed, "Well-played, man."

He smiled. "Glad my post-game pep talk got your mind off the soccer match."

I turned my head and kissed him, our lips meeting soft and warm, then harder, hotter, deeper. I spun around in his arms, his cock popping out of my ass, pressing up against my cock full-frontal. We clutched each other tight, kissing, then Frenching, our tongues twisting together, our cocks squeezing, sliding, hardening.

"Game's not over yet, stud," I breathed, staring into the guy's smoldering brown eyes.

He grinned, going down to his knees in front of my reinvigorated dick. Game on!

CAUGHT IN A TRAP
By Landon Dixon

He was dragging boxes out of the elevator, trying to keep the doors open with one hand while he wrestled cardboard with the other. I just had to lend my hand, help out a new neighbor move his belongings into his new apartment. It didn't hurt that he was drop-dead gorgeous.

His name was Carlos, and his new place was three doors down from my apartment. He was long and lean and bronze, with shiny, shoulder-length black hair, sparkling green eyes, a long, handsome face sporting a slender nose and dimpled chin. We hit it off instantly; incendiary, on my part.

I helped him unload his stuff out of the rental van parked down by the curb and lug the boxes and furniture onto the elevator and into his apartment. It was a hot day, like all moving days, and as one panting hour stretched into two, Carlos started shedding clothing. His jeans were the first to go, then his T-shirt; replaced by tight, white shorts and no shirt at all. His taut, mounded butt cheeks filled out the shorts in back, his golden-brown, toned torso with puffy, darker nipples filling out my field of vision in front.

Yes, I was staring; gawking, actually. My mouth hung open and tongue out not just from lack of oxygen due to all the exertion. I took every opportunity to bring up the rear – his rear. I let him bend down and lift the really heavy boxes with his long back and legs, his rounded bottom, watching the buttocks and muscles strain. And any time we entered or exited the elevator, or his apartment, I rushed to make it a tight twosome through the portals, so that we rubbed up against one another. A perpetual boner bulged my jeans, my balls sweating heavier than the rest of me.

"Whew! That's the last of it," Carlos said all too soon, looking around at his cluttered new home.

He plucked a towel out of a box marked "bathroom" and wiped the perspiration off his face and torso. I watched with unblinking eyes, absorbing every quiver of his long muscle fibres, the caress of that lucky, fluffy towel over his smooth, humped chest and protruding nipples.

43

"Hey, you want a towel? You look pretty damp yourself."

"N-no, that's okay," I stammered, picking up the used towel he'd flung back down onto a box. I rubbed my face in it, in the man's musky, sweaty, sensual scent.

I guess I moaned a little, too, kind of bit into the rub-rag to see if I could suck some of his essence right into my mouth and taste the man. Because his beautiful face wore a strange expression when I peeked my eyes over the top of the towel and looked at him.

"How 'bout a cold one?" he asked. "To cool down."

I gulped and nodded. The window air-conditioner was running full-blast, but, if anything, I was getting hotter, together with Carlos in that closed apartment, just the two of us. He handed me an ice cube-loaded glass of cola before I'd even managed to squeeze off a dozen strokes on my throbbing hard-on while he was in the kitchen.

We sat on his sofa and sipped our drinks. He started asking me questions about the building and the neighborhood. Nice, normal conversation. I choked out the answers as best I could, staring at his lovely face and body, wishing I was sharing his lovely face and body.

It was too much, too close, too hot. I had to get relief or burst my jeans and a couple of blood vessels.

"Can I use your bathroom!?" I blurted.

"Sure." He grinned bright, white teeth. "As long as it's just number one. I didn't bring any toilet paper with me."

"You're number one, baby," I murmured under my breath, as I scurried down the hall to the bathroom with a load in my pants.

I only noticed I still had my half-full drink clutched in my hand when I tried to close the door. The ice cubes gave me an idea, for cooling down and heating up at the same time. A wonderfully wet and wild idea.

I set the drink down on the sink, then stripped off my T-shirt, ripped open my jeans. My hard cock speared out into the open, out and up, happy for release and hungry for more to come. My nipples were engorged with arousal, and I quickly made them even harder, dipping my fingers into the glass and pulling out an ice cube, rubbing said cube over and around my pair of pink buds. They stiffened still more, areola pebbles prickling distinctly. I shuddered with the icy, erotic impact.

44

Glaring at myself in the mirror, I rubbed the melting cube all over my clean-shaven pecs, encircling and encircling my nipples. And, rapidly, the image of yours truly blurred before my half-hooded eyes, and the image of he-studly Carlos appeared. He had his back to me, was looking over his shoulder at me, smiling, as he slid his tiny white shorts over the twin spectacular humps of his bronzed buttocks. The ice cube liquefied against my heaving chest.

I scooped out another hunk of frozen water with my left hand, another with my right. I stuck the one in my ass crack in behind, rubbed it up and down my bum cleavage. As I gripped the other cube against my cock, shifted it up and down my erection.

"Yes!" I gulped, feeling the icy smooth dampness, the raw erotic burn. Gazing at Carlos bending forward, reaching back, grasping his beautiful butt cheeks and spreading them, showing me his cute little deeper browneye, for me to cram my raging cock into.

"Yeah, baby, I'll fuck you!" I hissed, polishing my cock with an ice cube, scrubbing my crack with an ice cube. "I'll stick my long, hard cock in that luscious ass of yours and fuck you so hard I'll come out your mouth!"

I was on fire, ablaze with passion. Water sprinkled down onto my puddled jeans and underwear at my feet, ran down my quivering legs, the ice cubes melting against the torrid heat of my pulsating cock and shimmering ass. I shoved the back cube right into my butt, popping it through my ring and into my chute. As my cock mentally penetrated Carlos's darling pucker and plunged full-length into the gripping, searing tunnel of his ass.

"Oh, baby! I'm fucking you, baby! Fucking your ass!"

I fisted my dick, splashing against my balls, pumping the other sliver of ice in and out of my bum. As I mind-fucked my new neighbor's delicious derriere.

"Fuck, you love it up the ass!" I hollered, jacking my dong barehanded now, pistoning my chute with my bare fingers. The ice had evaporated in the inferno of my molten lust. "You love me up your ass! Coming in your ass!"

I jerked, jolted. Hot, wanton semen sprayed out of my ruptured cock and splattered taps and faucet, two fingers hooking deep into my convulsing ass. I came and came and came, filling Carlos's glorious, gulping bum with my steaming ecstasy.

"You all right in there!?"

I shuddered to a stop, hand frozen on my cock, fingers up my butt. "Uh, yeah, sure! I'm all done! For now," I added in a whisper, winking at that lascivious hunk in the mirror.

# # # # # #

I left the shower running, stepped out of the bathroom and down the hall, peeked into my bedroom. Carlos was lying on my bed, on his stomach, naked, his taut, round, butt cheeks clenching and unclenching as he pumped into my bedspread. I bit my lip to keep from whooping for joy.

The black-haired beauty had taken my bait, one of my skin mags spread out on the pillow in front of him. He was ogling the fucking musclemen of *Gym Rendezvous 2*, as he fucked my bed.

The day after I'd helped him move in, I showed him around the building, introduced him to the outdoor swimming pool. It was another blazing hot day, with blazing gay possibilities, and upon my suggestion, we donned our Speedos and headed down to the dunk tank to "cool off."

We talked and laughed, I leered, lounging around the waterfront. Then, with the heat building up to coke furnace levels inside me again, I invited the jade-eyed Latino cock-charmer back to my apartment for a cold one. And after setting him up with a drink, I excused myself to grab a quick shower, knowing those porn mags of mine were already liberally spread around my bedroom, waiting for the golden boy to hopefully roam, read, reveal his true colors, which I fervently hoped and believed were rainbow.

Now, I was the one getting the house and crotch-warming present, staring at Carlos's smooth, lithe body, those humped and humping buttocks. I licked my lips and slipped inside the bedroom, in behind the guy. I was as naked as he was, my cock jutting out throbbing from my shaven loins. I take good care of my body, and now I wanted to take care of Carlos's good body.

I slid my knees onto the bed in between the man's long, parted legs, and reached down and grabbed onto his thrusting butt cheeks.

"Yeah!" he groaned, not even looking around. "I was wondering when you were finally going to make your move."

"Cocktease!" I laughed, squeezing the rich copper flesh of his ass. He pumped harder into the bed, making the pliable pair of bumpers jump in my clutching hands.

I rubbed them, caressed them, kneaded them, groping every smooth inch of his warm, luscious cheeks. I massaged them apart, gazing into the inviting crack of his ass, his puckered starfish. And then I spread them wide and ducked my head down and dipped my tongue into his butt crevice.

"Fuck!" he yelped, full-body shivering as my wet, hot tongue hit home.

I licked up and down his crack, lapping at his smooth, sensitive, heated butt cleavage. I swirled my tongue around his winking asshole, and he shivered some more. And when I speared my tongue right into his manhole, he mashed his face into the glossy pages and shuddered his rump in my face.

I took one long last dragging lick at his crack and then rolled him over onto his back, hungry to see if his front was built good as his rear.

It was, even better; his cock eight inches of cut, tan meat, hood mushrooming out delightfully from stiffened shaft. I grabbed onto the slab of beef before he did, lacing my fingers around the pube-fuzzed base and pulling upwards, slipping my lips over the crown.

He grunted and clutched the bedspread, staring at me. As I consumed his towering erection inch by pulsating inch, my stretched-out mouth sinking inexorably down on his prick, until I was kissing his abdomen and balls.

"Jesus!" he gulped, trembling in my deep-throat embrace.

I looked up along his ridged stomach and heaving chest and into his amazed eyes, thrusting out my tongue to lick at his sack. I kept him locked down like that, in the hot, humid confines of my mouth and throat, for a solid ten seconds or so. Then I started sucking, long and hard.

I slid my hands up onto his chest and pinched his swollen nipples, bobbing my head up and down, wet-vaccing his dong. He grasped my hands and pumped his hips, shooting head into my throat in rhythm to my sucking.

I alternated quick and hard, slow and sensuous, pulling and pulling on his cock with my mouth, inhaling the sweaty, musky scent of his balls and body. And just when I was about to disgorge his dripping appendage and try it up my ass for a change of pace, I felt the bed sag in behind me.

47

I twisted my head around, Carlos's rigid cock popping out of my mouth. Another big, nude, Latin dude had mounted the bed. He held his gleaming bronze prick in his hand, already slick with lube, beefy cap pointed directly at my upraised ass.

"Hey, Luis, you finally made it into town!" Carlos said.

"Yeah ... just in time," the Hispanic muscle-stud replied. "Got your note and decided to come on over before I unpacked." He slid his hand up his cock and smeared the gathered grease into my crack. "Glad I did."

"Luis is my roommate," Carlos explained, as I gasped with pleasure.

"Nice to know you," Luis said, scrubbing my tingling butthole with a pair of blunt fingers. "Don't let me stop what you were doing."

I nodded, and turned back to Carlos. He was holding his glistening dick up for me, and I lowered my mouth down on it again. Only this time, I actually did gag on the meaty pole, when Luis pushed his bloated hood against my pucker and plunged on through, gliding deep into my ass.

My muffled moan vibrated through Carlos's cock and body. Luis plugged me to the balls, then gripped my hips and pumped his, fucking my ass. My body burned, electrified butt stretched and stroked like I like it. I'd baited the trap, and I'd been caught in it – between two young, hung studs. It couldn't have worked out any better!

I sucked on Carlos's cock as Luis pistoned my ass. Luis's fingernails bit into my waist, Carlos's into my scalp; the butt-thumper banging his thighs against my cheeks, driving me up the ass; Carlos thrusting up into my mouth and throat, fucking my face.

The pace quickened, the tempo intensifying, men groaning and grunting, the bed creaking. Flesh smacked against flesh, cocks surging in sexholes. All three of us were sweating like the room itself, breathing hard. I gorged on cock, getting reamed.

I scrambled a hand off Carlos's clenched chest and grabbed onto my own flapping prick. Just as the guy howled, "Fuck!" and slammed my head down on his dick. He jerked, jolted by ecstasy, shooting hot semen into my throat.

Luis growled and shuddered, his pounding dong blasting my chute full of liquid orgasm – again and again and again.

I clung to my cock and managed one crank. That's all it took, with all that fire flaming into my mouth and butt. I exploded with orgasm, spraying onto the bedspread, spasming over and over on the end of those shooting cocks.

The boys down the hall have become a fantastic addition to the building, neighborly above and beyond the call of duty.

HORSE COCKED
By Landon Dixon

He was a stud in spurs. I ambled over to where he stood by the fire, put a hand on his shoulder, said, "How 'bout we rustle up some love?"

He turned and looked at me, the shooting flames of the fire reflected in his amber eyes. A smile creased his weather-lined face, and he tossed off the remains of coffee in his tin cup. "Shoot, I was wondering when you was gonna ask, pardner."

He threw his arms around me. I lassoed his tall, thin frame with my arms, our wet lips meeting, moving together with a fearsome passion. We were outriders scouting up ahead for the herd twenty miles behind. It was nightfall, and a day of close trotting with the silver-haired stranger who'd signed on at Abilene had left me hornier than a corralful of Texas longhorns.

I'd always been attracted to seasoned men, dudes with some mileage on their bodies and character in their faces, notches on their gun belts. And Jorge Martinez had all those things, a leaner, handsomer, more soft-spoken cowman I'd never seen, let alone roped. So, I'd made my play, and now I was punching lips with the beefcake.

Our Stetsons tumbled to the ground, as we consumed one another's mouths. Jorge tasted salty, savory, just as I'd imagined, his tongue jerky tough and whip-strong, wet as spring runoff, when it entered my mouth and thrashed around inside.

I slid my calloused hands down the man's straight back and onto his buttocks, grasping, groping the trail-taut mounds. As I fought a sexual duel with my tongue on his tongue, our slippery stickers entwining over and over. He gripped my face in his rawboned hands and really went to town on my mouth, feasting on the ripe, red facial feature like he was starved as I was for intimate male-male companionship.

Our shirts joined our hats on the grassy ground. It was a warm night, stars bristling the blackened sky, a full moon shining down on Jorge's lean, leathery, silver-haired chest, his pair of hard, tan nipples. I let my hands roam all over the rugged terrain of his chest, my own upper body bare and heaving, smooth as befitting my youthful years.

51

I cupped Jorge's firm pecs, popping up his firmer nipples, sucked one into my mouth and pulled heartily on it. He groaned, gripping my hair, running his long, sturdy fingers through my bushy black mane. I shifted my head west, inhaled his other stiff nipple, tugged on it with my bee stung lips.

Then I let my tongue mosey again, swirling it around the man's one nipple, the other. I felt his buds blossom even harder, tasting their rawhide texture, the pebble of his areolas, a few stray, damp hairs catching in my teeth. Jorge's whipcord body shook in my hands, and he tilted his head back, as if he was going to howl at the moon.

Instead, he pushed me back, busted the buckle on his gun belt wide open. The pearl-handled six-shooter dropped along with its slotted ammunition, and the buckle on Jorge's saddle-worn jeans was next to open. I licked my lips, tasting the man's saliva, watching him draw his Levis down slow and easy. His cock hung low from his hairy loins, long even semi-erect, just like I'd figured. I quickly joined him in full-blooded nudity, the pair of us keeping our boots on, just in case.

I walked closer, my prod bobbing up iron-hard, warmed by the fire, heated by the kisses, caresses, and cock of my trail mate. He gripped my prick in a hardy greeting, roping his strong fingers around the bloated shaft and stroking. I did the same to his cock. The shooter filled my hand, thick and vein-ribboned and pulsating. I thrilled at his touch and tug on my dick, surged with delight at the heft of his rod.

"Mind if I put my brand on you, amigo?" Jorge breathed, the pair of us kisser to kisser, cock to cock.

I looked into his eyes, feeling his pull, the beat of his cock. "I been hopin' you'd blaze my trail for a long time now."

He grinned, kissed me, lashed my tongue with his tongue. Then he let go of my cock and spun me around, bent me down, got me onto all-fours on the ground and squatted in behind. Bare-backing, out there under the big sky next to the roaring fire on the open range. I gripped grass and reared my rump up, shivering with the anticipation of that iron bar plumbing my bottom depths.

Jorge made his dick nice and slick with some handy bacon grease. Then he shot a pair of slippery digits in between my plump, pale buttocks and scoured my crack, lubricated my pucker. I moaned at the feel of his fingers on my sensitive manhole, my cock jumping, body flushing with animal heat. So help me, I couldn't hardly wait for that cock to plug me butt good.

He made me wait, poking his two fingers into my ring, sinking them chute-deep. He wiggled them around inside of me, just scratching the surface of my lust. "You're mighty tight, *compadre*. Think you can take all I'm dishin' out?"

I quivered, those fingers rotating sensuously in my rectum. Too long in the saddle had left me tighter than a tick in a burr, but I'd been busted by even bigger, so I knew I could take it. "Stick me, Jorge!" I rasped. "Pump my ass full of your cock!"

He grunted. The fingers eased out of me with a sucking pop, and sensation. Then I felt something bigger, thicker, more ominous banging on my backdoor – hood, and plenty of it. Jorge squeezed his crown up against my asshole. I wiggled my butt in anxious acceptance. He gripped my waist with one hand, his dong with the other, pushing the tip inside my tingling hole, popping my cork.

He busted my ass ring but good, his crown ballooning my pucker, getting swallowed, shaft following right quick, stretching, sliding, sinking into my anus. I tore at the short grass, that magnificent organ stuffing my ass, bloating me with feeling and fire.

Jorge delved deep right to the bowels, like I knew and prayed he would. His balls kissed up against my quivering haunches, his dick buried full and true. He let out his breath. I gasped for more. He gripped my narrow waist with both hands and went to work with his dong, churning my chute.

His stroke was slow and sure, sensual beyond measure. Then faster, harder, pounding. My anus burned, I was rocked to and fro by the force of his assault on my ass, his pistoning rod making my body and brain sing. The fucking friction sent my soul soaring, and I yowled like a coyote, taking it up the ass from a veteran cowman who plumb knew his way around hindquarters.

I tore a hand off the ground and grabbed onto my own jumping prong, pumped it in torrid rhythm to Jorge slamming my butt. His fingernails bit into my flesh, his pipe flushing out my ass.

I twisted my head around to look at the dude, pulling hard on my prod. His chest clenched and unclenched as he flung his hips back and forth, his back into the blistering work. His silver hair streamed down from his tossed-back head, and his entire body glowed bronze in the orange flare of the fire. He let out a roar, cock searing my tunnel.

I turned my head back around and frantically fisted my dick, feeling the hot spurt of the man's semen scorch my innards; one ass-embedded blast after another. I joined in, jerking, jetting, spraying the ground with my heated seed.

We spooned into each other's arms in front of the fire afterwards, still naked, Jorge' cock still lodged up my bum. The warm glow soon put me to sleep, right where I wanted to be.

# # # # #

"What's this then!? Been scalped of your clothes and bound bare-assed by some depraved tribe of Injuns!?" someone bellowed.

I blinked my eyes open, looked up at the trail boss, Captain Fellows. He was sitting high and mighty atop his big appaloosa looking down at me. I tried to get up, couldn't. I was hog-tied like a calf, buck naked as the night before.

"Dammit!" I grumbled, turning five shades of red – with both embarrassment and anger.

My horse was gone, my clothes and guns and grub.

# # # # #

My part in the cattle drive ended early, thanks to that no-good ass-skinner Jorge Martinez. It was a long, thirsty walk to the nearest town, and I cursed the man who'd corn holed me good and bad every dusty step of the way.

I was back on the trail quick enough, though – the trail of Jorge Martinez. And the trail was hot, like my seething anger.

I "borrowed" a horse and galloped south, all the way back down to sweet Abilene. And sure as shooting, in the fifth saloon I barged in and through, I found the dastardly Mexican silver fox, losing the money he'd made from selling my things in a backroom poker game.

"Hands up!" I hollered, kicking the door open, busting up the game.

Five men jumped to their feet like they'd been stung by a scorpion. One man remained seated at the gambling table – Jorge Martinez. "Pleasure to see you again, *amigo*," he stated calmly, taking a pull on his *cigarillo*.

I ordered the other men out of the room. One squawked about his money. I put a bullet through his bowler, and the door got mighty crowded.

"Stealin' a man's horse is a hangin' offence," I snarled at Jorge.

The southwestern elder was unperturbed. "You don't need no horse," he said, getting to his feet and unbuckling his guns, "when you got this." He drew his cock out of his pants, nice and slow, huge and getting huger.

I licked my lips, strode forward, pulled the man away from the table and his guns, by the dick. I tossed my borrowed rifle onto the table, unbelted my own breeches. "Where's Big Red, anyway?" I said, giving Jorge's prick a twist. Big Red was the seventeen hands-high palomino who'd given me so many years of good service.

Jorge grimaced, then grinned. He licked his thin lips with that silvery tongue that went so well with his hair. "Probably 'cross the border by now. I sold him to a Texican a week ago. Sorry, *compadre*. Can make it up to you, though."

I shoved the guy down to his knees on the floorboards, and he grabbed onto my rod hand and mouth. I shivered when his mitt clamped around my shaft, shuddered when his lips closed around my hood.

He pumped my stem, sucked on my cap. I rapidly inflated full-length, pulsating with wickedly delicious sensations. The old pro could wrangle an erection like he could stoke an ass furnace. He noosed my swollen shaft with two dry digits and stroked up and down, pulling on my bloated hood with his wet mouth, licking at my gaping slit.

I ran my fingers through his soft, silvery hair. He took encouragement from the gesture, boldly pushed his head forward, consuming my cock, sliding his mouth flaps down so that his fingers had to retreat all the way to the base of my prong. The savvy cowman had me swallowed up almost whole in no time at all.

I throbbed in the wet, hot, gripping hollow of his mouth, flushing with pleasure pure and simple. He bobbed his head, looking up at me with those smoldering brown eyes of his, sucking on my prick. He went up and down with a maximum of suction and a minimum of drool, blowing me more briskly and thoroughly than any dust devil ever could.

I groaned and pumped my hips to keep pace, fucking his rugged face. He reasserted his independence, however, pulling my shooter out of his maw with a moist pop and pressing it up against my belly, dipping his head lower, vacuuming up my balls. He swallowed my tight, wrinkled sack and tugged hard on it, making me buck.

Jorge looked up at me from my groin, his eyes glinting with satisfaction. He released my prick, let it slap down across his forehead, as he mouthed my pouch, juggled my nuts with his dexterous tongue. He was playing a tune on my testicles compelling enough to make me blow taps.

He sensed it and spat me out, kneed in behind me. I felt his knowing hands on my butt cheeks, spreading me, his tongue snaking up and down, licking at my crack. A ripple of raw delight rolled through me, followed by another, and another, in time to the man's tongue dragging my crack.

But I didn't like the fact he had my back. So I bucked him away with a bounce of my ass. Then I spun around and pulled him to his feet and pushed him up against the abandoned table. I bent him over the scattered cash and cards, riding his pants down low. It was my turn to brand him, long time coming.

I carry bear grease, and I used it, slathering my prick, Jorge's backside. I wasn't quite mean enough to avenge his treachery with a dry fuck. He flattened his palms out on the table and shuddered, as I spanked some sense into his taut, leathered cheeks with my hard-on. Before mounting him, cow poking into his pucker and ramming headlong.

I went in like greased lightning, sticking the man with every inch that I had, saddling up. He and I both groaned. For a guy far down the trail of life, he was still remarkably tight, infernally ally hot. I rutted around on the end of his rump like a dog wallowing in the dust. Then I held him tight by the waist and spurred full-gallop.

The table shook, money clinked, as I rocked, cocked Jorge with a ferocious intensity. I had some pent-up feelings I just had to let out, and his ass got the best of it. His tawny cheeks shivered non-stop, my cock plowing his chute in a blur. Even so, he still flexed his butt muscles, sucking on my prick even as I feverishly pumped.

The stuffy, smoke-laden backroom echoed with the crack of my thighs against Jorge's bare buttocks, like gunshots, fast and furious. Jorge moaned low and long. I hammered my shooter, balls spanking, cock spiking.

Then I bucked, blew, the steaming pressure too much for me. My cock erupted in the man's ass, and I sent molten semen pouring into his anus. Load after load spewed out of my pulsing iron, draining my balls and my body.

Don't know if he came. Don't care, neither.

I turned Jorge Martinez over to the local sheriff, charge: horse stealing; penalty: hanging. See, I liked Jorge and what he could do to and for me, but like most cowboys, I liked my horse even more.

Big Red was one hung stallion, even more so than Jorge.

I HATE YOU. BEND OVER
By Jamie Freeman

Jamie Freeman works for a large corporation, fighting the petty battles of the cube life and dreaming of a full-time writer's life. He has published dozens of short stories and novellas and is always unabashedly seeking out adoring fans and loyal readers. www.jamiefreeman.net or jamiefreeman2@gmail.com.

"Whassup, Mattie?"

My name's Matthew; most people call me Matt. This idiot called me something different every time he opened his mouth.

"Fuck you," I said.

"Surly," he said. "I like it." He grinned and dropped his briefcase on the floor next to his chair.

"I hate you so much it makes my scalp burn," I wanted to say. But I didn't. I just stared at the gray carpeted wall of my cubicle wishing I could throw a blood clot on cue and die, releasing myself from my inescapable incarceration with this back-slapping, hand-shaking, deep-laughing, sports-talking, suit-wearing, insider-trading, smarmy motherfucker.

"Hey, Mama's Boy, stop mooning over me or people will say we're in love."

I heard Wendy chuckle on the other side of the cubicle wall.

"Dude, I had the. Best. Weekend. Evar. Ev-aaar!" He slammed his hand down on the desk.

"What'd she charge you?" I asked.

He did a double take. "Very funny, douche bag," he said. "Hardy fuckin' har."

I just sat there pretending to be working, typing random letters on my keyboard to diminish his enjoyment of my curiosity.

He told me a long, crazy story involving his army buddies, a couple of hookers, two police stops, drunk driving, Lindsay Lohan and a Duane Reade bag full of cash. Total bullshit. I got bored about half way through and pulled up my work queue, downloading the first document and digging through my desk drawer in search of a pen.

"...so we just punched the bitch and ran like hell. It was awesome. You shoulda been there."

He laughed again and tapped away at his own keyboard, initiating his security sign-on and sniffing the contents of a couple of over-sized coffee mugs. He chose one with a photo of Obama wearing a Hallowell baseball cap. "Coffee?" he asked.

"I'm good."

"Yeah, I've heard that about you, Matteo. When're you gonna let me find out for sure." This last bit was whispered as he squeezed past me, pitched low enough for me to hear, but inaudible to those around us. He let his ample bubble butt slide against my arm. He left the cube door open. I waited until he was out of sight, around the first bend in the twisting warren of cubicles before I slid my hand into my lap to stroke the erection that'd sprung to life inside my khakis.

I grimaced and shook my head. I had a flashback to high school, being beat up in the student parking lot by Gary Stephens – the blond Nordic quarterback who'd haunted my masturbatory fantasies for years – and trying to hide my boner from his heckling buddies. Things like this always ended badly. Christ, these big, dumb assholes were gonna be the death of me.

Mario and I shared a cubicle about the size of two McDonalds booths shoved together. We'd been stuck together for about six months, ever since my former cube mate – Sharon "touch my titties" Fowler – was fired for sexually harassing one of the temps.

For me and Mario, it was hate at first sight.

He was infuriating: more handsome than he deserved, funnier than I'd like to admit, and sexier than I could stand. He had a thick, muscular body that bulged in all the right places, stretching his perfectly pressed white shirts and charcoal gray slacks. He had large, perfect hands and he shaved his head, which gave his face a feral, hungry look, his red power tie dropping from his chin like the lolling tongue of a wolf.

Despite his good looks and his suave demeanor, he was a total dick. He was a braggart and a liar. He stole credit for other people's work, found scapegoats for his own fuck-ups, swiped lunches from the lounge refrigerator, took coins from the coffee kitty to use in the vending machine, and plundered people's desk drawers after everyone else had gone home. I once caught him stuffing his briefcase with boxes of staples and paperclips. To be honest, the fact that he was stealing office supplies would almost have endeared him to me had forty bucks not gone missing from my winter coat the next week.

I hated him. A lot.

After my first two weeks with Mario, I submitted a form to Facility Operations requesting a cube reassignment. I was hopeful for a couple of days, but then I got hauled into my boss's boss's office where, with an H.R. rep named T.J. as a witness, I was accused of being a racist. With no clear preamble, I wasn't sure exactly where the accusation came from. I listened for a while and then asked what had prompted the meeting. T.J. handed me a copy of my transfer request. "It's not okay to hate Hispanics," he said.

My head exploded.

"I don't hate Hispanics!" I roared. "What the hell are you thinking?"

Martin, my boss's boss, leaned back in his chair, grinning and steepling his fingers as if he was getting a big kick out of the process.

"This is not funny, Martin," I snapped.

He shrugged.

T.J. inserted himself back into the conversation. "I think the best way to handle this is to get you some training ..."

"Oh, my God, T.J.. This is nuts."

"Your Remedial Diversity Training starts at 10:00 a.m. on Thursday in the small conference room."

"I don't need Remedial Diversity Training. I'm a half-Jewish, half-Catholic gay man from Alabama, for Christ's sake ..."

"Then you should be more adept at the whole diversity thing, don't you think?" T.J. was leaning forward with his elbows on his knees, projecting his talk show empathy in my direction. "Differences make us stronger," he said.

Martin was still steepling and grinning. Fucking bastard.

I "accidentally" knocked a cup of coffee off Martin's desk as I left the meeting, but I went to the class.

And I knew I would be stuck forever in that cubicle with Mario.

At the time, I'd been working for Hallowell Media for about five years. I was one of about a hundred underpaid technical writers crammed into cubicles on the fifty-second floor of an undistinguished Midtown office tower manufacturing news-on-demand for Hallowell clients. News-on-demand is a pretty focused "niche market" and explaining my job at cocktail parties was nearly impossible, even if I could do so without violating my employment contract and triggering a Blackwater-style wetwork termination clause.

Here's the gist of it: If you look at the arena of public political discourse in this country, the first thing you see are the divas. There's Glenn Beck, John Stossel, Keith Olbermann, Arianna Huffington, and pretty much anyone who looks and acts more like a circus ringmaster than a print journalist. These guys can say pretty much anything and be believed by a huge percentage of narrow-focused, bobble-headed Americans. Their power comes from outrage, challenge, theatrics, and storytelling; they've got no need for facts or references, footnotes or fact-checking. They transcend truth, as I like to say.

Hallowell Media had nothing to do with them.

We lurked behind the scenes, behind the next tier of journalists – the proverbial newspaper hacks and serious investigative reporters – producing facts and references, reports and studies, footnotes and fact-checks for them to uncover and report on. We provided the networks, the newspapers, the bought-and-paid-for-academics, and all the other corporate and governmental spokespeople with historical documents, studies, statistics, sound bites, and photos to support whatever our clients were pushing on the buying public at the moment.

We spent the better part of June and July 2010 producing gigabytes of "source material" about the safety of offshore oil drilling, the impossibility of oily rain, the resilience of ocean life, and the lack of financial ties between Big Oil and Big Politics. Our cup runneth over, like the sea floor at Macondo Prospect. Black Gold. Texas Tea.

I was rewriting an old Congressional report from the Office of Technology Assessment on "coping with an oiled sea" when Mario pushed past with a cup of coffee and a brown pastry bag from Starbucks. He bumped me and sent my chair into a partial spin.

"Dude, watch it," I said, shoving my elbow into his thigh. His leg was hot and hard as a desert stone; just touching him made my cock jerk.

"What's on deck, Matty-line?"

"Same old crap."

He gave me an arch look, but didn't say anything else.

I pulled open my desk, rattling the contents and grabbing my earbuds. I stuck them in my ears and clicked to a streaming radio station to block out further attempts at conversation. I could see him out of the corner of my eye, leaning back in his chair, sucking coffee through the lid, and licking icing from a pumpkin scone.

I pretended to be absorbed in editing a table of bioremediation estimates from the '79 Ixtoc I oil spill in Mexico. I was reducing the numbers in the old study by a factor of ten to accommodate lower future liability calculations and fighting to stay awake.

I'd been working for about an hour when I felt a lazy pressure on my shoulder. I pulled my left earbud out of my ear, ripping Freddy Mercury from stereo to mono, and flipping my chair to the side. Mario pushed his own chair back from mine, looking startled and guilty.

"What?" I said. My voice was so loud that an immediate silence rippled through the nearby cubes. A voice that had been murmuring into a phone – probably Earl or Larry – was suddenly silent. Wendy, in the next cube, stopped typing. Like hyenas circling a pair of their own locked in combat, they all kept their distance, but listened intently for weakness or bloodshed.

"What?" he said.

"What do you want?" I said.

"Chico, be calm. I was just looking over your shoulder."

"Well, stop it!" My voice was shrill; I felt like Jan Brady.

"Whatever." He looked at me with a lazy, hungry grin and leaned back in his chair. He moved his hand against his thigh, expertly drawing my eye downward to the rearing erection that stretched the front of his slacks like a python trying to push its head through low-hanging branches.

My jaw shifted; saliva squirted into my mouth like I'd bitten into a lime.

"Oh yeah." He mouthed the words, glancing up over the top of the cubicle and then back at me. I heard Wendy resume her typing. Earl or Larry went back to his phone call; sounds slowly returned to the veldt: the clicking of staplers and keyboards, the hum of printers and scanners, the shuffling of papers and folders. "You know you want this." Again his mouth moved; the words clear and crisp, but silent as a camouflaged predator.

My eyes traveled up from his bulging crotch across his thick, ridged belly and meaty pecs, across his neck and chin, stubbled even at ten in the morning, across his thick red lips, parted just enough to let me imagine the wetness beyond them, and finally up to his wide, brown eyes. He blinked slowly; I licked my lips nervously.

He wheeled closer to me, pulling his chair into alignment beside mine. To anyone who poked their head over the cube wall, it would seem as though we were consulting about the document on my computer screen. They might not notice how close our chairs were, how labored our breathing had become.

He reached into my lap, dragging his fingers across the hardening outline of my cock, the pressure just enough to be felt through the double layers of warm cotton khakis and jockeys. I drew a short breath. He raised his finger to his lips. Silence.

I hooked my right earbud, pulled it out of my ear, and dropped it in front of me, letting the faint, tinny music spill out across my desk. I leaned back in my chair, wincing when the aging plastic screeched in protest.

Mario leaned forward in his chair, tugging my zipper down slowly to hide the distinctive sound of metal teeth unlocking. Our faces were close enough for me to smell nutmeg and coffee on his breath. He winked, the skin around his eyes crinkling and forcing my lips apart in a reluctant smile. His fingers grappled with my button and then, in a swift motion, his cool fingers were inside, pushing the elastic band of my jockeys down beneath my rearing erection and big, heavy balls. In a flash, I was out there, bouncing beneath the steady trickle of AC that fell from the overhead vents. Mario glanced up, checking to see if anyone was around. He raised and pivoted his head, listening, cataloguing, identifying, and plotting the various sounds of the office on his internal radar screen.

I sat frozen with fear and desire.

When he was satisfied with his spatial analysis, he leaned forward, licked his lips, and went down on me.

I stifled a gasp as his lips slid down the length of my aching, feverish shaft.

He hesitated on the down-thrust, making sure I understood the power he now had over me. He began working me with an expert, silent attention. His mouth contained all the sound, holding the slurping, sloshing liquidity of the encounter firmly inside. My skin alternately flushed hot and cold. My heart thumped against my ribcage like an enraged gorilla denied access to his mate; the pounding resonated up through my body, the quiet hum of the office machines and low-pitched voices suddenly punctuated by the tympanic banging of blood inside my ears.

I writhed in my chair, holding my breath as I felt the tension building.

I put a hand on Mario's face, pushing against his flesh in silent warning as the locks began to open, one after another. I felt the gush of cum making its twisted way out of me and then I felt Mario's mouth tighten; he breathed deeply, but silently through his nose. The explosion jolted me so badly I thought I would fall out of my chair. It was as if a wave of sound had blasted through the cubicles like a bomb, twisting the room around me in a concussive maelstrom. I poured every ounce of energy left in my body into containment, of the growl that paced back and forth behind my clenched teeth; of the ragged breath that slipped threateningly from Mario's nostrils; of the blasting gusher of semen I'd just released into Mario's open mouth.

I concentrated on stillness, thinking I might have a stroke.

I heard the distinctive tread of Vanessa, the section supervisor on the carpet outside the cube. She was maybe ten feet away from the door, her trajectory slowing.

Four things happened in quick succession: Mario disentangled himself from my cock, sitting up and leaning forward in the direction of my computer monitor; Mario's hand pushed my chair up against the desk effectively hiding the remnants of our encounter; I flipped the elastic up, over my balls and my slick, shrinking erection; and Vanessa poked her head over the top of the cube door.

"Matt, is that report gonna be ready for go-live before three? We're gonna have half a dozen major servers pulled down – including one of the dot-govs – and Tina's getting antsy."

"Yeah." I was breathless, trying to sound calm and lucid. I decided to look up into Vanessa's eyes, flashing her a soothing smile and then, to reinforce the body language, I started to lean back in my chair. I felt Mario's hand holding the back of my chair forward and cut the gesture short realizing just in time what such the gesture might reveal.

"I was helping him review the numbers," Mario said. He ratcheted up his almost non-existent accent when he spoke to Vanessa, playing up to her sense of *la comunidad*, though she was Puerto Rican, and I was pretty sure he was Mexican. He sounded like the Taco Bell dog; I wanted to kick him across the room.

Vanessa's eyes shifted to Mario, pupils widening subconsciously with desire. She licked her lips and nodded. "You're breathing like a racehorse, Mario," she said.

He shrugged. "I was concentrating."

"This is not a complicated assignment ..."

"I'll have it to you on time, Vanessa." I cut her off, my cheeks flushing in awareness of the listening silence that radiated up from the cubes around us.

"Okay ... *bueno.*" She started to leave; I shifted in my chair. She turned back. "Gentlemen?" she said.

We both looked back up into her brown eyes, our faces incomprehensible muddles of emotions I hoped she would either ignore or misread.

"Three o'clock is good, but two is better."

"Yes, ma'am," I said.

And she was gone.

Mario let out a long shallow breath that turned to a low chuckle. The distant, syncopated strains of *Get Down, Make Love* drifted up from my abandoned earbuds. Somewhere off to my right, Dana was on the phone, cursing at her teenage daughter in angry whispers. I zipped, buttoned, and tucked, and then leaned back in my chair, the adrenaline in my body still whirring and pumping. My hands were shaking. Holy shit.

My career in professional deception springs from a long family history of anger, hypocrisy, and histrionics. That is to say, I come by my anger and hypocrisy honestly, growing up as I did, the son of a pair of Oscar winning actors.

When I was a kid, before she won her Oscars, my mother sometimes spent summers doing Shakespeare in the Park. I remember she was cast in a production of *Romeo and Juliet* one summer, and she was devastated that she was too old to play Juliet. She was probably in her mid-thirties at the time, but to her it was insulting that she should be cast as the nurse opposite a young soap opera star who, in a strange case of life imitating art, died of a drug overdose a few years later, her cold, blue body discovered laid out on her bed as if for a viewing. (My dismal scene I needs must act alone. Come, vial.) Typical of my mother's self-centered view of the universe, she later publically referred to the actress's death as a "belated casting critique from God." Her anger at "the Great Miscasting" stalked us through my high school years, the two aforementioned Oscars, three step-fathers, and six "visits to the country," as she referred to her frequent unfortunate psychological or addiction-related incarcerations.

One night shortly after she had separated from one of her husbands, and as she was beginning to pack her emotional baggage for another fortnight in the country, she spent an entire night in a giant rocking chair, legs drawn up beneath her, feet tucked beneath the hem of a blue kimono, repeating one of Juliet's youthful exclamations over and over. "My only love sprung from my only hate!" She delivered the line with increasing vehemence, pounding on the arms of the chair, her voice becoming cracked and clogged with spittle and bile.

She was a woman who never forgot.

I would never presume to understand the inner workings of the artistic mind, but the memory of my mother's pathetic, histrionic performance – equally mired, it seemed to me, in truth and falsehood – has followed me all these years.

I sometimes still hear her fist pounding the hard wood.

My mother collected sense memories like others collect rare coins. "My dear, I simply must remember what this moment feels like," she said when a delivery truck ran over my childhood pet dachshund Heidi; when all I wanted in the world was to forget.

Unhinged as she was, my mother was uniquely able to see that life is really just an intricate, interlocking dance of opposites: grief and joy, truth and deceit, terror and passion, love and hate. She knew these conflicting emotions for what they were: opposite sides of a single coin; heads or tails; shiny, precious objects to be collected and catalogued, and then called forth later, deftly manifested on stage, like a silver dollar from behind the ear of a credulous child.

I hated my mother. But I loved her, too.

Two sides of the same coin.

After the blowjob, Mario gave me a wide berth for a couple of days, diving with artificial exuberance into his work, skirting past me in meetings, and dashing out the door at the end of the day.

I watched him in smoldering silence.

The following Friday, I got stuck putting together packets for a Hallowell Media Board Retreat and spent most of the evening ensconced in the enormous copy center down the hall from our suite. I'd been working for almost three hours when I heard a fist pounding on the wooden door.

I glanced at the clock. It was after seven o'clock on a Friday. I figured the only people still left in the building were the security guards and housekeeping.

I was sitting in the middle of the floor, legs crossed Indian style, assembling stacks of identical, carefully tabbed and organized blue binders. The gold embossed Hallowell logo on the covers glinted in the stark overhead fluorescents.

"Come in," I yelled.

It was Mario.

"Oh, it's you," I said.

He grinned.

"Fuck off. I'm busy here."

"You don't mean that." The statement hung in the air between us; we both knew it was true.

Mario slid the bolt on the copy center door.

I smiled in spite of myself.

He kicked off one loafer and then toed off the other one while his fingers worked on his tie, then the buttons of his shirt, and then his slacks. He draped his shirt and T-shirt over a chair, then dropped his slacks and stepped out of them. He reached down to peel off his socks and stood in front of me in a pair of tight white briefs.

His body was tanned and muscular and covered with a neatly trimmed forest of dark hair. A stylized Aztec snake tattoo slithered up his body, looping over his shoulder to lick his left nipple. His cock, initially nestled softly and snugly inside his briefs, was stretching out now into a thick erection that nosed past the elastic waistband.

He reached up absently with his right hand, pinching his nipple and then sliding his fingertips rhythmically across the dark, quarter-sized areola just below the tongue of the tattooed snake.

That simple gesture, which seemed so real, so unplanned, brought me to my feet. I kicked aside a stack of empty binders and struggled out of my clothes.

Mario was there beside me in an instant, his fingers helping me out of my clothes, his hands running along my sides, my thighs, and my calves. He pushed his underwear down, dropping to his knees, and reaching up to slide my pants and underwear down to my ankles. He helped me step out of my clothes and then carefully peeled my socks from my feet. I dropped my T-shirt on the floor, and we were both naked at last.

He knelt in front of my bobbing erection, but surprised me by prostrating himself in front of me like a pilgrim before a holy shrine. In a moment I felt his tongue curling between the toes of my right foot. He sucked and licked his way across the arch of my foot, around my ankle and up my leg until his stubbled face finally scraped against the soft, pale flesh of my inner thigh. When I thought the sensation would overcome me, he crossed to the other thigh and began to make his descent, licking his way down my left leg, ending as he had begun, digging the curling tip of his tongue between my toes.

He let his fingers slide up the outsides of my legs and raised his eyes to mine. They were stern for a moment and then they melted into liquid brown pools. I wanted to dive into him.

I started to kneel, but his hands held me tightly in place.

"I'm not done," he said.

He went on to explore every inch of my body, licking, tasting and biting my skin, leaving red marks on my stomach, my chest, and my ass. When he finished his oral expedition, he stood in front of me for a moment watching me with those dark, aggressive eyes.

He stepped closer, so our bobbing cocks rubbed together. I pulled him against me, finally letting our lips touch. He was rough and verbal, different from the silence of our cube. He grunted when I slipped a saliva-slicked finger up his ass, but he moved against me, pushing against my hand and whispering, "Get the lube and the condom in my pants pocket and get me ready." I found a Trojan and a couple of packets of Wet in his pocket, lubed my fingers, and slid two and then three inside him. He moaned and moved his body around my fingers in a churning motion, reaching back and pulling his ass cheeks apart with his hands. The scent of him made my cock thump and rock against my stomach; my breathing became ragged.

He straightened up and twisted his upper body back to kiss me.

I put my hands on his hips, let the kiss get ragged and sloppy, and then I pulled back.

"Fuck me hard," he said. His pupils were wildly dilated; his skin was hot to the touch.

I aligned his lower body with my own; he twisted back again and I shoved him hard against the copier. He braced himself, his fingers hitting the pre-programmed copy button. The machine came to life beneath him, buzzing and spitting out a stream of white, warm pages.

"Do it, you dumbfuck," he said. He tried to stand up straight, but I pushed his shoulders down hard, slamming him against the lid of the copier. He fought me, pushing himself up again and bracing himself against the copier with his arms. His arm muscles stood out dark and ropey beneath the dusting of fur. He made an animal sound, part anger, part pleasure.

"You gonna fuck me, or what?" he snarled.

"I hate you. Bend over." I shoved his shoulders down and slid my cock inside him. The copy machine hummed and glowed beneath us as I fucked him, slamming into him, letting the mix of emotions and sensations bring us both to a growling, shouting climax.

My mother once told me she loved with my father from the first moment she saw his erect cock on screen. She was sixteen and she had snuck into a screening of *Child of Janus*, an experimental film by Zander Wolkins in which my father played a young man tormented by vivid dreams of mass murder. My mother described a scene in which Dad's character awoke from a turbulent nightmare, sitting up on a bare mattress naked and prominently aroused, his hair tousled and his face twisted in agony. That moment, she said, was the moment in which she knew she could love him forever. So deep was the terror in his eyes, and so eager the glistening tumescence of his cock that he must be capable of every imaginable emotional extreme.

Terror and passion, two sides of the same coin.

It was a year before she finally met my father. He was starring in *Penny's Retribution*, and she was playing a corpse at one of the crime scenes. The rest, as they say, was history.

Whirlwind courtship, fairytale wedding, photo spread in *People*.

I never knew the two of them when they were together, but the pictures from that time were curiously beautiful and melancholy, as though their marriage was a source of great love and great sadness to them both.

By the time I was born, they were engaging innocent members of the press in a publicly enacted divorce that catapulted the two of them – and their infant son – into the rarefied world of tabloid superstardom. "She hates him!" one of the *New York Post* headlines read. It was a calculated risk, but the decision to stage bitter confrontations in front of the press paid off for both of them. Within a year, my father had secured his first Oscar, and my mother had signed a three picture deal with Twentieth Century Fox.

When the dust settled, my father moved in with his boyfriend, and my mother moved on to her second husband.

Sometimes when my mother is boozy and maudlin, she tells me, "Your father is the only man I ever loved, Matty." She gets a dreamy look on her face and then she'll say something like, "God how I hate that fuckin' faggot." And I hear that, and I have to keep drinking until I hear the click and slide into nothingness. My only love sprung from my only hate.

Fucking Mario against the copier released the beast in me. Now, with something to hide, I was suddenly able to be openly hostile to him in a way I would never have contemplated before.

We had become so accustomed to constructing false stories to hide inconvenient truths that we created a world in which Matt and Mario hated each other without a second thought. For weeks, we argued in our cube, sometimes physically grappling over files and staplers and pens. Sometimes one or the other of us stormed out of the cube, slamming the door with an authenticity that would have made my mother proud. Sometimes Wendy would bang on the divider between our workspaces when she felt things had become too hostile, but everyone else avoided us in embarrassed silence.

One afternoon, we both ended up staying late to work on separate projects. By eight, we were alone in the cubicle warren.

Our eyes met in the growing darkness; he took my hand in his. I had to look away.

Mario did a quick reconnoiter, flipped off the overhead lights, and trotted back to the cube to find me standing naked next to our desks. The lights of the city behind me formed an intricate, pixilated, geometric backdrop toward which I turned as he entered.

I was playing contempt. I was playing insolence.

My body betrayed me.

I heard him unzip. I heard a meaty sound as he slapped his cock against his hand. I heard the foil condom wrapper rip, and then the slick sound of sloshing lube.

"I hate you. Bend over," he said.

"Fuck you, Mario."

My only love sprung from my only hate.

71

FACUNDO:
A FRANKY FERRO STORY
By Jesse Monteagudo

Jesse Monteagudo is a South Florida-based, freelance writer. Since 1993, he has contributed more than two dozen stories to STARbooks Press anthologies.

The sun was bright on that late August morning in 1973; and I was ready for the world. I was 18, cute and Cuban; the kind of boy Miami's gay scene was made for. I liked men and men liked me; and the summer of 1973 was an endless round of tricks and one-night stands. But there came a time when sex for its own sake wasn't enough, and I realized that I had to do something with my life if I was ever going to make money, move out into my own, and buy a car. So the first thing I did was find a job at a shoe store in Hialeah, which gave me the bucks I needed to move out of my parents' house and go to college, which is the second thing I did. My pal Joe Martinez (a year older than I) went to Miami College and seemed to do well there, so off I went.

Miami College was still new on Orientation Day 1973. From the moment I stepped off the bus, the college seemed to promise one new experience after another – and not just in academics. Like the Magic City, Miami College was a mix of races, colors, nations, and religions with endless opportunities that went beyond the classroom. Not certain what I wanted to do with myself, I signed up for some liberal arts classes including creative writing and *Español*. I also joined the Miami College Gym; for an 18 year old's body is a terrible thing to waste. It was my day off at the shoe store, so I didn't have to dress for the job. Instead, I dressed the way I wanted to: a light blue, long-sleeve shirt; dark blue short-shorts; black walking shoes and socks; and a backpack. It being 1973, my outfit didn't get much attention. At least until I got to the Orientation Desk.

"Looks like somebody's ready for class," said the young man who sat behind the Orientation Desk. The guy was 22 years old and very handsome; with dark brown skin, a bright smile and a short Afro. He wore a Miami College T-shirt that barely covered his muscular frame. He also wore a pair of tight blue jeans and a pair of leather boots. He spoke with a masculine but pleasant voice and with an accent. (Like me, most Miami College students spoke with a "Miami accent;" a combination of American English, Caribbean Spanish, and Spanglish.)

"I thought I'd dress down for school," I smiled. "I hear there is no dress code here."

"No, there isn't. But you can get in trouble with those short-shorts."

"I doubt it. You are the first one who's noticed them. But I came here for orientation, not to critique my outfit."

"Of course," my new friend replied. "So let's get you oriented. May I see your registration form?" I showed it to him. "Francisco Ferrer Ferro. That's quite a name."

"That's just my legal name. My friends call me Franky," I smiled. "I hope we can be friends."

"We'll see about that. My name is Facundo."

"Facundo?"

"Facundo Sarmiento. I was named after Domingo Sarmiento and his great book *Facundo*. I was born in the Dominican Republic but got my name from a 19th Century Argentine writer. That's what comes from having a dad who teachers literature at the University of Santo Domingo."

"I was born in Havana but grew up here in Miami. We might be related," I said. Like Facundo and other Dominicans, most Cubans have some African blood in them, though our skin color varies from light brown (like me) to dark brown (like Facundo). And though Cuba and the Dominican Republic went their separate ways two centuries ago, there is always the possibility. "Are there a lot of Dominicanos here?"

"There are a few of us," Facundo replied, as he stood up to shake my hand. "There are also Haitians, Puerto Ricans, Panamanians, Colombians, and Cubans, of course." On his feet, Facundo was quite a hunk, to put it mildly. He stood five feet, ten inches, a giant of a man to a boy like me who's only five-foot-four. His muscular body was even more impressive on his feet, as was the basket that pressed the front of his tight jeans. He smiled, an infectious smile that was hard to resist. He was a combination of brain and brawn; the best the Dominican Republic had to offer. "You are going to like it here, Franky."

"I already do."

"But you need to know your way around. My job is to help a new student, like you, on his first day of class. Have you been around campus? If not, I could show you."

Was Facundo coming on to me? If so, he would have to wait, for my first class awaits me. "I am sorry, Facundo, but my first class starts in five minutes. And I have a campus map to show me around."

"So you're all set, then! But perhaps we can meet after class. When are you through?"

"At five."

"Good! Meet me here at five, and I'll show you around campus." We shook hands, and Facundo began to assist another student. However, as I walked away to class, I managed to look back, and I saw him smile.

# # # # #

Facundo and I met at 5:00 p.m. at the Orientation Desk, now closed for the day. Facundo was as good as his word. Now carrying a backpack of his own, Facundo showed me around campus, pointing out each and every notable person, place or thing as we walked by. As it turned out, Facundo was a bit of a local celebrity, as women and men, students and faculty alike stopped us in our tracks to say hello, shake his hand, or ask him about his past experiences or his future plans. Facundo just shrugged it all off.

"I don't know what they're going to do when I graduate in December. Or, even worse, when I go back to Santo Domingo."

"How did you end up in Miami College?"

"I was a straight-A student. And I had a scholarship at the University. But I wanted to see the United States and especially Miami, where the boys and girls are hot and willing. Though Dad was not too happy with my decision, he gave in, took it for what it was worth, and contacted a friend who teaches here at Miami College. The next thing I knew I had a student visa and was on my way to Miami, where I registered for a work-study program. And I'm having a ball."

"You are very popular here."

"I get good grades, and I compete in a few sports. And I get along with people. It helps that I like both boys and girls. However, when given a choice, I'd rather fuck a hot Cuban boy's bubble-butt than some girl's tired twat. Especially one particular boy."

"You sure don't mince words."

"I never do. And don't act so naïve 'cause I know you're not. I knew you are queer for cock the moment I saw you walk up to the Orientation Desk, wearing those short-shorts. At first I thought it was quite nervy of you, dressed like that. Then I saw how cute you were, and I became interested. Then when you turned around and left I took one look at your hot *culo*, and I realized that you are a boy who needs to get fucked often. I bet you're not a virgin."

"I've been around the block," I said, which put it mildly. Though I was just 18, I was already on my way to become Miami's most uninhibited cock hound. My ass itched at the thought of being plowed by this muscular young Dominican who stood beside me. The fact that he was bisexual didn't bother me at all. "But where can we go?" I said, as a crowd of students walked by. If nothing else, Miami College lacked privacy.

"Just follow me," said Facundo, as he took my arm. The crowds seemed to get smaller as Facundo led me through a block of classroom buildings, an auditorium, a stadium, and a parking lot. Soon we arrived at an abandoned warehouse on the other end of the Miami College campus. Facundo turned on the light as we entered the empty warehouse, allowing me to stare at a graveyard of desks, chairs and other classroom equipment. "Here is where they keep the furniture, until they are needed. But don't worry; no one comes up here, at least not at this time of day."

"You seem to be familiar with this place."

"I first came here on Orientation Day, with a straight Cuban couple who gave me my first bisexual thrill. Students come here all the time to get high or to get laid. But I doubt anyone will come up here today, the first day of class, which is fine with me. I want you to myself," he said, as he grabbed me in a bear hug. As we kissed, Facundo grabbed my ass, holding it with all his might.

"You have one hot *culo*, Franky," Facundo whispered in my ear. "I've had my share of hot Cuban boy ass, but yours is the best!" While Facundo continued to grope my buns, he took my right hand and placed it on his crotch. He had a raging hard-on. "Do you want my cock?"

"You know I do. But I want to see it first."

"Then get on your knees and take it out, *Puto!*" Facundo ordered, as he pushed me down to the ground. "And while you're down there, suck my stiff dick." Now on my knees, I eagerly opened Facundo's pants, like a kid opening a Christmas gift, and took out his cock and balls. Facundo's cock was big and thick, at least ten inches long and as wide as a beer can. His massive *pinga* was hard as a rock and covered with a dark brown foreskin. A pair of low-hanging balls and a crop of black pubic hair completed the package.

"That's a man's cock you got there, Franky," Facundo laughed, as he shoved his thick, ten-inch cock inside my hungry mouth. "Do you think you can handle it? Now suck it!" As I began to suck, Facundo removed his shirt, exposing his muscular torso. Looking up at my Dominican lover's muscular chest and washboard stomach, it was all I could do just to keep sucking. Though I'm not the greatest cocksucker in the world, I know what I want and I wanted Facundo's dark Dominican sausage in my mouth and down my throat.

Meanwhile, the sight of a young cockhound on his knees, sucking his prick with all his might, only increased Facundo's ardor. Grabbing my head with his muscular hands, Facundo began to face-fuck me, filling my mouth and throat with his manhood. It was all I could do to keep up with my masculine lover. My tongue wrapped itself around Facundo's thick dick as it made its way in and out of my hungry mouth. Facundo groaned with pleasure, holding me tight as he continued to feed me his rock-hard sausage. Through it all, my own hard cock pushed against my shorts, begging to be released. For a minute, I thought we were going to come right then and there. But it was not to be.

"Get up, Franky," Facundo commanded, as he pushed me back on my feet. "I didn't bring you here just to get a blow job. I want your ass, and I want it now!" he roared, as he pushed me face down on a desk. Facundo then grabbed my shorts and pulled them down to my ankles. I did not have underwear on. "Now spread your legs, *Puto*! I'm gonna take that ass and give it the fucking it deserves!"

"Yes, Sir!" I replied, as I obediently spread my legs. Now naked from the waist down, I surrendered myself to Facundo's tough love. Facundo knew his way around a boy's ass. Taking my firm round buns with his strong hands, Facundo spread my cheeks apart, exposing my tender rectum. I sighed with anticipation as Facundo fingered the rim of my asshole. He then took some lube from his backpack, and used it to shove a greased finger up my anus, reaching deep inside to massage my tender prostate. Instinctively, I spread my legs even further apart, allowing my lover greater access to my hot boy pussy.

"Do you like that Franky?" Facundo asked, as he inserted a second finger inside my bunghole.

"Yes, Sir!" I replied, as sweat poured down my face. As Facundo continued to assault my tender *culo*, I felt a wave of erotic energy shoot through my body. Facundo smiled, happy that his finger fucking was driving me wild with desire. "Are you hot, Franky?" he asked. "'Cause you sure look hot to me!"

"You know it, Man!" I moaned. "My ass is hot, and I'm hot! But I need more than your fingers up my ass. I need your cock, and I need it NOW!" I begged.

"You better get ready, Franky, "cause you're gonna get the fuck of your life!" he boasted, as he greased up his own pinga. With his strong hands holding me down, my muscular young lover impaled me with his monster cock, causing me to scream with pain. But pain soon turned to pleasure as Facundo began to fuck me steadily, again and again and again. Meanwhile my own cock, equally hard, pushed against the desk, which added to my own pleasure. Soon I began to groan with delight, as I willingly surrendered to Facundo's savage fuck.

"You like that cock, don't you Franky?" Facundo teased, as he continued to shove his cock inside me. "This is a man's fuck you're getting; a fuck that you won't soon forget!"

"Fuck me, Facundo. Fuck me!" By that time the two of us had forgotten about Orientation Day, Miami College, or anything else for that matter. There was nothing in the world but Facundo's big thick cock thrusting its way into my helpless ass, again and again, with ever-increasing force. We were two muscular young animals, two young Latinos lost in the primal act of male fucking male. While Facundo continued to fuck my ass, I took hold of my own hard cock, fucking my hand with the same restless force. It wasn't long before Facundo's savage fuck led us past the point of no return.

"I'm coming, Franky!" Facundo yelled, as he thrust inside me one final time. "I'm gonna come inside your ass!" he screamed, as he shot his cum deep inside me. Facundo's orgasm led to my own climax, and I yelled with pleasure as I shot my jism on the desk. Having spilled our seed, it was all that we could do to fall into each other's arms.

"Welcome to Miami College, Franky," Facundo said, as we kissed passionately.

"Will I see you again?"

"Maybe not. I only fuck once, and I'm not the marrying kind. Besides, I'll be graduating and going back to Santo Domingo soon. But you don't have to worry. A hot Cuban boy slut like you will soon have guys waiting in line."

And so it was. Facundo Sarmiento was the first of many men, both students and teachers, whom I cruised, tricked, sucked and fucked (or more likely, got fucked by) in my years as a student at Miami College. But none of those hot *papis* would ever make me forget Facundo, the man who initiated me into gay college life. And it wasn't the last time. Facundo and I would get together again, in very unusual circumstances. But that, as they say, is another story.

ALL THINGS IN TIME
By Dick O'Connor

Born and raised in Southern California, Dick O'Connor is the pen name for a health professional/model/wannabe socialite currently residing in the San Francisco Bay area. This is Dick's first short story publication preceding his first novel. Email him at dick.oh.connor@gmail.com.

On the dance floor in a club during San Francisco Pride's Pink Party, I saw a gorgeous guy walk near me. Wait... I KNOW that face. In my sight was Melman, the "straight" guy I had a tumultuous fuck buddy relationship with years ago in college. He was still the sexy Colombian guy with striking dark eyes, exuding confidence and appeal in his faint accent. On his five-ten frame, his former slim build had increased to a more built and defined physique. *I see he stayed on the Crew Team after I graduated*, I thought in between loud bass drops and unintelligible lyrics in the club, the club lights highlighting his overall moreno complexion. Beautiful man, ugly name – I know.

Melman was accompanied by Fat-bian, my former housemate who facilitated drama between me and our other housemates years back, and Dieg-ho, a friend who ended up stabbing me in the back by perusing my ex-lovers after I moved; they were all commingling and partying on the dance floor. It was a trifecta of wrong. These three individuals were main points in my less-awesome phases in undergrad. So, of course, Melman approached me.

"What are you doing here?" I asked Melman with a puzzled look on my face.

He just stared at me, kissed my cheek, and walked on.

I stood aghast. I declared what I had hoped would never come – an absinthe emergency, Code Green. As a connoisseur, I had always had a 1.5 oz. novelty flask on my person in case such a disaster occurred. Disregarding security or onlookers, I ripped it off my keychain and chugged it warm like a spy biting a cyanide false tooth behind enemy lines, for this was hostile territory. Um, I then recalled splitting a few more Long Island Ice Teas with my "boyfriend" at the time (whom I had an "open" relationship with) and possibly picking a fight with a Sister of Perpetual Indulgence who I think won by kissing me, making me cry as the result.

After the Code Green at SF Pride that weekend, I had to contact Melman the next week. It was shocking to see him in a gay club at gay pride combined with him kiss me – a gay man – publically on the cheek. I emailed him to confirm that it was, in fact, him I saw and not some retrograde absinthe rouse.

"That was you I ran into at Badlands, right? Ha ha... the times have changed, my friend. So are you bi or full-fledged gay now?" the initial message wrote.

"bahahaha... yeah it was. it was a last minute trip my friends invited me too.. and lets just say i'm more open about it," he replied neglecting spell check.

"So that makes 2 yes'. Cool. Welcome. LA Pride is WAY better for next year FYI. SF Pride is just a cluster fuck. Have you bottomed yet?"

"No... Have you? Lol jk, but topped many times well I won't be here next year got a job in NY, so staying there for idk how long"

"Yeah and you also said you'd never be seen in a gay club so give it time... Ha ha. Anyway, Have fun in NYC. I like the energy there. The guys look like they just escaped from concentration camps though."

"Haha... Yeah Europe changed my mind about things, and thx, have a good one too"

That exchange didn't satisfy me and was unsettling. Back in our fuck buddy days in college, he flipped out for me telling people about us (although I did promise to keep my mouth shut) and on one occasion refused to even go into a frozen yogurt place with me, as to not be seen. The chat was only a band-aid to my unresolved issues with him. He still kept popping up in my head, as I wondered about his new gay life.

What was annoying was his online profile popping up reminding me of his new life with a blatant photo of him at Pride. A week later at work I took a break from my diligence and checked his profile. He had posted a recent photo of him in West Hollywood – my former stomping grounds. I had to message him.

"WeHo, eh? My old stomping grounds. So are you actually IN New York yet?"

"I Leave august 1st"

"Oh I see. You still live in LA until then, right?"

"Yeah But today I'm at [our former undergrad] for a day"

"I was there 2 weeks ago."

"You should have hit me up. What for?"

"A few of my undergrad buddies actually moved to the Bay too. So we all planned a road trip since it was the end of our school year."

"Cool"

"I'm headed down to SoCal for a week. We can catch up."

So we agreed to meet. I was giddier than a school girl who just started growing boobs. This guy meant a lot to me back in college, and I couldn't believe he would meet with me after our checkered past. I kept in contact with him throughout the week to confirm a good time to catch up before he moved to New York a few days later. It was odd getting lengthy replies from him with "lols" and "winky faces," as opposed to his previous "k" or "remember-to-leave-the-headlights-off" messages in the time we were hooking-up. Our meeting up again later that week was constantly in the back of my mind the next few days, never mind my family and friends I was initially visiting for the birthdays of both my mother and newborn niece.

I had the outfit planned in advance, a stricter workout routine, and a heavier skincare regimen due to a random and gross breakout of acne I had that made me look as if I had herpes. My goal was to have this play out the way I always wanted it to be: I wanted him to confirm his homosexuality in conversation, to credit the times we previously had, be seen in public with me, club with me, and just have a nice overall chat with perhaps a couple laughs sans any argument.

The day of, I was a nervous wreck. I squeezed in one more jogging lap around Santa Monica proper to calm my nerves before I showered and dressed; the primping rivaled the meticulous homecoming and prom preparation rituals I did in high school. "Weee... It's just like senior year," said Connor, my best friend of ten years who let me stay the rest of my vacation week at his apartment in LA up until I planned to meet with Melman. It was close to 8:00 pm, the time he agreed to pick me up, and Connor and I were attempting to act our age on the balcony while I waited. Just then Melman messaged me.

"Ohmygod, he's here already," reading the text to Connor."

"Ayyyyyeeeee!" squealed Connor, stomping his feet on the ground like the final dance scene from *Flash Dance*.

"I look okay?"

"Girl, your outfit is perfect and your hair is great and the dab of concealer covered the hyper pigmentation left over from that one herpes-looking zit."

"Great."

After he sprayed cologne in the doorway for me to prance through, Connor followed me out to the curb as he hid behind the apartment complex's gate to spy, sporting an eat-shit grin. I was nervous and posed as Melman pulled up the driveway. I got into Melman's car (surprised he offered to do all the driving for once) and tried to act natural.

Okay, do I make immediate eye contact? Do I greet him with a smile? Closed mouth or Texas pageant girl? I wondered as I buckled my seat belt. In the driver's seat, Melman looked sexy as all hell with a fitted button-down shirt (neglecting to button the top two buttons), tight pants (with just enough left to the imagination), and the familiar devilish smile (encircled by his boyish dimples) that effortlessly won me over years before.

"Long time, no see," he said. "I know, like two years? The last time we met up was before you went abroad that whole year to Europe, right?"

"Yeah, wow."

"I know."

"So which way to go?"

We had arranged to do dinner, drinks, and then dance in West Hollywood (which was still a major shock to me). I picked a sushi place beforehand, and we ate there. On the way, we did the usual catching up banter before any of the good stuff came out. Until the juicy point, the most pivotal topic I recall was directing his parallel parking job. In the restaurant, we ate as planned, and the buzz topics slowly surfaced.

"So what made you contact me?" he asked.

"Well it was funny running into you at Pride, and I wanted to see how life was for you. It was a shock to see you in a gay club after you once turned down an offer to go with me to one."

"Yeah, I guess. I was rolling, but I definitely remember you. It was interesting to hear from you. I thought you were a dick before but realized you were cool. I forgave you for telling people about us. I was debating on actually meeting up this week."

"Well, I'm glad we did. Just know, I have no agenda," I assured.

"I know."

"So... how did you come out? I'm a little late but welcome to the gay life," I smiled gesturing my arms open. Melman gave me some long story about making out with some Spanish guy who gabbed about it to his best friends in Europe. Then word caught on. Bottom line: he was out to friends but not family yet. "I brought home six guys that year and one girl, she was a mistake."

"They're all mistakes," I replied. He smirked. "So you still hang out with Fat-bian I saw."

"Yeah, when he finally came out ..."

"... that bitch's closet had a glass door!"

"Ha, yeah, but I messaged him when he came out in his blog. He told me I was his first 'boy crush.'"

"Charming. No wonder he hated me."

I continued to tell him of Fatbian's passive-aggressive nature as a housemate from hell and how he once tried to trip me and a boyfriend at the time in a club, preceding my threat on his life; this changed his mind on Fat-bian.

We chatted more about guys and our definitions of a "hook-up." The check came, I covered it (like a boss), and we went off to the Boy's Town section off Santa Monica Boulevard.

"So what's your number of guys, Dick?"

"Nope. Not a soul knows but me."

"Well I have my exact number in my head."

"I have a tattered piece of paper I've kept since high school with a legend classifying what act was done and how attractive they were."

"So I..."

"Yes, Melman, I marked you down for everything and... you were of average attractiveness..."

Another smirk.

"Let's go for those drinks now," I said.

At our first bar, Trunks, he covered the first round to which I ordered drinks by brand name.

"Jack 'n Coke and a Kettle-Red Bull," I asked the bartender.

After he paid, we sat in a corner and chatted more about our adventures the past few years.

"My New Year's was cool," he said making conversation.

"Did it involve a senator, a rented-out club across the street, and twin hookers?"

"No."

"I'm gonna win ..."

We finished those drinks and decided to bar hop, seeing as he had only been to two places in WeHo thus far. Might as well pick up the old reigns as his tutor ...

"Yeah, let's not do EastWest. They serve cocktails, not drinks," I advised.

At a place called Rage, I covered the next round.

"Uh ... yeah, a vodka-soda and a whiskey 'n Coke."

In the outdoor patio area, we sat, and I had a cigarette.

"You know, this place used to be the shit. Tonight should be Fuego night – Latinos galore ... This place had a mean cover charge, too, but once the recession hit they nixed that; they don't even use the second dance floor now. Pity," I explained.

"Ooh, I hear Paulina Rubio on. Who are your ladies of choice, Dick?" he asked, watching the monitors playing music videos.

"See, Ke$ha is my girl crush Level 11. I wanna party with that bitch. Britney is my Level 2, who I wanna be. Sarah Michelle Gellar is my Level 3, who I might impregnate."

I then offered to shotgun a puff from my cigarette, he declined, not realizing the obvious reasons behind my offer. He never liked cigarette smoke. I want our lips to touch, Dude. If carcinogens are the catalyst, then so be it. Still, he kept gripping my thigh in conversation and his body language was totally open to me. We sipped on that round, bull-shitted more, and then proceeded to a place across the street called Motherload.

"This place looks kinda dead," he said.

"Yeah, well don't get roofied here. Watch my drink," as I went off to pee.

When I returned, we went over to the small outdoor area to talk more. He explained his self-declared stance as a "mama's boy" and his status as the favorite of his siblings.

"The gay ones are always the mom's favorite," I explained.

"Well, she doesn't know."

"Right ..."

It was cute to see him finally open up about his home life. His mannerisms were more open, and he just came off as more "gay," whatever that means. It was a nice shift from his prior machismo. From there we decided our next round would be at placed called Fiesta Cantina.

"Smile to the straight drivers!" I told Melman as we crossed the street en route to the next bar, wrapping my arm around him.

"He he," he chuckled and timidly waved.

At Fiesta Cantina we ordered Long Islands. I said something funny (I think) and he leaned into me with laughter and kissed my shoulder. I almost tipped the bartender $20 in temporary retardation. Sitting at a table, we chatted about some more stuff, or so.

"I'm not a fan of karaoke," he told me.

"Eh, I can give or take, but this fool's rendition of Amy Winehouse is a double whammy of 'give,'" as I motioned to the bathroom.

Before I ventured off to pee again, I looked at Melman, wrapped my arm around his waist, and pecked him softly on the lips.

"I'll be back," I said.

Returning from the restroom on my makeshift runway, I sat in my chair and smiled at him.

"You made the first move this time," he questioned.

"Things change. I have, you have."

"True."

I leaned in for another kiss and was met with playful resistance.

"Oh, stop it. You always pull that shit," I grinned back at him.

"You know I'm always really attracted to you," he said.

Then we shared a deep kiss. The kind pent up after two more years of life experience on both ends. He was always good for that. The tranny that just finished her ranchera number gawked and yelped. More banter between Melman and I was said, sprinkled in with a kiss every few words, like old (mostly sober) times. We became that couple in the bar; I smiled.

"You know I can never be around you if I have a boyfriend, right?" I said.

"I take that as a compliment."

"Well, I think we'll meet up sometime again in life, like a year or so."

He nodded in definite agreement with a furrowed brow and glaring eyes. That made me smile, too.

"Things will always be weird – no – different with you, huh?" I asked.

"I think so."

"So, down these drinks and then dance like fools?" I suggested.

He nodded again and grabbed my hand to lead us out onto the sidewalk.

Inside the next club, Mickey's, we went to the bar for our last drink. I wanted to stay coherent to cherish the evening's promise, and I think he didn't get so hammered because he knew he was driving. We had gone drink-for-drink but were both tanks with the same undergrad pedigree, so we were merely buzzed.

At the bar ordering our drinks, I placed myself behind Melman and wrapped my arms around his waist, him lacing his fingers with mine. Then I softly kissed the back of his neck.

After we were handed our drinks and headed to the dance floor, we made a pit stop in the bathroom. I waited for him inside as he finished up at the urinal and kissed me on his way to the sink to wash his hands. I grinned and stood after. The bathroom service guy rolled his eyes and handed us paper towels.

The dance floor was packed, but all I saw was him. It was cute to see him dance to gay music and just be himself. I didn't know his body was capable of dance. We faced each other, kissed regularly, and moved our bodies (emphasizing the groin areas) to the beats. Then... a Britney song came on and my White ass was pleased. Thank you, Buddha.

"I LOVE THIS SONG!" I mentioned in his ear.

He then turned around and grinded his perfect ass on me to the song. I nestled my nose on that border between his hair line and neck, smelling his musk, kissed him fervently and sighed as I tightened my arms around his waist, him lacing his fingers with mine again. *Dick, drink some water, so you can preserve this memory.* Maybe this is that good Karma thing for doing a thankless, unpaid internship. Or perhaps it's the spoils for waiting around during a rocky three-year fuck buddy relationship.

Whatever it was, I know I was happy as fuck. The music tuned out and all I felt was him. My lips on his skin transferred all the latent and pent-up affection I was so scared to express to him while in undergrad. Back then I had the impression of him as easy to scare off, like a deer. I kissed him like Gomez Addams to Morticia Addams down from his ear to neck. He turned back and smiled to say, "I like that."

I liked it. And him. I had a guy that I seriously liked years ago in my arms again. The same guy who would have never stepped foot into a gay club, let alone, anywhere with me – especially not attached to me at the mouth. Making out on the dance floor became deeper, and he nearly ripped off my lower lip, but in a good way.

"Geez, does he taste good, Honey?" asked an on looking diva.

We just snickered and carried on. That continued on until the club closed when we decided to sober up at the local Pavilions super market with a gallon of water. At the check stand we debated on Doritos or Lays.

"Let's just get both, Babe," Melman suggested.

He noticed my eyes open wide.

"You're my babe tonight, Babe," he continued.

"Okay, Babe."

"I don't like 'baby,' sounds weird."

Melman just called me a pet name. And I just answered to it and called him one in return. Christ.

By then I was practically skipping back to his car. He joined in since his hand had been sealed to mine since Fiesta Cantina.

Melman just called me a pet name. And I answered to it and called him one in return. Contain yourself. I still had to process that.

"You'd have to change it to Mr. O'Connor. I can't change my name to yours since my professional name is already established. Dr. and Mr. O'Connor," boisterously explaining our names if we ever got married. He noted that. We then took a kiss photo on the street, for documentation of the night (as well as an online check-in, to be petty).

In the back of his car we ate and drained the gallon of water as we discussed our preferences of potential boyfriends and having children.

"I want a little girl to spoil, Babe," Melman said.

"I want a clone of me, no women involved – like Jango Fett."

He then gave examples of the languages he learned studying abroad in between small chip-flavored kisses.

"You have a lisp."

"It's Catalan," he retorted.

"It's a Latino lisp."

"Just kiss me, Guapo."

And I did. He then drove back to Connor's, my hand in his the whole time, and came upstairs.

Connor had agreed to let us use his bedroom while he was gone doing a graveyard shift at his design job. I opened the door with the key he left me, and we proceeded to the bedroom which was inexplicably locked.

"Goddamn it!"

The door did not have a typical key hole (save for a small circular hole) and could be only opened from the inside.

"Here, let me try. We have some like these at my mom's house," explained Melman as he grabbed a wire hangar and shoved it in the small opening of the door handle. My hoodrat attempt to use a credit card on the door had already failed.

"Hmmf, maybe I can unscrew the handle. Let me check my car."

He returned with a screw driver and a look of determination. On his knees he dismantled the door knob.

"Okay, that's fuckin' hot," I said as his criminal behavior triggered an erection.

We got into the room and began to undress casually. It wasn't so much a rush to get naked, more a calm undressing to prep for slumber. I still had remnants of my modeling figure, so I took my time – he looked great as always, sporting very sexy DKNY trunks filled in by his thick legs and bulge.

In the bed, we continued making out and went further. This time it felt better, more natural than his pilot runs. The physicality seemed to flow. I guess he had been gaining experience in Europe. It didn't feel like a quid pro quo task or a chore. We reciprocated everything one did to the other without effort, and his improvement was noticeable. He then assumed the top role in missionary position.

"I wanna top you," in remark to a comment I had made against bottoming hours before.

"No, I'm not tonight."

We wrestled around roughly a little more (which was our usual M.O.), and it was fun. I rimmed him, which he seemed to really like, followed by me dry humping him from behind, which he also seemed to like. I tried to put it in but couldn't breach the sphincter due to bad whiskey dick and nervousness.

Either way, we made out more, and he eventually turned around, assuming little spoon position. I wrapped my arms around him again, one under his neck and across his torso and the other around his waist; our legs intertwined as he grabbed my toes with his.

"Goodnight," I whispered, kissing the back of his neck and shoulders.

"Mmmmm," he replied.

"Sorry if I kiss you too much."

"No, I like it."

He began doing those little twitches one does as they drift into sleep. I was wide awake but didn't dare move from that position. I just reflected on the night and planted the occasional kiss on his back from time-to-time as he snored. I must have passed out sometime after.

The sun rose and the light woke us up. I was on my back facing up with Melman on my side resting his head on my chest. I kissed him, and he sat up. I had never enjoyed nagging someone about hogging the covers as I did that morning.

"Where is my underwear?" he asked.

"Hell if I know."

After we found them I wrestled them out of his hands.

"Ha ha, why can't I have them?" he said, plopping his head on my shoulder.

"I prefer you naked."

"Fair enough," as he turned back around to little spoon position.

He lingered with his peripherals locked on me to see if I'd wrap myself around him again – I did.

Minutes later, I restarted our sexy time. He moved behind me while I was on my stomach and dry humped, poking inside just a little. I didn't mind. After a few minutes of that, I flipped him around and did the same, using some lotion I found near the bed. We continued to literally just put "the tip in" with each other for a while. It was hot; I had never flip-flopped with a guy and I was enjoying it. At one point I had him on his back with legs in the air as I began to put my dick in him with deeper intent. He seemed okay with the notion as we made eye contact and he squinted his eyes. Connor then opened the door.

"AH!" I yelped as Melman and I shuffled for some blankets to cover us.

"O-M-G, I'm soooooooooo sorry," Connor whined as he closed the door.

Melman and I laughed as it slammed shut.

"That was your shot," he grinned as he placed me on my back. He lifted my hips and started pumping his dick to get harder. He gently put it in me half way. It felt good. I let him keep going and eventually found myself jacking off in syncopation. He kept a single rhythm with the occasional "figure eight" rotation he knew I liked. I was coming within a few minutes, tightening around the base of his dick. He then went faster and kissed me as he clenched his eyes and began panting.

"Ahhhhhh... I came in you," he moaned.

He came in me.

"Oh, God. I'm taking you on Maury Povich. Bitch, thas yo' baby!"

"Dat baby don't look like me!"

"Bitch, look at da eyes, look at da nose!"

After that exchange, it felt calm in the room. I was comfortable with him as he spooned me and rubbed my shoulders. We stayed and chatted more for about another hour. It was nice just recapping the night with him. And, yes, in the back of my mind I like that a part of him (in the form of seminal fluids) was with me – this is how bitches get pregnant.

"Well that was better than quickies in the back of my Honda, eh?"

"Yeah, but people still walk in on us in bedrooms," he replied.

"Yeah... I didn't have the pleasure of seeing you hop out a four by one dorm window immediately after this time ..."

We met eyes and had an unspoken sigh of nostalgic relief.

We both had to be places later on, him with family, me back in the Bay. We dressed and I walked him to his car. On the street I hugged him and leaned in for a kiss as he hesitated. Our eyes met briefly before I intercepted his attempt at a bland hug. In that moment, my eyes conveyed, "Just kiss me. Who gives a fuck out here?" We shared a brief kiss, and he drove off.

I showered in a daze. Then I looked in the mirror and was taken aback. I looked like I just short-changed my pimp that just choked me: hickies ALL over my neck. I noticed I left two small ones on him, beforehand, but mine looked awful. And I had a meeting the next day with colleagues! Fortunately, the Hoe gods smiled upon me and provided overcast the next day in the Bay, allowing me to wear a turtle neck inconspicuously.

On the long drive back to the Bay, all I could think about was my fairy tale night. Taylor Swift, herself, would have gagged watching us. Three years later I finally got from Melman the night of attention and appreciation that was long past due. All things in time.

ANGEL
By Taurus Blue

Taurus Blue hails from Baltimore, MD, and hopes to transition part-time writing into a full-time writing career. He works in law enforcement, which surprisingly, is not as glamorous as *Charlie's Angels* would have one believe!

When I first met Angel, he had saved my face from a disastrous kiss with the concrete floor of Urban, Milk and Associates, the real estate firm for whom we both worked. I was newly hired and happened to be walking in the hallway between departments in our division: Acquisitions. I tripped over my own boot and sailed head first to the floor. Angel, like the celestial guardians he is so aptly named, was walking by right at the very moment I went askew. His right hand moved firmly down my left side, a counterweight, stopping the trajectory of my fall to the concrete. An electricity traveled upward from where his hand stopped above my waist, to the top of my left ear. The tips of his fingers picked up ambient light as though dipped in alabaster. A moment frozen in time, forever afterwards, he was my hero.

"Thank you," I said, trying desperately not to lose composure.

"Hey man, anytime," he said with his crooked smile and a wink.

More often, now, he invades my thoughts. I don't think his seduction is deliberate. He just has a knack for being physically present in my sphere of existence at the oddest of times. There are moments we come into physical contact with each other. He might pass by and shake my hand or pat me on the back. The moistness of his strong calloused hands intrigues me as it grasps my own, ensnaring me in the lushness of physical promise. His body whispers constantly of secrets locked within the sinews of his quiet masculine form. The caress of his sweat soaked, T-shirted torso, hints at contours of alabaster clad muscles, drenched in light. The loose kiss of denim about his waist, almost painful in the description of his manly swagger, reveals nothing but the virility of the man.

The curls of his hair he keeps partially covered by different baseball caps, depending on the day. The dark locks he keeps clipped close, a blessed corona orbiting the bliss which is his countenance. Ecstasy, surely, the curve of his nose, the tiny curl of his upper lip. The vision of his tongue forced upwards, once, to meet his palate as he explains a word in his native language to me, a moment which enthralls my soul. He is from Mexico.

How pleasant. How profound. How platonic for him to express. How powerful for me to witness. The tumultuous creation of a cosmos of sexual tension, scary in meaning, scary for evoking such passion.

Overcome and swept away. The merest hint of his presence, either by the music of his keys bouncing on his thigh as he walks or the sound of his boot heels across the tiled floor, brings me alive and tears me apart. Shyness keeps my inhibitions in check, but bold danger lurks when I am embraced by the sweet caress of his tantalizing, mercurial brown eyes.

He was shy at first, Angel. Then we had an honest talk. Our first serious conversation. In the craziness that our days at work were, this moment shone as an oasis against the tumult of madness. This was the very beginning of something wonderful, something powerful. I asked what he really wanted to be doing with his life, rather than being our boss's everyman, like he was now. What he really wanted to be was his own boss, doing similar things, like he was now, but for himself. When I was asked the same question by him, the pat answers died away. An artist, an illustrator, I was happiest with pen or pencil to paper.

"You'll have to draw me, then. Tomorrow night, after dinner. I'll bring take out." He said. Final. No room for argument. Just like that. "I know where you live," he said, and he did. Our boss sent him to my house to collect me, once. In the snow. I opened my door and literally, there stood an angel, named Angel. The snow, caught in the stray curls of his hair not covered by his baseball cap, leant an ethereal glint to his unmistakable physical presence. The lively eyes and ready smile he always had for me, truly sparkled in morning light. The boss could collect me every dawn if he sent this divine Botticelli. Our boss was used to getting his way. I still did not know where Angel lived, however. Our conversation continued.

"What about children, Angel? Do you have any?" I asked.

"No."

"You should," I offered. "A *bonito* like you should have lots," I said, hoping he would pick up on my interest with the word.

"Nah," he said in his self deprecating way, "I am not *bonito*."

Beauty might very well be blind because this particular one sure was. Again, the tables turned.

"What about you? Do you have any children, do you want any?" He asked.

"When I was younger, perhaps. Now, as a thirty-year-old? No. They require too much energy."

Later in the day, I took a shortcut, traveling through the basement of our building, which was full of product, cases of paint, ladders and various tools, I bumped into Angel. I did not like going into the sub-level; it reminded me too much of a zombie movie with only one exit. I rounded a discarded desk and whom did I see sitting there?

"What's going on, Angel?" I said, pausing my swift pace. "Is everything OK?" I asked.

"Sure," he said, usually he was so much more expressive. Then, he added, "Just resting."

"Oh, hey while you have a moment, why don't you show it to me?" I couldn't believe my lewd side was on the loose, I couldn't stop the words. Something about Angel caught me off guard, destroying years of well honed self-control. He made me giddy, and I was more apt to act on impulse, like now.

He stopped me, raising a hand.

"I can't. Not here. Tomorrow night, change of plans, instead of take out we'll meet at the little restaurant up the street," he said, again, definitive, no room for argument.

"OK," I said, not sure what was going on, was my plan bearing fruit? Was Angel interested in me, even a little? We seemed to get along.

"You should know, they have microphones on this level and they can hear anything someone says." Now, his raised hand in the stop gesture made sense.

"Wow, I see, Big Brother really is watching, er, listening," I said.

My "outing" at work began innocently enough. One day he passed by my station, making derogatory jokes, as usual, this time about hot dogs.

"You must like sucking hot dogs, Del, huh?" Angel asked.

And my moment had come. I wanted to be honest, see if he could accept my true self. He was important enough to me to try. So, I pushed the envelope, in a rare moment of self affirmation.

"Yeah, what if I do?" rolled out of my mouth before my well honed ninja skills could stop the madness.

Of course, at that very moment, Aloysious Buck walked through my department. He regarded me, his eyes wide with disbelief at what he was hearing and whom he was hearing it from. His girlfriend and I were very close. Our sensibilities and personalities just meshed. She taught me what I know of our division, took me under her wing and protection. I never came out to her, but I was sure she knew where my leanings led. I learned all about the Spanish words for gay from her. Sometimes she would teach me, other times I heard her relating to her friends on the telephone using the words.

My response to Angel's jest was my liberation. Buck gave me a wider berth than usual in the days after my utterance, which may have caused a rift between him and Rosa Rosario. My boss. His girlfriend. Or maybe the world began to teeter on his shoulders, as his wife began to suspect his affair with Rosa, and Rosa was pressuring him for more of his time. She would confide in me, sometimes.

After the hot dog event, I began, what for me, was a full scale pursuit of Angel. Frankly, he scared me. Or rather, the emotions completely running over my usual rational, cool, calm, collected self, scared me. He was a vision, a force of nature. And he was humble. Simple. Uncomplicated. Full of life, though. There was a subtlety to the wearing away of the gates of my chastity. He was hard to read. He just had this way of looking at me that cut to the truth. There was something he was not telling me. And it made me nervous whenever he came around. Our orbits intersected more often, now. He wanted to show me something, share something with me, but didn't, as if he was afraid I wouldn't like what he revealed. The offer to join him for dinner was nice, forthcoming. I was excited.

Until I got to the restaurant and saw Michaelangelo Mixtli seated at his table. Now, I liked Michaelangelo. He worked in our building in the finance department. He was stocky and nice looking in a bookish sense. But there was something unusual about the way he stared at me through his glasses, when he thought I wasn't looking. It wasn't exactly revulsion painted there, rather, some inexplicable emotion. He was so caught in whatever expression gripped him that he did not realize I was regarding him, too. His face registered "if looks could kill," almost. I did not like to think about work in my free time. The script for my pleasurable dream date did not include Michaelangelo. Yet, tonight the fates were weaving their threads, for here he was. And just like the Sunday cartoons in the newspaper, I sported a dark thought bubble full of thunderclouds above my head. Angel, with his broad back to me, must have recognized the look on Michaelangelo's face, because he turned around without a word or gesture from his table mate. He stood and waved me over to their table. As I arrived beside him, he slapped me on my back and gave me one of his quirky crooked smiles. I was seated directly beside Angel, our legs touching. My body grasping such a small touch and magnifying it. I could not stand up or I would die of embarrassment, as parts of my anatomy strained against my blue jeans. I hoped neither my companions nor anyone in the restaurant took notice. Michaelangelo sat across from us. The two of them converse readily in English and Spanish.

Of course, my knowledge of the Spanish language was minor. The odd word here or there taught by Rosa or Angel. She taught me weighty words, he taught me naughty ones. *Pendejo* meant jerk, *coño* meant damn, and *cabrón* meant motherfucker. That was how he became my *Señor Cabrón*. He taught me that word, sending it my way one day as an insult in that playful way of his. I added the *Señor* in front of it, and he thought it was highly funny. So, he was forever *Señor Cabrón* afterwards. It made his mercurial brown eyes twinkle with more mischievous depth. Lighting up those very same eyes became my mission. He had his sad moments, despairing and deep. I wished I could spare him from such, but he was beyond my realm, presently.

Our dinner progressed well. Michaelangelo had a humorous side, which he rarely showed at work. His wit was scathing, biting, harsh and cruel, but funny just the same. Angel and I laughed good and hard during this meal. The drinks flowed. I became vaguely aware, as we had grown louder, that we three were drunk. They spoke natively; I just looked at them. Michaelangelo became Micky, to separate him from the evil looks beast. Micky would translate the gist of their conversation. They could have been calling me all kinds of names. But it did not matter; I was with my dream date, even though he did not know he was my dream date, and listening to their lyrical language transported me somewhere magical. I noticed the darkness outside the restaurant's windows had increased, and the servers were framing the door, a sure sign it was time for us

99

to check out. Mickey lived in the opposite direction of Angel and me. We bid him good night, and he departed into the dark. This night, I found out where Angel lived. We lived on the same street, he one block from me. I wanted to play up my drunkenness, pretend I could not make it home or forgot exactly where I lived, in the hopes of getting Angel to my house and into my bed. But I could not. Even drunk, I wanted no artifice with him; he was important to me. We came to his house first, which he shared with his brother and niece. I bid him *buenos noches* and perfected my drunken meander down the street to my front door on the next block.

At work, whenever we learned a new word in any of the languages present in our circle, be it English, Tagalog, Spanish or whatever was spoken in Guyana, Angel would move in close. He didn't have the personal space issues we North Americans have. I loved those moments. He moved in closer, once, as he called me a faggot and to my face! In the past, he would have been punched in the mouth for uttering such a word. The word left his mouth so cleanly, without malice, but I still flinched. A lifetime of defenses built up to survive such words still could not be overridden so easily. Our Guyanese version of Angel, Drake, defended me from the assaultive word, but there was no need. I knew Angel did not intend for his use to be mean, merely, a sort of pet name, like my *Señor Cabrón*. After learning the Guyanese word for monkey, Angel's face lit up.

"Aha! That's it! You have a little monkey face. Doesn't he?" He asked Drake.

"Yeah," Drake answered, looking at me as if to say I'm sorry.

I didn't care, for some reason, my being a little monkey face magnified the sparkle of joy within Angel's eyes. I didn't confide that I was called Curious George as a child. Angel's humor was offbeat, at times, but if the name pleased him, the name pleased me.

He and I had more serious conversations. He still owed me a dinner with takeout and a chance for him to model for me. He brought my favorites, from a Cuban restaurant a few blocks over from our street. *Mofongo*, which was some type of delicious pork dish, a sandwich *Cubano*, and fried *plantanos*. My treats, usually to myself, for lunch, which I learned about from my darling Rosa. Angel was wrestling with something as we shared the meal and some bottled beer. I look at his face. He seemed somber. Something was up. I knelt in front of him and held his hand with my own. His hands were warm and moist. "You look sad, Angel. You can talk to me. What is it?" I asked.

"Nothing," he said, very quiet was he tonight.

"Dude, you want to say something, you are all conflicted; your shoulders are slumped. Sometimes it is better to talk, Angel. Just get the problem out into the open. You can tell me anything. If I can help you, *Señor Cabrón*, you know I will."

He regarded me with those gorgeous brown eyes, hidden behind those thick eyelashes. I'd never seen him so serious. And now, I worried. He had been so quiet and brooding, more of late.

"That's just it," he said, looking at the sweaty beer bottle in his right hand and remained silent.

"Aggh, Dude, talk to me!" I exclaimed.

"OK, OK," he said. "There are men, and there are women," he stated, studying me, looking me in the eyes in such an intense manner before gazing at my hands holding my own sweaty beer bottle. "Then there is you. You are something – different. You exist somewhere in between. In the creation myth of my homeland, there is an old god, both male and female, from whom all other gods and humans sprang. You make me think of this myth, for you are similar, at least in theory. How do you explain this?" He asked, so serious, so intense. He really was searching for something, some truth. I hoped I was equipped to answer him to his satisfaction.

"Well, Angel. Everything is codified in terms of male and female. Sockets, language, the moon and the sun. Even humans. But strip away all the labels and what have you got? Human. You and I are humans, first. Strip away all else, language, country, job, clothes and what have you got? Two people. Two sexual beings. One of whom totally likes the other," there! I've finally said it out loud to the man I desired, without being lewd. I hoped.

His mirthful eyes went wide with anything but mirth. A look of surprise, not fear. His head turned slightly to the left, his eyes searching the floor.

"Who – who told you?" He stammered.

"What? Who told me what?" I asked, before realization enlightened me, and I stammered, "You … you mean …" and I stopped. I looked at the vision of beauty, the Botticelli, before me, as if for the first time. He stood in his manly way, confident, yet, tonight, so vulnerable. His brow, furrowed, his expression honest, open, confused. I smiled. This man! Angel, genuinely liked me. Was he so concerned about the rightness of what he felt?

"Angel. You like me?" I asked, incredulous. He whom I have been pursuing like the elusive jaguar of his homeland, could possibly return my affections?

"I do," he stated, in his simple manner. His eyes locked onto mine. His face stunned me. His face radiated an unabashed earnestness. The long lashes protecting the vulnerable eyes, those playful brown orbs of beauty. Something else colored his exquisite face. A sweetness, a delicate emotion I've never seen on him, but something more, something deeper. A hunger. A lust. Desire. I wondered if my own showed as varied, multilayered and complex. He continued. I was frozen in place, sure if I moved the magic of this moment would fade to nothing like a cloud against a mountain.

"I have done something for which I will need your forgiveness," he said, my heart sinking. There was such passion coursing through the statuesque man before me, his voice trembled. His eyes were moist. He moved forward and knelt on the carpet before me. He grasped my hands and looked up into my eyes. This could not be good; those words were not conducive to him whipping out a tiny box with a ring enclosed.

"I'm sorry," he said, tears flowing. His actions, his vulnerability, burning into my soul. "I don't want to offend you. The dinner ..." and he looked away.

"Offend me how? The dinner? With Micky? Oh." My mind filling in blanks and jumping to conclusions. "I see. You and Michaelangelo. Makes sense, wow," I said, reverting to Micky's unabbreviated name again.

"What? No," he said, eyes back on mine, with another quirky questioning smile. "Micky, he is my friend but just a friend, he's married. He has been kind to me. He is gifted."

My mind again jumped, imagining precisely how "gifted" Michaelangelo might be. Perhaps it was my turn for some evil looks. Angel's eyes searched mine, almost pleading. His tug on my soul, on my very being was threatening to engulf me.

"Uh-huh," I said, inflecting my words in such a way as to be sarcastic. I am missing something terribly important to this kneeling man before me. "Just tell me, Angel."

"Micky is psychic. The dinner was arranged, so he could read you." He grabbed me about the waist, tight, his face

102

smashed against my abdomen. His next words, muffled, somewhat. "I don't want you to be mad at me."

I loosened his grip about my waist, because if he remained where he was, he was going to feel a very hard piece of flesh poking against his chest.

"What did Michaelangelo tell you about me, Angel?" Wondering if Circe of The Dinner revealed anything worthy which would have any real bearing on Angel or me.

"He said there are very powerful spirits about you. He said those spirits would brook no foolishness. He said you were like a tempest , or more like the calm before the storm. If I wanted to be with you, truly, I had to stop being afraid and learn to understand you. I had to stop, take my time and learn you."

"Micky said all that?" His short nickname reinvoked. I was flattered.

"Yes. There is more. He said if I could fathom crossing the bridge to get to you, get to know you, we could build a solid foundation. I want that. I want that with you. If I am totally honest, I want you. I have always wanted you. I was hesitant at first at what I was feeling. I did not want to enter into anything lightly with you, without a deeper meaning, a deeper connection. I always thought I would end up married with five or six children. I almost lost you, bothering with my stupid fantasy."

"What fantasy? We can still get married and have six children, if you really want such a life," I said, with my most serious face. "And you were this close to losing me," I sayid, as I held the thumb and forefinger of my left hand about a half inch apart.

He laughed. I kept my face serious. He looked on, nervous, his eyes questioning. Then I laughed. Our laughter joined together.

"Seriously, though, Angel if you want a large family, you shall have a large family," I said.

"Let's start with you and me first," my hero stated, matter of fact, with no room for argument, as if such was the simplest thing. "You think me a superstitious fool?"

"No, Angel. I have a lot of respect for you. You are one of the most level-headed of twenty-four year olds I've met. You are one of the hardest working people I've ever seen, and you do so without complaint. I know you have integrity and ethics. You will work towards your goal tirelessly if it's important to you. My question is, however, what if Micky had never done a reading or what if he predicted doom and gloom for us?"

"Don't have to worry about that, because he read what he read. End of story."

I had to learn to let go and stop analyzing every little detail. "Well," he said. "Now that the difficult stuff is out of the way, I promised to pose for you," he began to undo his belt buckle. I stopped him because I needed to concentrate on him without the lust, at least for this first sketch. I wanted to capture him devoid of the slant my sexual objectification would add. I wanted to capture him simple, true and pure as I saw him in my romantic sense, untainted by my lewd side.

# # # # #

The love letter lay atop a heap of alabaster rose petals spilling over the large maroon pillow on the bed. The tall man with the dark, curly, brown hair and jovial brown eyes picked up the letter with his large, strong, right hand and lifted the flap of the folded parchment paper with his thumb. The corner of his mouth rose, transforming the curl of his lip into a slight, crooked smile. His stance, legs spread wide apart, denoted the quiet confidence of the man. His strong body was clothed in a navy blue, short sleeved T-shirt and blue jeans. The universal uniform, or so his lover claimed.

Dear Angel,

So many times you have freed my soul. The jingle of your keys and the approach of your footsteps, instantly get me hard. Your quirky little looks. Your laugh and love of life. The curls of your hair. The curve of your nose and the curl of your lip.

The way you stand, so confident and sexy and self assured. The moist but firm grip of your handshake. Even your risqué jokes compliment the pleasure which is you. If you are reading this missive, you have found and bravely crossed the bridge to our future. Tonight, prepare to have your pleasures multiplied endlessly and often, as I hope to elicit boundless joy to match what you have so graciously given.

"You bet," the attractive subject of the love letter said aloud, his crooked smile a full-fledged grin. He walked over to the wall, where the drawing, sketched on the night of the takeout dinner, was framed. His little monkey face was talented. The composition was casually centered and drawn with relaxed contours. Angel marveled at his likeness staring back from the glass frame. Del saw the most amazing things in him, which

Angel scarcely believed he possessed. But the drawing expressed love. Tender, simple, pure.

Del slipped his hands under Angel's arms from behind, pressing his body close, breathing in his aroma, reaching up and caressing Angel's pectorals through his T-shirt. Angel leaned his head back. Del pressed his lips to the back of Angel's neck, right at the hairline. Angel's body erupted with Goosebumps and the flame of desire. He turned to Del, picked him up and laid him on the bed of rose petals.

"These are alabaster, like your skin," Del said, placing the fingers of his right hand in the thick brown curls above Angel's left ear. Angel engulfed the mouth speaking those words with his own. The first kiss, their saliva, a strand connecting them to the infinite. The kiss, so passionate, immobilized Del, his heart pounding fully, his breath frozen. Mercurial brown eyes searched his for something they both shared. Both bound in the simmering depths of their emotions would no longer be denied. His large warm hands tenderly caressed the sides of Del's face, before moving slowly over his body. Every movement an expression, a dance, a reassurance. These are the words in the song of a man, secure, completely in tune with his body, his feelings, his mind. Each move, slow, deliberate, enticing.

Angel's fingers crept under the edge of Del's faded orange T-shirt and began to unveil the flesh of Del's belly. Each inch, as he pushed that edge up, was followed by a tender kiss. Del's jean clad hips bucked in anticipation. Angel placed his left hand just below Del's belly button to still the movement. The heat of that hand radiated, and Del was close to erupting. He looked into Del's eyes, continuing as before. The shirt made it just below Del's armpits, and he raised his arms so it could be lifted off. Angel complied. He dropped the shirt on the floor beside the bed. He started to lift his own, navy blue T-shirt. Every inch raised, revealing the smooth, glowing skin beneath. Angel's arms crossed as the shirt was lifted above his head. A whimper escaped Del's face. The sight of the naturally muscled Angel's naked torso and the bounce of his curls as his head emerged from the T-shirt seared into Del's memory. His hands reached up, caressing the pectorals again, unencumbered by the fabric. Angel's dexterous fingers reached for the button of Del's jeans. A little moan was Del's response. Angel smiled, his crooked one, with a mischievous look in the eyes, he unfastenned the button and unzipped the zipper. He slid off the bed, grasping the jeans at the ankles and yanked the pants from Del's body. He cocked his head and grinned when he saw the state of Del's erection. His member pointed toward his chin. Angel unzipped his own jeans and turned his broad back to Del. He turned to make sure Del was looking, smiled, and slowly lowered his jeans from his tight muscular bubble butt. Del whimpered, again, but yelled aloud when Angel, one hand on the bed, hopped clear onto Del's chest in a swift movement of muscle, limbs and member. Angel looked at the sweet face of Del taking in and enjoying the sight of his body. He was always surprised by Del's attraction for him. He followed Del's wide eyed gaze to his thick, long, low hanging, uncut member. He pressed the tip down onto Del's chest and rolled it from side to side.

"It's not hard, yet," he stated, leaning in closer, to savor another slow, gentle kiss. "I have something else to tell you, monkey face," Angel said, before adding, "I hope you will not think less of me." His eyes, usually so full of humor, were quite serious.

"You're not going to tell me that thing grows to twice the size it is now?" Del stated, joking.

"Nah," Angel smiled and leaned in, his head to Del's left ear, his lips pressing lightly as he whispered, "I am a virgin." He brought his face back in front of Del's and regarded him from eye to eye.

Del leaned his head forward and pressed his forehead to Angel's. "I am, too."

Now, it was Angel's turn to look surprised. He shook his head, the quirky smile in place, he asked, "At thirty? *Coño!* I thought I was late! I was saving myself for you."

"No, I was saving myself for you," Del said, reaching over to the nightstand and grabbing a jar of lubricant.

Slathering generous portions of the stuff on each other, Angel slowly entered Del, who held his breath. Angel pressed forward and was rewarded with a gasp from Del as the wide head of Angel's member slid past the sphincter. He moved slow and steady, in and out. The young men's senses building before crashing together, realizing they had found each other, enmeshed as one inside the other. A new sensation added to their song, a revelation. They belonged together. Del's arms held Angel close as Angel began to moan, he was near the eclipse of pleasure. The friction of his slow, steady back and forth and his pressure from within sent Del over the edge; his hips bucked as his salt spilled between the two men. His forceful ejaculation spurred Angel to climax inside the warmth of Del's body. Their kissing, languid, not rushed. Each committing to memory the feel and touch of the other. Love consummated.

As his little monkey face slept, Angel reread the love letter. He remembered the day he fell in love. Del was quite loudly and vehemently arguing with their boss, the man who could fire either one of them in an instant. But that did not stop his love. The skinny man was defending Angel with a strength, a passion, and an energy that was quite scary, had he not known the man. They looked as if they would come to blows. The face of his love a mere inch from the boss's. In the history of their work world, this was unprecedented.

The incident. Somehow, a key from Angel's key ring went missing. A considerable amount of items went missing from the storeroom, Angel was blamed and forfeited an entire paycheck to cover the cost of the missing goods, which was criminal because his paycheck was anemic. But once Del heard what had happened, the wiry man oh so calmly and smoothly walked into the boss's office and began Armageddon. Every excuse the boss conjured, Del countered. The injustices Angel suffered were unfair, who could prove he was the culprit, keys went missing all the time. Items were stolen, often, and no one forfeited a paycheck. How dare Angel be accused of such, all the years he has worked without complaint for the boss, a man akin to a thief himself, paying the hard working Angel a pittance and then taking the paltry thing back was beyond insult. He should give the man a raise or better yet, the deed to one of the small apartment buildings and let him manage it for all the grief he had been given and continuously endured. And as violently loud as the words had become, they ended quietly. Del was sent home early that day, as was Angel.

Unbeknownst to all, a detective had been hired. Seems a lot of things went missing at the business, for years. The culprits were caught after the investigation: a pair of Somalian brothers who were connected to all types of nefarious dealings with unseemly sorts, possibly helping to spearhead the pirates assaulting ships off the African coast.

That was the day.

When Angel was sent home, he began down the block but did not stop at his door. He kept walking, finding his way to a basement apartment, as he had once before, in the snow. When he rapped upon the window, the door opened, revealing a puffy, red eyed, trembling mess of a wiry man. At the sight of the vulnerability of the man who had just unleashed World War III, Angel pulled him close, kissed him atop his head and moved across the threshold, shutting the door.

"Hey, now, monkey face, what's all this? Huh? Why are you crying, why are you trembling? Don't! Shhh."

"Oh Angel, I am so sorry. I think I managed to get us fired," Del stated, fresh tears flowing.

"Maybe, El Gordo, but we shall find new jobs," Angel stated, in his matter of fact way.

"But Angel, you don't understand. I won't be able to stay here. I won't be able to pay the rent or my bills or eat or anything, and I got you fired! My big mouth, I should have kept it shut," Del stated, through more tears.

"Nonsense, bonito," Angel stated, hugging his love tight. "You worry about things too much, sometimes. It makes you a sad monkey face," Angel said, his crooked smile and twinkling eyes causing Del to smile and punch him in the chest, lightly.

"Oww, that hurt," Angel lied.

"Serves you right, you *pendejo*. I do not have a monkey face," Del stated, smiling, though he had been called by that moniker even when he was little.

"Angel? Are you here to deliver the bad news? Am I fired?"

"I haven't heard anything, Micky will tell us, if anything should go down."

"Right. So, why are you here?" Del asked, looking so timid and shy, quite unlike the behemoth of half an hour prior.

And Angel told him the truth. "Because anyone who would go against our boss, toe for toe, without fear, stand up for a man in such a way, even though he might not be able to love you the way you love him, and leave the building walking, instead of on a stretcher, is worthy of the best love I can give," Angel said, pounding on his chest to emphasize the "I." After that show, Angel knew this thin fella was a keeper, and Angel vowed that day, he would never leave his side.

# # # # #

As an apology from the boss, Angel received the deed and keys to a tiny, three-apartment building. It was a start. I resigned. I couldn't continue working on a job where I was at odds with the boss, though he stood redeemed with his generous gift as apology. He did not want to let me go, said I was like a storm, the only person, other than his wife, to stand up to him and tell him the truth whether it hurt or not. But leaving his employ freed me to spend more time with Angel, who hired me. Angel Enterprises, L.L.C. was borne from a small, three-apartment building, infused with blood, sweat, tears and love.

COMPROMISING DREAMS
By Mark Apoapsis

Mark Apoapsis does not currently have a website but may be reached at mapoapsis@excite.com.

I woke up in the dark, not knowing where I was. It was still the middle of the night; no light was coming in through my window. I had the feeling something had awakened me. Maybe the dream I'd been having. I'd been having anxiety dreams ever since learning my apartment building was being torn down, especially when the official eviction notice had arrived before I'd made any progress in finding a decent place I could afford. The dreams generally involved my still being in the building, forgotten as it was torn down around me. The worst ones were frightening, involving wrecking balls suddenly crashing through the wall. The best ones were steamy and yet humiliating, with hunky construction workers walking along the girders they'd laid bare and discovering me still in my bed in my boxer shorts. Tonight's dream had started as one of the good ones and ended with a nightmarish twist: a construction worker hauling me out of bed only to lose his balance and fall through the empty space that used to be my floor, screaming all the way down. I'd jerked backward onto my bed just in time to keep from sharing his fate, and had woken up.

I relaxed as I came to my senses. Not only was I safe in bed, but my housing problems were over. At the last minute, a week ago Thursday, I'd found someone looking for a roommate. The apartment was only ten minutes from work, and most days we carpooled, since Arturo worked two floors above me in the same office building. After weeks of online searching, I'd stumbled across his ad on a physical bulletin board in the cafeteria, alongside such things as before-and-after photos for weight-loss schemes I certainly didn't need, and before-and-after photos purporting to prove that aliens were building a colony on the moon.

The rent was about a third of what I'd been paying at my old rent-controlled place, for a larger and nicer apartment. Granted, I'd had the old place to myself, while here I had to

111

share everything except my bedroom. But my bedroom was bigger than my old one. I didn't mind that it lacked a window.

Arturo had not only let me move in right away and not requested a deposit – I'd had to practically force even the first month's rent check into his hands – he'd helped me move my stuff, starting right after work that very day. I'd protested that I had two perfectly sturdy friends lined up to help if we waited until Saturday. We did finish the last of it on Saturday with Bernie and Barry's help, in less than two hours. In past moves I'd always bought pizza for anyone helping me, but Arturo fed everybody with lasagna left over from the tray he'd made me the first night, the best any of us had tasted. When that ran out halfway through, he apologized for underestimating the appetites of four big strong guys after so long cooking for one, and the minute he'd helped us haul the last of the boxes up the stairs, he was back in the kitchen whipping up homemade burritos to order while my two friends helped me start unpacking.

"If you ever want to trade," Bernie had told me in the privacy of my new bedroom as we worked, "I might consider it." He grinned fondly at his partner. "It would almost be worth giving up the sex in exchange for the cooking."

"I wonder if Arturo has picked up on you guys being a couple," I had said. "It would be interesting to see his reaction."

"Have you come out to him?"

"Not yet. Normally, I would have, but I really, really needed this place and wouldn't have had time to look for another one, as you well know."

"Too bad you're allergic to cats, or our couch would have been better than nothing," Barry had said.

"If you don't mind the hour's commute," Bernie had added.

"I'm really hoping this will work out. Especially after tasting his cooking."

"He's not bad to look at, either. Did you see those abs, when he mopped his brow with his shirt?" He'd given me a playful shove. "Dude, it's so easy to make you blush."

# # # # #

Since I was awake and usually needed to get up to take a leak at least once a night, I decided to get that out of the way, so maybe I could sleep uninterrupted for the remaining seven hours. I spent some time hunting down where I'd thrown my bathrobe; living alone I hadn't had much need for it and kept it in the bathroom, but now that I had a roommate I was keeping it in my bedroom but hadn't yet settled on a standard place for it. Not that it was likely I'd run into anyone between here and the bathroom at this hour. Finally, I found it, put it on, and unlocked and opened my bedroom door. Immediately I noticed that the kitchen light was on. Then I saw Arturo's profile; he was standing at the dining table with a mug in his hand, his back to the kitchen. He turned to face me, the light from the kitchen ceiling fixture spilling over his smooth brown torso from the side and casting his chest and abdominal muscles into sharp relief. He was clad only in boxers.

He asked, "Sorry, man, did I wake you?" He seemed slightly embarrassed, which at the time I assumed because a near stranger had unexpectedly walked in on him in his boxers. Like me, he'd been getting dressed in the bathroom after his shower for the week I'd lived here, and undressing in his room.

"No," I said, "I woke up on my own. A bad dream."

"Oh?" He seemed interested. "Have you been getting those a lot?"

"Only since I started worrying about the eviction. I should be okay in a week or so. When I was in school I used to spend the first couple of weeks of summer vacation dreaming I'd flunked a test and the last couple of weeks dreaming I was looking for my new classroom."

"One of my younger brothers used to have dreams exactly like that. Seems unfair, doesn't it?"

"Do you have a lot of siblings?"

"Just the two younger brothers in college, and one older one."

I nodded and headed to the bathroom. When I came out a couple of minutes later, Arturo was still where I'd left him, and still in his boxers. If it had been me, I'd have taken the chance to put something on. I actually felt slightly uncomfortable wearing nothing but my bathrobe. It was one thing to expose myself in the context of sex to men I never expected to see again. The nudity was part of what was arousing. Walking around with my chest hair curling out in front of my new, presumably-straight roommate, a guy I was going to see every day for who knew how long, was a new experience for me. I didn't even like changing in the locker room at the gym, so I drove there in my gym clothes; anyway, the gym I'd chosen had private shower stalls with individual changing areas.

This was silly; I only had to make it from the bathroom door to my bedroom door on the direct opposite side of the living room with a slight detour around the couch. "Goodnight," I said, angling my body self-consciously away from the dining nook as I passed.

"Are you going right back to bed, man?" There was something wistful in his voice.

"Well, tomorrow's a work day. I feel tired all day if I don't get six or seven hours." And I'd gotten less than an hour so far.

"Tell me about it. I'm afraid of being passed over for a raise this year because I've made so many mistakes. I miss out on sleep a few nights, and I'm stumbling around like, like a ..."

"Zombie?" I prompted, thinking for a second that he didn't know the word in English. Then I realized how stupid that was, since he seemed to be as fluent as I was; I was sure he'd grown up here and was bilingual. He had only the faintest accent, just enough to make him even sexier.

He shivered. "Great. Now I'll start having that one again."

"Oh. Sorry. Is that why you've been having trouble sleeping? Nightmares?"

"You have no idea."

I was tired, but he'd been very nice to me, and he seemed to want to talk. "Want some company?"

His dark brown eyes looked pathetically grateful. "Would you? I hate to make you lose sleep, but maybe just until I can work up the nerve to get back in bed?"

"That bad, huh?"

"Want some hot chocolate? I was just about to make myself another mug."

"Sure. Maybe with marshmallows."

"Sorry, man, I don't have any marshmallows."

"But I do."

His dark eyes lit up like a kid's. "You're kidding? You brought marshmallows?"

"I think so. In the box labeled 'Kitchen Cabinet, Dry Goods.' I haven't unpacked it yet."

"I kind of wish 'Kitchen Junk Drawer' had been the one you hadn't unpacked," he grumbled good-naturedly. "We now have three corkscrews and four can openers, thanks to too many guys moving out in a hurry."

As we sipped our hot chocolate with melted marshmallows, Arturo said, "Armando used to make it just like this for me when I had bad dreams."

I was intrigued. There was no mistaking the affection in his voice and his dark eyes. "Who's Armando?"

"My older brother."

The fondness was still there. Nothing like what I felt for my own brother, or for any other person.

"I can spike it with some brandy or rum if you want," he offered. "I've been avoiding that so far out of nostalgia, I guess, and also because it would be too easy to overdo it. That's probably why I haven't bothered to take the padlock off the liquor cabinet, even after my last roommate moved out. He was an alcoholic."

"Ah, that explains why you had a room available. Did he give you any trouble when you kicked him out?"

"I didn't kick him out. It was his idea to leave after two weeks."

He seemed uncomfortable with the topic, so I changed the subject by complementing him on the hot chocolate – honestly enough; it was the best I'd had in as long as I could remember.

"Thanks. It's Armando's recipe. It has cinnamon and a little peppermint."

"Good cooking must run in your family."

"Both of my parents work in the restaurant industry. They were under the impression that their sons' career options would be limited to busboy or cook, so they made sure we all learned to cook, so we'd always be able to support ourselves. And actually, I did work my way through college as a cook."

I asked him where he went to school, and told him a little about my own college and family. This was the kind of late-night talk I'd always fantasized about having with a roommate in college but had never had. Arturo had pulled up a chair right beside me when he served the hot chocolate, sitting so close that the left sleeve of my bathrobe grazed his bare right shoulder when I wasn't careful.

"It's nice to get a chance to hang out with you, man," Arturo said, long after we'd each finished our second cup.

"What do you mean? We have dinner together every day. I used to usually eat a rushed meal on my own, but your awesome cooking has convinced me to change that. We also talk when we're doing the dishes. Although I told you, it's only fair if I do all the cleaning."

"Like I said, I don't agree. Cooking is fun and cleaning isn't."

He'd insisted on doing his share of the cleaning and on helping with the dishes. I felt like I was taking advantage of his good nature. Also, to be honest, he had a habit of standing closer to me than I was used to straight guys standing, and he had a disconcerting way, when we were doing the dishes, of reaching right through my personal space. It would have felt threatening, coming from most guys, but I liked him enough that it only felt disturbingly intimate. He didn't seem to notice that it bothered me.

"By the way, we should work out some everyday domestic details at some point. We don't have to do things the way I'm used to. For example, we can turn the air conditioner down even further at night if you want, especially for the summer. Everyone's different. You're not the first roommate to wrap up in a bathrobe when I was comfortable in shorts."

"Oh. No. This is fine. A little hot, if anything, but at least we're conserving electricity."

"And I promise to let you know if I'm even thinking of bringing a girl here, especially overnight. You have a right to walk around your own apartment without worrying some chick will see you in your underwear and freak out. Or worse, the opposite."

"The opposite of a chick?"

He laughed. "The opposite of freaking out." He'd been looking me in the eye; now he glanced down, almost admiringly. "I don't want to have to compete with a hunky, hairy-chested gringo."

"Oh, come on! You think I'm competition for you?" I fiddled with my robe self-consciously.

"Not on purpose, I'm sure. And I promise not to take anyone away from you if you find her first. But anyway, you can be sure I won't bring a girl home without telling you in advance."

"Thanks."

"Can I count on you to do the same?"

"You mean warn you before I bring anyone over?"

"Particularly girls," he said.

"Sure. Don't worry about it." This would have been a perfect moment to come out to him, I thought, but I wasn't ready, and I didn't want to blow it just when things were going so well.

"Thanks," he said.

The moment had passed. Maybe some other time, when he had more clothes on. With a yawn that was only half feigned, I said, "Thanks for the hot chocolate. Now I really should get back to bed." I had set my empty mug to my right to get it out of the way. Now I reached for it, but Arturo said, "I'll take care of them." He reached past me, the fine black hairs on his forearm actually brushing against the fabric of my robe and even my chest hair. I tried to ignore that. "Hey, aren't you going to let me do any work around here?" I moved the mug out of his reach.

"The hot chocolate was my idea, so I should wash the cups. Do I need to wrestle you over this?" He playfully grabbed the nearest lapel of my bathrobe and turned me in my chair to face him, incidentally baring my left flank and nipple. I reflexively scooted my chair away from him, knocking over the empty mug on the table.

He let go of my robe and held his hands up, palms toward me. "Sorry, man. I guess I don't know you well enough to be horsing around like that."

"It's okay," I mumbled, pulling my robe shut and tightening the belt before standing up. I hadn't been expecting that. I was no stranger to near-strangers ripping my clothes off, but usually I gave them permission first, explicitly or not. And usually, I could expect it to lead to sex a few minutes later, which clearly was not something that would even occur to Arturo. I hoped the loose folds of my robe hid my body's reaction to that expectation. "Try to get some sleep."

# # # # #

I awoke to the sound of Arturo's voice coming through the thin wall between our bedrooms. He was crying out in pain. "What do you want from me?" He cried out sharply again, like he was being struck. "Please, just let me go!"

I scrambled out of bed, not even stopping to locate my bathrobe, and fumbled with the still-unfamiliar knob to unlock it. The lights were all off, the living area only dimly lit by what light spilled around the curtains. I was still sleepy enough to be confused about the layout of my new apartment, but then I saw the dozens of LEDs to my right from Arturo's impressive array of entertainment equipment that he'd been so eager to share with me. I hadn't decided yet whether to sell my flat screen or set it up in my own bedroom. I'd probably need to hook up cable, since reception would be bad here for up to half the day, like it had been everywhere this year. But so far Arturo and I had enjoyed watching things together on cable or DVD on his big screen, which put mine to shame. It was huge enough to make me wonder what he was compensating for.

By the already-familiar multi-colored constellation of his entertainment system, I was able to navigate to Arturo's door, which was on my left. The floor plan was coming back to me. It was very simple: My door opened onto the living room, his onto the dining nook, which was adjacent and not separated by any walls.

I knocked hesitantly. There was no response, but Arturo again howled in pain. I pounded the door with my fist and called his name. He was whimpering something in Spanish.

I tried the knob. It wasn't locked. I eased it open. I saw Arturo lying in bed, face up, with his eyes closed, sheets twisted around his legs. His chest, gleaming with sweat in the moonlight, twitched slightly, and he howled again and pleaded in Spanish. I heard several sentences starting with the word "No," and he sounded bewildered and frightened.

When I'd rushed to his aid, I'd been sure someone had broken in and was doing something awful to him, but now I remembered the conversation we'd had – was it hours before, or only minutes? – about his nightmares. I stepped through the door and debated shaking him awake. Maybe I should go back and find my bathrobe first. But was it really necessary to wake him up? He'd probably wind up lying awake, and then finally falling back asleep only to have another nightmare. It had happened once tonight already.

I watched for a while longer, because I was unsure what to do, not because I was enjoying the chance to stare at him without him knowing it. He really was nicely built. He had a smaller frame than I, but he obviously worked out, and he kept himself extremely trim despite the temptations of his own cooking.

I noticed absently that he'd basically lied when he told me he had the larger room and that's why he was charging me well under half of the rent. He'd generously given me the larger room, although admittedly his had a window. He'd left the curtains open, and a fair amount of moonlight came in, or maybe streetlight. I took advantage of the situation to check out his view out of curiosity. Nothing spectacular. I'd been right about the sources of the light: in addition to some light from streetlights below, the gibbous moon was high in the sky, a little past its first quarter.

I left, shutting the door, and went back to bed. I couldn't get back to sleep, of course, between the noise and the guilt of letting him suffer. Finally the pleading and cries of pain subsided, and I started drifting off to sleep. Then the silence, and my sleep, were shattered by a scream of terror that chilled me to the bone.

I leaped out of bed, fumbled with my door lock, and rushed into his bedroom without even knocking. He was in the same position I'd last seen him, breathing hard. I knelt at his bedside and took both his shoulders in my hands and shook him. "Arturo! Wake up!"

He awoke with a start and clutched at my biceps. He had strong hands. He stared at me without really seeing me. Then his eyes focused, and he relaxed. He didn't let go, though, so I didn't either.

"It's okay," I said quietly. "You were just having a nightmare."

"Thanks, man," he said, sounding shaken. "Sorry I woke you."

"*No problemo,*" I said with a grin.

"Probe-blame-oh," he said, gently correcting my pronunciation. He released his grip on my arms. I took my hands off his bare shoulders. This was the basically the first time I'd touched him except for a handshake when we met and another when we'd sealed the deal.

I backed off and said, "Sleep well. Pleasant dreams this time."

"I hope so. You, too, man."

I left him straightening out his twisted sheets and tucking them around his body again.

# # # # #

I was having a very pleasant dream about being dragged from my bed by burly, shirtless construction workers who had just knocked down my bedroom wall. It was broad daylight in the dream, and they were going to string me up from the girders in my shorts, as a warning to other tenants who'd ignored their eviction noticed. But first, they were going to ...

When I woke suddenly from that dream, the fourth time in one night I'd been awakened by screaming, the one silver lining was that I was proven right: waking Arturo up hadn't stopped the nightmares. I didn't have to feel guilty about hesitating to try it again if it wasn't going to do him any good.

I went and shook him awake again.

"I'm so sorry, man! Now you know why the room was available. I should have bought you some earplugs. I didn't know this was going to happen again."

He looked more vulnerable than I'd ever seen a man look, and I don't mean the fact that he was stretched out before me almost naked. Seeing my normally cheerful and confident roommate reduced to this pathetic state, with tears in his eyes, was tugging at emotions I didn't know I had. I'm not always the most sympathetic person in the world, and naturally I was irritated at losing sleep, but I found myself saying, "Earplugs? How will I be able to know when you're having a bad dream and need me to wake you up, then?"

His face lit up with a smile.

I said, "Do you want to try to get back to sleep, or do you want some more hot chocolate?"

"I'd love some more hot chocolate. I'll make it, as long as ... could you get the syrup out of the fridge?" He made it sound like a big favor.

"Of course," I said. We went into the dining nook together. I couldn't help glancing back at my bedroom, wondering if I should make him wait while I looked for where I'd thrown my bathrobe, but decided not to. He hadn't put anything on either.

As I peered into the fridge, he said, "There isn't anything unusual in there; is there?"

"I'm a gringo, remember, a guy who barely knows how to cook anything not in a package. You have a lot of stuff in here I've never heard of."

"I don't suppose the top shelf is full of severed, bloody hands reaching out to pull you in?"

"Nope."

"Didn't think so."

"Why, were you in the mood for some?"

At least that got a laugh. "I think I'll stick to the hot chocolate. The syrup's in the door."

"Trust me," I said, taking the syrup out, "you've got one of the least horrifying refrigerators of any guy I've seen. Look, everybody has dreams like that sometimes."

"Yeah, but all night? Every night?"

"Every night? Did I sleep through a whole week of you waking up screaming?"

"No, it comes and goes. But once it starts, it takes weeks until I get back to normal. My roommate left me a week into the first episode. We'd been roommates two years! Also, my girlfriend stopped sleeping with me, and eventually we broke up. I keep trying to find roommates, but none of them ever stayed more than three weeks. One or two nights of this shit, and they're out of here. "

"Have you talked to a therapist?"

"I'm not crazy!" he snapped. "I don't need help, like some neurotic housewife!" Those were the first angry words he'd ever spoken to me, and I was immediately sorry for the suggestion.

"Of course you're not," I assured him. "I was just worried about you, man."

He folded his brawny arms over his leanly muscled chest and glared at the table.

I offered tentatively, "I read that soldiers sometimes get recurring nightmares after a battle."

It seemed to be the right thing to say. He unfolded his arms and looked me in the eye again.

"How did it start? Did something bad happen to you?"

"No. That's the strange thing. I was fine, and one day, right in the middle of an ordinary week, they just started. I must have gone two weeks without sleep. Then, just when I thought I couldn't take anymore, they stopped just as suddenly, and I thought I was okay. Then, after a couple of weeks, they came back. After that, I did try one thing: going to church. I'd never even set foot in a church since high school, except for weddings and when I was visiting family. I went a few times. I didn't help at all. It just made me dream of demons and the tortures of Hell for a few nights instead of the usual stuff."

"What's the usual stuff? Sometimes you sounded like someone was torturing you or something. Do you remember anything when you wake up?"

"They seem silly, now that I'm in a bright cozy kitchen talking with a friend, but when they're happening, they're terrifying."

Maybe it was the cocoa, but I felt a warm glow at hearing Arturo call me "friend" for the first time. The growing warmth further down, of course, was definitely not due to anything as innocent as cocoa. I reminded myself firmly that the fact we were both sitting here in our boxer shorts didn't mean anything was going to happen. This flavor of relaxed intimacy was a new and confusing experience for me.

I said, "Maybe it would help to talk about them. Especially if they seem silly now. I promise not to laugh."

"Man, it is so nice to have someone to talk to again."

I resisted the urge to put a comforting hand on his bare shoulder, and just smiled encouragingly.

"They always start out the same way. It's in black and white. I'm in a desert. I'm not wearing a shirt, and the sun is baking my back, even though I can see it's nighttime, but my chest is freezing. Some kind of monster is attacking me. I never see what it is."

"That sounds awful."

"That's not the worst part. The dream shifts to something even worse after that. Different each time, but really nightmarish stuff. Flayed corpses. Heads with dangling intestines that fly around and strangle people. Sometimes everything will seem normal and then – well, that's why I was scared to open the fridge."

"It was just a dream."

"Sometimes I think I woke up and it turns out to be another dream, so..."

"Oh, yeah, I get those, too, sometimes." Half-jokingly, I said, "I just hope I'm not having one now that I'm not really in bed back at my old place being evicted at the end of the month, dreaming I found a great apartment with a great roommate." A handsome and extremely well-built roommate who thought nothing of sitting beside me in his boxer shorts. It did seem too good to be true, and yet it felt real.

"Don't worry, man. It's August, and you're safely out of your apartment and settled here. This is real." He gripped my forearm, as if to reassure me or maybe himself of its solidity, and stroked the hair above my wrist with one fingertip. He eyed my chest speculatively, as if making sure he could count every hair there. Now he was making me nervous again.

We finished our hot chocolate and went back to our bedrooms. I had a dream where we were officemates, and he was sleeping in a sleeping bag stretched out on his desk in the darkened office while I kept watch. Suddenly, I saw a dark shape slip out of the shadows. Before I could warn my sleeping comrade, it darted to Arturo's side, opened the top drawer beneath him, and started rummaging around. Another joined it. They were wearing dark business suits with hoods that hid their faces.

"Pen thieves!" I shouted. "Arturo! Wake up, *compadre*! Pen thieves!"

My comrade sat up groggily, saw what was happening, and screamed.

I woke up and realized that Arturo really was screaming again. I was getting better at finding my doorknob and unlocking it in the dark. I padded over to Arturo's door. He'd left it ajar, and I didn't even bother to knock. I stood there watching his bare chest rising and falling with shuddering breathes in between screams. Not only was it clear why he couldn't keep a roommate, I was beginning to wonder how he'd survived many roommates without being smothered in his sleep. I guessed that suggesting tranquilizers would be as offensive to his pride as suggesting a therapist had been. If the liquor cabinet hadn't been padlocked, I'd have considered pouring a bottle of whiskey, or whatever he had in there, down his throat in the desperate hope of knocking him out for the rest of the night. That might not hurt his masculine pride so much.

Finally I sighed, unable to let him suffer any longer, and shook him awake.

"Sorry," he said despondently. "If you want to move out, I'll understand. I'll give you your money back."

"I'm not going anywhere," I assured him. "I just wish there was something I could do."

"You just saying that to be polite?"

"No, I'd do anything to help you."

He hesitated. "You really mean that?"

"Sure," I said, surprised to realize I really did.

"I feel funny asking this. I never asked any of the other guys ..."

"Try me."

He seemed uncomfortable. "It's just that, like I said, I haven't had nightmares since I was a little kid. And never this many even then. But when I was a kid, I usually only had

123

nightmares when I had to sleep alone. Could you ... stay with me?"

"Sure. If it'll help. I'm not getting any sleep anyway." I rubbed my arms. "It's going to get a little chilly, though. Let me get my robe. And a chair."

"*Cabeza de chorlito,*" he muttered, smiling at me.

"What's that?"

"Knucklehead," he said, not without affection. He pulled the covers back and patted the mattress.

"You want me to ... sleep by your side?" I asked incredulously.

"I'm sorry. I know that was way too much to ask. I barely know you. Forget it, man."

Before he could talk himself out of it, and before I could stop and think through all the very good reasons why this was a bad idea, I climbed in beside him. His spare pillow was soft and inviting, and it was nice and warm under the covers. I was very careful not to let our shoulders touch, and I folded my hands primly over my chest, like a corpse or a vampire. Still, my right arm was so close to his left that I could feel the warmth radiating from him.

"Thanks, man," he said, sounding surprised. He reached over with his far hand and firmly clasped my right hand where it rested on my chest. "I really appreciate you doing this."

"Well, if it makes you feel more secure. If it feels like you're sleeping with one of your brothers."

"You don't feel like any of my brothers," he laughed. He released my hand and rubbed his palm around in my chest hair playfully. "Maybe I'd mistake you for my teddy bear."

"Hey," I said in mock indignation. No one had ever called me a bear before. "First of all, I'm not all that hairy. Secondly, teddy bears are plump."

He moved his hand down to probe my flat, reasonably firm abs. "Okay, so you feel like a very under-stuffed teddy bear who goes to the gym three times a week."

Now I felt complemented. I only wish I could stick to that regular a schedule. "Your brothers all have smooth chests, like you?"

"Not a chest hair among us."

We lay there in silence for several minutes, as I tried not to picture his two college-aged younger brothers, or even his beloved older brother, each with a different variation on Arturo's good looks, all lined up shirtless for my inspection. Finally, I said, "How do you know?"

"Huh?" he said sleepily.

"It just occurred to me that I have no idea whether my younger brother ever got hair on his chest. He and his wife do have a pool at their new house, but the one time I visited them, we didn't use it."

"Armando has the whole family over for Thanksgiving, Christmas, *Cinco De Mayo*, and Fourth of July," Arturo explained. "Our parents sleep in my niece's room, and she takes the sofa. Or the floor if someone brings a friend. My younger brothers and I share the little guest room and all pile into one bed. We even have pillow fights sometimes, just for old times' sake. Sometimes Armando can't resist joining us."

"Sounds like fun."

"Yeah, I guess it is," he said thoughtfully, as though he'd been taking it for granted, the way I would if someone had said to me a couple of months before, "Isn't it nice to have a roof over your head" or "It's great to know that white-collar jobs you're qualified for are open to you."

He yawned. "Well, good night, man." He closed his eyes, still lying very close to me and making no move to roll away.

# # # # #

I was walking down a long corridor lined with doors. It went on forever. Echoing from somewhere far ahead of me, I heard the sounds of whips cracking and a men crying out in pain. I tried to reach the sound, but it didn't seem to get any closer.

Then, suddenly, I realized I was at the right door. I touched the knob, and it swung away from me, opening out onto a stark, starlit desert landscape with jagged rocks all over. A line of men clad only in loose pants that looked something like pajamas was shuffling along, barefoot in the dust, chained together by shackles around their bare ankles. They were of assorted ages and ethnicities, and the whole scene was in black and white, like an old movie. In their arms they carried baskets full of rocks. I wondered how they could carry such a heavy load; many of them didn't even look as if they were in particularly good shape. I saw other chain gangs in the distance, some also composed of men wearing nothing but pants, some with veiled people in long shapeless gowns that I would have called "flowing" except that not the slightest breeze stirred them, and they just hung limply, swinging with every step with dreamlike slowness.

I spotted Arturo, dressed like all the other men, but with no chains running through his shackles. I recognized him even with his back to me, kneeling in the dust, head bowed. Two other men were kneeling beside him, but I ignored them, even though both were shirtless and one was just my type. All I cared about was that Arturo was writhing out in pain every few seconds, soundlessly begging for mercy from some unseen tormenter. I stepped through the door to run toward him. I found myself moving in slow motion, the way you do in dreams where you can never reach your goal or get away from whatever is chasing you. But I covered the distance between us quickly enough, even though every step seemed to take forever.

I usually dream in color. This was the first black-and-white dream I could remember. Then again, I usually don't know I'm dreaming, but part of me knew this was a dream inspired by Arturo's descriptions of his own. I was lucky I wasn't having one of the really horrible nightmares he'd described, at least so far.

While I could still see the men screaming and pleading, everything was now utterly silent. This wasn't just like a black-and-white movie; it was like a silent movie without the organ music or title cards. Everything cast inky shadows like an over-exposed photograph. It was a very clear night; the Milky Way was easy to pick out, and I could see extra stars in the middle of the Big Dipper that I remembered only from camping trips.

As I got closer, I noticed that the shadow Arturo cast was not only unnaturally dark but was the wrong shape. I eventually discerned that it was merged with the shadow of an invisible man standing beside him, holding a several whips, maybe a cat-o'-nine-tails. It separated itself, and for a moment I thought it looked more like it was cast by a tentacled monster than a man with whips. I saw lines of sparks playing across Arturo's back each time he writhed and cried out. As he doubled up, Arturo's separate shadow still seemed wrong: too angular to be the shadow of a man.

My slow-motion running finally got me to his side. I hauled him to his feet and dragged him away from his invisible tormenter, toward the nearest chain gang. The enslaved men didn't look exactly happy with their lot, but at least they weren't being tortured.

The next thing I knew, I had chains around my own ankles, linked to the ankles of a skinny guy a little younger than I, with hair that looked as if it might be sandy blond if I were dreaming in color, and to the whole line in front of him. I hadn't noticed what I'd been wearing up until now, but now I saw that I was dressed identically to the other slaves, and could feel the sun beating down on my naked back, even though it was nighttime and I could see the stars. I glanced back and was blinded for a second before a man's head eclipsed whatever light was illuminating us. I was relieved to see that it was Arturo, his ankles chained directly to mine. Unlike the brightly illuminated backs of the men in front of me, my roommate's face was little more than a silhouette against the night sky, but my eyes adjusted very quickly until I could see the dramatic starry backdrop behind him and recognize his features. He smiled wanly at me, and his mouth moved but no words came out. We were each holding a basket, like all the other guys I could see. When I saw the blond guy ahead of me pick up a rock and put it in his basket as we shuffled along, I followed suit. As I straightened, an angular shadow on the ground moved, and I glanced back and saw that Arturo was emulating me.

It seemed to go on a long time, although my arms didn't get tired. We eventually reached a hexagonal hole set into the side of a small hill, and I emptied my half-full basket into it when I saw the men in front of me each emptying his as he passed it. Arturo had only gathered a few.

# # # # #

I was in a hallway of doors again. I opened one and saw a banquet table filled with an assortment of my favorite desserts. I left that door open and tried the next out of curiosity. Behind it was a beautiful beach with the bluest water and the whitest sand I'd ever seen outside a travel brochure. I wouldn't have it all to myself, though; there were already people sunbathing, splashing each other in the surf, playing beach volleyball. But that was perfect because unlike any beach on this side of a TV screen, it was populated entirely by young people with perfect bodies. And all male, and all my favorite types.

I was about to step through when I heard a scream from down the hall. I sighed and waited to wake up in my bed. But it sounded again without the dream fading.

I abandoned the second door and walked further down the hall. I quickly found which door the scream was coming from and yanked it open. Unlike the brightly colored scenes behind the first two doors, this one was dimly lit, and looked like an old black-and-white movie. Exactly like an old black-and-white movie, the kind where zombies shuffle slowly toward people who are running for their lives and yet somehow seem to catch them. A crowd of vacant-eyed people were shambling, arms outstretched, toward Arturo, who had run into a small room that had no escape routes: no windows and only the one door, which zombies were shambling toward from either side. They'd reach it any minute, and Arturo was screaming, with his back to the wall. I could tell he'd had one narrow escape already; his T-shirt had been ripped to shreds, and there were scratches across his belly as if something had been intent on disemboweling him using only human fingernails.

I jumped through the door and ran into the scene. There were zombies on either side of me, but they didn't horrify me; they looked like the bad makeup job in an old movie I'd seen once. I'd watched it out of curiosity, only a few years back because my parents hadn't let me watch it as a child, claiming it was too scary. And the zombies were moving laughably slowly. I slipped into the room ahead of them. Arturo looked immensely relieved to see me.

"Come on," I said. I was glad to find I could speak here. I grabbed his shoulder. "We can outrun them. Or do you I need to carry you on my back?"

The doorway to the long hall I'd come from had apparently disappeared behind me, but the front door of the house was unblocked by zombies. I dragged Arturo past the two hordes lurching slowly at us from either side, and we ran outside and down a long country road. The zombies were giving chase, but we were putting more distance between us with every stride.

"Dude, they're moving like ten times slower than we can. Who's the knucklehead now?" I said teasingly.

# # # # #

I woke up to find Arturo sound asleep beside me, sleeping on his side, facing me, one leg pressed against mine, covers still neatly drawn up to the middle of our torsos. I watched his chest rising and falling in untroubled sleep. The moonlight, which was coming in at a lower angle now, accentuated his muscles. His

Marcus Anthony

face looked relaxed, unguarded, trusting. There was something incredibly hot about him lying at my side, exposed and defenseless like that. He'd only known me a week, yet he trusted me. I drifted back to sleep contentedly.

# # # # #

The next day at work, I went up to Arturo's cubicle to see if he wanted to go to lunch. I hoped I hadn't waited too long past noon and missed him. I tried to glance at my watch, but its face was blank, and I remembered that the battery had recently given out. Certainly everyone else seemed to be out to lunch already. I passed one empty cubicle after another as I wended my way through the random maze of cubicles that filled his whole floor of our office building. His absent coworkers were running some very bizarre screen-saver programs, each one different from the last. I didn't remember having seen any of them before.

Arturo was in his cubicle, all right, working at his computer, with his back to me. I was surprised, though, to see that shoulders were bare. Had he actually taken off his shirt at the office? That would be a strange thing to do, even at lunchtime. I didn't see his discarded shirt anywhere in his small neat cubicle.

He swiveled his chair around. "Hey, man," he said. "What's up?"

He'd taken off more than his shirt. I swallowed hard and pretended not to notice the obvious fact that he was naked. Not that I minded a bit!

I didn't think they'd let him into a restaurant without shirt and shoes – though I supposed that pants were not technically mandatory – so I abandoned my plan to ask him to lunch. "Um, I was just wondering if I should stop at the store on the way home and pick up some ingredients for dinner. What were you planning on making?"

"Yeah, sure, we could stop and get something if you want. We carpooled, didn't we?"

"Oh, right. I forgot." Had he been properly dressed in the car? Come to think of it, which of us had driven? I couldn't think of anything right now except his perfect, leanly muscled body sitting so casually naked right in front of me, his skin an even brown from his handsome face down to his bare feet, broken only by pubic hair. And he didn't particularly have to

129

compensate for anything with his huge video equipment, as far as I could judge from what his uncut cock looked like in its flaccid state.

"We'll figure it out on the way home. Now get out of here." He said it in a friendly tone. "I have a report to finish for my boss in ten minutes." He turned back to his computer.

"Ten minutes? It's lunchtime. Everyone's gone to lunch."

"Huh? No it isn't." Before I could stop him, he called out, "Mr. Smith! You're still here, right?"

"Why?" I heard someone answer from another cubicle. Then, closer: "Have you finished your report?"

Frantically, I tried to place my body in front of Arturo, but he stood up and stepped in front of me, giving me an excellent view of his smooth and muscular ass. "Not quite yet, sir," he said.

His boss gaped at Arturo's nakedness, then burst out laughing.

"What's so funny, sir?" Arturo asked in confusion. I stepped in front of him again.

Several other people came by to see what the joke was. All of them doubled up, laughing and pointing at poor Arturo. Belatedly, I managed to get in front of him again. I looked back at him apologetically, wondering if I should tell him what was wrong. He, completely clueless: distressed that everyone was laughing at him, but finding out the reason was only going to make it worse. So I said nothing.

Finally, he glanced down and realized with obvious horror and astonishment that he'd come to work totally naked. "*Mierda!*" he swore loudly.

I awoke with a start. Arturo had also jolted awake, apparently at the same moment.

"Another nightmare, Arturo?" I asked in concern. "Or did I wake you up?"

"Oh, man!" he groaned, placing his pillow over his face.

"You okay?" I asked.

He took the pillow away. "Yeah, another nightmare. Not quite as bad as usual."

"Want to talk about it?"

"No way!" he said, sounding more sheepish than shaken. "How are you doing? You been sleeping okay here?"

"I just had an incredibly vivid dream of my own."

"A nightmare?"

"No," I said. "A very nice dream, actually."

"I'm glad one of us is having nice dreams. Well, go back to sleep, man. Sorry I woke you out of a good dream. Hey, what time is it?" He reached across my bare chest to turn the clock radio to face us. It was the wee hours. I glanced at the window and saw the moon was below tree level, which meant some time had passed.

"That's the first time in days I've slept more than an hour without waking up screaming. Thanks, man!" His hand gave my bare chest a friendly pat on its way back.

"My pleasure," I said with complete honesty.

# # # # #

When I awoke to the sudden blaring of a Spanish radio station, my first thought was that I was in a hotel room and that the maid had been the last one to change the clock radio's tuning. Then I felt a man's hands on my chest, and opened my eyes to see a hot, half-naked Latino crawling over me. Fortunately, I woke up enough to recognize my new roommate, Arturo, before I could do something inappropriate.

He turned off the radio and said, "Sorry, man."

I focused my eyes on the display to read the time. "Why? We should be getting up, or we'll be late for work."

"I mean I'm sorry I had to climb all over you."

"*No problemo*," I said, stretching lazily.

"Not bad," he said with a grin. "You pronounced it pretty good this time, for a gringo." He swatted playfully at my chest with his pillow.

"You're in a good mood this morning."

"I'm just really glad you were here. I think it made a big difference. I actually got half a night of decent sleep once you joined me. How did you sleep?"

"Very well, once ... you know."

"I really owe you one, man. Well, I'd better get up and start breakfast. You can have the shower first."

"I'll be along in a minute," I said. I wanted to get the erection I'd woken up with under control first, or maybe slip into my room and get dressed while Arturo was out of sight.

"Don't worry if you want to snooze for fifteen minutes, I'll make sure you don't oversleep. I'll have coffee and some breakfast burritos waiting."

"You really feel like cooking after half a night's sleep?"

131

"Don't worry; I can do burritos in my sleep."

It was true. I'd seen him make them in five minutes, not counting getting the rice steamed.

He shook me awake awhile later. I smelled fresh coffee and fried bacon. Neither of which was half as enticing as the hand that was casually gripping my bare shoulder. He'd put on some baggy walking shorts and a tight T-shirt. "Sorry to wake you, man, when it's my fault you're still tired. But unless you want to call in sick to work or miss breakfast, it's time to get up."

"OK. Give me just a couple minutes," I said. My erection had returned.

He went back to the kitchen. I waited thirty seconds and then made a break for my room. I picked up a bundle of clothes, and carrying them strategically in front of me, I headed for the bathroom for a quick cold shower.

# # # # #

We carpooled, and we did pick up fresh ingredients for dinner. It reminded me of the vivid erotic dream I'd had, but I didn't comment on it, for obvious reasons.

"You have no idea how nice it is to not come home to an empty apartment and cook dinner for one," he said as he dished out the *chile relleno*.

"It never bothered me, eating microwaved food alone, but I can see how it could get lonely."

"Yeah, it sort of did, but it's more than that. Good food is one of the great pleasures of life, and the pleasures of life are meant to be shared with friends."

As he helped me clean up from a dinner that was lavish even for him, Arturo said, "I don't know about you, man, but I'm bushed. I was thinking of going to bed early, no games or videos or anything."

"Yeah, I was going to do the same."

He reached past me for a dish on my side of the sink, covered with residues of guacamole and salsa, both of which he'd made from scratch. His arm brushed my chest, but it didn't seem like a big deal; at least I had a shirt on now. He started to say something, then seemed to lose his nerve.

"Are you going to be all right?"

"I don't know, man?"

"So what do you want to do?" I asked as neutrally as I could.

He looked at me hopefully. "Same thing as last night? Is that okay?"

"Sure, if it'll help," I said off-handedly, my heart pounding. I knew this wasn't going to lead to anything, but I was getting an erection nonetheless.

# # # # #

After we'd finished the dishes, I went and brushed my teeth carefully. I was still hanging around uncertainly in the living room when Arturo finished brushing his. I followed him into his room, where he turned on the light and began unselfconsciously stripping.

When he was down to his shorts, he looked up and down my fully clothed body and said pointedly, "You're gonna at least have to take your shoes off, man." He sat down and waited.

I sat down beside him on the bed and untied my shoes. Arturo watched me, seeming amused.

"You can just toss your clothes on the floor," he said. "That's what I do."

I tossed my shoes in the corner, then shyly pulled off my shirt.

"What's with you, anyway?" he teased. "I've already seen you in your shorts, and you've got nothing to be ashamed of. You're in great shape, man."

I tossed my shirt on top of my shoes, followed by my socks, then finally my pants. At least there was no embarrassing tent in my shorts at the moment.

I dreamed again about being part of a chain gang in the desert. Arturo and I were in a different gang this time, near the front. I didn't recognize any of the other men chained to us from the first dream, so at least I got to admire fresh meat, but again most of it wasn't worth looking at. If the tempting scene I'd passed up behind Door Number Two the previous night had been like an all-male version of *Bay Watch* or your average gay porn flick, our chain gang was more like what I could see on any public beach in the country, except for being all adult men. Over the shoulders of the men chained in front of me, I could see another shirtless all-male chain gang ahead of us who looked much leaner. For some reason they were all Asian, not like my own motley crew. I glanced back at Arturo to see how he was doing. He was calmly filling his basket with rocks, and in fact had already gathered quite a few while I'd been checking out the fresh meat. I surveyed the men behind him. Beyond them, I thought I could see one of those gowned and veiled chain gangs. I had a theory that those were the female ones, but they were carrying exactly the same average load as the men. For that matter, the scrawniest men behind Arturo were tirelessly hauling the same loads as the brawniest. I realized another strange thing: none of us were even sweating. I shrugged inwardly. Dreams weren't supposed to make sense.

# # # # #

My bladder woke me up in the middle of the night. Arturo was sleeping on his stomach with his shoulder pressed solidly against mine and his fingers curled in my chest hair. He didn't stir as I slipped out of bed, or when I climbed back in and moved his arm to his side to give me room.

# # # # #

I'd always preferred Dracula movies to zombie movies, and maybe that's why I next found myself wearing a cape and strolling around in a castle as if I owned it. I somehow knew Arturo would be here, too, and I was searching the rooms looking for him. When I found him, he whirled around to face me, looking frightened. As well he might.

I hoisted him off the ground by his belt with one hand and shoved him against the stone wall. With my other hand I tugged his collar aside, so I could get at his neck. I began nuzzling it, but what I really felt like sinking my teeth into was the meaty muscles of his chest. So I ripped his shirt wide open – and was horrified to find he was wearing a large cross around his neck. I dropped him and backed away.

"Yeah, that's right," he said, holding the cross out in front of him and advancing on me. "The Church hates your kind." He backed me into a corner, and I panicked. Everything turned misty, and I found myself in another room, standing next to a coffin. Gratefully, I opened it and climbed in, still fully clothed, and closed the lid over me. I would be safe here. I realized it was early to go to sleep – the curtains over the arrow slits the room had in place of windows showed no trace of the dawn filtering through – but soon the total darkness in the coffin was broken by faint traces of pink shining through the cracks, and I lost consciousness.

I awakened suddenly when the lid was raised, letting in blinding light. Arturo was leaning over me, shirt still hanging upon and cross swinging uncomfortably close to my nose. He had something long and hard in his hand: a wooden stake.

"Turnabout's face play," he said, ripping open my lacy shirt. I felt him poke me in the chest with the point of the stake, and saw him raise a mallet, but I was helpless, paralyzed. He brought the mallet down hard …

… And I woke up in bed with a start.

It was unusual for me to have such easy-to-interpret symbolism in a dream. Before I'd met Arturo, my dreams had always been meaningless, much like my sex life. I looked over at my sleeping roommate beside me. He'd rolled onto his back, and his face was relaxed, his head thrown back, throat exposed. I'd known when I moved in that any meaningless sex would no doubt have to stay outside the apartment. I wouldn't be bringing any tricks across Arturo's threshold without his explicit invitation. And I was afraid to ask. He'd implied he wasn't very religious, but knowing his upbringing, I could guess how he'd feel about it. And now, with him sleeping so trustingly beside me, how could I tell him that I was attracted to men, that it took all my self control to lie here beside him and not press my lips to his neck, just as a first stop? What had I gotten myself into?

# # # # #

I slipped back into the recurring dream about the chain gang almost as soon as I closed my eyes. It wasn't surprising that my subconscious would choose a recurring dream that involved shirtless men, but you'd think it could be doing a better job of populating it with men who looked good with their shirts off. Fortunately Arturo was ahead of me, so I had at least one set of nice back muscles to watch as he worked, but the guy ahead of him and the one behind me looked like they spent more time on a couch or behind a desk than at the gym. The crew ahead of us were much skinnier, some maybe too skinny, and for some reason they were all dark-skinned this time: Indians, like some of the guys at work only thinner, and some of the blackest black guys I'd ever seen. In the distance, I glimpsed one crew that seemed to be made up mostly of blonds. Even further away, there was another dark-skinned group I could only see from the waist up since they'd crested a hill a couple of miles away.

135

The hunky guys sharing a chain with me looked all the better for their rarity, and if they minded being ogled they couldn't do a damn thing about it. I got a good look at some of our own crew when we followed a curving path around some low hills.

But sometimes, I got tired of trying to spot the rare hot guy and just studied my own toes trudging through the sand as I waited for the dream to be replaced with a more interesting one. I could never see the shadows of my toes as I lifted my feet; my shadow seemed to be wearing square-toed boots.

# # # # #

We got a full night's sleep, and I felt fully rested when the Spanish suddenly blared out of the radio. I woke up immediately, but lay still with my eyes closed and allowed Arturo to climb over me to turn it off.

He was in a great mood all day and cooked another tasty breakfast and a lavish dinner to celebrate his first good night of sleep in the face of the strange dreams. He didn't tell me what he'd dreamt, although he hinted that it had been almost pleasant, and I wasn't about to tell him about my dream featuring us ripping each other's shirts open, or how it felt to have my mouth on his neck or his stake prodding my chest. I thought it was better not to admit I was dreaming about him at all. If his own dreams had been pleasant and not for sharing, I assumed they were about women.

# # # # #

I was getting used to stripping in front of Arturo and crawling under the covers with him. I was also getting used to finding myself in the recurring chain-gang dream. Arturo was always in it, chained directly to me, and we were always trudging on a dusty desert plane, in and out of shallow depressions, always heading toward a low hill a couple of miles away that we never got closer to.

# # # # #

My men had captured a large cadre of the rebel forces and were leading them single-file to where the firing squad awaited. Each prisoner had been blindfolded and his hands bound behind his back. They were still dressed in their khaki uniforms that blended with our dusty surroundings, but their shirts had been unbuttoned. They walked barefoot on the hot baked ground; their shoes and socks having been confiscated.

I hardly glanced at their faces as they filed slowly past, but one of them caught my eye. "Wait!" I ordered. They halted the line, and I pulled off the blindfold of the prisoner I had chosen. He was a handsome man. Fairly young, like most of them. About my own age. His dark eyes glared at me sullenly as I gestured for my men to continue leading his comrades to their death. Two guards held his arms, awaiting my orders.

"Strip him," I said.

Obeying without hesitation, they ripped the shirt from his body. He was a fine specimen, much too good to waste. His legs were just as powerful as his chest, I noted as my men pulled his pants down. Then one of them grabbed the captive's ankles and lifted his feet in the air while a second one held him up by the armpits, and a third man pulled his pants off entirely. Then, finally, his boxers were forcibly removed.

The naked prisoner tried to put on a brave face, but he was trembling. I raked my eyes hungrily over his helpless body, then said, "Take him to my office and chain him to my desk on his knees. We're going to have fun these next few weeks."

Rage gave the prisoner the temerity to speak. "Forget it!" He spat out the words with insulting familiarity. "I would rather die now, like a man."

He needed to be taught his place. I snapped my fingers, and one of my men handed me a box with two cables coming out of it. I knelt at the man's feet – since he was so reluctant to kneel at mine – and clamped the two steel alligator clips to his ball sac. I had the satisfaction of hearing him stifle a whimper as the metal teeth closed on his loose flesh. Then I threw the switch.

He screamed and writhed in agony as electrical current surged through his balls. "Stop, please! I'm begging you!"

This was more like it! He'd also suddenly switched to the respectful mode of addressing me, I noted with amusement.

"I'll do anything! I'll tell you the combination!"

The combination? That sounded interesting. I switched off the current, and he slumped limply in my men's arms, totally defeated.

"What is the combination?"

"13-41-33," he said miserably.

I detached the clamps and stroked his balls gently as I committed the number to memory. Then I said, "Chain him under my desk. If he gives you the least amount of trouble, use the device on his nipples." I gave his balls one very gentle squeeze before releasing them, to remind him that they were mine now, along with the rest of that perfect body.

# # # # #

I woke up with my heart pounding. What made the dream even more unsettling was the fact that it had left me with a hard-on. I looked at Arturo, who was sleeping quietly but was drenched with sweat, his chest gleaming in the moonlight now shining directly through the window. The prisoner in my dream had looked exactly like him.

I got up, shut the door quietly behind me, and went to the kitchen. For the first time, I wished I'd asked Arturo to take the lock off the liquor cabinet. I could use a stiff drink right now.

The padlock was a combination lock. The dream had seemed so real that I was seized with an irrational desire to try out the combination from the dream. Well, it couldn't hurt. No one was there to see me make a fool of myself.

"Thirteen," I muttered to myself. "Forty and one. Thirty and three."

The lock clicked open.

Now I really needed a drink. I found a bottle of Scotch in back, behind the Kahlua, brandy, Irish Cream, and tequila, and helped myself. Twice.

# # # # #

By the time I was dressed that morning, Arturo had an omelet ready for me. "I already ate mine," he said. "Sorry about that, but we're in a rush."

"You make omelets on days when you're in a hurry?" I asked incredulously.

"Sure. It's no trouble."

"What do you make on ordinary days? Soufflés?"

He laughed. "You want one or not?"

"Sure. Whatever kind is easiest. Whatever you already got out for yourself."

"Swiss and cheddar with salsa and onions."

"Sounds delicious."

"Anyway, it's the least I could do. Thanks to you, I actually got a great night's sleep. I didn't wake up once last night."

"No dreams?"

"Oh, I had a couple of interesting dreams, but no monsters, nothing like what I've been getting half the time for the last few months. I think you'll be the first to know if the ones that make me wake up screaming come back."

While he was in the shower, I tried the combination lock. Surely I'd dreamed the part about getting up and opening the lock from a combination Arturo had revealed under torture.

It opened. And the cabinet contents were just as I remembered.

# # # # #

After dinner that evening, we played a fun two-player video game. It was based on an old TV show. We each built a robot on-screen and then set them loose on each other in a battle to the death, controlling them with our joysticks.

"Wouldn't it be cool if we were operating real robots somewhere, like the ones on the TV show?" I said.

"That would be a little expensive," he pointed out. "They get destroyed with every game."

Afterward, we watched a pretty good action-adventure movie.

"Want to make it a double feature?" Arturo asked, picking up the plate holding the remains of the homemade nachos we'd demolished. "It's Friday night, after all."

"I'm a little tired," I said. "Feel free to watch one yourself. I can probably sleep through it with the door closed."

"I used to stay up late to avoid the dreams. It's easy at first, even eleven o'clock would do it, but after awhile they catch up with me and even 3:00 a.m. isn't late enough to avoid them. But I'm not afraid of them tonight. If you're hitting the sack, I'll join you."

# # # # #

That night I had the recurring black-and-white dream about being on a chain gang trudging through the desert. I was beginning to enjoy those. The route the chain gangs followed at this site happened to make a turn at the base of a cliff, giving me a good view of the other gangs in profile. Amid the endless variety, I could always find some who were worth looking at. Tonight, I even had a broad-shouldered hunk directly in front of me, treating me to a close-up view of well-developed back muscles. And as before, Arturo was right behind me, so I could get a glimpse of his abs and his friendly grin whenever I cared to glance back. The basket he was holding out today held far more rocks than mine; he was getting into the spirit of this dream, and I was getting distracted by the scenery.

I was returning half asleep from my nightly trip to the bathroom when I heard male and female moaning from the bedroom. I pushed open the door, which was ajar, and was startled to see Arturo astride a woman with long blonde hair and improbably big breasts who was lying on our bed. I should have backed out of the room, but I found myself transfixed, watching the two naked figures in horrified fascination. The blonde was moaning Arturo's name, saying cheesy things like "Oh, it's so big! Give it to me, Arturo!" that might have come out of straight porn – assuming straight porn was as badly scripted and acted as the stuff I was more familiar with. I tried to focus on the more appealing aspect of the scene: Arturo's sweaty torso and the occasion glimpses of the base of his dick emerging for another thrust.

Arturo opened his eyes for a moment, saw me standing there, and grinned, then went back to what he was doing with renewed enthusiasm, as if he appreciated the audience. When he'd finished, with appropriate theatrical sound effects from his female partner, he said, "You know, for a guy who keeps waking up with a morning hard-on, you're not showing much reaction to the free live sex show."

"I hoped you didn't notice that," I said, mortified.

"It's a little hard to hide something like that from the guy you're sharing a bed with. It's no big deal, man. It happens to me a lot, too. Definitely not worth making us late to work over because you can't leave the bedroom until it goes down."

"Can we not talk about this in front of your, er, friend?"

"Oh. Sorry, man. You're right. Speaking of the chick, it's your turn, if you want." He didn't even look at her for permission for this strange offer. That probably meant she was a prostitute, but still. But she turned her head and looked at me invitingly. I said, "Uh, no thanks." I backed away until I hit the wall behind me. I felt my bathrobe hanging there from a hook, and quickly put it on.

"I understand," Arturo said, climbing off her and approaching me. "Lots of guys think sloppy seconds is gross."

"It's not that," I said, honestly enough. "She's just not my type."

"Well, there's plenty more where she came from," he said, gesturing at where the far wall should have been. Dozens of busty naked women rotated slowly by, sitting in provocative positions on a carousel like those found in restaurants displaying desserts, or in airport baggage claim, holding luggage. But there were no old bags on this one.

He put his hand on my robed shoulder. "Take your pick. We can share her, if you like. That would be hot, wouldn't it? You first, of course. Or you can have her to yourself. You don't even have to let me watch, but I'd really like to see you enjoying yourself."

"Look, Arturo, I'd just like to get back to sleep."

"Let me pick one for you. You like redheads?" He swept a svelte redhead into his arms and held her out invitingly. "No? How about Latinas? I prefer something a little more exotic, but I'll have what you're having, if you're into it." He put the redhead on the floor and picked up an attractive woman with skin matching his own. "Come on, man, don't just stand there, with all this tail available!" He strode across the room again and yanked my robe wide open, then pulled the belt loose and shoved the robe off my shoulders. I tried to stop him, but he was too fast and too strong. It was like I was frozen to the spot. I was at his mercy.

"Oh, so now you're getting hard! I knew you weren't a monk." He bent down and pulled the waistband of my boxers gently over my erection, then yanked the boxers down to my ankles. "Oh, yeah! You can't tell me you're not in the mood for sex."

"Why are you doing this?"

"Because I just got laid, and now only one thing will make the evening even better. I want to see you enjoy yourself, too." He forcibly turned me to look directly at the selection. "Just pick one, already! Or two."

Just then I saw a man rotate into view amid all the distasteful female flesh. He was a little scrawny for my taste, but sometimes that's fun; if they like dominating bigger guys, the mismatch makes it all the hotter. And he had a nice-looking dick I would love to coax to hardness with my tongue; even soft it looked like it would be a big one. "I'll take that one," I said, pointing.

"What, the guy?"

"Yeah. The guy."

"He's all right, I guess, but seriously? With all those hot chicks to choose from?"

"You said it was my choice."

"All right," he said, rushing over to the carousel before the man disappeared into the wall, and grabbing his shoulder to haul him to his feet. He muscled him over to me. The man came along willingly enough until Arturo forced him onto his knees facing me. He looked over his shoulder at Arturo uncertainly; he seemed disappointed he wasn't getting Arturo. I couldn't blame him.

"Yeah, that's right, faggot," Arturo said. After a split second I realized the word wasn't aimed at me. I also realized he hadn't used the word faggot at all, but a word in Spanish that meant the same thing. "Suck my buddy off real good, now," he continued, still speaking Spanish. He shuffled forward until the man's head was trapped between our bodies, and his own semi-erect cock rested on the guy's bare shoulder along the side of his neck. He grasped my shoulders and watched my face as I was sucked off. "That's better," he whispered, squeezing my shoulders in rhythm with the mouth on my cock. "I want to see you body wracked with pleasure."

# # # # #

We both slept a little late Saturday morning, but Arturo was up by the time I arose. He'd put on some sweat pants but nothing else, and was making breakfast with his shirt off. "You're up!" he said happily. "Great, I'm starving." He put some bacon in the pan and began cracking eggs. "I've also got some pancake batter ready to go. I hope you like pancakes because I want to celebrate the best night of sleep I've had in a long time."

"I love pancakes." I was awkwardly holding a bundle of clean clothes in front of my crotch.

"I'll start them as soon as you take care of that."

"Take care of what?"

He flipped the sizzling bacon, flinching almost imperceptibly. I realized that hot droplets of oil were hitting his chest, and that cooking shirtless was a kind of subtle machismo. "Do you think you're the only one who needs to jerk off in the shower to get rid of his morning hard-on? You're not fooling anyone. We talked about this."

"Did we?"

He paused to think. "Oh. Maybe we didn't. I just dreamed we did."

The chill that ran down my spine had nothing to do with my lack of a shirt. "That's weird. I had the same dream."

"It must not have been a dream, then."

"It was a dream, unless you installed a luggage carousel in your bedroom."

He dropped the spatula in the frying pan and turned to face me, slack-jawed.

"I'm freaked out, too," I said.

"This carousel," he said slowly. "Did it have chicks on it?"

"And one guy."

"How – how can this be?"

"Damned if I know. But check this out." I put down my clothes – my erection had subsided anyway – and stepped over to the liquor cabinet and opened the lock.

"I'd almost forgotten that dream. You got the combination out of me under torture, man!"

"Hey, it was only a dream. I wasn't myself. I dreamed I was ..."

"Yeah, I know. Anyway, if I hold you responsible for what you did to my balls, I also have to give you credit for saving me from being torn apart by zombies."

"Damn right you do. I'll be back in a minute. Just let me get dressed."

"I'll get the pancakes ready. Maybe if we hurry we can enjoy them before I wake up."

I realized what he meant: He thought he was dreaming. I let it pass and got dressed. Either we were both awake, and he was wrong, or I was dreaming him, in which case there was no point in arguing with a figment of my imagination.

We ate in thoughtful silence. Everything felt real enough; I could feel myself chewing, and other mundane details.

"Well, the pancakes taste too good to be true," I told him as I cleared the dishes, "but other than that, this doesn't feel like a dream." Arturo had even put on a T-shirt. If I was dreaming, why would my handsome shirtless personal chef put on a shirt?

"I'd say 'thank you,' but what's the point? I've got to be dreaming this. It's the only explanation."

"I'm telling you ..."

"Of course you would deny it, if I'm dreaming you up." He didn't bother to turn to look at me.

I let the water run in the sink and opened the refrigerator to get out the pitcher of ice water we kept there. Then I poured it over Arturo's head.

"What the fuck!?" he sputtered. "What was that for?" He pulled off his sopping, ice-cold T-shirt. The ice water had also darkened the crotch of his sweat pants, and he pulled those off next. I realized this was the first time I'd seen him naked in real life. If this was real life. His body was literally everything I'd dreamed it would be.

"If this is a dream, wouldn't getting ice water dumped on you wake you up?"

"Not if I'm only dreaming the ice water, *cabeza de chorlito!*"

I had to think for a moment to remember what that meant.

"That means, what, 'knucklehead'?"

He advanced on me, calling me several other words I didn't understand. That as much as anything convinced me I wasn't dreaming now; I'd understood his Spanish effortlessly last night, and come to think of it, in the dream where I'd had him tortured, both of us had been speaking Spanish.

Eventually, after he'd tired of holding my head down in the sink while he ran cold water over it, he pulled me out, holding me by my wadded-up shirtfront, and got the ice cube tray out of the freezer with his free hand. He threw me down on the floor, clear of the kitchen tiles and onto the carpet, so it didn't hurt much, and as I got up on my hands and knees he pushed me onto my back and straddled me. Setting the ice cube tray down beside me, he leaned down, not seeming to care that his swinging balls were grazing the hair that trailed down from my navel, and pushed my T-shirt all the way up to my chin.

"Apologize for the ice water," he demanded in English.

"I'm sorry I dumped ice water on you," I said meekly.

"Now," he said, holding the ice cube tray upside down over my chest, "apologize for torturing me, even if it was a dream."

"I apologize for the shocks," I said, wincing as a drop of cold water dripped onto my own nipple.

"Beg for mercy," he said.

"No."

He pressed the ice briefly against my chest and asked again.

\# \# \# \# \#

"I guess we really are awake," he finally admitted, handing me the towel he'd gotten for me when he'd finally let me up. He'd wrapped another towel around his waist and draped one over his shoulders, hiding his nipples, which were as shriveled as mine.

"Would you have done that to me if you'd known that?"

He grinned up at me as he bent to pick my slightly damp shirt up off the ground. "Probably." He went to put our wet clothes in the washer. "We need to figure this out. Can I get dressed first?"

"If it's not a dream, I guess you've got free will," I said.

# # # # #

"I was pretty sure that having you sleep next to me was changing my dreams for the better, but I didn't know you were fucking entering my dreams," he said. "How are you doing that?"

"Fuck if I know! Nothing like this has ever happened to me before. You're the one who was having all the dreams before we even met."

We were sitting together on the couch, a little closer than I would have chosen, dressed in dry clothes.

"You mad at me?" He punched me lightly in the arm.

"What, for the dreams?"

"I meant for the sink and the ice."

"No, I had that coming."

"I normally don't get anywhere near that rough except with close buddies I've known a long time, but, well, you know ..."

"Yeah." It already felt like I'd known him forever.

"I'm glad you're not mad at me. You're a great roommate, and I hated living alone. I was really glad when you moved in. And now, on top of that ... well, I not only like you, I need you, man. At night."

No one had ever told me he needed me before, not in so many words, and with such a sincere, vulnerable expression on his face. "Oh, you could probably tie me to the bed if I don't come willingly," I said, trying to make a joke out of it. My cock stirred at my own suggestion; I was glad I was wearing pants.

# # # # #

"What a hot dream last night, huh?" Arturo called from the shower, later that week.

We'd had four that I remembered, two of which had been the usual recurring dream. "The second one? Where we were, like, super villains?" That had been hot. Arturo had been my partner or maybe henchman, dressed like me in a sleeveless tunic that showed off our arm muscles, as he pulled on a rope and hoisted a dripping cage holding three men out of a vat of yellowish liquid, lit from below by a green glow. In the dream I knew they were superheroes, our archenemies whom we'd somehow captured. I couldn't say which ones they were, since their costumes had already been dissolved away before the dream started, at least the part that I remembered. But I had some guesses based on the colors of the occasional shred of clothing still clinging to their naked bodies. One of them had shreds of blue cloth sticking to his chest and legs, a few fibers of red stuck in his pubic hair, and his toes were sticking out of the tattered remains of red boots. Another had green shreds clinging to his body. The third had apparently been wearing no bright colors, just black and gray.

"Yeah, right," Arturo said sarcastically. "Sure, that was a blast. But hot? Seriously? You know which one I mean. The one we just woke up from. You remember the one with the three-way?"

"Oh, that. I thought it was a little creepy, to tell the truth," I said, wiping more steam off the mirror, so I could see to shave. I'd showered first, and of course I'd put my pants on before I'd opened the door to signal Arturo the shower was all his.

I heard him turn off the water. "Creepy? You mean the way she lowered herself down onto us like a spider?"

"Yeah, among other things."

In the mirror, I saw him opening the shower stall and getting his towel off the rack as he said, "I should have realized. You used to be shy about even being touched, and there we were with our shafts pressed against each other, our balls mashed together ..."

"No, it wasn't that," I assured him, looking at him over my shoulder.

He raised the towel to his head, exposing his hairy armpits, letting the water sheet down his smooth brown body for the moment as he dried his hair first. "What, then?"

"Just the whole spidery female thing, I guess."

146

He looked at me thoughtfully in the mirror as I shaved and he slowly dried his sides, then his chest and belly. Finally he said, "Would a spidery male have been better?"

"Let's just say that a certain freelance photographer college student would have been more welcome in my dreams."

"Really? Even if you got to choose between him and, say, his girlfriend? The way she looked in the movies?" He finished drying and knotted the towel around his waist.

I turned to look him directly in the eye, even though my chin was still half covered in shaving cream. "Definitely."

"Wow. I know you did that once in a dream – chose a guy with an infinite supply of female flesh handy – but dreams don't exactly count. Even our dreams. Well, I'm really touched you would share that with me, bro." He put both hands on my shoulders and looked me in the eye. "I know we haven't known each other that long, but I already feel like I can tell you anything, too."

That wasn't the reaction I'd been expecting. I'd expected, given his culture and the teachings of his parent's religion, that he'd be freaked out, at least temporarily. I also figured he had every right to be furious at me, no matter how tolerant he normally was, for not telling him sooner, and allowing him to believe he was sharing a bed with someone who had no possible interest in his body. That's what I'd expected. What I'd hoped was that he was so modern that he'd shrug and treat it as no big deal. It hadn't occurred to me he'd be touched, like I'd just trusted him with my darkest secret.

Then he drew me unselfconsciously into a hug, which really took me aback. The skin contact still felt erotic to me, but I was getting a little more accustomed to it. I buried my nose against his damp shoulder, inhaling the clean scent odor of him half-hidden by the fragrance of the bar of soap we shared.

# # # # #

The next night, we decided to make the chain-gang dream more interesting by competing to see who could collect the most rocks. Arturo had an off-the-wall theory that it was like a game, with the dream that followed being the prize for the winner. The previous night, I'd collected more rocks, and we'd had a dream about naked superheroes. Then he'd collected more rocks and we'd had that disturbing she-spider dream. If he was right, it was the most boring game ever, especially compared to the video game where we were operating robots. Then again, what other two guys could say they played a full immersive VR game with each other in their dreams?

I didn't point out that there wasn't always a clear winner. We might have different tastes, but he'd admitted to enjoying having helpless superheroes in our power, and I'd secretly enjoyed the part of the other dream where his genitals had been pressed against mine.

Tonight Arturo was in the lead, and I was chained behind him. All the shadows had gotten shorter over the past week, making it harder to spot small rocks. There were a lot of guys ahead of us on our chain, and of the rocks they missed, he managed to pick up almost every single one before I could reach it. Once, we passed a cluster of three rocks and he was had his hands full with the first two when the third one came into my reach. I was about to grab it when he kicked it with his bare foot, and it sailed away in with dreamlike slowness. He grinned at me over his shoulder. I tried to give him the finger, but I couldn't make my fingers do that, so I settled for giving the equivalent gesture with my forearm.

# # # # #

My men had just set up camp, and my aides and I were surveying the surrounding jungle, when I stumbled across two of my men who had snuck away from camp. I knew the names of most of the men under my command, and I recognized José Ramón kneeling at the feet of – what was his name? – oh yes, Arturo. Their uniforms were in disarray, and their helmets lay on the ground, and Arturo was being pleasured by José Ramón.

I sighed in frustration. I'd thought we'd weeded all the fairies out during the long sea voyage. The few that hadn't bled to death under the lash or during the keelhauling had been abandoned on the next available island. Yes somehow we missed one. I would never have suspected José Ramón of being one. And it baffled me that Arturo would be stooping so low now that we'd made landfall. He'd done this more than once at sea, which I could almost understand; certainly he hadn't been the first or the last to seek sexual release on the long voyage. But why now, when he would soon have access to all the native girls he could possibly want? They'd soon be the spoils of war when we sacked the city, along with the gold bricks rumored to pave its streets, the chocolate flowing from the fountain fabled to sit in its public square. It made no sense. We were so close to the pyramid that whenever there was a break in the canopy we could look up and see the natives, tiny in the distance, carrying sacks of cacao beans up the steps and chocolate bars wrapped in golden foil down the other side.

I was going to have to reprimand Arturo this time. But first, there was the faggot to deal with. José Ramón! Who would have guessed? He was a hot-tempered man built like a bull, short and thick-necked and broad-shouldered, not the sort I would have expected to debase himself in such a fashion.

After a brief court martial, with my aides testifying they'd witnessed the offense, I pronounced the sentence: "José Ramón de la Sueña, as your commanding officer, I find you guilty of sodomy." I paused. It had been easy enough at sea to find traditional painful and humiliating methods of punishment that also relieved the men's boredom. I couldn't keelhaul him here, and we'd left the lash on the ship so the officers could keep the crew in line. If I waited until after we'd conquered the city, I supposed I could have the men stone him with gold bricks from the street or have him drowned in the fountain of chocolate. Unfortunately, we couldn't leave a faggot in our midst even that long; it was obviously too much of a temptation for the men, when they should be thinking of the battle ahead.

I was still trying to decide on a suitable punishment when I caught sight of a tribe of pigmies emerging from the jungle, dressed in feathers. I'd always thought pigmies were found in Africa, not South America, but what else would you call perfectly proportioned mature-looking men whose head would barely reach my waist, even if their skin was the reddish bronze of the local savages and not the deep black of the African? They began to sing:

José Ramón! José Ramón!
That silly little maricon!
A real man would put up a fight
And not be made a catamite.
So now, by order of the court,
He'll reenact your favorite sport,
And go down fighting, on all fours,
His comrades turned to matadors!

# # # # #

Stripped naked, José Ramón looked more bull-like than ever, with his hairy legs, hairy barrel chest, and large swinging balls. I assigned two horsemen to be picadors. Their job was to hamstring him with their lances. With that accomplished, he was indeed on all fours, robbed of any hope of dying like a man. Howling in pain and rage, he charged the three men I sent in next, who scattered at the last minute and circled around him, each one bravely lunging in to attack his shoulders and chest with makeshift *banderillas* while his attention was focused on the other two.

After a long period of torment, I sent in the man I'd assigned to be matador put him out of misery. I'd chosen Arturo, the very man José Ramón had allowed to rob him of his manhood. By this time, the condemned man's chest hair was completely matted down with blood, and he was as weak as one might expect such a man to be. Arturo teased him for a moment with his red cape, proving his dominance, then finally forced him to the ground on his belly and raised his sword, aiming for a spot between the cowering man's shoulder blades.

It must have been that moment, while we all were distracted, that the natives attacked, taking us completely by surprise. Full-sized natives; I wasn't sure what had happened to the pigmies. All I knew was that there was a moment of confusion, and then all my men lay dead around me and I was being dragged off, stripped of my boots and helmet but not my armor, with gold chains around my wrists and ankles.

# # # # #

Having marched me up the endless steps of a pyramid, the rough stone tearing at the tender souls of my feet and the sun above the forest canopy baking me in my steel armor, my pagan captors laid me flat on my back on a stone altar at the top. They stretched my armored limbs out and bound them to the corners of the altar with the gold chains. Their king – or was he their high priest? or both? – loomed over me. He bore a striking resemblance to Arturo, the man José Ramón had been caught with, except Arturo of course was a Spaniard, while this man's features had the distinctive cast of a native, and his skin was reddish bronze, not just tanned like my man Arturo's.

The priest produced a can opener, stuck the sharp tip into a weak spot in my breastplate and began prying it open. The half-naked savages around me began removing the armor on my arms and legs. Each had his own can opener. That explained why we had so many in the kitchen drawer, I realized vaguely.

Soon they had me stripped of my armor. Underneath, I was wearing a white shirt and a tie. The pagan king brought a stone knife to my throat; I thought he was going to slit my throat, but he had no such easy death in mind for me. He used it to cut my tie off. Obviously the savage had never seen such a thing and had no idea how to remove it non-destructively. Then he ripped my shirt open, exposing my bare chest. The savages murmured to each other in their uncouth language at the sight of the black swirls of hair covering my chest, so much more manly than their own smooth torsos. A dozen hands reached out to touch it. For a moment, despite my helpless situation, I took pride in my own inherent superiority.

Then one of the savages took out a can of shaving cream and began coating my entire chest and belly with the foamy white cream. I watched in helpless horror. The king then held a razor before my eyes. Its plastic handle was stained with old blood from previous sacrifices, but its twin stainless-steel blades gleamed in the tropical sunlight. A fresh sharp refill. He drew it across my chest gently, almost lovingly, leaving my creamy white skin as smooth as his own reddish bronze skin. He shaved me all the way down to my belly, and beyond, robbing me of even the trail of fine hair that runs down that private and sensitive area between my navel and my pubic hair. I realized then that the rest of my clothes had somehow been removed; I was stretched out utterly naked before him. The savage even had the gall to trim away the top of my pubic hair, evening it out as a barber might trim a man's beard. Then, as a final humiliation, he took my balls in his hand as if he owned them, and smeared shaving cream all over them, too. He then lightly ran the razor over my sac, removing the hair even from there, leaving it feeling even more naked and vulnerable.

By this time, I had admitted to myself that I was totally in this savage's power and could only be grateful that he had chosen to cut off nothing but hair. Then I saw that he was wielding his stone knife again. "No!" I pleaded. But he placed it, not against my balls, but against the hollow at the base of my throat. He drew the blade gently down the center of my naked chest. The skin parted neatly. He cut another line horizontally above my navel, and again along my breastbone. Then he handed the knife to an acolyte and stuck his thumbs into my chest, peeling my skin to either side like an unbuttoned shirt, so that the muscles underneath stood exposed and quivering before him. He was so skillful that not a drop of blood was spilled, and I felt not the slightest pain. I did feel intense fear and humiliation. I was determined not to disgrace myself by allowing him to see it.

His fingers felt rough as they explored the chest muscles he had laid bare. I arched my back, groaning helplessly.

He said something in his barbaric tongue that I sensed from his gloating tone must have meant "I've got you now." He slid his calloused hands into my chest, carefully removed my pectoral muscles, and laid them aside, like so much meat waiting to be barbecued. He paused to finger my bare ribs. I was surprised to find that it tickled. My ribs had always been ticklish, but somehow I'd always assumed it was the skin that was ticklish, not the ribs themselves.

He grasped one rib in each strong hand and pulled. My ribcage swung open with a creak. I whimpered as my organs lay exposed and glistening, completely unprotected from his invasive hands. My heart was beating faster and faster in panic, I could see.

The priest admired the view of my exposed organs, then reached in with his bare hands and got a firm grip on my heart.

"Please," I moaned. "I'm begging you, sir." But it was no use. His simple mind was incapable of understanding Spanish, and I didn't speak a word of his primitive language. With a tug, he pulled my heart free.

It beat rapidly in his hands, as though trying to escape, but he held it tightly. He stroked it with his thumbs, and it slowly calmed down. I could feel his calloused thumbs, could feel his fingers caging it in as it expanded against them with every strong beat.

He toyed with my heart for a long time, and I almost began to trust him not to hurt it. Maybe he would put it back where he'd found it, and let me go back to find any of my men who'd survived the attack. Or at least let me remain here as his slave. The thought of being a slave to a barbarian was humiliating, and there was no telling what obscene things he might do to me. Yet, it might be the best option I had left.

I only realized the foolishness of that wish when I saw an acolyte approaching with a plastic bottle of Hershey's syrup on an ornate golden platter. The king held out my heart and the half-naked young savage poured the syrup over it. Needless to say, it was once again beating frantically.

The king's dark eyes gazed directly into mine as he brought my heart to his lips. I felt his nose prodding between the ventricles, the tip of his tongue running along a large vein. Then I felt the rasp of his unshaven cheek, before his perfect teeth bit down into the muscles of my heart.

# # # # #

I think I cried out as I woke. Arturo blinked at me. "*Caramba!*" he whispered. "Some dream. Are you okay, man? Scared?"

"By a stupid dream?" I said. "No way!" But my voice sounded shaky even to me.

He pressed his palm lightly against my chest. "Your heart's pounding a mile a minute," he observed.

"No it isn't," I lied.

He burrowed his fingers into my chest hair to make contact with the bare skin above my heart. "Yes, it is. Admit it, man, you were scared!"

"No more than you used to be!"

"True enough. And this was a particularly weird one."

"Weirder than zombies?"

"Especially the first part. Why would I have some faggot give me a blow job when I could just as easily dream about real sex?"

"You seemed to be enjoying it, from where I was standing."

"Well, yeah, which makes it even more ..."

"Wait, did you say the first part was the weird part? You do remember the second part, where you cut my heart out of my chest and ate it, right?"

"It tasted great, man," he said teasingly. "Too bad we woke up when we did."

If only, I thought, I could get him as interested in nibbling on my external organs. I grabbed his wrist and tried to remove his hand from my chest. He resisted, grinning playfully.

"I was taking you apart, piece by piece, man!" he gloated as I managed to pin his wrist to the pillow beside his head. "It was great!"

"Shut up and go to sleep," I said, glowering down at him.

He chuckled and relaxed against the pillow. I reluctantly released his wrist, resisting the temptation to do a little nibbling of my own. I settled in beside him, and we soon fell asleep.

# # # # #

I woke up suddenly when Arturo ripped the covers off of me. I blinked against the sunlight. He'd already put pants on, though no shirt or shoes yet.

"Time to get up, man," he said cheerfully.

I groaned and tried to roll away from the light streaming in through the window. Arturo grabbed my shoulder and rolled me flat onto my back again. He pinned my arm above my head and dug his fingers into my armpit. "Come on, get up."

"I'm not ticklish," I lied.

He ran his fingers over my ribs and proved me wrong. "I knew it. Just like in the dream."

The dream came back to me in a flash: Arturo as an Aztec priest-king fingering my exposed ribs as I lay helpless on his altar. But I recovered quickly, grappling with Arturo and eventually pulling him against me and holding him down.

"Okay," he panted, "that's enough. We don't have time for this, man. Not on a weekday."

I let him go, wondering just how much time he'd be willing to spend wrestling on the weekends.

"Get in the shower," he said, with a parting playful slap on my chest. "What kind of omelet do you want?"

# # # # #

"Admit it, I was right about the winner-controls-the-next-dream thing," Arturo said as we watched a mixed martial arts bout on his big screen. It was a hot Saturday afternoon, and rather than spend half our pay on electricity we were dressed in not much more than the fighters on the screen. He was slouching in his usual spot near the center, with his left arm stretched along the back of the couch, bridging the gap between us, his fingertips almost brushing my shoulder. Our bare feet were propped up on a common footrest.

"I still think it was a coincidence. Anyway, I don't think you exactly 'won' the first part of the dream."

"What do you mean?" He scooted a little closer and slapped me on the shoulder. "I got a blow job, and you didn't. Plus I got to totally dominate the guy afterward."

"On my orders."

"Go ahead, then, slack off on the chain gang from now on. See what happens to you." He leaned closer and drew his finger down the length of my bare torso as if he were cutting me open from clavicle to navel. I shivered, and not from fear.

He said, "This time I'm actually going to miss the dreams when they stop."

We watched the end of the bout, then played a few rounds of our favorite video game, each taking great delight in destroying the robot the other was controlling.

# # # # #

I did slack off a little in the next recurring dream, and Arturo beat me handily. We wound up dreaming we were robots in an arena – not controlling robots; it felt like we were the robots. Mine was well-armed and had an armored shell like a turtle, but had the same vulnerability as a turtle: Arturo's robot had a spatula-like weapon with which he flipped me onto my back, wheels spinning helplessly. My underbelly was not well protected at all. I couldn't see anything except his wheels through the narrow field of view of my black-and-white camera, but I felt his tools pry open my access panel and root around in the delicate nest of wires and sensitive circuitry inside. He could have shorted me out instantly at that point, but he took his time, taking me apart piece by piece and laying the pieces out in front of us. There wasn't a thing I could do about it.

# # # # #

"I don't remember having any dreams at all last night, do you?" I asked later that week as we washed the plate from the nachos we'd eaten while watching a movie. We'd found that shirtless action heros appealed to both of us, maybe not quite the same way. Neither of us particularly cared for the obligatory love-interest scenes, but if we wanted to avoid those subplots, we figured we were pretty much limited to movies set in prisons or submarines, and even then it wasn't a sure bet.

"The last two nights," Arturo said, "I had just a few not very vivid dreams, and you weren't in them."

"Same here."

"It's been about the right amount of time. It's, what, two weeks since they started?"

"Is that all? Yeah, I guess it's only been about three weeks since I moved in."

"They've been starting later and later, haven't they? That's the way it always is. Then I stop having them, unless I sleep really late."

"So you've got a good couple of weeks before you have to worry about nightmares again?"

"Yeah, and I kind of miss them. They stopped being nightmares the minute you joined me. Oh, well." He took off his shirt and headed toward his bedroom.

"You calling it a night, then?"

He opened his door and turned around. "Yeah, I'm a little tired. You coming, or you staying up for awhile?"

I followed him in, unbuttoning my shirt as I went.

# # # # #

"We should go out tonight," Arturo said in between rounds of our favorite video game on Saturday. "My old roommate and I used to do that, but I haven't gone out since the dreams first started and he moved out. I don't like sitting in a club myself trying to hit on chicks. It makes me feel like a loser. But he and I had pretty good luck picking up women together."

"Um, Arturo, I thought I explained to you ..."

"Oh, right. Well, could you at least play along, if we find a couple of hot girls?"

"Anything for you," I said sincerely. "Tell you what; you can have my share, too."

"That's not the kind of three-way I've ever fantasized about, although I know some guys who do. Fantasize, anyway."

"Have you ever fulfilled yours?"

"Nope. Closest I ever came was a four-way make-out session. I was sitting here in this very spot, my roommate was here" – he patted the spot between us – "and the girls were on the ends of the couch."

I looked down at my seat in exaggerated distaste and scooted next to him.

"You nut," he said, laughing and throwing his arm around my bare shoulders. "It didn't get heavy or anything until we went to our rooms. The girls were almost fully clothed, and he and I were wearing about what you and I are now. More: socks and long pants." It was another hot day, and we'd seen no point in wasting money and contributing to global warming by keeping the thermostat low just, so we could wear more clothes.

"Another round?" I asked.

"Let me get us another couple of beers."

I debated scooting back to my usual spot while he was up, but stayed where I was. He handed me my beer and sat down about half an inch from me. We had to move further apart when we started to play again, just for the elbow room in using the controllers, and even then we kept accidentally leaning into each other as we played. He didn't seem to mind at all, and I found the skin contact less distracting than I'd expected; I guess I'd gotten used to it in my sleep. It felt warm and friendly, with only a slight erotic undertone for me.

# # # # #

That evening I drove Arturo to his favorite straight bar. Pausing outside the door, he said, "Undo a couple of buttons."

"What?" I asked stupidly.

"Show off your hairy chest, man," he explained, impatiently undoing a button on my shirt himself. "Some girls love that."

"Uh, Arturo, I thought I explained ..."

"Even better. Give anything you catch to me." As an afterthought, he undid a second button. "There," he said, clasping my shoulder. "You'll make a great babe magnet."

So I spent the next few hours helping Arturo flirt with pairs of women. It was actually fun, though, just to be spending time with him outside the apartment, and I liked the music. There were plenty of cute guys to admire, too; and the fact that they were oblivious to my interest only made it more fun to cruise them.

"Maybe we should try for one of each, so you can have someone to take home, too," he suggested.

"Yeah, because going after women accompanied by men will really improve both our chances of getting lucky."

We did find two women who seemed interested. I felt a little awkward, especially when Arturo left me with them while he went up to the bar to buy us all drinks, but I did my best to be – what do straight guys call it? – a good wingman. They seemed to believe what I was saying about how kind and generous Arturo was. It probably helped that I meant every word I was saying. "And you've never tasted anything like his cooking," I said, launching enthusiastically into descriptions of my favorite dishes.

"Yeah, I love to cook," Arturo said, coming back with the drinks. "I just wish I had more people to cook for, just once, than me and my roommate. Half the time I make too much and we eat leftover the next day when I'd rather be cooking something new."

I had to admire the skillful way he'd steered the conversation where he wanted it to go. A few minutes later we'd invited the pair of them to dinner the next day.

# # # # #

"I can probably still come up with an excuse if you'd rather make this a romantic dinner for two," I said, watching Arturo set candles on the table.

"Dinner for two would have been too obvious a come-on. This way is less threatening. If they decide they don't like us, everyone can always pretend it was just a dinner."

"You keep saying 'us.'"

"Sorry, man, I just keep forgetting. I can't believe you'd pass up someone like that. The redhead, I mean. The brunette seems more into me, although if you have a preference ..."

"For the last time, I have a fucking 'preference,' and it doesn't involve either of them."

"Suit yourself. Thanks for playing along."

"Well, I haven't had to lie, and I've never heard a woman complain that she wasted a whole evening having a romantic dinner and didn't get laid."

We picked them up in my car. I shouldn't have been surprised when Arturo moved to the back with his date, but somehow I'd watched too many episodes of *The Flintstones* to see that coming. During dinner, Arturo started a conversation about movies, which led to the redhead mentioning one that just opened in the theaters.

"Wasn't that the one you've been wanting to see, man?"

"Yeah," I said, lying for the first time.

"Maybe there's a showing you two could go to."

# # # # #

"You owe me big time, man!" I yelled at the shower the next morning.

"Sorry, were we that loud?"

"That, too, but I was talking about how I had to sit through a two-hour chick flick, so you could make your move."

Arturo turned off the water and opened the shower door. Looking at me seriously, he said, "I already owed you more than I can ever repay, even before last night. You know that."

I pulled his towel off the rack and tossed it at him. "So, are you going to call her?"

"No ..." he said, drawing the word out as if I'd asked something ridiculous, and he had to say it slowly, so I'd understand. He began toweling his hair vigorously.

"I guess this wouldn't be a good time to start a relationship, if you're expecting to go through another cycle of waking up screaming in a couple of weeks."

"Uh, yeah. That's why I'm not going to get serious with her."

"I noticed she left before midnight. Did you sleep okay on your own?"

"You were still up when she left?"

"You expected me to sleep through that?"

"Why didn't you come in after you heard her leave? I changed the sheets right away." He looked almost hurt.

"Oh. I didn't ... I just ..."

"Hey, no big deal, I understand. You didn't feel like getting up once you'd gotten settled. You were probably just starting to doze off."

I spent the rest of the day not daring to ask the question of whether I should go back to joining him, now that there was no reason for it. But he'd made it clear enough by telling me he'd changed the sheets for me. I guess we'd both gotten used to having a warm body next to us. Certainly it had felt strange to me that night, to be sleeping alone again.

Arturo spent the rest of the day – hell, most of the week, with this satisfied smirk on his face, and whenever he caught my eye he would give me a big grin, even more affectionate than usual, and that was saying something.

"What?" I would sometimes say, by word or gesture. And he'd always reply, "I got laid! Thanks to you, man."

The third or fourth time he said that, I protested that I wasn't that good a wingman, and he could have easily gotten laid without me. After all, he was a good-looking guy, and could be very charming. He replied, "It wasn't just that. How good do you think I look and act when I haven't had a decent night of sleep in two weeks?"

I gave up arguing, but it went on for days: "I got laid! Thanks to you!" Often accompanied by a slap on the shoulder or a playful poke in the ribs. Especially when I wasn't wearing a shirt. Like when we were undressing for bed, or just getting up.

# # # # #

Another weekend arrived without our having had any more dreams, other than the ordinary kind. "We should go out again tonight," Arturo told me over breakfast. "By next weekend, the dreams could come back."

I'd been expecting that, since it had made him so happy the first weekend, and was glad it was time again, for the same reason. "Sure. Same place?"

"No, it's your turn to pick a place. We need to get you laid. Pick some place where you'll have a chance of picking up a ... um, another man."

"What, like a gay bar?"

"Why not?"

"I thought the idea was to go someplace together."

"That's the idea. You came with me last week. It's only fair. You were a great wingman, and it's time for me to return the favor."

"I appreciate that, buddy, but it isn't really necessary. As long as I stay in my league, I stand a very good shot at finding someone on my own. It's easier to talk most men into a one-night-stand than most women, if they're interested at all."

"But I want to help. I owe you that and a lot more. It couldn't hurt to have a wingman, right?"

"Well, actually ... Someone might assume I was already taken, if they see me already talking to another man."

"You really think someone would mistake me for your ... um, you know?"

"Arturo, very few straight men hang out in gay bars. If you go there, they'll assume you're gay. Didn't everyone assume I was straight at yours?" Even though I was with another man, and obviously close to him. "Or every day on the street, for that matter. If they don't think you're with me, you're going to get hit on. A lot more often than I was last weekend. Men are a lot more aggressive and straightforward, especially when they're not dealing with women."

"I'll risk it. I want to hang out with you, and I want you to get laid, buddy. You do want to get laid, don't you?"

"I'd be just as happy chilling out here with you." I gestured in the direction of the screen and game console. "Taking you apart, piece by piece."

"Not that I don't enjoy stripping away your weapons and breaking you down to your component parts, but you can lose to me any night. Tonight may be the last chance for either of us to get any action for awhile."

I was surprised at myself, but the prospect of sex with some stranger actually seemed like a less attractive option than playing a video game with my straight roommate, with our physical bodies intimately rubbing shoulders side by side in the middle of the couch even as our robot bodies tore into each other on the screen. And the truth was that I enjoyed losing to Arturo at least as much as winning, even if I couldn't admit it to him.

But, I couldn't talk him out of it. He insisted on driving me to a gay bar, arguing that if nothing else he could be my designated driver, so I could enjoy myself. He even helpfully made himself scarce whenever I went up to someone.

That was how I lost track of him for twenty minutes or so at one point. When I found him again, his shirt – a bright red dress shirt I'd never seen him wear before tonight – had been unbuttoned even further than he'd had it when we'd entered the bar, and that dumb self-satisfied grin he'd worn most of the week was back. I thought I was misreading him until he shouted in my ear, "Can you keep a secret?"

"I think I've been keeping a big one, not telling anyone about our dreams."

"I wouldn't admit this to just anyone, but I told you I'd trust you with anything."

"Sure. I won't tell anyone, I swear."

"You know how I thought you were nuts, to ever choose to have sex with a man when there are perfectly good women around?"

"I don't think of it as a choice."

"Well, I no longer feel you're nuts."

"What?" It was fairly noisy, of course, and I'd thought I'd heard him say something unbelievable, that he didn't think I was nuts for preferring men. Either that, or he was saying he wanted to feel my nuts, which seemed only slightly less likely.

"Dude," he said, drawing me close with an arm around the shoulders and speaking intimately into my ear, "I just had the best blow job in my entire fucking life! Every other one I had to plead for for months, buy flowers, cook special dinners. This guy did it right out in the alley, and he was incredible!"

"I don't believe this!"

"Maybe he'll do you, too. I can try to find him again. I think I remember what he looks like. Wouldn't that be cool, if we both took turns on the same guy? Hey, do you think he would do me again at the same time."

He took off on his self-appointed errand before I could recover from my amazement enough to protest that I was holding out for someone who made house calls. I mean, what's the good of having an understanding roommate if you still have to have sex in back alleys?

"Your boyfriend?" said a stranger, coming up behind me and leaning close to me in a seductive way. I took a good look at him, knowing Arturo's presence provided me with a tactful way of getting rid of him if I didn't like what I saw. But he was really hot. Not ideal, a couple of inches shorter than I and a little skinny – I prefer them well-muscled – but compared to most of the guys who'd propositioned me so far tonight, he was young and lean and handsome, far too attractive to reject out of hand. And white, which personally I find the second most attractive ethnic group, all other things being equal.

So I told him the truth: "No, he's just a close friend. My roommate. He's straight. Just here to keep me company."

"Too bad. If I could get the two of you bent over a bed, I'd enjoy taking you both at once."

"That sounds hot," I said, leaning closer and allowing him to play with my chest hair. I hadn't had a chance to submit to a smaller man in years, and he seemed to be aggressive enough to pull it off. "Too bad it's not majority rule. Would you settle for just me?"

# # # # #

A couple of hours later, we lay naked and spent in my little-used bed. My trick – I'd forgotten his name, even though he'd shouted it in my ear in the bar – was drifting off to sleep in my arms. I'd never been a big fan of letting sex partners spend the night, normally preferring to have the bed to myself. Tonight, all I could think of was Arturo in the next room. He'd retired to his room, with many a leering look, while my trick and I had still been pawing each other on the sofa. I found myself actually craving Arturo's familiar touch, the warmth of his body right next to mine, the weight of his head when he pillowed it on my chest. Was that sick or what? I was lying there with another gay guy I'd just had consensual sex with, who seemed content to sleep next to me, and all I could think about was how I could get rid of him, so I could sleep with my straight roommate whom I couldn't have sex with.

I'd long since developed a set of tricks for getting sleepy tricks out of my bed, short of rudely shaking them awake and bundling them into a taxi. I tried one now. "Want to take a shower with me?"

"Fuck, yeah!"

Under the warm spray, we helped each other get clean, and then we started getting dirty. I was on my knees, and had him halfway to his second orgasm of the night, when I heard the bathroom door open. I'd gotten out of the habit of locking it these past few weeks, and Arturo and I had gotten pretty casual about coming in to urinate or shave while the other guy was in the shower.

"Oh, sorry, man," he called. "I didn't realize your, um, guest was still here." He was just a blur of brown flesh tones pixelated by the frosted glass. I could just make out that he was wearing light-blue boxers tonight, either the solid ones or the striped ones. I realized about all he could see was that there were two naked white guys in the shower, one standing, the other kneeling.

"You don't mind, I hope," Arturo continued, and moved out of my field of view, around the corner to the toilet.

I stopped what I was doing – he was getting limp in my mouth anyway – and stood up, making a shushing gesture.

"I hope he's half as good as that guy in the alley," Arturo called.

I turned off the water. I didn't hear any tinkling sounds. And Arturo rarely got up to urinate in the middle of the night.

"You guys done already? Or just waiting for me to leave? Because I could be standing here a few more minutes at least, at this rate."

I'd never known Arturo to be pee-shy, at least when it was only me in the shower or at the sink. "Did you really have to piss, or did you just come in here to mess with me?"

"Would I ever mess with you, man?" Arturo said in mock innocence. He stepped back into view, and without warning, opened the shower door. He spared only a glance for my trick cowering behind me, but looked me up and down, grinning wickedly. "You know, man, I feel like I see you naked all the time, but technically this is the first time."

"Everything you dreamed of?" I asked, glaring defiantly.

"Exactly what I've been dreaming of."

"You told me he was straight!" my trick stage-whispered.

"He is. I think. We're just kidding around. Sort of."

"Is this the kind of prank straight guys play on each other in frats?" he said wonderingly.

"How would I know?" I said.

"Look, man," Arturo said, "you don't need to share everything you own with me, but I figured it couldn't ..."

"You want a blow job, man?" my trick asked my roommate eagerly, almost shoving me aside as he stepped in front of me. I noticed he'd started to regain his erection.

Arturo looked past him at me. "Did he finish sucking you off?" he asked me.

"Not exactly," I answered quickly, before my trick could correct him.

"I don't want you to miss out, so you first. Unless he can do us both at the same time."

"Fuck, yeah!" my trick said eagerly, stepping out of the shower.

I got out, and Arturo put his arm around my shoulders and drew me close, hip to hip, skin to skin. "Start with me, then go back to him, and keep trading off." He pulled his boxers down with the hand not clamped around my shoulder. My trick had the expression of a man who couldn't believe his luck and expected to wake up at any moment. A very real possibility, but I doubted it. He sank eagerly to his knees, letting the fingers of each hand trail down Arturo's smooth brown torso and my paler hairy torso on his way down. Arturo placed his outside hand on the back of the man's head. I reached down with my own outside hand and interlaced my fingers with my roommate's, and we guided his head toward Arturo's cock.

I felt every twitch, every shiver of pleasure as Arturo enjoyed his second blow job of the night – his second male blow job ever. After a moment, breathing hard, with amazing self control, he nudged the kneeling man's head over to my crotch for a turn. I was fully hard again by now, just from watching Arturo being pleasured by a hot guy. I gasped as I felt the warm mouth that had just been on my roommate's cock enveloping mine for my first blow job in quite awhile, not counting the recent dream.

# # # # #

I woke up in Arturo's bed, with his head pillowed on my chest. My hand was resting on the back of his neck. I had a vague dreamlike memory of carrying him back to bed in his satiated languor. I stretched contentedly, and Arturo woke up, lifting his head just enough for his ear to clear my chest hair.

"Morning," I said. "I couldn't believe it when you opened that shower door. Or was that a dream?"

"I don't know. Did you get your little friend's phone number, so you can call and ask him?"

"No."

"Then maybe we'll never know for sure. Does it even matter?"

"Well, since you were kind enough to leave my heart in my chest this time, I guess it's not so big an issue."

"I think it's too early for the dreams to come back. Anyway, I'm glad you were a good sport about it. I've sometimes fantasized about how hot it would be if my roommate walked in on me while I was with a girl."

"In your dreams, buddy! But it was hot. And the next part was even hotter."

"I never would have expected my first three-way wouldn't even involve a girl, but I always wanted to share that kind of pleasure with a guy I liked, side by side." He tousled my chest hair and rolled off me toward the edge of the bed. "Pancakes?"

"You're going to make me fat if you keep this up."

"I'll monitor the situation closely," he said, pulling the covers down to my waist and patting my flat belly. Then he did a double-take. "It was no dream."

"How do you know?"

"Because you always sleep in your boxers." He yanked the covers down to our knees. He was clad in boxers as usual – he'd managed to pull them back up last night, or I'd done it for him, as I vaguely remembered – but I was stark naked. I hastily crossed my hands over my crotch.

Arturo laughed. "Seriously?" He pried my hands away and pinned them over my head. I resisted only a little. "Like we have anything to hide from each other? Although admittedly, this is the first time I've seen you soft. Kind of pathetic looking – oh,

165

wait! There you go. You still thinking about last night? How we had him on his knees, pleasuring both of us?"

I didn't answer. I was breathing hard.

He still had his weight on my wrists, pinned against the mattress, as he looked down the length of our bodies. "Now I'm starting to get hard, thinking about that."

"I was first," I said. "I get the shower first."

"Want to just jerk off here? Together?"

So we did, side by side, shoulder muscles touching like when we were playing video games at the center of the couch and manipulating our joysticks.

# # # # #

I woke from a fairly pleasant dream about the chain gang in the desert. For once the guy right ahead of me, the one whose ankle shackles were directly linked to mine, had been in good shape, judging from his nicely sculpted back and slim waistline, and from what glimpses I got of the side of his chest when he'd twisted around to look at me. He'd been openly checking me out. It seemed pointless to try to break out of my chains and do anything about that, and even his back was just out of reach, so I kept trudging along, but I didn't pick up many rocks that night.

Arturo was still sound asleep when I woke up, even though sunlight was streaming through the window. I looked in the closet and realized I'd used up all the clean shirts I'd cached there, so I padded off to my own room to find one. My own room looked unfamiliar, I'd spent so little time there. I even noticed a door I'd forgotten existed. Probably another closet, but I couldn't remember ever opening it to look until now.

It wasn't another closet. It was a bathroom, twice the size of the one I'd been sharing with Arturo, with a gleaming gold faucet and brown marble sink. Instead of a shower stall, it had the most enormous tub I'd seen in a private home, big enough to actually hold a full-grown man. I usually preferred showers anyway, but I missed the occasional hot soak. Why hadn't Arturo mentioned I had my own private bathroom?

I had to try it out, of course. A moment later, I was soaking in steaming hot water, naked, with my eyes closed.

"I knew it!" Arturo's voice said.

I opened my eyes and saw him standing by the tub, already fully dressed. Before I could work up the motivation to ask what he meant – I was so relaxed and comfortable that I didn't want to expend even that much energy – he continued, "I picked up way more rocks than you, so I expected to have the upper hand in this dream. And sure enough, here you are sitting in my soup pot, totally naked." He produced a kitchen knife and began slicing a peeled potato into the water.

I wanted to point out that it was clearly a hot tub – I was pretty sure we didn't own any soup pots big enough to hold me – but I was still feeling too relaxed and lazy to speak. I passively let slices of potatoes and carrots bounce off my chest into the water.

"How're you doing, man?" Arturo said after I'd soaked awhile.

It was great, and I wanted to ask him to join me. There might just be enough room if we got friendly. But all I could manage was the word "Fine" in a slow lazy drawl.

"You getting soft yet?" He plunged his arm into the water, pushed some half-cooked vegetables out of my lap, and grabbed my cock, which was indeed as limp as a wet noodle from soaking in hot water. It didn't even harden at his touch, surreal as that may seem. This just felt sensual, lying there and letting my straight friend handle my cock. He moved behind the tub and placed a hand on each shoulder, kneading my muscles. I leaned into the massage, groaning softly in pleasure as he dug his thumbs in. My muscles had already loosened up from the hot soak, but now I felt downright ready to melt into a puddle.

Arturo released my shoulders and dipped a ladle into the water and lifted it to his lips. "Mmm! This is gonna be good! Needs something, though. Maybe a little olive oil." He drizzled some olive oil over my chest and began working it in with his hands.

Something started buzzing harshly. Arturo looked puzzled. Then he appeared to decide it was an oven timer: Over his shoulder I saw an oven appear out of thin air just in time for him to turn to it and push a button. The noise continued, and he fiddled with it to no avail.

"Damn," he said. "You know what? I bet it's …"

I woke up to find Arturo leaning on me to turn off the clock radio. "Yeah, it was the alarm," he continued. "I set it to use the buzzer because I got tired of waking to traffic reports." He collapsed on top of me. "Just as it was getting good, too. How did it feel, being cooked down to a soup?"

"Like being in a hot tub. Relaxing. How did I taste?"

"Delicious. Just like you smell."

"Oh, come on! Don't be gross."

"No, really. I like the way you smell, man. Sort of nutty and musky. I wonder if that's what you really would taste like."

"You'll never know," I said, stretching lazily.

To my amazement, he pinned my arms and nuzzled my open armpit. "Hey!" I protested automatically.

He ignored me, to my secret delight, and started licking my armpit, still pinning my wrists firmly above my head. I made a show of struggling, arching up against him, feeling his warm skin against mine. Music seemed to be playing somewhere far away, matching the rhythm of our playful struggle. I could make out the words: "In the semidarkness, my heart is filled with you. Your music is a dream that resonates with me." Or words to that effect. In Spanish.

Arturo gently sank his teeth into the muscle near my armpit, not quite hard enough to hurt, and proceeded to nibble his way down my chest in the general direction of my nipple.

The music stopped. I felt Arturo climb over me, back onto his side of the bed, having turned off the clock radio. "Well, that was ... interesting," he said.

I opened my eyes – well, the third time's the charm. Arturo and looked at each other uncertainly. I had the definite feeling that in reality, his tongue had never been anywhere near my armpit, any more than I'd been simmering in a giant soup pot before that. But I was equally convinced that he'd experienced it, too, just as surely as if he'd really done it.

# # # # #

"The dreams are getting cut off earlier and earlier by the alarm, did you notice?" I said around a mouthful of chips and guacamole.

"Yeah, we must be almost at the end of another cycle." He gestured with a chip. "Maybe we should stay up late on Friday and sleep in on Saturday so we don't miss out."

A glob of homemade guacamole flew off his chip and landed on my chest, near my shoulder. "Oops. Hold still."

I shivered in anticipation, wondering if this was another erotic dream. Could it be he was really going to clean me off with his tongue in our waking life? But he only wiped it off with a napkin.

# # # # #

I found myself in the familiar desert chain gang setting. I knew I was dreaming, and yet it was hard to think back on the events of my real life. With some effort, I recalled our dream-free weekends taking turns choosing a bar, and a night that the dreams had returned, just as Arturo had predicted from experience. Had that been last night, making this the second night in a row after the break?

The dream was less pleasant than usual. The guy I had in front of me tonight was a huge pasty mound of flesh. Not only was his brightly lit, pale shapeless back the last thing I wanted to look at, but was so wide he completely blocked my view of the guys chained ahead of him. I focused on anything but him: On glimpses of Arturo behind out of the corner of my eye. On the way my toes didn't seem to cast the expected shadows each time I took a step; my shadow looked as if it was wearing square-toed boots. And most of all on picking up rocks.

I was rewarded with a very pleasant dream, although, as usual, I didn't realize it was a dream. It seemed perfectly natural at the time to both of us to leave the car at work and fly home. It was such fun, we couldn't understand why we didn't do it every day; it was so easy to get airborne once we'd kicked off our shoes. We headed roughly in the direction of home, but higher than necessary, chasing each other through the clouds, whooping and laughing. Arturo wrestled my shirt off and sent it fluttering toward the ground far below, exposing my chest to the moist chilly air of the next cloud he hauled me through by my ankles. I jackknifed in midair and grabbed hold of his shirt. He let go of my ankles and struggled to hold it down, but I managed to expose his navel, then six inches of smooth brown skin above it, and then suddenly ...

... I was awakened by the sound of clattering dishes and rowdy male laughter in the kitchen. I heard the muffled sound of several male voices speaking in a bantering tone. It sounded like it might be Spanish, but I couldn't make out any words. I swung my feet out of bed, padded sleepily to the door, and pushed it open.

"Hey, you're up!" Arturo said delightedly. "I've been waiting to introduce you to my brothers." He was serving a plate piled with an improbably high stack of pancakes to three men seated at the table. "Have a seat, man."

169

Muzzy-headed, I shuffled over and took one of the two empty chairs. Where had Arturo been hiding the guest chairs? I hadn't realized we had three extra ones.

"This is Armando," he said, putting his hand on the broad shoulder of the oldest one, who looked very sharp in a business suit, and was if anything even handsomer than Arturo. He was only a few years older, but somehow exuded maturity and wisdom.

Armando gave me a very firm handshake. "I've heard a lot about you. It's great to meet you."

Then Arturo introduced his younger brothers. Danielito was in his sophomore year, and Diego in his senior year, at different colleges. Both were very cute, with boyish good looks, casually dressed in T-shirts and jeans.

"I guess he's better than nothing," Armando said suddenly.

"What do you mean?" Arturo asked, offended. "He's the best roommate I've ever had."

"Roommate? You're not fooling anyone. I'm just saying, any regular source of sex is better than nothing, if you can't keep a girlfriend."

"Armando! What the fuck are you talking about?" Arturo looked shocked and betrayed. "He's just my roommate. He's not like that. In fact, he brings home other guys to do it to." His tone suggested that somehow the fact that I had sex with other men proved in his mind that I wasn't *that way*, which made no sense.

Armando scoffed. "Then why don't you let him wear any clothes?"

I looked down and was mortified to discover that I'd stumbled out of the bedroom without getting dressed, without even throwing on a robe. I was wearing nothing but boxers. And my fly was gaping wide open, with pubic hair curling out and the middle of my shaft in full view of the men on either side of me.

"Well, he just got out of bed," Arturo said.

"And what's this for?" Diego asked. He'd gotten up without my noticing and was now rummaging through our junk drawer; he triumphantly held up a collar on a chain. "It's too big for a dog." He dodged around Arturo and was suddenly behind me. "But just right for a man." He snapped it around my neck. "If you can call someone like that a man."

"Take that off him!" Arturo yelled, snatching a large knife from its wooden block and menacing his brothers with it.

"All we're taking off him is the shorts," Danielito said tauntingly, taking hold of my waistband of my boxer shorts.

Arturo advanced on them. Armando said, "Arturo, *tranquilízate*," which I unthinkingly understood as meaning "Chill out." It occurred to me that I wasn't sure they hadn't been speaking Spanish all along, but that thought was derailed when I felt Danielito yanking my boxers down. At the same time, I saw Arturo slash at his beloved older brother's arm with the knife. Armando doubled up in pain, clutching his arm. Diego was holding the choke collar tight in one fist while his other arm pinned my arms to my side. Danielito straightened up and got between us and the enraged Arturo, who slashed at him. His younger brother howled and spun away. His shirt had a long diagonal slice through it, and I could see bare brown skin through it, and a long shallow cut beginning to bleed.

Everything got confused – I'd never full woken up and couldn't deal with this – and the next thing I knew, I was on my knees in front of Arturo. My roommate was wrapped in Armando's powerful arms and I had Danielito's hands clamped on my bare shoulders. Diego holding my leash.

"Take off the pants," Armando ordered. I knew he meant Arturo's pants, since I was already stark naked. Danielito pulled his brother's pants and boxers down around his ankles, and Diego forced my head against my roommate's crotch. Arturo was getting a little bit of a hard-on despite himself. I did something I'd normally never dream of doing, even though I'd wanted to, because it seemed to make sense at the moment. It wasn't my fault, after all.

Arturo gasped as I took his cock in my mouth. With the skill of long practice, I began caressing the underside with my tongue, using my lips to roll his foreskin away from the sensitive head it protected, and slowly teasing him toward full erection, then toward climax.

At the moment he came, we both woke up. We were wrapped around each other, face to face. Arturo pushed me away, more in panic than in anger.

"I'm so sorry, man!" he said. "I don't know where that came from, I swear! And my real brothers would never, never act that way."

"It's cool. It was just a dream. I understand that. I should have known. I mean, you wouldn't really attack your brothers with a knife."

"If they were doing that to you, I might. But they never would, of course."

I didn't want to admit that I'd found it sort of hot. The only problem was they hadn't asked my permission, but given that it was a dream, that seemed forgivable.

"You have nothing to apologize for," I said instead.

"That must have come from some deep, dark corner of my psyche that I didn't even know was there."

I hesitated. "How do you know it came from your subconscious?"

"Because I can't imagine any part of you wanting to be forced into that! Whereas I ... Well, I guess I enjoyed the blow jobs I got from the guys in the bar a little too much and wanted more of the same. And man, if that were real, you'd be the champion hands down. I know it's a horrible thing to say, but I actually enjoyed it. I'm sorry, man."

I was silent for a long time. Finally I said, "It's not a horrible thing to say."

"Really? Yeah, I guess you're right. It's not like it was real, after all."

I hesitated again then finally said, "Exactly. If you can't cut loose and have fun in dreams, what's the point of dreaming?"

"So you forgive me?"

"Seriously? You're begging forgiveness now? It's not the worst thing you've done to me in a dream."

"Really? What was worse than that?"

"Cutting my beating heart out of my chest and eating it?" I reminded him.

"Yeah, I guess." He licked his lips.

# # # # #

After work the next day, Arturo called each of his brothers and talked for awhile in Spanish.

"What's new with your brothers?"

"Diego's complaining his TV reception is getting bad in the afternoons again. He told me a couple of weeks ago it had gotten better. I told him he should get cable and offered to pay until he graduates and gets a job."

"Did you ask them about their dreams?" I asked impatiently.

"Yeah. I told them I had a weird dream about them. None of them remember dreaming about me in a long time. Their dreams sound pretty boring." He grinned and me fondly. "Looks like this is just you and me. By the way, they all say hi."

"But they've never even met me!"

"I talk about you a lot. Hey, have I ever showed you their pictures?"

"No. Do you have any?"

"Of course! Lots."

"I'm curious to see if they look like what I saw in the dream."

They did, more or less. Diego and Danielito had more mature faces than I remembered, even in their high school graduation pictures, let alone the more recent ones. I noticed something in Armando's wedding pictures, where Arturo had been his best man: "Hey, Armando looks at least an inch shorter than you."

"Does he? I guess he is. I never thought about that."

"He looked much taller in the dream." I remembered him towering over Arturo as he held him from behind. He'd been much taller than I, and I was a bit taller than Arturo. I saw it again in a picture of the four brothers in casual clothing: Armando was the shortest of the bunch, though not by much, and Diego the tallest. Armando was wearing a tight tank top in that picture, and he looked well-built, but no more so than Arturo. Certainly he wasn't the imposing broad-shouldered figure from the dream.

The wedding pictures were old enough that Diego looked as if he was in his late teens at most, and I saw a pimply kid who could only have been Danielito. It was the first time in my life I'd seen childhood pictures of someone I'd been in a sexual situation with, and I found it vaguely disturbing and acutely embarrassing.

"So Armando's been married for several years now?"

"Yes, and he would never cheat on his wife."

"Well, technically, that's not what ..."

"Yeah, I know," Arturo said, clearly embarrassed. "He made me do it. But they way they were treating you in the dream, we're lucky Diego and Danielito and maybe Armando didn't gang-rape you instead of just, you know ..."

173

"Yeah, we did get lucky," I said, slapping his shoulder affectionately.

"They'd never do that. Armando would have stopped them, not helped them, but they'd never do it in the first place. They're good kids."

"Men," I corrected. "Good men."

"Yeah, I know."

"Even if part of you will always think of them as your baby brothers."

"They're good men. And they'd never be stupid enough to think I'd want to do that to you."

He had an odd way of putting things like this. Had we been in the same dream? The way I remembered it, he'd been helpless when I, not entirely unwillingly, took his cock in my mouth. I was getting the feeling that even if we'd been alone and I'd had him bound hand and foot, he'd think of it as him "doing it to me" even as I stripped him and sucked him off. But all I said was, "Dude, it was just a dream."

Not seeming to hear, he continued, "Even if they thought that, they'd be crazy to think I'd do it to you right in front of my own brothers! You should come with me next Thanksgiving, so you can meet the real guys instead of figments of my imagination."

"Figments of our imagination," I corrected. "Wait, really? Do you mean that? I wouldn't want to intrude on a family gathering."

"It's cool. We'll find you a place on the couch or something. Diego brought his roommate from college last year, so why shouldn't I bring mine?" He chuckled. "Of course, if he brings him this year, you may need to wrestle the guy over who gets the couch. But I know you can take him."

# # # # #

Late in the night, after Arturo beat me at the chain-gang game by cheating again, we dreamt about Thanksgiving. Armando was still wearing his suit, but he'd ripped one sleeve off and wrapped a white bandage around his wounded shoulder. Danielito was shirtless, with a long white bandage pasted diagonally against his brown chest. As for me, they were having me for Thanksgiving dinner, all right. I'd been stripped, hogtied, shaved, baked to a golden brown, and arranged on the table with an apple in my mouth, preventing me from begging for mercy as forks were shoved into various parts of my anatomy. Arturo just laughed and watched his brothers tormenting me. They remarked in Spanish about how tender I was, and Arturo gestured at me with his own fork, suggesting particularly tender parts of me they might want to focus on. He had something speared on his fork that I hoped was just a sausage; my hands would have instinctively flown to my crotch if they hadn't been tied to my ankles.

We woke up, and Arturo was still laughing at me. "Is that what you think will happen if you come to Thanksgiving?"

"I suppose you'll tell me they won't do that either?" I joked feebly.

"Well ... I might." He rolled on top of me, pinned my arm above my head, and sank his teeth gently into the knot of muscle that stretched from my pecs to my armpit. I put up a token struggle as he began to nibble, but we both knew I was strong enough to stop him if I really wanted to.

When I woke in the morning, there were no toothmarks. I wondered if it had been another dream. I didn't bother to ask Arturo; I knew he'd remember it regardless. I wondered if the distinction really mattered, when it was just between the two of us.

# # # # #

"Let me get this straight," Bernie said sometime not long afterward.

"No pun intended," Barry interjected.

We were in my living room, and I forgot where Arturo was. When I thought about it, I vaguely remembered my friends getting me drunk in a bar, maybe for my birthday. It didn't occur to me how strange it would be for Arturo not to have insisted coming along.

Bernie glared at his partner and continued, "He loves his brothers more than you can possibly fathom, but he loves you even more than them."

"Probably. Don't ask me how I know."

"And you share a bed, even though you've got your own bed."

"Well, there's a good reason for that. Or was."

"And you, Mr. One Night Stand himself, would rather lie in bed with him, cuddling, than go out and actually get laid."

"Did I really tell you that?"

175

"We got you pretty drunk," Barry put in.

"And you have wet dreams about each other."

"I didn't say wet dreams. Did I?"

"But erotic dreams. You, I could understand, but him, too?"

"Erotic dreams?" Barry asked. "I just thought he said they 'share all the same dreams.' Which sounds like a great basis for any kind of relationship, but it doesn't have to be more than a friendship."

"No, he was talking about actual literal dreams. Weren't you? You're drunk and not always making a lot of sense."

"Yeah, he has erotic dreams about me as often as I do about him." Exactly as often. "At least, I would call them erotic."

"So, to summarize, you love each other, and you have this physical relationship, cuddling and roughhousing ..."

"And licking," Barry said. "Don't forget licking."

"And he has erotic dreams about you."

"All true, pretty much."

"Explain to me again how he's not gay."

"He doesn't think about it that way."

"Are you guys talking about me?" asked Arturo sleepily. He was standing in the doorway of our bedroom, wearing nothing but his boxers. I had no idea how much he'd heard. How had he gotten the door open so quietly?

"That must have sounded weird," I said apologetically. I looked at my friends and realized that they were both dressed in leather jackets, no shirts underneath, just chains, and leather chaps. That probably looked surreal to him. Bernie was even wearing a leather collar that looked suspiciously like the one I'd dreamed of being forced to wear.

"It's cool," Arturo said. "It's not like I'm not used to this by now."

"You are?" all three of us said in unison, as if this were a movie.

"Sure. This is a dream, of course."

He might be right. My memory was very confused, although that could be all the drinks. My mind was filling in a back-story, vague memories of being plied with drinks, being helped up the stairs. But it wouldn't be the first time my mind made up an explanation when confronted with an inconsistency in a dream. It seemed more reasonable that, just as I'd had a dream where I'd walked out of the bedroom in my boxers when Arturo was with his brothers, now he was having one where he was in his boxers and my friends were here. Classic enough kind of dream. The only surprise was that we'd each been wearing even boxers.

"Yeah, I guess so," I said. "I wonder who's in control of this one?"

"Easy enough to find out. If I'm in control, I would make your buddies strip you naked right now."

That would be a dream come true for me. Although I doubted the "true" part. My friends gave me an incredulous look, but I mouthed Do it. Some silent communication passed between the two lovers, and then they each grabbed an arm.

I put up a token struggle, but I doubt even a real struggle would have made a difference. They were big guys; I'd long since sized up Barry as being strong enough to trounce me single-handedly, and even Bernie was probably a match for me all by himself. They stripped me to the waist as Arturo watched, then Barry wrapped his arms around me and lifted me off the ground while Bernie removed my shoes and socks, then pulled off my pants, and after a slight hesitation, my boxers. If this turned out to be really happening, I definitely owed them one.

"What do you want us to do with him?" Bernie asked Arturo, putting a meaty hand on my bare shoulder.

Barry, still pinning my arms to my sides, added, "Your wish is our command."

Arturo grinned. "Of course it is. Stretch him out on the table and drizzle him with chocolate syrup."

The dumbfounded look both my friends gave me was priceless.

"Fridge," I whispered helpfully. "Bottom shelf in the door."

When they muscled me onto the table, I knew it was a dream. I'd doubted it until now, but Bernie and Barry were monogamous. And yet there was Bernie, actually opening the refrigerator while Barry held me down with a hand on my chest and Arturo held my ankles. Barry's tight pants revealed a bulge. Surely the big guy hadn't been harboring secret desires for me all these years? This had to be a dream.

The syrup wasn't cold, like it should have been, as Bernie dripped some into the hollow at the base of my throat and began drizzling it down my upper chest.

"You actually left the syrup on the counter," Bernie mentioned, as the dream caught up with the inconsistencies and tried to explain them away. He laid down a zigzagging trail of syrup that narrowly missed one nipple, crossed my pecs, tangling in my chest hair, then passed squarely over the other nipple and coated it, and continued in a narrowing zigzag down my chest and onto my belly before reaching my navel, which he filled to overflowing.

"You can stop right there," Arturo said. "No way am I licking it off any further down than that."

Barry sounded surprised. "You – Lick – I was sort of expecting you to order us to do it." Like they would.

"No, you guys just hold him down. He's all mine." Arturo leaned down and nuzzled the hollow of my throat and began following the trail of chocolate down from there, back and forth across my chest, slicking down my chest hairs as he cleaned them. His tongue passed teasingly close to the first nipple, and I shivered in anticipation as it slowly approached the other, and arched my back when I felt the moist warmth against those sensitive nerve endings. The whole thing was extremely vivid: the feel of my friend's tongue, the warmth of his skin against mine as he rested his weight on me. I had my eyes closed by this time.

He paused in the middle of my chest, saying, "I'm surprised you guys are still here. I'd expected you to disappear by now." Then he went back to what he was doing, ignoring my friends, until he finally reached my navel and dipped his tongue into the remaining pool of chocolate.

Finally he was finished and hauled me to my feet. "I don't even want to think about what you're going to do to me to get even for this, the next time you're in control. But it was totally worth it."

"For now, I'm yours to do with as you like," I said meekly. I noticed we were alone in the room now. Bernie and Barry had somehow disappeared when things started getting interesting. I hadn't heard the door shut, but then again, I had been just a little distracted.

"On your knees, then, and pull my shorts down with your teeth," he ordered.

I knelt naked at his feet and did as he asked. He had just the beginnings of a hard-on, nothing like the raging one I had – which he was politely ignoring, though it was in full view. He put his hands on my shoulders and drew me closer, kneading my muscles as he did so. I began coaxing him to full hardness with my tongue.

Once I'd finished pleasuring him, we both collapsed gently to the floor together. I distinctly felt the carpet digging into my bare skin for a few moments, but then I felt myself slipping into a deeper sleep and the dream fading away. Arturo's voice dragged me back. "How long will it take us to wake up?" he asked. "The dream doesn't usually last this long once the action is over."

"I don't know," I said honestly. We sat up, and I threw an arm casually around Arturo's bare shoulders. "I'm starting to fade. Maybe you could make us some coffee while we're waiting?"

THE GATOR GUY
By R. W. Clinger

R. W. lives in Pittsburgh with his pet alligators, Esmeralda and Galen. Gator guys are his weakness, of course. R. W. can be reached by e-mail at <u>kenitorico@verizon.net</u>.

1. MONSTER IN MONTABA

I moved from Boston to Naples, Florida, because of work, which consisted of a management position. My employer, RailSave Incorporated, stored valuable computer data for high-end clients – mostly financial groups along the eastern coast. Wealthy establishments in Key West, Miami, Washington, D.C., New York City, and Boston. If the world imploded, RailSave Incorporated claimed they would still have their clients' data.

My transition to Naples was rather harmless. Winter turned into summer overnight. I went from wearing February sweaters to knee-low shorts. I gained a tan during my first week at Montaba, the miniscule hacienda next to the Gulf where I lived. Happily I left the Boston cold behind, sucked up the cheery sun, and learned my new position at RailSave. Naples welcomed me with open arms, shared its Latino culture with me, and saved me from the northern clutch of an icy winter and miserable Massholes.

No, I didn't have a boyfriend. Instead, I lived alone at Montaba, or so I thought I was alone. Three alligators resided in the blue-green canal out back: Mo was ten feet long; Larry was nine feet long; and Curly was eight feet long. I assumed the three were a family and a little pissed at me for moving in. Honestly, I kept my distance from the scaly trio and never found myself outside by the canal. The screened-in patio was as far as I went. There, I watched the gators nap in the sun, swim in the canal, lounge under the palms, and feed on the fishes. The gators had their space, and I had mine. Who said two different worlds couldn't function as one?

One Monday morning in late February changed that idea of content living, though. I rose from my bed, took a piss, showered, shaved, climbed into a tight T-shirt the color of the

181

Floridian sky, and slipped into a pair of khaki shorts and matching sandals. Ready for work, dressing down for the day, I headed into the kitchen for a cup of coffee, a freshly picked orange, and ...

"Holy fuck!" fell out of my mouth.

On the middle of the kitchen floor sat Mo. The greenish black lizard stared at me with its beady black eyes, which suggested that Mo wanted me for breakfast. Behind him, the west screen on the patio was ripped open and dangled from its stainless steel frame. Since the day I arrived in Naples, I hadn't locked or closed the sliding glass doors that separated the screened-in patio and pool area from the rest of the stucco bungalow. Mo had obviously broken through the west screen, discovered the kitchen, and found himself caught between the quartz island and the dishwasher/sink area.

The gator was pissed. Anyone could have determined such an elementary assessment when Mo opened his toothy mouth and snapped it closed. The reptile tried to move to the right and left but couldn't. The poor bastard was really caught where he was, unable to wiggle free.

"Shit, Mo ... What did you get yourself into, pal?"

He snapped his steel-like jaws again, left out an uncomfortable groan of sorts, and gave me a look that said: "Help me, bud. I can't do this on my own."

I heeded Mo's request, jumped on the Internet in my bamboo-decorated study, and Googled: alligator rescue Naples.

A list of 200 or more sites popped up on the screen, most of which were foundations or non-profit groups and organizations that protected Florida's wildlife. One website stood out from the rest: THE GATOR GUY. Curiosity meandered through my fingertips, and I clicked on the site. The page was comprised of a number of alligator pictures, the company's address, e-mail address, and phone number. A brief description regarding The Gator Guy said: "Have a Gator problem? Call me. 24 hours a day. 7 days a week. Will rescue gators and find them good homes. Low fees."

What the hell, right? I dialed The Gator Guy's phone number, listened to the line ring three times, and then a Latino-sounding female said, "*Hola!* The Gator Guy. How may I help ju?"

I told Lucia my problem.

"Ju need to make an appointment."

"I don't think you understand me. I have an alligator in my kitchen. He's trapped. I can't get my coffee."

"*Aye dio mio!* I send café to you, *señor.*"

"I need the Gator Guy, not coffee. An alligator needs to be removed from my kitchen."

She called me something sweet in Spanish, told me to hold, came back on the line a few seconds later, and took my name, address, and phone number. Once that was accomplished, Lucia added, "Gator Guy help ju in half hour. No café, though."

I thanked the woman and ended our call.

# # # # #

I called into the office late, stared at Mo, and told the gator everything was going to be fine, not that he believed me.

Approximately forty minutes later, the Gator Guy arrived. He pulled up in his flaming red Dodge Ram truck, which hauled a massive gator cage behind it. The *chico* parked in the seashell-covered drive, climbed out and ...

My God, I had never applied my intoxicated stare on such a handsome man in all my twenty-seven years of life. The Ecuadorian stood at six-two, weighed 190 pounds, sported cocoa bean-colored eyes and matching spiked hair. His biceps gleamed olive-colored perspiration in the morning's diligent sun. The twenty-nine-year-old man was tapered from his massive shoulders down to his narrow waist. He was dressed in a white tank top that outlined every ripple and curve that designed his muscular chest, mud-stained khaki shorts, onyx-colored booty socks, and rugged Under Armour boots.

"*Buenos dias*, Paulo." He held out his right hand for me to shake with his good morning.

"How are you, *señor?*"

"*Bien. Gracious.* My name is Manijo Dulce. I understand you have a gator in your bedroom?" he asked, and raised his adorable eyebrows with interest.

"My kitchen," I corrected.

"Oh," he mumbled, maybe semi-disappointed that we wouldn't be visiting my bedroom together.

"Follow me." I led him to the kitchen, and Mo stared up at us.

"That's a big one. Just the way I like them," Manijo chanted. "I'll have him out of here in a second."

I stepped aside and let the gator guy do his thing. He wrestled with the gator and practically rode the animal. Manijo bounced up and down because of the reptile's fury. Kitchen cabinets and the Kenmore refrigerator were scratched. The dish washer had a bowling ball-sized dent in its front. Eventually, the gator guy got the beast under control and used duct tape around Mo's snout, tied up the lizard's feet in a harmless manner, and wrestled Mo into the patio room, then outside, next to the narrow canal. Manijo used a gurney on wheels to tote Mo to his truck. The gator was safely rolled inside the massive cage, covered for protection, and ready for its next residence, somewhere along Lake Okeechobee.

When Manijo came back in the house with his bill, I passed him a glass of water. In doing so, I said, "There are two other gators in the canal. Can you haul them away with Mo?"

Manijo sucked down some water, flexing his right bicep. Then he walked through the kitchen, into the screened-in patio, and observed the beautiful sun-gilded day and the green-blue canal that led to the warm Gulf. "No gators here."

"Trust me, they come around."

He turned away from the screen and faced me, smiled, and took me in from head to toe, but not in a sexual manner. The gator guy consumed my semi-brown skin tone, Panamanian lips, amber-colored eyes, 175 pounds, and my five-ten frame. He did a second once-over of my lean torso, studied the cotton-covered package between my legs, licked his lips in a discreet manner, and said, "I'll come back for the other gators."

I didn't believe the man. Good help was hard to find, even when it came to removing giant reptiles from one's backyard in Naples, Florida. "When will you be back?"

He passed the empty water glass back to me and began his exit. "Don't know. I'll have Lucia arrange something with you. In the meantime, pay the bill I gave you. We accept all major credit cards."

I was about to tell him that the sooner he came back, the better. I didn't want another alligator in my kitchen, among other rooms in my abode. To no avail, though, the guy split with speed. He waved goodbye over his right shoulder, yelled out his thanks for the water in thick Spanish, and vanished from my gator fiasco, but only for the time being.

2. A JOB TO DO

Two nights later, I was working in my office at home and heard some ruckus outside in the driveway. With a Corona in hand, I flicked my Notepad off and found myself at the front door of Montaba. There in the evening's blue-purple twilight that coated the seashell drive was the gator guy with his truck and massive cage. He jumped out of his Ram's cab, gathered up some equipment from the vehicle's bed, and started to carry the goods around the bungalow, heading towards the canal, Larry and Curly.

I rushed outside with my beer and was on his heels. "Hey, Manijo! ... What's going on?"

The handsome guy wasn't wearing a shirt since it was ninety-three degrees and his chiseled chest gleamed with model perfection. An extreme heat wave had tackled southern Florida and wasn't letting up anytime soon. At the side of Mantaba the gator guy spun around in the blue-silver garden light. In his hands were a camera, a stainless steel lunchbox, and a laptop. Not that I really cared what he was holding, since my eyes strayed to his firm and hairless pecs, solid nipples, rigid abs, and the thin line of dark treasure trail which fell from the base of his concave navel into his khaki shorts.

"Gator hunting, pal. Didn't Lucia call and tell you I would be here?"

"She didn't."

"Sorry about that, Paulo. Sometimes she does a great job, and sometimes she doesn't. I still love her as a sister, though." He spun around, trotted into the backyard, closed in on the canal, and began to set up his camera. In doing so, he prattled, "This should do the trick tonight. Night vision always helps. Gators like the night. It's feeding time for them. The camera has a wireless connection to the laptop. We can watch your lizard buddies from inside the house. If we don't feel like watching the laptop's screen, a sensor on the camera goes off and will alert us of a gator's movement. I can then react when the time is necessary."

"What's in the lunchbox?" I inquired. Anyone attracted to the guy would have asked. Maybe he had other gadgets that he would use that night to capture Larry and Curly.

"A protein bar, sandwich, and Diet Pepsi."

"Your lunch?"

The rough guy nodded his adorable head, smiled at me, and added, "Yeah. A guy's gotta eat when he's working the night shift."

"So you're spending the entire night here?"

"Lucia should have cleared that by you. Sorry again."

"It's alright," I admitted, "I'm learning a lot of gator stuff from you." Plus, he was the hottest Latino man in all of Florida: hearty-sized, intelligent, motivated, forward, and quite interesting. Truth was I wanted to get him out of his tight khaki shorts and have my way with his bronze skin. Something told me that the convex shape between his thighs was a massive cock. Meat that was surely ten inches long and two inches wide. A piece of beef that needed to be licked, sucked, and pushed into my Latino rear for its indisputable pleasure. Trust me, alligators were not the only creatures that liked to eat meat at night.

That sex-gig was only my imagination running away from me. The gator guy and I were not going to fuck around together. He had a job to do, which I was paying for, and I had ...

I'll tell you what I didn't have instead: a boyfriend. Someone who looked like Manijo Dulce with his masculine charm, self-assured manner, and unlimited sexiness. I craved a guy like the Latino to peel my clothes off and have his dirty way with me. Straight or gay, I really didn't give a shit. I merely wanted and needed some male companionship in my life, masculine body against masculine body, even if it turned out to be a one-night stand with a guy who was fixated on lizards.

Once his wireless camera was set up near the canal, and his laptop was open and running on the screened-in patio, we found ourselves in my kitchen, and I offered the gator guy a Corona.

"Love one," he supplied, grinning from ear to ear.

"What will your boss say about you having a beer?"

"I am the boss," he confessed. "I started The Gator Guy about five years ago. Best thing that could have happened to me."

"And your sister works for you?"

"Lucia does. Our parents are deceased. She lives in the house where we grew up. I have a hacienda near Coral Cove."

"North of here?"

"Yes. You got it. Obviously you're new around here."

I gave him my Boston history, a chat about my Latino mother and my German father, and how I ended up in Naples because of my job.

"Do you have a girlfriend, Paulo? A guy with your good looks probably does."

I shook my head. "I'm single. My last boyfriend was named Cooper. He decided he liked Irish guys instead of Latinos. I couldn't compete with that skin tone, and we broke up."

Manijo didn't at all seem taken aback by my queer confession. He sipped his Corona, enjoyed the beer, and eventually asked, "How long ago were you with Cooper?"

"Eight months. Last spring."

"Does he still talk to you?"

"Nope. We've both moved on. He's in Chicago, and I'm here in gator world."

"I'm single, too," the gator guy replied. "Lucia is begging me to get a man in my life and settle down."

"A man?" I inquired, wondering if I misheard him. "You're queer?"

He rubbed a massive palm up and down his chest in a rather seductive manner, shared a masculine laugh, and admitted, "Queer as Tinker Bell. What can I say? I like poles instead of holes."

"I didn't get that when we first met. I mean, I thought about it, but that was because I wanted to ..." I closed my yap, having said way too much. What did I want from the man, though? I wanted to suck his hard nipples, dive my wet and hungry lips against his tight navel, and travel my pointed tongue down and over his treasure trail, into his thatch of thick, triangular-shaped man-hair above his semi-erect knob. I wanted to lick and lap at the hairless flesh on his inner thighs. I wanted to pivot my mouth over his upright shaft and cover his tube of flesh with my narrow throat. I wanted to create a night with him that I could have titled 50 Shades of Gay and ...

"You're a sexy guy, Paulo. I rather like you. Shame on Cooper for ditching your cute ass."

"You like my gators more."

He shook his head. "Not really. I like to protect the gators."

"Because they're a lot like you. Strong. Unafraid. Hulking."

"And sometimes biting, don't forget."

"I can't see you as biting," I confessed.

"Keep me around, and you might see it."

187

Maybe I would do that. For now, though, I had other things on my mind. I sipped my Corona, swallowed the liquid down, wiped my mouth with the back of my right hand, felt subdued a touch, and said, "Tell me more about the gators."

"I'd like that."

"Something told me you would."

Manijo said, "Gators are the largest reptiles in North America. Unlike the crocodile they have a broad head. The beast's tail accounts for half its length. There are over one million alligators in the state of Florida."

"What do they eat besides fish?"

He rubbed the center of his plated chest and gradually moved his palm over a firm pec. Maybe he was teasing me, maybe not. "Turtles, birds, and other reptiles."

"How long do they live?"

"Up to fifty years in the wild."

"How do you handle them, gator guy?"

He gave me a wink with a smile, and replied, "Like a rough and wild Latino man in the bathtub, of course. Why don't I show you?"

We put our beers down on the kitchen counter, and he straddled me from behind. Once there, he said, "You have to be gentle with the gators." His breath lined the back of my neck, my right shoulder, and an earlobe. "Gators like to be loved, Paulo. They're very much like men. Open your heart to them, and all the good things come out."

I laughed. "You're shitting me."

"I am," he chortled and breathed on the splay of my neck again. He gathered my hands at the front of my stomach and added, "I usually use plastic straps to tie their little legs together. It doesn't hurt them. Then I wrap duct tape around their snapping jaws, just to keep them under control."

An erection built at my center. I was windswept and in a state of uncivil wonderment by his chatter, and his mound of beef next to my bottom. His chest grazed my back and sent me into a spin of excitement. How tantalizing it felt to be in a man's arms again, particularly a dark-skinned Latino's with massive biceps, a steel-plated chest, and a similar sexual hunger as my own.

My hands were released. Then one of his palms fell to my stomach, lifted my T-shirt, and grazed my fuzzy navel and sculpted abs. The appendage dropped a little more south and discovered the khaki-covered stiff tool between my thighs. "What do we have here, Paulo?"

"A very bad gator."

"You think I can tame it?"

"Maybe. I'm not sure. It's pretty wild."

"What do you say I give it a try?" he inquired, squeezing the tube of meat between my thighs, obviously into our gig, prepared to fully seduce me.

3. DESPAROS! (Shooting!)

I was spun around and kissed. Our mouths met with such tenderness and bliss. My heart pitter-pattered within my chest like a high school boy's. Everything about the kiss was poetically cleansing and a robust emotion that clarified that he wasn't about to hurt me in any way. His tongue delved into my mouth, pulled away, and delved again. Lips brushed together with hungry speed and agility.

The gator guy pulled away from me with a sting of spittle hanging off his bottom lip, which he hurriedly and sexily wiped away with the back of his left hand. With quickness and much skill, he reached down to my hips, discovered the bottom of my skin-tight T-shirt, and simply yanked the cotton up and over my head with a hefty pull. Entranced by my medium-sized build, Manijo studied my hairy pecs and the thin line of dark, masculine hair that traveled southward bound along the plane of my built chest, into my navel, and then continued down into my Rufskin shorts. His right fingers danced over a firm pec, pinched its tender nipple, and then traveled down and over each of my pumped abs. Fingertips grazed my navel and teasingly rerouted their travels northward, stopping at my chin. Once there, the stranger simply whispered in his thick Spanish, "*Te quiero.*" (I want you.)

We kissed again: tongues danced together; rounded chins melded and brushed each other; chests combined and nipples were glued together with male perspiration. That second kiss was an explosion of lust between us; an unstoppable rush of man-connected-to-man euphoria. Heat was discovered between us. Fire could have easily caught the alligator-damaged kitchen aflame. Sweat from our nicely built bodies could have sizzled the countertop, tile, and appliances because of its volcanic heat.

He removed his mouth from my mouth and it strayed down and along the veins that lined my shaven neck. His extended tongue brushed my left shoulder, left pec, and found a home at my nipple where he diligently sucked. His palms discovered my sides and slowly fell to my semi-muscular hips. Eventually their fingers found exactly what they were looking for and pulled my shorts and Aussiebum briefs down to my knees.

A mere few moments had passed, and the man's mouth was aligned to each of my abs at various times. Cautiously, he carried out his hunger for my upright body as he fell to his knees. What greeted him beneath my navel was nothing less than a manscaped patch of Latino curls above my eight inches of cut tool. A whiff was carried out as he inhaled my Panamanian scent and dark skin. He moaned with delight and ...

I almost fell to the kitchen floor as his lips met the top of my cock. The man's tongue waved around its cap and caused a grunt of fulfillment to lift out of my lungs and mouth. What followed was nothing less than spectacular. Manijo's mouth and throat fell over four inches of my dick and his head began to rock to and fro, providing the stiff piece of protein with overwhelming friction.

Intoxicated with each other, we blissfully swayed east and west in opposite but concurrent actions. Both of us huffed, grunted, and murmured in states of erotic satisfaction. Together, we slammed into each other, fell apart, and slammed into each other again. That action of cock-to-mouth ensued for the next three ... eight ... fourteen minutes, until I was ready to explode my goo into his system, coating his organs with my man-spurt, and drowning the handsome Latino with every drop of cream that I could muster.

No, I did not blow my thick and sticky churn inside the gator guy's mouth or throat. Instead, I quickly pulled away from him, and forced him to end his blowjob. I pushed on his shoulders and called down at the man on his knees, "Use that reptile on my ass, man ... I want to feel it inside me."

"I like when a man demands things from me." Manijo stood, planning his next sexual adventure with my skin, looking keen to connect with me yet another time, but in a different way.

"Of course you do."

In a matter of seconds, I was spun around at the island in the kitchen by his meaty hands. I placed my palms on its quartz top, ready for what the lizard guy had to offer to me.

Manijo spanked my tight bottom with his left palm and instructed, "Get out of your clothes and prop your leg up on the counter, guy. I have some work to do on your ass."

He did indeed, which prompted me to listen. Once I kicked my shorts and Aussiebums across the kitchen tile, I did as my ass-assailant instructed and stretched my leg upwards, settling it on the island. Once that was accomplished, the gator guy fell to his knees again and started his naughty mouth-duty on my rump.

Laps, licks, and a taste-festival of playful sorts were carried out on my bottom. A dozen or more pulls to my rear with his fingertips occurred. The man's extended tongue entered my fissure, exited, and entered again. That consistent action continued for numerous minutes: probing, pushing, pulling, pinching, and pounding. I huffed over the island, seemed to lose my breath, and felt somewhat dizzy. An intoxication of lust wavered from the base of my spine to the base of my neck because of his feisty work on my behind. My bottom was slapped, bitten, and fingered, sometimes all at the same time. The gator guy pleasured the both of us to the fullest.

Once, and only once, he pulled his face and fingers away from my taut rump, and chanted in his thick Spanish, "*Quiero que golpear.*" (I want to bang you.)

"Bang away, pal. Don't hold back. I'm ready for whatever you have to fuck me with."

# # # # #

Honestly, I got exactly what I asked for regarding the Latino behind me: a steady and rough pounding by his ten-inch, condom-coated flag. Manijo gripped my hips with his palms and fingers. One rush of his cock jammed and released in my man-crevice, which excelled into many. After ten minutes of his east and west motion, I was left in a surreal world of gator guy bliss. Perspiration flew off my forehead and drizzled the kitchen's appliances. Moans of glee echoed off the room's walls. The island, although solid at one time and tight against the floor, began to loosen and wobble to and fro because of the Latino's steady and relentless bolting.

Spanks occurred to my bottom. Bites were applied to my left shoulder. I felt the man's carved abdominals on my lower back. Again and again his hip-thrusts crushed me against the island. Numerous blasts with his ten-inch dick rushed inside my rump, quickly exited, and rushed inside again.

Together we glided, swayed, bucked, moaned, sweated, and carried out a wayward adventure between our naked bodies. Smacks, yelps, and grunts echoed off the stainless steel appliances. My flesh was gripped, licked, and kissed by the Ecuadorian positioned behind me. Suction over his pulsing and ramming cock was persistent. Congealed, we bumped into each other, pulled away, and collided yet again ... again ... and again.

"*Voy a hacer llegar,*" (I will make you come.) he groaned behind me, bashing my butt. "*Es que! ... No deje de!*" (Do it! ... Don't stop!)

Manijo reached around me with his right arm. His hand and fingers discovered the tool between my sweaty thighs and gripped its eight inches of length. With aggressive motion, he started stroking the cock up and down, attempting to get me off. Swift and perpetual jerking occurred. One cock-jack was followed by five ... nine ... twelve jacks.

"*Desparos!*" (Shooting!) echoed within the kitchen. As a jolt of deep contentment waved throughout my core ... as I became numb and confused in front of him ... as he continued to manhandle the beef between my legs, I sprayed my load on the floor, the side of the island, and spilled some of the hot cream on his right hand. Under his spell, heaving for breath, I felt chaotic and bliss-filled at the same time. Seed kept blowing out of my dick. Arc after arc was released with such ease and offered nothing less than an emotional state of euphoria.

Perhaps my orgasm sent him into his own condition of Latino elation. Two jacks to my ass were carried out ... a third ... a fourth, and then he released his junk from my behind. The condom was removed, and he informed in his native language, "*Estoy drenaje, tipo.*" (I'm draining, guy.) Manijo griped his cock in both palms and started to maneuver his fists in a north and south motion on the piece of meat. Over my right shoulder, spent and heavily breathing, I witnessed his hips in pulsing motion. The man was fucking his own hands, getting himself off. Four juts turned into eight and an echo of lust was heard within the kitchen, which was then followed by a spray of white and sticky cream over my spine, both shoulders, the back of my neck, and on both ass orbs. Manijo's load was everything I thought it would be: thick, bittersweet smelling, and glistened in a brilliant pearl-white hue.

After he came, he pulled me up to his sweaty chest. The gunk on my back sealed our bodies together. I turned my head to the left, and we kissed like lovers. The kiss lasted a minute or more, post-sexed and fiery, and bitingly delicious. And what followed was obvious: showers and a naked night's light sleep in his Latino arms as we listened for the camera and laptop to chirp with noise of a present alligator or two.

4. NAUGHTY YOU

I woke the following morning to an empty spot next to me on the bed, and a bill on the island in the kitchen for Curly and Larry's removal at dawn. Naked and pissed, I reached for the piece of manila-colored paper, began to study the gator guy's fee, and felt a smile of lost seduction surface at the edges of my lips. His hourly rate for the alligators' removals was scratched off. In its place was Manijo's script: "XXXOOO." Underneath the letters was a brief statement in red ink: "Naughty you. I will pick you up today at six for dinner, Paulo. We can listen for more gators in your canal tonight, or other things. Something tells me you want to wrestle with me again, which I'm willing to do." The note was signed MD and a tiny alligator drawing with sharp lines was etched below his initials.

The smile on my face grew, as well as an erection between my legs for the stranger and his needed touch. And there, that place where he had seduced me for the first time, I anticipated his return and aggressive man-handling, or whatever else he wanted to sexually carry out with my manly and Latino hide.

PANAMA DAN
(a novella)
By R. W. Clinger

ONE – AWAY WE GO

I wanted Panama Dan inside my tight and bulbous man-ass, having the hardest man-crush on the guy. His sexiness was the purest sin. One look at the five-eleven zoologist, and I melted like a puddle of pudding. Never did I miss his television show on WTUR, Channel 4, in Naples, Florida. My knees grew weak because of his Latino dark skin, scruffy cheeks, soft-brown eyes, and chiseled chest. The dimple in his chin just about rocked my world to slivers. The man was delicious like no one else I had ever seen, and local. Again I took in his thick jungle tan shorts that were snug against his hips, the khaki Guayabara shirt with its sanded print and six buttons, Wellco sage boots, and Tillie Airflo hat. When four o'clock at the office of Millbourne & Mosser Insurance struck, I made sure I was watching him, glued to his kids' show: *Panama Dan and His Wild Animal Adventures*.

"Close your mouth, darling, you're drooling," Vivian Lynn, my best friend of eight years, sidekick, fag-hag, confidant, personal assistant, and blonde bombshell whispered into my left ear. "He's really not all that."

"He *is* all that," I wooed, in lust for the man, glued to the forty-two-inch Sony.

Viv and I were alone inside the break room, which looked exactly like my office: tinted windows, beige carpet, stainless-steel everything. She rolled a seat up to my side, placed her head on my right shoulder, and added, "He is all that, isn't he?"

"In more ways than we know."

"Your Mr. Right."

"The man of my dreams."

"Your Prince Charming, Casper."

"So out of my league."

# # # # #

I knew too much about Panama Dan. Viv thought I was stalking him, but I wasn't. His real name was Danielito Eban Estar. His birthday was August 18. The sixth child of seven to Francisco and Isabel Estar of Bisira, Panama. He liked Italian food, had a fear of flying, never used drugs and drank a little, but didn't have a problem with his alcohol. He moved to Florida when he was eighteen, attended Miami University, and obtained a master's degree in zoology. He was thirty-two years old now and worked at WTUR for the last dozen years. The zoologist created his hit show from nothing, built it up to the empire it was, and grew wealthy. The Naples show went national in 2009. And the marketing behind it was a complete success: stuffed animals, board games, video games, lunch boxes, erasers, pencils, clothes, rub-on tattoos, cartoons, DVDs, music, and whatnots. Panama Dan made over ten million bucks last year. The man was definitely out of my league. Someone better than I. Royalty in Naples and the rest of the United States, which meant there wasn't a chance in hell he was ever going to be my boyfriend.

# # # # #

Viv consoled me as I watched Panama Dan play with a red-and-yellow coral snake on the Sony. She rubbed my back with a palm and said, "He talks to stuffed animals, Casper. Maybe he isn't your Mr. Right."

"Beatrice the Beaver is cool. Who doesn't love Beatrice? I would talk to her if I could."

"What about the hammerhead shark? Tell me you don't like him?" Viv inquired.

"I love Harry, and Panama Dan does, too. They are best friends. Harry always gets him out of trouble."

Viv clarified, "I'm rolling my eyes."

"What can I say? ... I like Danielito. So what if he talks to stuffed animals."

"He's a child in a man's body. There's a lot of immaturity there."

"He's young at heart, brilliant, and the man drips of money. The man is a genius in my eyes. He sold his idea and it worked."

"You have your own money."

"Not until my parents die."

"Twenty million, right?"

"Something like that. My accountant knows."

"You can buy a guy like Panama Dan when your parents finally kick the bucket."

I laughed at Viv.

She laughed at her own comment.

And Panama Dan started to sing a playful song about the snake wrapped around his right wrist.

"My God," I whispered, "he makes me hard." I readjusted my ass in the uncomfortable seat, felt a semi-boner pop to life between my legs, and sticky seepage at the top of my cock in their Pistol Pete underwear.

"This is sinful," Viv said. "You're getting hard over a kids' show. Isn't that illegal?"

"I'm getting hard for Panama Dan ... It has nothing to do with the kids."

"If I had a dick, I'd be hard for him, too," Viv added, removing her palm from my back. She stood, stretched, and said, "We should get back to work."

"Go without me. There's ten minutes of Danielito left."

"You'll have to stay late and make up the time."

"The guy is worth it."

Viv started to leave the break room, paused, and called over her right shoulder, "Don't be jacking off in here ... People use this place to eat."

I laughed.

She laughed.

And Panama Dan started to talk to Harry the hammerhead shark about snake bites.

Ten minutes later, Panama Dan smiled at his audience, waved goodbye, and sang, "Away we go, kids." He swung from one jungle vine to the next through the Panamanian jungle. Baby monkeys sang an upbeat song about jungle travels and Panama Dan. Sloths tossed bananas and coconuts to and fro. Stuffed toucans whistled. Baboons beat on drums. A tiger shifted its tail from left to right with the melody.

"So long, you succulent piece of Latino man-ass," I said to the Sony, stood, adjusted the hard dick underneath my khakis, and flicked the television off. Smiling from ear to ear, daydreaming about being locked in Panama Dan's arms, swinging from vine to vine in a navigated jungle with him, I eventually walked back to my office, sat behind my desk, and pushed insurance papers from my In Box to my Out Box, lusting for Danielito Estar the entire time.

TWO – ACCIDENTS HAPPEN (REAR-ENDED)

Flamingo Boulevard was jammed packed as usual. On a good day I could get back to Sunset Cove and my mini-hacienda in twenty-five minutes. That particular day in July was hell and ninety minutes stared me down. Trucks and cars of many sizes and different colors, busses, and taxis were bumper to bumper. At a snail's pace, we slid along the concrete. A Bentley Mulsanne was in front of me with a license plate that read BIGBITCH3. Behind its wheel was a brunette female texting. The Cube behind me was a candy apple red color. Two high school-aged Hispanics lounged in their seats and listened to loud rap music. I was driving a three-year-old Nissan Frontier, which was charcoal black, had a few dents, and terrible gas millage.

Putting along gave me enough time to check my pretty boy Latino face in the rearview mirror: curly cinnamon-colored hair, matching eyes, slender nose, Ecuadorian skin tone from my mother, no wrinkles around my mouth at thirty, clean-shaven cheeks, and a rounded chin. I was six-feet tall, not bad to look at, but not a supermodel, either. I was average any way a stranger wanted to gawk at me: financially, physically, and intellectually. Casper Reginaldo Dasio at your service. No one spectacular. Mundane. Plenty to work with to get a date, but a chain of men was not following me around as my personal sexual entourage. Too bad.

I was just about to phone Viv to see if she wanted to spend the ninety-three degree evening in my screen-covered pool with a pitcher of margaritas when an abrupt jar sent my Frontier jolting forward, snapping the seatbelt against my chest, between my solid and hairless pecs. Crunching metal sounded in my ears. My neck snapped forward with a quick motion, flew against the headrest's seat, and caused a slight dizzy spell to take over my consciousness. Horns blared. Jackasses yelled obscenities out their windows; I think it was the two teenagers behind me in their Cube. And glass sounded like it was cracking all around me.

My first instinct was to slam on the Frontier's brakes, which I executed with skill. The last thing I wanted to do was hit the Bentley and Miss BIGBITCH3. My second instinct was to throw the truck into park, which I carried out with speed. Next, I shook my head and realized that I had clearly been struck from behind; a rear-ender had occurred if there ever was one. It wasn't my first accident on Flamingo Boulevard, and it certainly wasn't going to be my last.

A quick glance in my rearview mirror told me that a bumblebee yellow Hummer had tried to squeeze between my rear bumper and the Cube's front bumper. Mr. Hummer totally misjudged the distance between the two vehicles and nailed me from behind; I would learn later that the Cube was unharmed and the high school kids drove away from the scene.

Road instinct for me kicked in again, and I popped the truck into drive, steered it off the side of the road, into Rushdie's Scuba Gear Underworld. In doing so, rubber smelled like it was burning, the truck barely moved, and the sound of metal continued to peel apart, providing a strange crinkling noise.

Mr. Hummer pulled into the empty lot behind me. I sat in my Frontier and attempted to calm down. My heart raced within my chest, my neck throbbed, and my hands were jittery. After a few seconds of calmness, I gathered my Millbourne & Mosser insurance card, registration, and license. Ready to battle with Mr. Hummer, I climbed out of the Frontier, stepped into the steeping heat, and ...

To my surprise, low and behold, I immediately decided to forever bow to the queer gods of a distant heaven. Shock discovered me as I made eye contact with the Hummer's owner: the sexy and alluring, drop dead gorgeous and Latino television star, Panama Dan!

Yes, my mouth fell ajar, and I thought I would simply drop to the shell-covered parking lot in hopes that Mr. Hot of the Block would pick me up in his hulking arms. Sultry sparks of man-lust immediately burst from every pore on my average-size and average-looking body. A wave of excitement rushed through my center and caused the tool between my legs to go instantly semi-hard. Perspiration lathered my cheeks and forehead. Dizziness swept over me, and a loss of oxygen occurred. My legs started to tremble, and I believed my tongue was hanging out of my mouth like a dog's.

There was my Mr. Prince Charming, the man of my ultimate queer dreams, right before me. A knight in shining armor who was wearing skin-tight shorts the color of the Mojave Desert. A beefcake of a man in his tight T-shirt who I imagined would jack a load out of his nine-inch tube of veined rod, into my open mouth, feeding me his bittersweet cream. Mr. Perfect. Mr. Roll-Me-Over-And-Fuck-Me-Hard. Mr. Debonair and Marry Me. Just what I was waiting to have ram into the rear of my Frontier, among other items of interest that I owned.

"Shit," he swore, squinting his eyes and studying the damage to my truck: crinkled bumper and side panel, mutilated wheel well, fucked up tail light, among other issues. Panama Dan rubbed the back of his right hand across his mouth and added, "What the fuck was I thinking, man?"

My father said that a man who used vulgarities was a man who had a limited vocabulary. My father was dead, though – God love him. In truth, I found a man who swore sexy as hell and a total turn-on. A potty mouth on a man was a pure sign of masculinity in my opinion; an Alpha male characteristic that would often cause me to drop my summer shorts, spin around, and wiggle my ass for his upright and ready-to-ram-me cock. Bottom line: the more the potty mouth on a man, the more horny I became.

I kept my work chinos and Pistol Petes up on my hips and consoled him with: "No worries. The damage can be repaired."

He shook his head with a pissed off look on his adorably handsome face and insisted, "I'm sorry, guy. Really, I am. I misjudged the space between you and the Cube. My bad."

"Our car insurance companies can handle it. We can switch information, and they can do the dirty work."

Panama Dan nodded his head, continuing to take in the Frontier's damage. "I don't think you can drive it. Your bumper is kissing your left, rear tire."

I wondered if it would be too much to ask the Latino stud if he wouldn't mind kissing my rear. Such a request was out of the equation at the moment, though. Instead, I said, "I have a friend who can tow me for free."

No lie there. Toby Shant worked in the field for Millbourne & Mosser; one of my straight buddies who wouldn't mind lending me a hand. He lived a few miles away and could be at Rushdie's Scuba Gear Underworld in just a few minutes. All was good.

Panama Dan ignored my comment as he bent over in front of the tire, pulled metal and plastic away from its rubber with his bare hands, admired his labor, and grunted in his thick Spanish accent, "I think you can drive it now. The tire doesn't look punctured."

Positioned behind him, I studied his tight and bulbous ass, his strong looking back, and wide shoulders. My gaze took in the man like a glass of iced tea on the hottest day in Naples. I hungrily moistened my upper lip with a quick tongue-lick and thought of the nastiest things that he could maybe accomplish with my naked bottom. I was mannerly, though, and cleared my throat. Then I decided to toy with him a touch and asked, "Don't I know you from somewhere?"

Mr. Hummer stood and turned around. The man struck me with his pearly white smile and a glint of humility in the corners of his butterscotch-brown eyes. He held out his right paw for me to shake and finally introduced himself, "You probably know me from television. I'm Panama Dan."

I shared a befuddled and weak look with him that told the Latino beefcake that I hadn't the slightest clue what he was talking about. Then I shrugged my shoulders and shook my head, playing with him.

"The kids' show on WTUR?"

Again, just to tease him, I shook my head. I jacked his hand and replied, "I'm sorry. I've never heard of Panama Dan."

"I do the same thing that Jeff Corwin does, and Jack Hanna."

I lit up with a polite smile. "I know those guys. Very famous. Very handsome. They like to play with animals."

He continued to smile at me, although part of him was probably deflated inside because I claimed I didn't know of his successful kids' show. He seemed to forget about his career then and said, "I'm Danielito Estar. Nice to meet you."

"Casper Dasio," I said, and allowed his strong paw to pump my average one. "A pleasure."

"Again, Casper, I'm sorry about this."

"Accidents happen," I replied, winked at him in a suggestive manner, released my hand from his, and found my insurance information to share with the zoologist.

THREE – EAT ME UP, PANAMA MAN

Twenty-four hours later I received an unfamiliar phone number on my cell. I thought about not taking the call, but what the hell. What did I really have to lose, right? I stopped eating a slice of vegetable lasagna and Caesar salad, discovered the Sprint phone next to the Noritake plate on the three-person table in front of me, and pressed the TALK button. "This is Casper. How may I help you?"

My greeting sounded professional, but it had to be. A few of my clients had been given the number and were maybe trying to contact me because of an emergency, or they simply needed answers to basic questions that pertained to their insurance policies.

"Mr. Dasio?" The voice was deep and sexy, somewhat alluring and quite masculine. I didn't know who exactly it belonged to, but was interested in finding out, since it was Latino.

"Yes. This is he."

"Casper, this is Danielito Estar."

"Who?" The tone in my voice clearly stated confusion, although I really knew who it was. The one and only Panama Dan that I had secretly fallen in love with while watching his show on WTUR for the past year.

"I bumped into your truck yesterday on Flamingo Boulevard."

"You bumped into my what?" I played with him, grinning from ear to ear.

"Your truck. I rear-ended, Carlos."

"Yes. Of course. Now I remember you." Truth was how could I forget the beefy Latino man and his handsome voice, eyes, hair, and broad shoulders, among other sexy body parts that designed his impeccable frame? In the past day, I had thought of him fucking me numerous times, rear-ending me without my clothes on again and again. Sometimes with his clothes on and his cock exposed, and other times completely naked. Either way I imagined the zoologist, I stung with a rigid-hard boner spiked between my thighs. Other side effects included: a rise in my temperature, sweat on the back of my arms, and a shortness of breath. All were clear signs of my unconditional lust for the local television star. And all caused me to grow nervous and somewhat dizzy until they passed.

"Casper, our transaction is not over."

Of course our transaction was over. Both of us exchanged insurance information, license numbers, telephone numbers, home addresses, e-mail addresses, and cell phone numbers.

# # # # #

And following his Hummer-bump into the rear of my Frontier, we parted the scene of the accident on good terms: masculine nods of our pretty boy heads and shaking hands.

Panama Dan had apologized to me for his careless driving, which I accepted in full.

Thereafter, I drove away in my mangled Frontier and traveled the three miles to Justin's No-More Junkers, one of my straight friend's garages. There, my truck could be repaired at a minimal fee and be back on the road in no time, thanks to Justin's skilled and Latino grease monkeys.

Following the drop-off at the garage, Justin decided to give me a lift home. Think Chris Pine with those dazzling blue eyes and five o'clock shadow. Not Latino, which is what I liked in a man, but close enough.

Justin drove like a maniac: too fast, carelessly, without patience. He zoomed to my house with very little to say. Once he dropped me off at my mini-hacienda, he called over his Audi's front seat, "I'll call you about your Frontier. Don't worry about it, pal."

"Sounds great."

"No worries."

"Not when my truck is in your hands," I admitted, told him goodbye, and was finally home from work.

# # # # #

"How is our transaction not over?" I asked Panama Dan, fully interested in what his reply was going to exactly entail. My voice reeked of cockiness, but it wasn't intentional. Honestly, I didn't mind hearing from the stud since he sent my sexual hunger for his delicious looking bod into an unstoppable spin and powerful overdrive.

He cleared his throat. Was he nervous? Maybe. Did he always do that? I didn't know. Then he calmly replied, "I really don't know how I ended up with your insurance card, but did. I must have accidentally kept it and failed to give it back to you yesterday when we exchanged information."

Before I responded, I leaned a bit forward, pulled out my G&B wallet from a back pocket, opened it, and thumbed through all of its contents: two credit cards, Florida license, gas card, registration information for the Frontier, AAA card, and a receipt for a Chinese dinner with Viv from two nights ago. To my surprise, I didn't discover my insurance card inside the wallet and informed the sexy Latino of such.

"I can drop it off if you'd like. What do you say?"

"I would hate to impose on your tight schedule, Danielito. You're a very busy man."

He sort of chuckled on his end of the line, but I really wasn't sure why. "It's hardly an imposition, if you want to know the truth. Honestly, I wouldn't mind seeing you again."

"Me?" I questioned, completely caught off guard by his last statement.

"Yes, you."

"Why me?"

Our banter sounded ridiculous for two adult men. How young and innocent we acted, immature and rather mundane.

"Because you have all the qualities I'm looking for in a guy. You are single, aren't you?"

"Terribly and unfortunately."

"And you're queer, like me, right?"

My God, he was becoming quite personal, and somewhat intrusive, but I seemed to enjoy it no less. When was the last time a local man had taken an interest in me? I couldn't even remember. I wasn't pertaining to one-night stands either: men who I sometimes picked up at the queer bar called Below the Sun and fucked around with them, getting my rocks off. I meant a guy who was serious about me and saw more than my dark-skinned good looks, which consisted of my Latino skin, impeccable smile, and nicely crafted chest. I had a soul, and a brain. Did Panama Dan get that? Maybe so. Maybe not. Only time would tell.

Before I could respond to his arrangement of dropping off my insurance card, he cleared his throat again, which was definitely a sign of being nervous, and added, "I have a better idea."

"I like a man with ideas." It was the truth. Who wanted dead weight around for company? No one.

"I want to have dinner with you tomorrow night."

"Wednesday?"

"Yes. If you're not busy, of course."

"Trust me, I'm never busy." A sudden alarm went off in my head, something thunderous and daunting, and ... Danielito wanted to invite me over to his house for dinner, eat me up, and toss me to the curb. Panama Dan was like every other man out there: find me, fuck me, and dump me.

"Maybe we can change that, Casper. What do you say?"

204

I thought about telling him to fuck off, that I didn't want a one-night stand with him, that I was worth more, and that my skin was valuable and I wasn't about to just hand it to him for a night's pleasure. I kept my trap closed for some reason, though, and agreed to his gig. "Tomorrow night, right?"

"Yes."

"What time?"

"Seven o'clock."

"I can do that."

"I hope so."

"Bring a suit. I have a pool."

Again, I agreed. Before ending the cell call between us, I asked for his address, although I already knew it, and I thought to myself: He's playing a game with me. The guy just wants my ass. I'm sure of it. Whatever.

FOUR – BONER APPETIT

2787 Gator Drive had a sprawling driveway constructed out of seashells. The beachfront estate was called La Selva, which meant The Jungle in Spanish. Three bright-white stucco balconies overlooked the Gulf. Projecting downspouts hung from the house's flat roof. A loggias wrapped around the right side of the edifice. Palm, willow, and eucalyptus trees decorated the property. A fenced-in pit of massive gators was to the far right. In the distance, peeking through the high palms was a giraffe. An elephant sounded in the distance. An ostrich walked around the left side of the house and greeted me. Its beady eyes suggested betrayal, not that I cared. Domestic cats of different hues were sprawled on the front verandah.

Panama Dan met me in the drive, pushing Brutash, his pink-necked pet ostrich away from me, preventing the animal from pecking my eyes out. The estate owner caught my interest immediately because he sported a pair of beach sandals and Pistol Pete shorts in periwinkle blue. The material was snug around his muscular contour and detailed his shape: two-inch thick cock and ripped thighs. My stare studied his inflated pecs and their brown nipples, which were oversize. The man's navel was puckered and a string of black hair fell into the pair of shorts. Danielito seductively rubbed his cut abs, smiled at me, and shared, "You came."

205

Not yet, but I wanted to on his massive chest or in his mouth.

He hugged me; a handshake was obviously out of his repertoire. In doing so, his bulky chest aligned with my own: my T-shirt covered pecs met his bare ones; our stomach's brushed together; cotton-concealed cocks kissed for the first time. His embrace was mighty and unyielding – exactly what I wanted at that time from a chiseled man.

"Did you bring a suit, Casper?" He lightly patted my back, gave it a rub, and eventually pulled away from me.

I did bring a suit. And a towel. And a pair of flip-flops to use at the pool. "It's in the car."

"A rental, I presume?"

"Ford Fiesta."

"Very gay, but likable."

"I'm sure Ford has sold many of them."

"To all the gay guys in the world." The zoologist walked me into the house where I met: Perilya, a giant gray pig; Ortho, a Tamandua anteater; and Victor, a scentless skunk.

Following my introduction to his friendly animals, he asked if I wanted something to drink.

"An iced tea will do fine."

"Long Island alright?"

"What the hell."

I was given a tall glass of the cocktail and then taken on a tour of La Selva, which consisted of four bedrooms, two rhinos, many turtles, a handful of snakes, and twenty or more domestic cats, none of which I could remember their names. Once the tour ended, he escorted me through his quartz kitchen, outside, and on a jungle-like deck where he had planned for us to share dinner.

Ferns, palms, and a variety of Florida flowers (swamp sunflowers, goldenrod, and porterweed) outlined the deck. Beyond the deck was a narrow, cobblestone pathway that led to the Gulf. Danielito pointed to the trail and said, "I have a decastyle portico out there. It's quite nice to sit in while the sun sets."

"Great place you have here."

He was humble and said, "It's home. Nothing special. Everyone needs a place to sleep."

We walked back into La Selva again where I enjoyed my strong drink at the quartz bar. I watched the bare-chested cutie prepare us dinner: artichoke salad, grilled salmon with gazpacho sauce, and a side of Napolitano skillet pasta. For desert, he claimed, "We're having raspberry cookies."

"My favorite."

He turned around from his work at the counter and winked at me. "You're a tease."

"Some guys think so."

I studied him at work. My eyes consumed his broad shoulders, splay of muscular back, beautiful ass, thick thighs, and his arms in motion. Shame on me for wanting to stand behind him, pull his Pistol Pete shorts down, bend him over the counter, and allow my extended tongue to have its feisty and pleasurable way with his rump.

"Why are you single?" he asked over his right shoulder, grilling the salmon.

"I have no idea."

"You a serial killer?"

"Not that I'm aware of."

"A heartbreaker?"

"No. I don't play that game."

"A cocktease?"

"No."

He spun around with grace, held a filleting knife in his right hand and a wedge of lemon in his other hand. "Let me guess, you don't fuck around with guys because you have a religious deal with God."

I shook my head, took a long sip of my drink, swallowed, and replied, "Not quite."

"You're really straight?"

I laughed at that. "Never. I like dick a little too much. Plus, I have a thing for male Latino ass."

He waved his knife at me and admitted, "Me, too."

"I would have never guessed you liked cock. You look like a ladies' man all the way."

"Trust me, if I get you out of your clothes, that wouldn't even cross your mind."

Again, I laughed. "Although I think you're the sexiest guy in Florida, my clothes are not coming off."

"We'll see about that." He gave me another wink, turned back to his preparation of the food, and showed off his back and ass to me yet again, which I found utterly pleasurable.

The history of Panama Dan was learned over our shared dinner on the patio. He liked to read mysteries, attempted painting and failed, and never missed a Sunday off. He claimed he would never live anywhere else in the world. "Naples is my home. These people are my people. No matter how famous I become." His last boyfriend was Samuel Batting, a blond assistant that he became too close to. He added, "Never mix business with pleasure. That was a mistake I made." I learned Samuel enjoyed Danielito's cock more than he did his job, which he failed to do. The man's work piled up and ... Panama Dan had to fire him. The hardship passed quickly. He said he ate a lot of ice cream to get over Samuel. He ran, too, but he really wasn't fond of the task. "I like to take care of my body. What fag doesn't?"

I told him about my parents, my job as an insurance salesperson, and the two thousand dollars' worth of damage that he caused to my Frontier. I mentioned my likeness for cats, although I didn't own one. Topics entailed making cocktails, Jane Goodall, the Naples Zoo, and how I liked pandas.

He laughed at me.

I laughed at him.

# # # # #

We drank heavily, although we probably shouldn't have. We seemed to have a bit of chemistry together. The conversation between us was smooth, and there wasn't a single pause that floated in the space that separated us. We flirted with each other, playing a dating game of sorts, careful not to give into some heavy petting or kissing.

And eventually dinner and desert had ended, and he asked, "Do you want to get your suit and take a swim together?"

"Sure. I think I'd like that."

"I'll meet you by the pool."

"I won't be long." I stood and ... something cold and scaly glided along my right ankle. It was smooth and ridged at the same time, somewhat soft, but not really. I looked down and saw a red, white and yellow snake slither around my ankle. A gasp escaped me and every pimple on my body rose with fear.

"What's going on?" Danielito asked, obviously aware of the fear on my face, and my sudden surprise.

"Snake ... ankle ... bite," the words tumbled out of me, but they made no sense. I wondered what kind of snake it was.

My dinner date stood and shuffled quickly around the table. In a matter of seconds he prattled, "It's Butch. Stay still. He usually slithers away from humans when they're around and leaves them unharmed. Let me handle him."

"Butch?" I questioned, fearing that I was going to be bitten.

"He lives in the wet grass to the right of the house. I don't know what he's doing out here."

"What kind of snake is he?"

"A coral, which are very typical for Florida."

What transpired next was predictable and scared the hell out of me. When Panama Dan slowly bent over and went to reach for Butch, the snake decided to bite me. Sharp pain arced through my right ankle because of the snake's pointed but rather small fangs. Butch released his neurotoxin into my system with speed, unclenched his bite, and ...

"Fuck," Danielito chanted, "the little shit bit you." He snatched up the snake in two hands and vanished off the deck with Butch. Less than a minute later, he was at my side without the slithery beast in his hands. My date fell to his knees next to me, investigated my bitten ankle, and shared, "You need some antivenom right away. Butch's bite has the power to take down your respiratory system in just a few hours."

"I only have some minor pain."

He looked up at me, shared a serious look, and said, "Trust me, you can die from this. Let me handle it."

I think I passed out then, but not from the snake bite. Panic maybe settled into my core, and I felt dizzy and light-headed all in a matter of seconds. Before blackness surfaced behind my closed eyes, a string of thoughts quickly zigzagged through my mind: Panama Dan is sexy as hell, but dangerous. First, he hit me with his Hummer. Now, his snake bit me. What's next? And why do I still like him?

FIVE – REGARDING LAST NIGHT

I came to inside an unfamiliar bedroom decorated in different shades of green. Vanilla-colored tile covered the floor. A single window overlooked the Gulf. A doorway escaped to a balcony and a bright, new day. Warm wind found its way into the bedroom and caressed my naked shoulders and cheeks. My shorts, shirt, and sandals were missing. I felt hungry as my stomach rumbled. The room smelled like lilacs although there wasn't a vase of them to be seen; their scent was strong and almost overwhelming.

Just as I was about to climb out of the queen-size bed, Panama Dan entered. He was bare-chested, sported a pair of bright red Rufskin shorts, and no sandals. He carried a bamboo tray in his hands, which he placed on my right side, next to my chest. The tray held a glass of orange juice, a plate of scrambled eggs, and two slices of buttered rye.

"You're awake, sleepy head."

"What happened? And what time is it?" I knew it was daylight, and my right ankle stung a bit and felt itchy. Maybe my new friend could fill me in on the rest.

Danielito stood at the base of my bed and detailed the tale of Butch and the snake's biting episode. "It's about ten o'clock in the morning. You passed out from shock before I gave you an antivenom. Do you remember me injecting you with it?"

I shook my head. "I can't recall anything."

"I'm not surprised. You've been sleeping like a baby all through the night. Are you hungry?"

"Ravenous." I sat up in the bed, removed the glass of orange juice from the tray, and guzzled it down.

My host discovered a bamboo chair, slid it from the corner to the side of the bed, and sat down. In doing so, he coached, "Thatta boy. Drink and eat up. You have some energy to replenish."

I felt dizzy and confused, exhausted and undernourished. The orange juice tasted remarkably soothing. I downed the remaining drops, eventually lifted the china plate off the tray, and helped myself to the eggs and toast. Between the delicious bites, I inquired, "What happened to my clothes?"

He chuckled, blushing. "You looked uncomfortable with them on, so I decided to take them off."

"What else did you do to me while I was asleep?"

"Nothing that you should be concerned about. I was a complete gentleman." He leaned over and took a slice of the toast from the china plate, nibbled at a corner, and placed it back where he had found it. After chewing up the corner and swallowing it down, he inquired, "How's the ankle feel?"

"The good one ... or the one that your snake removed?"

He chuckled at me in a playful manner. "I'm really sorry about last night. Butch was out of hand."

"Butch obviously doesn't like me."

"Not to worry, my friend, I like you."

"You're just saying nice things to me, so I don't sue you."

Again, he chuckled, which was boyishly cute and rather sexy at the same time. "Can I ask you a serious question, Mr. Dasio?"

I shoveled a mouthful of eggs into my hatch, started to chew them up in a busy manner, and nodded my head.

He studied my chest like an art piece: dipping navel, ribbed abs lining stomach, and pert nipples because of the summer's soft wind. His eyes strayed to my shoulders. Although they weren't beefy like his, they were still nicely defined. Surely he wanted to reach out and graze one of his fingertips against a part of my body. Never had a man analyzed me with such bliss tucked in the folds of his eyes and handsome smile.

"Why are you looking at me like that, Danielito?"

"Like what?" His stare strayed to my white boxer-briefs and the tubular package that was hidden under its cotton. I was quite sure he wanted to peel the material away with his teeth and lips, fulfilling a hungry desire for my skin, and other manly details that comprised my body.

"You look like you want to accomplish something naughty with me."

"Just a kiss perhaps."

Our eyes locked together and held for the longest of seconds. My heart thumped erratically within my chest and the back of my hands started to perspire because of nervousness. No longer was I interested in the meal on the bamboo tray. Other things had surfaced regarding my appetite. Like the man sitting by the strange bed, absorbing my Latino skin, and everything about me. "That seems innocent enough."

"It is harmless."

"Prove it," I challenged him. "But only if you really want to."

The moment turned rather naughty, I admit. Danielito leaned into me, closed his eyes, and applied his lips to mine. Hunger was found. Saliva mixed. The single kiss became something bold and strong and relentless. My world was knocked off its axis, and my limbs became weak. I lost oxygen and my chest rose and fell with excitement. His kiss was intense and unstoppable.

He didn't pull away.

I didn't pull away.

Something wildly erotic stirred between us. The blending was unlimited and irreversible. Had the country started to rock to and fro by a wicked earthquake? Did a volcano erupt and fill the bedroom with searing lava, melting our flesh together? I thought so on all accounts, weak against him, and without trepidation regarding our intimate connection.

When did he eventually pull away from me? Three minutes? ... Six minutes? ... Nine minutes? I was unsure. I wanted the kiss to last longer, and other things to occur between two naked men. How greedy I became for the man to join me on the queen-size bed where we could meld together even more with steeping erections, racing heartbeats, hungry mouths, and unrefined ejaculations.

Such erotic actions failed to transpire, though. Instead, the man sat in his chair and smiled at me. His Panamanian face turned a rose madder hue with embarrassment and a noticeable longing. He simply whispered, keeping eye contact with me, "You're late for work."

I was, by a few hours. Jokingly, I inquired, "Are you kicking me out?"

"Never." He shook his head and continued to blush. Perhaps he was still caught up in our shared kiss, lost within the refined texture of its folded memory. "You can stay if you'd like."

His handsome eyes told me that he wanted me to spend the whole day with him and not leave anytime soon. I had responsibilities to carry out, though: my job being on the top of its list, grocery shopping, and paying my bills on-line. "Thanks for the option, but I really have to go."

"When will I see you again?" His right hand reached forward and grazed my chin in a soft, careful, and caring manner.

"This weekend. Saturday. We can spend the day together. What do you say?"

"I like that idea."

"Me, too." Something romantic glimmered at the corners of his tranquil eyes. I really wasn't sure exactly what their pools suggested (lust ... love ... tenderness ... longing ... something between a zoologist and insurance salesman that could last for years to come ... Latino men combined by a carnal hunger and cocks) but could have easily fallen under their remarkable spell.

"My clothes, may I please have them?"

He fetched them for me. While passing the heap to me, he said, "Really, you don't have to go."

"I must."

"You do?"

"I do."

"Such a pity. We could have had a great time together today. I'm sure something exciting could occur between us."

"Saturday I can be yours. Call me with the details."

# # # # #

Less than ten minutes later, I was driving away in my rented Ford Fiesta, chatting on my phone with Viv; she had the day off and was spending it at Tarpon Springs with her wealthy aunt. I spilled all of the juicy details with her pertaining to my date with Panama Dan. At first, she was outraged that I had been bitten by Butch, but then immediately calmed down when she learned that Danielito had given me an antivenom and took care of me.

"Obviously you were in good hands," she admitted.

"I was. He's one of the best zoologists in the world. The man knows what he's doing. I wasn't even in any danger."

"It sounds like you really want to see him again."

"I do. We had a great time together. It was simple and sweet, and he was a complete gentleman, minus the Butch incident."

"I bet you'll be in the sack with him in less than a week."

"Never," I laughed, although she was probably right.

"Trust me, I know you better. You get something in your head and then you want it in your ass."

I laughed at her, rolled my eyes, and barely kept the Fiesta on the road. Eventually, I said, "I have to go. Home calls for me, a shower and shave, and then work."

"We'll chat latter, darling. Thanks for the update."

I glowed inside, delighted with our friendship, her emotional care for me, and invaluable support. Following our conversation, I beamed from ear to ear with a smile and thought of Panama Dan: the way he rubbed my chin and his eyes twinkled with likeness. Half of me wanted to spin the Fiesta around and drive back to La Selva to hold him in my arms for the rest of the day. That was a preposterous thought, though. Life called for me instead, and I followed its yelp with struggle. Danielito would have to wait for my return in the meantime, and survive by the memory of our date tucked in the folds of his mind, between his temples.

SIX – CLUB SUSTANTIVO (HEAT)

I had other friends besides Vivian Lynn, of course. Queer, manly friends that I was platonic with. Latino queens that I went clubbing with and had an unbelievable time in their company. Friends that I had met at Miami University and kept after graduating. Carlos. Alejandro. Silas. All three were from Nicaragua. All three were single and worked at Lord Glass. LG specialized in making/shipping drinking glasses. Blue collar men with Latino good looks, beefy bods, and relentless sexual hungers. Men who were players to their cores. Jockish pricks who picked up young and attractive American boys of age. Young men that they wanted to fuck, having no care to know their names. Men who made me laugh, feel boyish, and knew how to have a good time that was maybe considered dangerous.

Friday nights we hung out at Club Sustantivo. Once there, we partied like kings. The place was always hopping, wall-to-wall gorgeous fags of different sizes and colors. Marines. Professors. Twinks. Cops. Clergymen. Politicians. Bears. Office boys. College jocks. Cowboys. You name it, they were there. Queer rock filled the underground club: Humble Tripe, Girlyman, Pansy Division, Hey There Cowboy. The place rocked it out.

Two bars shaped like a split diamond were positioned in the center of the club. Bare-chested jocks with clean shaven chests served longneck bottles of beer, fabulous appletinis, and whiskey shots, among other festive drinks. Red, yellow, blue, green, violet, orange, and silver-white beams of light flashed on and off overhead. Dance floors in front of the bars welcomed energetic fags to get their grooves on. Drugs were present: meth, coke, Rugby, Splied, and Yuff. The bathrooms were not a place to piss. Instead, one fucked inside, preoccupied with the notion of getting off. Sex lurked within every corner of the gay bar. Blowjobs were carried out against the walls. A twink was getting his ass licked by a Marine. Two cops were kissing on the dance floor; both had their cocks pulled out of their denim jeans, connecting. The place was wickedly fun. Sweat flew off dancing bodies. Nipples were kissed and licked. Cocks were sucked. Beer was splashed over college bodies. Tips added up for the bartenders.

Silas found me at the bar. His sultry brown eyes locked with mine. I knew that he was on an upper, hyper and blown away. Sweat clung to his forehead and cheeks. The bear was shirtless and sported broad shoulders, pumped pecs, and swollen abs. He held a beer in his right hand, which was almost empty. I had seen him with a blond boy only minutes before, dancing and kissing next to a wall. I imagined Silas would take the boy home and have his way with him. History proved that Silas sometimes took two boys home on the same night, disposing of both after he had his sexual way with the pair. "You look lonely," he said, cuddling up to me.

"I'm not. Just enjoying the sites and my drink." I was on my third whiskey sour and felt quite comfortable. My goal was not to get drunk, since I had to drive home. In truth, I would probably have to take a cab home. Better safe than sorry, right? Too many guys at the club got blitzed and climbed behind the wheel. Arrests occurred. Accidents were accomplished. Deaths sometimes happened. I didn't want anything bad to transpire to me or someone else. I was sure to be responsible and end up back home without any damage accomplished whatsoever.

"Don't you want to get laid tonight?"

I shook my head. "There's a guy I'm interested in."

"Who's that?"

I told Silas all about Panama Dan. In fact, I rambled a bit, which maybe was overwhelming for my friend.

"I commend you, *chico*," Silas said, patting my shoulder. "You have more morals than I do. I simply use men up and toss them away."

"We're all different. To each his own."

"You're so cool not to pose judgment on me. Some guys would think I was a slut."

I shook my head. "Silas, we've been friends for a long time. I get you. Life is all about having fun. You certainly have your fill of that, don't you?"

He took the last of his beer down and placed his empty bottle on the bar in front of me. The bartender exchanged it for a new one.

I called out to the hazel-eyed bartender with his golden boy pecs, "I got this one." I tossed a few bucks on the bar, handed Silas his beer, and said, "Enjoy."

"Thanks, bud."

"Any time."

Silas was about to say something else, but his blond friend leashed his arms around my friend's bearish middle, and pulled him away, onto the dance floor.

Not even five minutes later, and I was hit on by a Mario Lopez look-alike at the club. The steamy Latino found a seat beside me at the bar, clinked his vodka on the rocks against my whiskey sour, and introduced himself, "I'm Fredrico. A lot of guys call me Freddy."

"Nice to meet you, Freddy. I'm Casper."

"Like the ghost."

I frowned, hating when people said that. "Not quite."

He apologized, which I totally respected. Then he asked, "You alone?"

I nodded my head, studying his lime green tank top and his chiseled chest. Freddy had a tiny star-shaped scar on his left shoulder, but it was hardly noticeable. "For tonight I am."

"You want to dance?"

"I can't dance. I might be Latino, but I don't have the dancing gene in me."

"That's too bad. I would love to get close to you on the dance floor." He moved a hand to my T-shirt covered chest and pressed his palm over my right nipple. He gave the pec a gentle squeeze and rolled fingertips over its nipple. Following his suggestive act, he inquired, "Would you like to fuck me, Casper?"

"I would." Why was I nervous? The party boy was like every other guy in the club: horny, hard, and ready to fuck me. I shouldn't have been nervous. The thin hairs rose on my limbs. Perspiration formed under my arms.

"You think I look like Mario Lopez?"

"I do."

"What do you say we go into the bathroom and you can lean me over the American Standard sink and have your way with my tight ass?"

I swallowed saliva down the back of my throat, took a sip of my cocktail, leaned into his left ear, and said, "Although your offer is tempting, I can't do that. I'm holding out for a zoologist."

He backed away from me with speed, acting like my honesty was a shock to his system. "I thought you were single?"

"I am."

"But you have a zoologist in your life, right?"

I clarified, "I'm trying to obtain a zoologist in my life. I don't have him yet."

Freddy took a chug of his vodka on the rocks, swallowed the strong drink down, wiped the back of his left hand across his beautiful mouth, and said, "Will you let the zoologist fuck you?"

"I probably will."

"I like that idea," he admitted. Then he added, "You're not going to fuck around with me, right?"

I shook my head. "Sorry."

"I respect your honesty, man." He shook my hand and off he went with his Mario Lopez looks in search of a guy to bend him over the club's bathroom sink. Freddy shuffled away, on his sex-quest, and left me to my whiskey sour.

To my utter surprise, I saw Panama Dan on the opposite side of the club. He talked to a gingerhead with plump lips and sparkling, blue eyes. The television star was dressed in his normal attire: khaki shorts and shirt, bootie socks, and boots. The two talked for quite some time, kissed once, and drank from the same beer bottle. When the bottle of beer was empty, Gingerhead ordered a new one.

Danielito did not see me opposite him. Once, his gingerhead friend made eye contact with me, but just for a second. Their ten-minute conversation turned into fifteen minutes. They laughed, connected their chests together, and held hands. Then the zoologist took the redhead into a semi-dark corner where they heavily kissed with extended tongues. Their hands found inflated pecs, sweaty biceps, rounded shoulders, and ribbed stomachs. Heat was discovered between them and an irreversible blending that I could not pull myself away from watching.

What transpired within that corner was nothing less than wayward pleasure between the two men. Gingerhead pressed the zoologist against the wall and lathered the man's neck with his tongue and passion-driven kisses. Panama Dan's shirt was ripped open – a plastic button or two went flying off the material and became lost within the club – and his Latino torso was braised with steady licks, a few bites, and some minor sniffing. The man's pert nipples and mounded abs were enjoyed by the redhead. Then, Danielito's club friend fell to his knees, unbuckled the zoologist's khaki shorts, and removed the nine inches of cock out of the material and started to blow him off.

I shouldn't have watched but couldn't help myself. Truth was ... I should have simply walked out of the club and let the two men go at it without my voyeuristic and uncivil behavior. How nasty, yet erotic it was to view such a scene. How unfair. How ...

I stayed at the club. God, why did I stay? There, I watched that naughty and dirty act, caught up in its nasty-niceness, observing every second of their disgusting and pleasurable intimacy unfold.

Gingerhead's face moved to and fro with speed. His right hand held onto Danielito's swollen shaft. When the redhead needed oxygen, he pulled his lips and throat off the zoologist's tool. He licked the man's balls, one after the other, and held up Panama Dan's crank by its rounded cap. Following his tongue-laps, Gingerhead continued to blow the man who lived at La Selva. One head bop by the younger man turned into a dozen. Such feisty but predictable motion ensued, of course. My guess was that Gingerhead was bound and determined to get the television star off.

Danielito held onto the back of the younger man's head with both palms, riding his face. He thrust his cock into Gingerhead's throat, paused, and banged another inch into the redhead's system. I imagined the zoologist grunting while carrying out such an act. Honestly, I couldn't see his vocal cords in motion in the modest light of the corner. As his blowjob was carried out – a perfectly executed rhythm – he squinted his eyes and gritted his teeth. His Latino cheeks and forehead turned a crimson rose color.

Feeling numb, I gawked at their erotic play when I shouldn't have. Yet, I was entranced by the two men, under their spell, completely caught up in their obscene and satisfying act. I was helpless at the club, unable to move. Dry-mouthed, wide-eyed, and wordless, I analyzed their motion: the way the zoologist bucked his hips into Gingerhead's face; how the redhead obeyed his thirst for the local star, coveting his cock in the rear of his throat; Danielito's aggression and how he held the back of the younger man's head; Gingerhead's head-bobbing, up-down-up-down; the look on Panama Dan's face, which suggested he was going to blow at any second; the quick and steady motion the redhead used in strumming Danielito's balls; the relentless rise and fall of the zoologist's torso and ...

Yes, I should have bolted from that indecent and naughty dance between the two. I should have knocked off my drink and rushed out of the club, running away from what was about to transpire next. The inevitable. The predicted. Insanity for me.

Panama Dan came. Speedily, he released his dick from Gingerhead's mouth and reached down for the tool's mass. His right palm held the base of his dick, and he sprayed white gunk against the redhead's right cheek, the length of his neck, and his chin. Danielito was like a spigot that was turned on at full blast. Unending amounts of spunk flew out of his post. A vat of the shit. White rain.

I left ... finally. Shame on me for staying so long. How dirty I felt when I rose from my seat at the bar and exited the club. How brutally windblown. How unsure I was and in complete disbelief of the zoologist because of his flesh antics. My mind was scattered and my emotions were depleted. How maddening that moment was for me. A disaster at hand. An unfortunate, yet stimulating, event that I had unintelligibly stayed and watched.

Drunk and confused, I stumbled to the parked Fiesta. Out of my mind, outraged, hard between my legs, beyond pissed, excited, I climbed behind its wheel, started the engine, and zoomed home ... to safety ... to my mini-hacienda ... to clarity and aloneness. Just me. My solitary life. Singlehood forever.

SEVEN – CASPER, ARE YOU THERE?

On Saturday morning Viv couldn't believe what had transpired at Club Sustantivo and gasped when I shared the news with her. We were drinking Arabian coffee in my sitting room, sunbathing in the August sunrays. She was wearing a cream-colored summer's dress, flats, and arrived in a broad hat made of straw. The hat sat next to her on a satin settee. Viv sipped at her coffee, relishing the blend. "Who was the guy Danielito was with?"

"I really don't know. Nor do I want to know." I was on my fourth cup of java and felt a solid buzz. My hands shook and my heart raced. Beads of perspiration decorated my forehead, even in the air conditioning, which was set at sixty-eight degrees.

"Obviously the zoologist is a player."

"A player I won't be spending the day with."

"What if he calls, darling?"

"I intend to ignore him."

She shared a look with me of support, grinned, and remarked, "He's a pig." I loved it when Viv became a little spunky. Zest seemed to work well on her. She looked sexy with attitude, and much younger.

"Like most men. Maybe that's why I'm still single," I confessed, regretting going to the club the evening before.

"Perhaps. I really thought he was going to be the right guy for you. Obviously I was wrong."

"Last night was disgusting and erotic at the same time. It made me sick and horny. It was an emotional train wreck for me"

"Such a shame. How damning." She crossed her legs in an elegant manner and shared a sigh.

"I know. Tell me about it. I'm not proud to say that I was so pissed off I drove home from the club drunk. You know I hate to do that."

"So irresponsible," Viv said, waving a finger at me. "You know better."

"I plan to do nothing for the rest of the day. Vodka calls when noon comes. Part of me is severely crushed. I just may spend the day in my pool. Be a kind friend and join me, Viv."

"I can't, darling. I have a spa treatment in an hour with Fernando." Viv liked her beauty time. What woman didn't? Heated lava rocks and aromatherapy for her elegant looking skin were her friends. She lifted the coffee cup to her lips, but didn't take a sip. Instead, she asked, "You're sure it was Danielito last night?"

"Of course I am sure. He's one of a kind. He's Panama Dan. Who else in this city dresses like he does? Who plays the part?"

"You pose a very rational explanation, luv. I'm sorry for inquiring." She took a sip of her coffee in an elegant manner, crossed her legs in the opposite direction, found comfort for her ass, and attempted a smile.

"And I apologize for being snippy."

"You wear snippy well, my friend."

"You should spend the day with me in my pool. Please, Viv, I beg of you."

She shook her head. "Fernando will be outraged if I miss my appointment. He's a spicy queen when rubbed the wrong way."

My opinion of the man was rather brisk and catty, which I chose to keep to myself. "I can't believe you're going to leave me all alone when I'm submerged in this dramatic state."

Viv rolled her eyes and pressed her lips together. "Don't be silly, Casper."

"I feel heartbroken," I shared, attempting to play with her emotions. Had she spent the day in my pool with me, her company would have healed my open wounds. "Please, if you walk out on me today I'll play Adele all day long and probably drown."

She laughed. "You're silly."

"And don't forget that I'm remarkably broken."

Again, she laughed: heartily, with a broad smile, lifting her shoulders. Once she calmed down, Viv said, "Actually, I have a splendid idea."

I leaned forward ever so slightly and prattled, "I'm the kind of guy who likes splendid ideas."

"You spend the day with me at the spa. We have facials, massages, and aromatic therapy. You'll be pulled out of your drama within seconds." She was finished with her coffee and placed her empty cup between us on the Chippendale table. "We can call it a queen's day out."

"Which one of us is the queen?" I inquired.

She giggled. "You, of course."

"Of course."

Not five minutes later, the phone rang inside my bedroom where I was changing my attire for a day spent with Viv and Fernando. I accidentally picked the house line up before looking at the caller identification to see who was calling. "Hello," simply fell out of me with ease.

"Casper," Panama Dan chanted my name.

I curled inside, sick to my stomach. My mind buzzed with anger at myself for picking up the call. Rage boiled under the surface of my skin. I pinched the bridge of my nose and felt cold all over.

"Casper, are you there?" His voice was nothing more than a whisper. He sounded distant, perhaps lost, and a million miles away from me.

He was probably wondering why I hadn't called him regarding spending the day with him, as we had planned two days before. I couldn't bring myself to do that, though. Viv and I had determined quite clearly over coffee that he was a player and someone I shouldn't have in my life. I couldn't speak to him and wouldn't. Shame on me for picking up the phone. What the hell was I thinking?

"Casper?"

There was heavy silence on my end. Could he hear my heartbeat thump within my chest? Could he determine the panging between my temples, which was bringing on a head-splitting ache that only an afternoon martini could take away? Could he ...

"Casper, I can hear you breathing and know you're there."

He couldn't. Danielito was lying. He was toying with me, again.

My hand shook against the side of my face. The phone almost tumbled out of its weak grip and cracked against the marble floor. A pool of saliva collected at the back of my throat, but I didn't swallow it down. I felt weak and pale and dizzy and breathless.

"Casper?"

It was time to hang up, which I carried out with a sharp abruptness. Within seconds I pulled the phone away from my ear and pressed the OFF button on the device. Flushed and flummoxed, I tossed the phone to the bed and it bounced once ... twice ... and sat motionless. I looked at the device, shivered, and whispered, "Player."

"Baby, what's wrong?" Viv found me a few seconds later. "You've lost all the color in your face. You're shivering." Her eyes scanned the phone on the bed. Immediately, she gripped me in her arms and clung me to her breasts. "Baby, did that player call you?"

"He did," I whispered, caught completely off guard by Panama Dan's call. "I accidentally picked up the phone."

She brushed a palm over the back of my head, soothing my wounds. "That bastard."

"Really, it was my fault. I shouldn't have done that. I wasn't thinking."

"I have you, luv. Not to worry. Viv is here for you."

I knew that. I would always know that. Viv Lynn was my dearest friend in the world. My personal fag hag. My rock. The woman I was supposed to marry if I hadn't liked dick. There, I felt safe in her arms, coddled by her, and protected from the bad man we called Danielito Estar.

EIGHT – QUEEN-THERAPY

Fernando's Spa was a place where an everyday woman or friendly fag could feel like a noble queen. Although Fernando himself disliked me, and I abhorred him to the fullest, he did have a worthy establishment. His staff consisted of fifteen men and women: acupuncturist, herbal specialist, physical fitness trainer, dietician, two masseurs, an aromatherapy specialist, and others. The staff wore white from head to toe and barely spoke. Zen was found in every corner and offered endless bliss. The reason I decided to take Viv up on her offer was simple: I did feel a little broken over the zoologist, and I knew that Fernando would ignore me, keeping his distance, since we shared a racy past.

Our history was ugly. Bottom line: we dated off and on throughout the last two years. We kissed occasionally on such dates, and once we went all the way. Although Fernando was beautiful with his Latino skin and fall-into blue eyes, and he knew how to ride a man's ass to the fullest XXX degree, our chemistry together lacked immensely. I was night, and he was day. Throughout time I had learned that our indiscreet battles consisted of politics, religion, money, and gay rights. The basics of our relationship was purely elementary: he was a dog person, and I preferred the company of cats. To keep my distance from the man was rational.

Showing up at his spa was scandalous, a bit ballsy, and certainly dangerous for me. I had Viv's company, though, and knew she would protect me like a valiant heroin from Fernando's differences, safe within her proximity. Viv would not allow the man to insult me, particularly since she was dropping a considerable chunk of change for our Saturday girl-time at the spa; I learned later that day that her wealthy uncle, Jackson Marlow, had picked up our tab.

We spent the late morning in a mud bath while listening to the sounds of melodic harps, which dispersed from ceiling speakers. We were served mineral waters and Tibetan tea. Following our baths, Chinese masseuse worked the pain out of our shoulders, legs, and backs.

Face down on a comfortable leather masseuse bed in a plain room decorated in light browns and calming whites, half-concealed by fluffy white towels, and feeling Chen's knuckles roll against my naked spine, I listened to Viv ask, "Why are you hurting over Danielito when you hardly even know him?"

I sighed heavily out of contentment for the massage and my companion's valued company. "Our destinies entail us as being together."

"How do you know that?"

"I just did." I spoke in past tense, already learning to recover from the zoologist's inflicted pain.

"Perhaps it was love at first sight."

"I think so."

"You believe in that, Casper?" Her tone suggested judgment, but I ignored it, enjoying my morning man-therapy at the spa.

I fully did believe in love at first sight. If the stars and moons in the Milky Way were lined up in just the perfect positions, destiny occurred. One could also gain information about their futures by soothsayers, Tarot cards, and palm readings, which I was very much a strong believer in. "Come on, Viv, you know me better than that. Of course I believe."

"We all have something to live by, don't we?"

"Absolutely. If we didn't, I hardly believe we would find any happiness in our lives at all."

"Perhaps I agree with that."

Chen continued to work my back over, which felt pleasing and rather medicinal. Her fingers were like magic on my muscles, tendons, and ligaments. Clearly, I was dough under her labor, relaxed and calm.

Viv asked, "What if Panama Dan shows up at your doorstep today, tomorrow, or the day after?"

"I'll politely ask him to leave."

"What if he doesn't leave?"

"I will provide him with a vat of details concerning the blowjob he received at the club last night."

Viv giggled. "You're bitter."

"I really liked him. I was in love with him even before we met in person."

"You fell hard."

"I was hard for him," I mischievously replied, delighted with her company and intriguing conversation.

Chen kept professional overtop my horizontal body. Not once did she squeak with a sound. Viv's masseuse was also quiet, respecting our conversation.

"Perhaps another man will come along and make you hard," my sidekick chanted, enjoying her massage.

"I can only hope so. I cannot stay single forever."

"A mechanic of sorts."

"An English professor."

"An underwear model," she shared, giggling.

"Oh, Viv, I like that."

"An underwear model who is a mechanic on the side."

"Stop, Viv," I teased, giggling with her, settling more into my massage, my best friend's uplifting company, and Chen's delightful fingertips that added a soothing pressure to my shoulder blades.

# # # # #

Noon at Fernando's came and went. Viv and I had Tahitian salads for lunch and bottles of chilled water. Following lunch, we enjoyed an hour of meditation in the Shanghai Room. There we bowed our heads, pressed our palms together, sat with our legs crossed, and hummed, sinking into an abyss of nothingness mixed with numbness.

Once our meditation hour was up, I decided to take a cab home because Viv wanted to stay behind at the spa and have a discussion about the nutritional value of the kiwi with a straight musclehead named Juan Senti. The guy was from Ecuador, a dietitian with almost-amber colored eyes, a massive chest, and tree trunk-size thighs. Juan worked under Fernando for the last year. The processional was twenty-seven years old, stood over six feet tall, and knew how to flirt with the spa's female cliental, which always brought them back to the establishment where they spent loads of their money; Viv just happened to be one of those women, of course.

Bottom line: Viv wanted to stay behind and try to boff the muscular Latino again; a task she carried out successfully three times before. My friendly companion was not shy about her involvement with the sexy dietician. Details clarified that the Latin American hottie was massive in the cock area. She exclaimed after her first sexual encounter with the beefy man that Juan's dick was no less than eleven inches long and two inches wide. "He was like getting fucked by a baseball bat, if you want to know the truth, darling. Not that I'm complaining, though. The guy tops like a freight train and enjoys some heavy duty rough play."

So Viv was on the sexual prowl for Juan, his muscular beefiness, and baseball bat-size cock. Whatever my friend wanted, she always got. How dare one stand in her way or they would be pushed aside without much candor.

I left Viv to her sexual, dietary needs, called a cab, and waited patiently for it to retrieve me from the spa and carry me home. The wait was short, which pleased me. Once the green-and-white PT Cruiser arrived, I climbed in its back seat, told the driver my address, and settled into a comfortable and rather mundane ride home.

At approximately two in the afternoon, the Naples taxi pulled up to my mini-hacienda and ...

"Shit," escaped my lips as I stared at Panama Dan's bumblebee yellow Hummer parked in my seashell-covered drive. The semi-naked zoologist was sprawled over the vehicle's hood, sunbathing. Danielito sported Oakley sunglasses, no shirt, a skimpy pair of Rufskin running shorts, and no shoes or socks. His bare skin baked in the sun's golden rays. The blinding light glazed his Latino pecs and their firm nipples. Because the Rufskin was snug against his middle, the man's private parts looked extra-large. His pumped biceps glistened with light perspiration and his sculpted thighs reflected the day's bright light. When the taxi pulled into the drive, the actor sat up on his Hummer's hood, lifted the sunglasses from the bridge of his nose, took a gander of my body in the backseat of the PT Cruiser, and beamed a rather pleasant looking smile of excitement.

I almost told the taxi driver to turn the cab around and head back to the spa, needing Viv. Such an instruction never transpired, though. Instead, I sucked up my hardship, mumbled something indecipherable under my breath, and decided to confront Panama Dan, ending the emotional madness that had caused me to feel somewhat sick.

Less than a minute later, I paid the cabbie, stepped into the day, and visually consumed Danielito on the hood of his Hummer. As the taxi drove away, leaving me at my residence with the promiscuous zoologist, I stood my ground and inquired, "Danielito, what are you doing here?"

He sat on the edge of his hood with his legs hanging over its front, right panel. I admit the man looked tasty-hot and completely rugged. The label Latino cowboy instantly flitted through my mind, and I unintentionally licked my lips. My gaze studied his puckered navel, tight looking abs, rounded shoulders, and his beaming smile.

"I thought we were going to spend the day together," he said.

"I changed my mind. That isn't going to happen."

"You don't like me now?" He sounded like a little boy when he asked me that, which was sweet in itself and delicious sounding.

"I don't."

"Can I ask you why?"

I was snotty and bitchy to the nth degree. "You can ask, but that doesn't mean I will tell you why." My feet and legs carried me to the mini-hacienda. Once there, I unlocked its front door, turned the knob, and was just about to step inside. Before doing so, I called over my right shoulder, "Get out of here, Panama Dan. We should have never had that dinner together the other night. You can leave on your own, or I can call the police to have you removed from my residence. You choose."

He raised his arms with a questioning and helpless look smeared over his face. In doing so, he called out rather bluntly, "What did I do to piss you off?"

"Just drive away, Danielito. As far I'm concerned, we never met." I slipped inside my abode, closed the door behind me, felt my heart break in two symmetrical pieces, and almost cried. I held it together, though, and kept my composure as a strong man, one who just happened to badly need a vodka on the rocks, or three, and right away.

Minutes later, the vodka over ice went down smoothly. One drink turned into three. By the sixth one, I was totally smashed, naked in my pool, and was talking to myself, slurring my words.

No, I didn't tell the actor that I had seen him at Club Sustantivo the night before, fucking a man's throat, blowing his load over the stranger's face. No, I failed to be a man and confess to the zoologist that I didn't want anything to do with him because I felt that he was a player. Shame on me for not sharing that.

Truthfully, I believed we were from two different worlds. My life did not entail a list of men whom I bagged in public at a queer bar. I was more settled than that, less wild and sexually mature. My fuck-and-dump days were long over and ... obviously, his weren't. Panama Dan liked his cock, possibly from numerous young men such as the one he fucked last night. I wanted something and someone more serious. I had a standard to live up to and maintain, a basic criteria of the type of man who I wanted to have at my side, in my life permanently, and one that I could call my best friend, without him straying from my cock and other intimate parts. Truth was Danielito Estar was not for me. And I was not meant to be his boyfriend, lover, or someone of importance. Case closed.

NINE – MISTAKEN IDENTITY

One week later I decided to start my life over again and felt better about who I was as a single man.

My Frontier was back in the drive and fully repaired. The grease monkeys at Justin's No-More Junkers did a fine job. Justin treated me like gold and only charged me a portion of the bill, which made me very happy.

Eight days after my tryst with Danielito, and I found myself at Club Sustantivo again, which had more men inside it than a skink flick star. The ultra-modern music roared and drinks were clicked together in dramatic toasts. The club was filled with queer pilots, bankers, sexy dentists, firemen, greasy mechanics, and a dozen or more different types of men. Four shirtless bartenders worked the two bars, zipping to and fro. The college boys were earning the best tips. Dollars built within their tip jars, proving just how busy the club was.

I stood against one of the dark walls with a longneck bottle of beer. Some young, fun, and filled with cum guy with small ears and Channing Tatum good looks decided to hit on me. Channing ground his middle to my middle, pinched one of my nipples through the Rufskin tee I sported, and whispered in my right ear, "You a pitcher or a catcher, man?"

I was calm and cool, and not at all interested in the guy, although he was quite charming, dazzling, handsome, playful, and horny. My mind was elsewhere of course, completely lost in Panama Dan, hurt by the man because of his sexual antics as a player. I was blue. Such knowledge of his promiscuous actions deflated me, especially since I placed the actor on a high pedestal and was wholly convinced that he was my Mr. Right.

How exactly long would I stay somber because of Danielito's man-with-man gigs? I really wasn't sure. Long-term seemed an appropriate and accurate measurement. Just enough time to heal, but not exactly enough time to completely forget about him.

To answer the young Channing Tatum look-alike regarding his question whether I was a pitcher or catcher I simply smiled and rattled off, "Sorry, pal ... I don't do baseball."

In a huff, the guy said, "I was talking about fucking around with you."

My mind drifted for a few seconds, and I started to think of insurance terms behind my eyes: active participant, waiver of premium, hazardous activity, residual benefit, valuation reserve, aggregate limit, net premium earned, total loss ...

Channing was not pleased with my silence and inquired, "What the fuck is your problem?"

"Go away," I said in a moderate tone, not to piss him off more than I already had. "I really don't like easy guys."

Channing held up his right hand and gave me the finger. "Fuck you, man. A dozen or more dudes in this place would like to fuck around with me."

"Go for it. Don't let me hold you back."

He called me an asshole and pulled away from my chest. Before I realized it, he was lost among the many queer bodies, vanished from my sight, and left me alone with my blues.

How was I not intoxicated after drinking eight longnecks? In fact, I was stone sober. My stomach was calm, my vision wasn't blurred, and my head was completely clear. Because of my condition, eight longnecks turned into twelve. Then I started to feel a thick buzz, which was comforting and rather enjoyable. I only wondered how many more longnecks I could enjoy before I became inebriated, unable to stand, and passed out.

Another guy hit on me. The handsome Guatemalan with his chocolate skin and matching eyes discovered me against the wall. Brooks was his name and he wore a white cowboy hat that I thought was a Stetson. I learned almost immediately that the guy was new to the city and liked to smile. He grabbed my belt buckle with some hearty force, drew me toward him, took a whiff of my left pec, licked his lips, and said in his thick Spanish drawl, which I found delightfully sexy, "I'm thinkin' you should be under me."

Honestly I thought it a great pick-up line and enjoyed what he had to say. Plus, I wouldn't look so bad under his naked skin since he was rock-solid hot. A laugh actually spilled out of my lips and then I hit him back with: "Will you be wearing anything while I'm under you?"

"Hopefully not."

"You intend to ride me like your horse?"

"Whatever it takes to get you off."

"Flattering. I rather like the idea."

Brooks was terribly good looking, and I would have gone home with him had I not felt like an emotional pile of dog shit. He was definitely the type of guy I wanted to be under. The man's build was Herculean-like and his face was magazine stuff. Think William Levy with a darker hue about his skin and eyes. I was pretty sure he could fuck like a wild animal since Guatemalans had the reputation as such but decided not to take him up on his provided invitation.

"Sorry, guy. You're really nice to look at and you seem to be pretty suave. The truth of the matter is simple, though. I'm a little blue tonight and just want to be left alone."

"I can respect that," he said, smiled, and leaned into my left cheek. The Latino cowboy shared a kiss to the cheek, pulled away, and smiled again. "You take care of yourself, man. Get rid of the blue and try to have some fun tonight."

Brooks left my side and saddled up to the bar between two Latino jocks who immediately took an interest in his cowboy good looks. Both started a conversation with the stranger.

Good for him, I thought, pleased to know that he could bounce back and recover so quickly from my rejection.

As Brooks flirted with the two bar boys with his indulging charm, I decided it was time to release my bladder and take a piss break from the queer masses. Quickly, I guzzled the last two inches of the somewhat warm beer, enjoyed my discovered buzz, and discarded the empty longneck on a nearby table covered in empty cocktail glasses, shot glasses, and two ashtrays filled with a variety of cigarette butts.

Upon my travels to the distant bathroom to empty my load a little, I zigzagged through the throng of young men, most of which were Latino and bare-chested. Inebriated fags discovered every nook and cranny on my body. Fingers pried at my bottom. Palms rubbed against my torso. Pecs were pinched by straying fingertips. The place was a meat market and I was its prized mass of edible beef. Such men who were present among the dancers, pick-up artists, minglers, and drinkers had unstoppable libidos.

Cautiously, I worked my way toward the pissing facilities in fear that I would tumble into a bear's massive paws and forever be lost there within his relentless lust. Jocks of different sizes wanted to eat me up, devouring every inch of my tasty body in their drunken and not so pretty stupors. Musicians wanted to rock the house with me. Daddies wanted to toy with the junk between my legs. And others simply wanted to grind their tools against any part of my available body, desiring to get off and shoot their sticky-white loads on or inside me.

The bathroom was shoulder to shoulder with horny gentleman. How many men were providing other men with blowjobs? Who were the twinks getting it on near the urinal? What dude had his hand on my ass and gave it a squeeze while he licked another man's ass? Who tried to slip his palm into my shorts to tease my jewels? What bad boy fingered my abs?

The bathroom was no place to urinate; I had determined, but I had to really go, unable to hold my piss flow in a moment longer. The many longnecks I had consumed were finally catching up with me, and urine was going to spray.

No, I did not share my private moment of pissing with a certain horny somebody in the restroom. An episode of golden showers did not transpire between my cock and a dog in the men's room. No one fell to their knees with an open mouth and allowed me to piss inside their system or all over their face. Instead, I kindly and patiently moved through the crowd, apologized for my nettling, and discovered the handicapped stall with its available toilet.

Two men were naked in the stall. Both were Latino and looked like dancers. Had I not been feeling blue over Panama Dan, I would have taken a quick piss, stripped down to my bare bottom, and labored over their chiseled nakedness. Sex with the handsome couple did not transpire, though. Rather, I excused myself, found a way behind them, felt a naked cock jab me in my thigh, listened to one of the gentlemen groan with pleasure, heard slurping and kissing, and safely stood in front of the toilet bowl, ready to carry out my business.

Next, I unzipped, released my pisser from cotton, and started to unload my urine, which tinkled in the blue water.

Behind me, one of the naked Latinos asked, "You need help with that, man? I can hold it for you."

I looked over my right shoulder and saw that both jocks were watching me take a piss. Not that I really cared, though. I had a job to do and was getting it done, no matter what. Good for me.

Before I could say anything in return, the other naked jock said, "Yeah, we both can help you with that, chico. Piss on us if you want."

Leakage was already happening between my legs in an overpowering rush. I didn't want to take the fun out of the duo's naked bliss, but had no interest in sharing my piss with them. "I've got it handled up here. Thanks for the offer, guys."

"If you change your mind, we're right back here. Let us know," one of the jocks said.

How nice of the pair. How convincingly sweet and kind. Or, were they just being selfish like every other guy in the club, willing and ready to get their rocks off with some man-on-man-on-man actions, which included a downpour of golden showers? No thanks. I passed.

I finished my piss, steered my way around them, was man-handled like a toy, and found myself outside the stall and in the cluster of men within the small bathroom. Calmly I worked my way through the homosexual mass, felt a number of pinches, pushes, probes, and spanks. Queer deviants took advantage of my availability within the restroom's confines. I had become meat for their carnivore needs. A sex thing younger than thirty that they possibly wanted to do the most naughty things to and with. Pretty prey for their desires.

Eventually, I escaped the sexually hungry men in the bathroom and returned to the main part of the club. Once among the athletes, military men, and blue collar workers, I absorbed The Pink Assholes' new tune, which flooded down from the overhead speakers. "Rock My Rump" echoed within the club, and the faggots went crazy over the hit, dancing at full speed. Although I did enjoy the local band and their nationally syndicated hit, my attention was unexpectedly elsewhere.

To my horror, surprise, and unfailing dislike, my view caught Panama Dan with two young men against one of the bars, which was directly in front of me. What I saw was unappealing and assaulted my eyes. Struck with shock, I stood motionless among dancers next to the dance floor, and stared at the zoologist and his hedonistic behavior.

Danielito sported nothing more than his shorts, which were unzipped. His massively plump cock swung left and right between his legs like a pendulum. Behind his limp dick were his swinging balls. Having both arms lifted above his head, one of his predators, a blond Georgian boy of maybe eighteen, licked and lapped at one of Panama Dan's armpits. The other boy, a black-haired somebody who I had seen numerous times before in the club, but was unfamiliar with his name, was on his knees, ready to suck the zoologist off.

There, I absorbed the sexually unsatisfying as the three labored over each other: kissing, fingering, caressing, licking, lapping, and sucking. Danielito's skin was mercilessly used by the youthful pair, obviously caught up in their game of queer lust. How pleased he looked with his mouth ajar, legs parted, and his chest heaving for breath. Excitement seemed to twinkle in his semi-closed eyes. The man rocked forward and backward, growing hard within the one boy's mouth. The action among the three was disgusting and richly unseemly as the trio processed their public sex.

I was disgusted by the sight at hand. I felt ridiculous in the club, witnessing my Mr. Right's sexual antics again. A feeling of bemusement passed throughout every vein in my body. Anger caused my legs to wobble. My heart jumped within its chest. How could such an event happen once in my life, let alone twice? What kind of fool was I to even think about visiting the club and relaxing with seven ... eight ... nine ... a dozen longnecks? The place was the actor's hangout. Why did I think he wasn't going to be there, enjoying some open sex among club-goers?

Just as I was about to leave the club ... just as I was about to spin on my heels and find my way home, back to my seclusion and blues ... just as I was about to call my life shit, something life-changing occurred. Something dramatic. Something oddly perfect. Something unplanned.

My cell phone vibrated within my Go Softwear shorts against my right testicle. Within seconds I pulled it out and – to my utter surprise and confusion – saw a text message from the zoologist. Danielito wrote: "want to see you. need to talk. I didn't mean to piss you off. talk to me."

Another message was followed by the first: "call me, Casper. better yet, come over. I want to see you."

I was confused and looked up. My attention was drawn to the zoologist with his two play-things. I took in Danielito's work with the pair: he thrust his hips into the black-haired young man's mouth and pressed the blond's face into his armpit. The actor had a look of pure pleasure in his eyes that robustly glinted. All three men were sweating and heavily breathing. The black-haired man was ravenous and ate the zoologist up. The blond continued to eat Danielito's armpit, nuzzling his face inside the concave structure.

What the hell is going on? I thought. Puzzlement cradled my mind, nestling itself between my temples. I didn't understand what was happening. How could Danielito be sexually involved with the duo at the bar and text me at the same time? Was my phone broken? Did the actor's text messages come in at a later time after he sent them to me? I was just thinking that possible when ...

My phone buzzed again. Three quick vibrations occurred in my hand. An incoming call from Panama Dan was happening. Yet, wasn't he next to the bar being sucked and licked and coveted by the pair of young men? Wasn't the zoologist a player who was preoccupied with his lustful game of public sex?

Bafflement discovered me and rocked my world. I looked up and saw the actor busy with his male friends, clarifying that he wasn't calling me. In fact, the Danielito at the bar was busy doing other things, which I found naughty, rather prolific, and distasteful.

Curiosity found me, and I decided to take Panama Dan's call. Although the club was obnoxious with noise, I held my cell up to my left ear and hollered into the device, "Who is this?"

"Danielito," he confirmed. Same smooth and attractive voice. Same Panamanian accent. The same guy that had spent the night with me when I was bitten by his snake, Butch. The gentleman who cradled me in his arms throughout the night and didn't take advantage of my skin.

"Where are you?" I sounded rude and obnoxious.

"Waiting for you at La Selva. I was hoping you would stop by for a drink, and we could talk about what's bothering you. I want to know how I can make this better between us. I really like you, Casper, and ... I don't want you to get away from me.

Something tells me it's too late to try, though, maybe even foolish, but I'm willing to risk my heart for that ... and you."

I began to sweat, unsure of what was happening. The Danielito Estar at the bar was not speaking to me on his cell phone. Instead, he was busy with his tag team boys and some heavy duty sexual antics. My legs wavered, and my heart thumped radically within my chest. My head was spinning, and I thought I was going to vomit. I asked, "Aren't you at Club Sustantivo?"

"Where?"

"Club Heat. Aren't you here?"

"No. I don't hang there ... But someone who looks like me does. Or so I've heard. Some guys think he's my twin, but he's not. Is that where you're at?"

"Yes ... with you."

He laughed at me. "Trust me, I'm not there. I'm cozy with my animals at the estate. Why don't you leave there and stop by here?"

It was all making sense now. The guy at the bar wasn't Danielito Estar. It was just a guy who happened to look like him. A twin of sorts. A queer someone who was a player and could pass as Panama Dan's identical brother. It was a mistaken identity on my part. Not the same guy. Not the zoologist that I liked. Someone who just happened to look like the actor. A certain someone that I knew but wasn't the same man at all. Instead, he was someone completely different, and easy with his flesh, unlike Danielito.

Bottom line: I fucked up. Big time. There were two men who could pass as twins in Naples. One was a zoologist who I thought was my Mr. Right, and the other guy was a man-whore who liked to have sex inside Club Sustantivo. Two different men who just happened to look alike.

Guilt found its way into my soul. I had abandoned Danielito because I thought him promiscuous and a nasty player. I believed he was having random sex with a variety of Joes in public. I judged him when I was in no position to. The zoologist wasn't the same guy that was with me inside the club. I questioned the actor's integrity and ...

"Casper, are you there?"

"Here," I said, snapping out of my thoughts of guilt for treating him so badly during the past few days.

"You coming over tonight? I think you should. Butch misses you."

I rather liked Butch, even if he didn't like me. And I liked the zoologist more, everything about him. As a smile of satisfaction surfaced on my face, and my mind turned from disgust for Panama Dan to heartfelt tenderness, I replied, "I'm on my way. Give me a couple of minutes. If you don't mind, I will need a drink when I get there."

I could hear a sense of strong happiness in his tone as he replied with: "It will be waiting for you, guy. I can't wait to see you again."

I called Viv on my drive to La Selva, but she didn't pick up her cell phone. My excitement about the evening's events with the zoologist was overwhelming, and I wanted to spill my emotions to her listening ear. Viv was my best friend and adored such tales that occurred within my single life. She would have been thrilled to learn that I was about to mend my ways with Danielito Estar. In fact, she would have bubbled up with supportive laughter regarding my decision to visit Panama Dan.

We didn't talk, though. Viv had her own life and was busy doing something. Therefore, I left a voice message for her: "Viv, I'm heading to Panama Dan's estate. I think we have things worked out. A total misunderstanding on my part. I'll call you tomorrow and will share all the wicked details with you. Love ya, gal. Have fun. Be safe."

TEN – SEXUAL CAPERS

I arrived at La Selva approximately twelve minutes later. Warmness coated my insides as excitement raced from the base of my spine to the back of my neck. My hands were shaking, and I felt dizzy and unsure of my cellular antics with the zoologist. Part of me was embarrassed by my infantile behavior regarding Danielito's look-alike at Club Sustantivo. The same part of me rose above the situation and continued with my evening. In due time, I would share the situation and its crazy details with the actor. In the meantime, I had other things on my mind, like permitting the zoologist to wrap my body inside his hulking arms, and prompt him to drag his tongue along my neck, among other masculine body parts.

As promised, a drink waited for me upon my arrival. Kamikaze shots sat on a plastic tray inside Panama Dan's living room. Candles were lit. Jazz was playing. The man was dressed in nothing more than a pair of khaki shorts and a blooming smile, which I found adorable.

"It's hot tonight," he said, passing me a Kamikaze shot.

"You're hot," I admitted.

"To us," he shared a toast, clinking his shot glass against my own.

We guzzled the shots and went for seconds.

"You want to tell me why you've been acting weird? I understand the chase when it comes to men, but you're an extremist at it."

"Soon," I admitted. "Now is not the time. I promise to be on my best behavior from here out."

"I was worried you didn't like me. One minute you seemed to be into me ... and the next you were ignoring me."

"Don't think that. I adore you. You're my Mr. Right. I'm here right now to prove that I like you."

"Prince Charming," he corrected.

"That, too," I agreed, forgot about the shots and fell against him, hungry for everything he had to offer me in my white collar world.

His hulking frame compressed against my own in an unforgettable kiss. The embrace we shared was nothing less than Earth-shaking. The kissing transpired with heat and we became inseparable, lost in each other. My tight neck was eventually licked as well as my chin in a rather sloppy but hungry manner. His lips found my lips again, and his tongue delved inside my mouth. He removed my tight tee, yanking it up and over my torso. The material was dropped to the floor and forgotten until morning. Danielito's lips dragged across one of my firm pecs and then the other. His extended tongue lingered over each nipple, pleasuring me. His fingers discovered my abs, rolling their prints over my design with much care.

To tease him, I tried to pull away from his appetite, but he grabbed my hips with both palms and secured me next to his face. His tongue met my indented navel and rolled around its shallow flesh-pit with pure delight. The man moaned and groaned beneath me as he fell to his knees. Fingertips discovered my shorts, which were promptly removed. Perhaps he was stunned to learn that I was not sporting underwear as a light gasp escaped his lips. Not that such a discovery deterred his work. Within seconds his right hand found the already erect knob between my legs – eight swollen inches of cut dick. The hand started to jack the tool up and down in a feisty manner. His mouth found the tip of the cock, and he started to suck on my meat while he yanked its tubular and solid length at the same exact time.

I wavered above him. My legs almost gave out, and I started to fall to the floor. The moment was far too erotic between us to prevent such an event from transpiring. It was as if I had simply lost all control of my frame and turned into man-jelly, losing my balance because of the windswept moment with him.

The zoologist was on task and tightened his grasp on my hips, preventing me from a dangerous tumble. His fingertips dug into my skin, muscle, and bone, keeping me upright. While that challenging moment transpired, he never let his moist lips fall off the erect spike between my wavering legs. In fact, his hunger for my Latino skin only heightened, and he lodged the veined beef down the back of his narrow throat, which he didn't gag on, having experience with such naughty tasks.

Balanced again, no longer as windblown, I decided to thrust my cock into his system, and shifted to and fro. My hands discovered his shoulders and gripped their triceps with brutal force. I rocked back and forth, caught up and into his throat-ride. My hips bucked his face and caused grunts of pleasure to leak out of the corners of his mouth. And my balls, grossly extended in their Latino sack, slapped against his chin and part of his neck.

How long did the actor on his knees blow me? Ten … thirteen … seventeen minutes? Neither of us really knew. We moved together in opposite directions, building friction between us. The candlelight was forgotten as well as the jazz playing in the living room. No longer were we in need of shots or talk. Instead, our connection comprised of one male longing for another male with persistent appetites.

Eventually, he pulled away from me and instructed, "Kick off your sandals and shorts. I have other plans for you, man."

I listened. What man who just happened to lust for the zoologist wouldn't? Once my sandals and shorts were lost, Panama Dan spun me around, directed me to plant my palms on the back of the rattan sofa, and added, "Separate your legs and bend over."

What transpired next was improbable: heaven parted, all the gay gods fell out, and each offered the two of us ecstasy.

Positioned behind me, still on his knees, the zoologist pulled my rump apart and lathered my Latino-tight hole with his tongue. Murmurs of pure elation floated out of the man's mouth as he swabbed my bottom with delight. A tirade of licks and laps occurred, which sent me into a state of euphoria. There, half-positioned over the rattan sofa, gripping anything that I could to keep my balance, I felt his outstretched tongue inside my man-cavern, which quickly pulled out, darted inside, and pulled out again.

Once, he found the brave notion to spank me, which I fully enjoyed while gritting my teeth. His left palm struck my left, rear orb and a throbbing sting caused much delight to meander throughout my masculine core. The slap was everything I wanted during our connection. In fact, I desired a few more just to keep me in the game, but the man behind me didn't follow through with such naughty antics.

One tongue-delve to my bottom turned into numerous tongue-delves. Danielito's fingers pried my rear open, and his Latino face brushed against my most sensitive area. Grunts and growls of pleasure exited the man's mouth as his lengthy tongue continued its work on my center. "More," escaped my lungs, demanding the man to taunt and titillate my opening. Wet slurps were heard, prosaic licks transpired, and ...

He was only teasing me, I knew. Danielito pulled away from my rear, stood from his knees, and called down and over my back in his thick Spanish, "*Quiero hacer.*" I want to do you.

Seconds passed, and Panama Dan found a condom, lube, and my compact ass. Naked now, sporting a nine-inch uncut tool between his legs that was decorated with a triangular patch of groomed pubic hair and hairless balls, he rolled plastic down and over his shaft. Over my right shoulder, I saw him add lube to his swollen dick. Wasting no time, he steered the tip of the pole against my warm and constricted rump, ready to trespass inside my guy-harbor.

Without further ado, my ass was banged by all of his nine inches, which caused desired pain to mollify inside my core. Sanity was lost for a brief moment ... two moments ... three moments. I gasped, losing oxygen as his nine inches thundered inside my body and took harbor against my intestines and other organs. I ground my teeth together and gripped fingertips into the rattan sofa. My body grew stiff under his forceful touch, which caused my mind to spin in all directions with utter wonderment.

His banging was consistent and rough. The man hung on my hips with vise-like grips. His clean-shaven balls thwarted repeatedly against my balls, which knocked together in a state that offered much bliss. The actor's V-area of pubic hair bristled against the upper part of my rump as he thrust his weight into me, pulled away, and thrust again. Bolt after bolt to my man-hole continued for the next few minutes.

He whispered behind me in Spanish, "*Tu eres el chico mas caliente.*" You're the hottest guy.

I replied in my own Spanish, "*Mas rapido ... Espolon que.*" Faster ... Ram it.

Danielito listened, and whiplash discovered me. My head flew forward and backward as his prominent banging transpired. A loss of air was discovered, my toes bunched up, and I felt a roll of prosaic bliss that mixed with lust cascade throughout my middle.

Panting occurred between the both of us. Together we rocked east and west in hyper motion. Perspiration flew from his chest and splatted against my back. Challenging grumbles of contentment filled the living room. He woofed once ... twice ... three times and ...

"*Que viene,*" I'm coming escaped me.

Without even having my eight-inch rod being touched, spew shot out of the tube of meat as if it were a spigot. Stream after stream of ooze decorated the back of the rattan sofa and the living room floor. The sticky cream flew out of my shaft and nailed both my feet and Danielito's.

The thumper behind me laughed and confessed, "I made you explode."

"It's your turn," I rattled off, still enjoying his pick inside my behind.

Panama Dan's thrusts quickened. A rhythmic banging occurred to my back side and his grips on my hips became more stringent. Thump after thump numbed my bottom as his motion became manic and uncontrollable. Another woof escaped the man, which was followed by a long growl of infinite pleasure.

Half of me believed that Danielito came inside the condom that separated our bodies. That wasn't the case, though. Rather, he was just getting ready to blow his load when he yanked out of my rear with an abrupt motion and told me, "Stand up and spin around ... You're going to wear my load."

I did as he told me, still flag-hard between my legs, ready to be glistened and sticky by his Latino juice. There, both of us now stood behind the rattan sofa and faced each other, and I watched the man begin to work his massive bolt in an overexcited manner. Both of his hands moved north and south on his cock. Danielito puffed his cheeks, released air from his lungs, and bucked his fists with some heavy-duty thrusts.

"Shoot it," I coached him. "Don't hold it in."

"*Casi.*" Almost.

# # # # #

If the truth be told, he came with only a few jacks to his beef. Veins popped to life in his massive thighs, his balls jangled between his legs, and his eyes glazed over with a sense of enjoyment. Sweat clung against every ab that designed his ripped torso and his breathing intensified with numerous grunts.

"Animal," I called him in English, prompting him to finally shoot.

"Now," he replied, on fire and ...

Three long strings of Latino goop flew out of his rod and splatted against my chest. The white churn hung against my rigid nipples, ladder-like abs, and decorated the cock that was upright and still hard between my legs. Another string of his ooze flew against my balls, which hung from the orbs like a monkey from a jungle tree.

Following our blowing session, we kissed: with tongues, locked together as men in post-lust, compressed as boyfriends and long-term lovers. Spew gelled our torsos together, sealing one man's body to the other. Our still-firm cocks also kissed, aligned together in bliss.

When the kiss ended, Danielito pulled away from me, yet still held my torso against his own, and said, "You're naughty."

"Like you."

"You're more naughty."

"The only way you want me to be, of course."

# # # # #

We showered together following our naked play. Under the warm spray, our Latino chests collided, and our cocks were limp, but only temporarily. Much kissing was shared as I told him about my evenings at Club Sustantivo, the man who looked like him, the player who enjoyed public sex, and the mistaken identity.

"People have told me about this guy. He even wears the khaki shirt and shorts."

"I swear he looks just like you. A twin. Your brother. If you hadn't texted me or called ..."

"It doesn't matter. I would have still chased after you. You found a place in my heart and ... I wasn't about to let you go."

"Was I one of the wild animals you often chase on your show?"

"Exactly. Except, you're my favorite animal."

"Your new boyfriend."

"My new lover," he corrected with a blistering smile, squeezing me against his hulking chest.

"I like that," I said, and decided to grab the bar of Lever 2000 and started to soap down every part of his body for the next twenty minutes ... until we decided to have a go at round two of sex, unwilling to separate.

THE EDITOR

MARCUS ANTHONY is a writer and editor, residing in Newport News, Virginia. He holds a special place in his heart for Latin men.

g ... ...g ...ight jeans, so tight yo

earing any underwear. "Excuse me," I said, having a hard time look

linded by that bulge in his crotch, "but don't I know you?" "Maybe

ind of t   bout

with Ray   God,

t loser?   in?" h

aid. "Lik   s stron

ce body   e on (

lly, he l   I eve

a up to t   any id

istaking   e san

a, I coul   ery lo

ood raci   ne sw

ing with   e in s

we go   behir

ill see   in pu

ed?" he   vent t

rivacy.   grabk

hard. I

k, tracir   t, so

ed it, ha

with my   bing

obing, I   a cock

he sound of unzipping filled the small space. I don't know who's h

but before I knew it, I had his rod in my hand, and mine was in hi

t to do?" he asked, his tone challenging. I knew exactly, and sank